I0664120

The Girl Who Flew Too High

Daniel Basil Lyle

LylePublishing

Sulphur, Oklahoma

The Girl Who Flew Too High

Copyright © 2015 by Daniel Basil Lyle

ISBN 978-0-9794101-8-5

Published by LylePublishing
505 W. 12th Street, Sulphur, OK 73086
(www.LylePublishing.com)

Printed by CreateSpace, an Amazon.com company. Available from Amazon.com and other retail outlets. Also available as an ebook on Kindle and other devices.

LCED12222018

DISCLAIMER and FORWARD

Although this book draws heavily from some of the author's own experiences, all characters in this book are fictitious. Any resemblance to real persons, living or dead, is purely coincidental. Although the historical Galileo is depicted in this book, his words and behavior are fictionalized. This book is a sequel to "*The Girl Who Danced With Snakes*," beginning where that book left off.

Chapter 1

PUNISHMENT

Yes, it is often hard to discern
Between retribution and reward
When you are at the center of conflict
Thinking you're doing all the right things
But lacking a perspective of space and time
You lash-out, without thought or consideration
The baby knocking over his glass filled with milk
The teenager popping drugs, chugging alcohol
And adults just looking for a casual hook-up
Left without food, clarity, or self-respect
Thinking they are still cruelly denied
Looking for someone else to blame
When they need to learn more
To grow into maturity
Painful but necessary
Lifting heavy weights
Reveling in the chain gang.,,
Eashoa's Lament, 1:9-13

Tommy found himself lying face-down in a luxurious meadow.

"Again?" he laughed, rolling over to look up at a deep blue sky.

Overhead, fluffy white clouds floated past. Around him, many red and blue flowers sprouted. A thick layer of green grass cushioned his back. Off to the side were thick woods. And further away to both sides he could see the tops of high mountains.

He was back in the verdant valley that once was the dry desert of the Wilderness of Judea.

"Thank you, Jesus!" he happily smiled, enjoying the soft sunlight. "You sent me home!"

He just lay there for a minute, grateful to have this wonderful present. Just a few moments before he was spinning out of control into a *vast white void*—seemingly abandoned by Eashoa, a manifestation of the Creator presenting Himself as an old, grizzled military man! Sally knew him earlier as Jesus. And now that very same magnificent Deity had transported Tommy to a place of ultimate safety.

What a great guy!

Sally and Dave had also been there with Tommy in what they termed "*sub*-subspace", a level of reality that enclosed and contained the Creator's "*Multi*verse", a vast collection of an uncountable number of linked, pearl-like *Uni*verses! But Tommy sadly concluded that he and his friends must have made Eashoa angry—because he tossed them all away into the featureless, white void...

—to fall back down to Earth!

"That was really strange..." Tommy mused, frowning as he lay staring up at the blue sky. "Why did he get so mad at us? I was being a good boy...I think?"

But then again, Dave and Sally were getting rude with the elderly gentleman, asking him very disrespectful questions. Maybe Jesus wasn't angry with Tommy, just with the two adult humans?

Tommy knew full-well that he was just a boy-sized android—a biological "robot" housing an advanced computer intelligence originally constructed by Sally. He wasn't a *real* boy for the Creator to need to reward or punish!

"Oh well," Tommy grinned to himself, brightening up. "I'm sure it will work out. Mommy and Dave are probably around here somewhere. I just need to find them."

Still clutching Dave's laptop to his chest, Tommy slowly sat up. Even when tossed into the void he didn't let loose of the laptop. Wow, that was clever of him! Maybe the laptop's programs could help him find Dave and the others?

He carefully got up to his feet and looked around. Yes, it was the exact same valley he'd departed from...except...?

"Oh my," he gasped, looking now at the valley's surrounding mountains.

They were clearly smoother and lower than he remembered. They were worn down. Also, the sun overhead was considerably larger and redder.

Tommy realized he'd been sent by Eashoa to a point far *beyond* when he dived into the time portal to travel back to ancient Greece!

"Yep...maybe a *hundred million years* or more into the future beyond when I was here last," Tommy nodded to himself, carefully calibrating the wear on the mountains, the size and redness of the sun. "I wonder if anyone's still living here—and where are Mommy and Dave?"

He now strode purposely through the meadow, marveling at the many colorful flowers surrounding him. Large insects were fluttering and buzzing around, busily drinking nectars and carrying pollens. The soil beneath Tommy's small feet was rich and spongy, healthily adorned with industriously digging worms.

Down below in the middle of the valley the central river was still flowing, but smaller and slower than Tommy remembered.

"And where's the animals?" Tommy mused as he walked along clutching the laptop, looking under the bushes and in the forest for signs of critters. "And where's the birds?" he frowned, looking up again into the vividly blue sky.

In fact, where were the *four-winged black birds* that before had actually talked to him? They told him that he was somehow *related* to them. Hah! That was really stupid. He wasn't a bird! But they also said that Sally created them as well as him. Say what? And the birds also told him that he was supposed to be a "Prophet" who brought the "End Times" to their world!

"Huh...me a 'Prophet'?" Tommy snickered. "That's funny! I'm just a little boy—well, maybe a *smart* little boy," he congratulated himself.

Suddenly he realized that he was exactly where Dave's homemade hut had been. But now there was no trace of it. In its place were just more grass and trees. And Dave's cultivated fields were replaced with yet more wavy meadows. It was as if Dave was never there?

"Well...it *has* been a hundred million years or so," Tommy sighed to himself. But he'd hoped the hut had miraculously survived. He liked the hut. It was so warm and cozy! But now there was just nature...lots and lots of nature—but with no animals or birds.

"Huh?" he frowned, starting to get worried.

Surely there were some humans around somewhere?

"I have to get up *really high* so I can see everything," he nodded to himself firmly. "Even if there's no towns close, Mommy and Dave are probably out there wandering around just like me. Up high I can see them and wave hello!"

So, with a definite plan of action, he trudged up a gentle slope toward the mouth of the valley, the highest point around, whistling happily to himself.

It took several hours to reach the valley's elevated mouth, but the sun was still shining in the sky, brightly illuminating everything. Tommy saw that the source of the river—now only a meandering stream—originated from an artesian well, streaming from a crack in the rock where water under pressure was steadily gushing up and out. And above the artesian well was a cliff leading up to the highest mountain peak.

"Well, I guess I better climb up that mountain," Tommy cheerfully grinned, looking up at the towering, sheer cliff looming above him.

Carefully tucking the laptop safely into the back of his sturdy Greek tunic, he leaned over to tie the straps of his small sandals more firmly. Then Tommy methodically began climbing up the cliff's face. He knew he could probably find a safer roundabout route to the peak, but didn't want to take the time. The direct route—if he didn't fall and kill himself—would put him at the top before the sun set.

He wanted to know his circumstance as soon as possible. If there was a nearby town he should be able to see it. Plus he wanted to locate Dave and Sally, who'd been tossed away into the white void along with him. He hoped they'd followed or preceded him to the valley. And they might be hurt and need his help! Their mushy flesh-bodies weren't near as tough as his sturdy android body.

Tommy quickly discovered, however, that free-climbing was more difficult than he'd thought. He had extensive files on how to do rock climbing in his internal databases, but that involved anchors, ropes, and attachment devices. Grabbing onto protruding rocks and cracks using only your fingertips and toes was just plain hard work—and dangerous!

Halfway up, clinging to the sheer rock face, Tommy was starting to regret his rash decision. He knew he should have done a better odds-assessment, plus a detailed visual mapping of the cliff face. But looking up he spied a series of ledges and broken rocks that lead to the top.

So rather than go back down, he continued on up...inch by tortuous inch.

And in just another hour he pulled himself up and stood on the top of the peak, looking out over the entire valley. The sun was still up, but now hung low on the horizon—casting the valley into long shadows.

"Wow...that was hard!" he gasped, rapidly sucking in large volumes of air. He'd expended a lot of his internal energy stores getting to the top so fast. He felt uncharacteristically weak, maybe something to do with being exposed to *sub*-subspace? He was going to have to eat something soon to maintain optimal internal processes. He'd seen plenty of fruit and nuts out in the forest, so that wouldn't be a problem once he climbed down.

But, regardless of his present physical condition, he'd made it all the way to the top.

He cupped his small hands, drew in as much air as he could into his lungs, and shouted out as loudly as his powerful artificial lungs could muster: "MOMMY! DAVE! WHERE ARE YOU? I'M UP HERE! YELL BACK IF YOU CAN HEAR ME!"

He heard his own voice echoing-back from down below. If Dave and Sally were out in the valley, they'd hear him.

He paused, listening carefully for a reply...

But there was nothing.

He peered intently at everything visible below.

There was still nothing—not only no humans or towns, but no animals or birds. *Where are they? What's happened to them?*

Puzzled, Tommy turned around to look beyond the valley in all directions and saw...*sand*—lots and lots of sand dunes, stretching to the far horizon.

It was then that Tommy realized the valley was an isolated *oasis* of life! Everything else around...was dead.

"Is this all there is?" Tommy frowned.

He sat on the rocky peak and opened the laptop. Fortunately the entire outer surface of the laptop was solar panels. It could operate—hopefully for years more—just on sunlight. That was fortunate as there didn't seem to be an electrical outlet left in the world.

"Maybe...I can get a signal...or receive an answer to a broadcast from the laptop?" Tommy mused as his small fingers danced across the keyboard.

If there was any radiofrequency activity, he should pick it up. If there were satellites beaming signals, he'd receive them. And even though his broadcast range wasn't large, just a few miles, from the high mountain peak he might still reach the Dinosapiens or Martian Snakes in any surviving nearby cities. Plus, he was sending up a signal that should weakly communicate with any orbiting spaceships or satellites.

He looked at his readouts expectantly, waiting patiently...

But there was still nothing.

Gradually, as the sun sank past the horizon, Tommy came to the grim suspicion that he was the *last person* on Earth!

If that was true, then *why* had Jesus sent him here?

And then—like a burst of light in a dark room—Tommy realized his purpose, his Mission.

"Oh, I see," he nodded thoughtfully.

Yes, he knew his body was going to wear out eventually. But his sturdy robot construction should last for years. And before he finally stopped functioning, he knew had a solemn duty to fulfill. Eventually, aliens from other worlds might visit Earth. There should be a *testament* waiting for the visitors that documented humanity's brief existence.

...not just a stone monument or archeological remains, but something substantial to *tell the story* of mankind!

Maybe no one would ever read it. Perhaps God would be the only one ever to see it. But Tommy knew in his heart that his job was to write it.

Why else did he arrive back on an empty Earth in the far future with a solar-powered laptop in his arms?

"Ok," he said, determined to accomplish his task. He sat cross-legged on the top of the peak with the slim computer balanced on his lap. "What would Mommy like me to call it?"

He accessed writing techniques recorded in his vast internal database while mentally comparing each possible word to the accumulated literature of mankind throughout all recorded history.

One book in particular jumped out: the one that Dr. David King had written when he'd thought he was the last surviving human—*The Luminary Chronicles.* Tommy had found it in Dave's hut on a disc, scanning it visually into his memory banks. As the Snakes built the Time-Tunnel Tommy had a lot of time to study and analyze the book. It was surprisingly well written. He particularly enjoyed its free-form poetic cadence, crispness, intellectual depth, and verbal emotional sweep.

Yes, he'd write his in the same format, attaching a transcript of Dave's book as an addendum.

"This is going to be a big job to say goodbye to all the humans..." Tommy mused, frowning.

Above him, a noticeably smaller-looking moon now shone down, having retreated from the earth over the last billion years from when humanity last ruled the planet. But the stars still twinkled overhead in their full glory.

Yes, in all of time and space, there was once the Human Race. And for all its many failures it was still a remarkable species. Tommy's job was to engrave its *tombstone.*

By the glow of the computer screen Tommy carefully typed out his first words, mumbling them aloud as he did: "*Homo sapiens* Eulogy, Chapter One—*Garden of Eden...*"

It was going to be a good book.

Daniel Basil Lyle

Chapter 2

<u>SUPPRESSION</u>

Yes, you can't always get away from what's bad
But many times it can be pushed away or minimized
Though the wisdom of that approach is debatable
When the poison seeps up and everything spoils
How much do you fight evil versus conserve strength?
And where is the "tipping point" that makes sense
To stop "putting up" with the negative and take action
Going on the attack rather than strategic retreat
You've got to make that painful choice
Or you are doomed to fester,
Falter, fall, and die
A sad defeat...
Eashoa's Lament, 2:28-32

"Hey, Mr. David—follow me!"

Dave lay sprawled on a smooth, linoleum floor looking up dazedly at a grocery shelf that was filled with various pharmaceuticals.

It was hard to see anything clearly. It was dark...

And his body hurt all over, as if he'd just fallen down a rocky slope.

"Hurry, hurry!" a large, dark-skinned man urged him.

"What?" Dave groaned, levering himself up to sit swaying on the hard floor. "W-where am I?"

He winced at particularly fierce pains in his left arm. Feeling at it with his right hand he noticed several large lumps.

What the hell is going on?

He vaguely remembered just a moment before falling through an *infinite white void*—helplessly spinning away from Sally and Tommy...

"There's been a power failure, Boss!" the man said, grabbing him by his arm and urgently hauling him to his feet. "The store cameras, they all be off! But they'll be back on quick-like. I gotta get you outta here. Come on!"

"I...don't know...?" Dave mumbled.

"And don't forget these, Mr. David!" the man said, his dark-skinned hand grabbing a *couple of pillboxes* off a shelf and jamming them into a side pocket on Dave's dangling Greek tunic. "Miss Sally said you gonna need them real bad!"

"Sally...she's here?"

The dark-skinned man grabbed him by his left arm—making Dave groan in pain—and yanked him down an aisle.

"Stay low!" the man cautioned, putting a finger in front of his lips. "And be real quiet."

Shaking his head to push back the dizziness, Dave did as directed—ducking low, trying not to let his sandals "slap" as he followed the uniformed gentleman.

He could hear other people in other aisles talking loudly, the squeaking wheels of shopping carts, and loud shouts by employees saying not to worry—the power would be back on shortly.

Dave feared that any moment they'd be seen and caught!

But the gentleman in front of Dave was expertly leading him this way and that through momentarily unoccupied aisles...then on into a secluded delivery dock at the back of the store.

"Here you go," the man softly said, undoing a lock and opening the door wide.

It led outside.

Right behind the store Dave saw a thick grove of medium-high trees...

—that seemed *ominous*, a dangerous destination in an unknown darkness!

The man noted Dave's confusion and fear.

"Go! Git! You be safe out there!"

"What? But...?"

"You done it before!"

"I did?" Dave asked in confusion.

"Ah...you don't remember," Kyle nodded, squinting nervously. "Sally said you might not. I is Kyle, one of the store-slaves here," the man hurriedly explained. "Sally be a good friend of mine. She needs your help, Boss! But you ain't no use to her or to yore self if you is caught by the Keepers."

Keepers...yes, the "Peace Keepers"—Dave groggily remembered. They were the brutal police in Sally's alternate Dimension. They were "storm-troopers" enforcing an authoritarian regime that ruled the United States of America with an iron fist. The Keepers had full judiciary authority. According to Sally they could and would execute you on the spot for even trivial offenses!

It made for a very orderly, obedient, and perpetually *terrified* society.

"You know," Dave tentatively responded, now recalling how he and Sally got out of tough jams before, "one of their *guns* might be very helpful."

"Oh, right Boss," the man grinned, his white teeth gleaming starkly against his black skin. "Ah will just go ask one of the Keepers for one of their guns and they'll just hand it to me, nice-as-you-please."

"Oh, sorry..."

"Look, Sally done told me you'd be back one day during a power failure, so ah's kept my eye out for you," he said. "I cain't get no gun for you but I *do* gots me spare coveralls and boots that I hid here that nobody's gonna be missing. So if you gonna be takin' time to dawdle here, *take* them. You know you cain't be running around in that *dress*."

Dave grimaced down at his aristocratic Greek tunic. Just 2,500 years ago in the past, in ancient Athens—where he'd been just a day previously—his clothes were quite fashionable!

Kyle urgently pushed the coverall and boots into Dave's arms.

"Thanks," Dave said, gratefully accepting the modern-day, nondescript clothing articles. "But where do I...?"

"Get to your Momma's house," Kyle urged him, pushing him roughly out the door. "I'll be by when I kin."

Right...he was back in *Sulphur, Oklahoma*—where in his Dimension his mother lived. He'd grown up in that small town. But this was a different place. This was where he'd unknowingly crossed over to the other human Dimension and first met Sally.

"Oh no!" Kyle exclaimed, cringing back...

—as floodlights behind the building flickered brightly on then abruptly back off, interrupting Dave's returning memories.

"Git! Git!" Kyle urged him again, waving frantically towards the woods before slamming the door solidly shut.

Dave didn't need any more urging. He heard dogs starting to bark at the noise of the slamming door.

As the lights again came up, Dave just managed to dive into the thick woods, wincing as he fell onto his hurting left side. He scrambled up to his feet and ran heedlessly into the darkness of the low forest.

He had no idea what was happening. He only knew he had to escape. And the dark woods were his only option...

Sally was worried about a lump on the back of her upper arm.

It was tender and tight.

It hadn't been there the day before and she didn't remember getting hit on her arm. But then again, what with their escape from the Spike-Ships, battle with the Demon, the Obelisk smashing into the control room, struggling to activate the spare-parts DE-generator, being whipped around through *sub*-subspace, their subsequent violent passage through the Black Hole, and then horrendous crash onto this new planet in another Universe—she'd been banged up enough for a *thousand* bruises and lumps to appear on her body!

She shrugged, moving the sleeve of her shirt back down to cover the tender lump.

"Are you injured, Sally?" Dennis kindly asked as he entered the jumbled engine room of the Dinosapien Starship.

"Oh, it's ok," she said, shrugging. "I'm just sore, is all. Nothing to worry about."

"Good," he sighed. He looked very tired, barely able to keep his big orange eyes open. He had the large, oblong head of a young T-rex, complete with gaping jaws and lethal, pointed teeth. Plus he had razor-sharp, long claws on his three-toed hands and powerful legs. His long tail thrashed about nervously.

"Are your Duplicator Units running?" she joked with him. She was still busily trying to salvage the ship's Dark Energy-generator's burnt and melted parts.

They'd thought that the engine room was totally destroyed when the alien DE-generator exploded. Indeed there was plenty of damage. But some components were salvageable.

"Sally, you know that we need a working DE-generator to power them," Dennis seriously replied, apparently not realizing she was joking. He sagged onto all fours next to where she was working. Impulsively, she reached out a hand to pat him on tenderly on his hard snout as he continued: "We might use the Obelisk. But we can't get it to do anything either. It's depleted of energy or broken, one of the two."

"I know all of that, Dennis," she sighed. "I was just making a joke, is all—to relieve the tension."

"Oh...a joke...alright."

He didn't seem amused.

"But I *am* trying to provide the vast energy needed to get them going," she continued.

"And how's that working out?"

"Well, I'm afraid I can't yet give you enough energy to warm up even a cup of tea," she shrugged, remembering how this whole incredible rollercoaster ride had begun when Dave couldn't get his "cold-fusion" device to function. His "Device" led to the discovery of how to fracture Subspace and generate high amounts of usable, concentrated Dark Energy.

But now that they only had an inert Obelisk and two destroyed DE-generators they were simply dead in the water.

Outside, there was no plant life—just inert rocks and volcanoes as far as the eye could see. Yes, there were single-celled organisms similar to Earth bacteria, algae, funguses, and lichens. Far off there were oceans, detected in their fiery descent. That's where the oxygen in the atmosphere apparently originated. But there were no higher organisms. In fact, it was much like early Earth, or how Mars was hypothesized to be before it died: warm, wet rocks with simple life and atmospheres.

Earth kept its molten metallic core which generated a static magnetic shield that protected its atmosphere from the solar wind—eventually allowing complex life to evolve. Mars didn't, losing even the simple life it had on the surface—though deep underground in a large network of caverns life did survive. Maybe someday Sally's new, highly volcanic world would evolve complex life on its surface, but that might be billions of years in the future if ever.

They couldn't wait around billions of years for their next meal of tasty vegetables or meaty steaks. Their stored rations—already low when they'd crash-landed on this planet—would last the crew only a few more days.

They were facing starvation and death.

"Sally," Dennis sighed, "If you can't get the spare parts or the Obelisk generators to work—then we've got no hope. We can't get back into orbit to try to find a new planet. We thought it wouldn't be hard to get our Starship working, but that was wildly optimistic. All we've got is ion drive, which is only sufficient for pushing us around in weightless space, not launching us up into orbit. We can't generate food. We're on emergency power now. We lack solar panels for generating electricity. Our batteries are fast fading and..."

"I know all that!" she snapped at him. Then, more softly, she continued: "I'm sorry, Dennis. I haven't slept for three days now since we crashed onto this God-forsaken rock. I'm not thinking straight anymore. I've no idea why the Obelisk isn't working or what the chances are for getting this cobbled-together generator going. What isn't melted or crushed was fried from the lethal radiation when the Spike-Ship generator exploded."

She sagged back out of the twisted mess.

Tears of frustration began pouring from her wide green eyes. She couldn't stop sobbing.

Her good humor was depleted.

"Please, Sally," Dennis said, putting his scaly arm up over her shoulders. "Don't despair. Alice and George say our dung-garden is still intact. Once our stored food is depleted, their potatoes and other vegetables may keep us going for a while. We've got air and water plus lots of dung. Sure the sunlight lamps need power to run, so they are down. But we've rigged up mirrors to shine the weak sunbeams here into the ship and onto our garden. So there's still hope."

"But I *don't like* those fecal-matter potatoes," she wailed. "I want your Duplicators to cook me up a nice tasty steak!"

Dennis snorted in disgust. She knew they'd reversed roles. It wasn't long ago she was rebuking *him* for complaining about eating dung-vegetables instead of tasty synthetic protein cubes!

"You know that we Dinosapiens are vegetarians," he admonished her. "We don't eat bloody animal meats. We left that behind millions of years ago in our evolutionary development."

"Oh, you'll quickly revert to your genetic imperatives," she griped, remembering how he'd done that previously while at the center of their original Galaxy. She tried to stand up straight but staggered even in the weak gravity of the smaller planet. "You'll be pulling out the contents of those Tubes scattered out there and gobbling them like they were giant hotdogs!"

She immediately regretted her words, seeing the horrified look in Dennis' rapidly blinking orange eyes.

"I'm sorry, again," she quickly apologized. "I know you wouldn't eat us little humans, no matter how hungry you were getting."

At least, she *thought* they wouldn't. But she wasn't going to tell her intelligent dinosaur friend that.

There were a million Tubes of time-frozen humans scattered across the arid plain outside the downed Starship. They came from the shattered, split-apart Harvester spaceship. Indeed, a big job of the surviving Dinosapiens was gathering them up. But there were far too many to fit into the Dinosapien's Starship where a small "private" collection of the Demon's resided, already filling their cargo hold to bursting.

"I suppose they *might* make a nice source of protein," Dennis now joked, breaking the sudden tension. "In fact, you're looking quite tasty yourself!"

"Oh, you!" she huffed at him, "bopping" him on his flat head with a balled-up fist.

"I think you should get some rest," he gently suggested, sweeping her up in his strong arms and carrying her away toward her quarters.

She yawned deeply, barely able to keep her eyes open.

"Maybe things will look better...in the morning," she agreed while swaying in the strong arms of her considerate dinosaur friend.

"Just don't eat me!" she sternly warned him, drifting off to sleep in his arms. "I'm too tough for you. I'd give you indigestion."

Periscus and Socrates were set to eat a feast fit for a king.

Periscus noted that Socrates had a sour expression on his wide, fat face. But Periscus disregarded the expression of his ungrateful "friend." Socrates looked unhappy even when he was happy.

The feast was laid out on long wooden tables in front of a series of large huts. The adults sat at one central table. Around it, on smaller tables, the different ages of kids were seated together. Many wooden bowls contained delicious-looking cooked vegetables, breads, meats, and desserts.

Periscus quickly discovered that during the workweek everyone ate whatever they needed for sustenance at whatever time was convenient. But on the last day of the week, Saturday, the entire village came together for a communal meal.

This was the Athenians' first time to experience the regal spread.

"Let us say grace," Snake solemnly said at the head of the table, bowing his head and folding his hands together in front of him.

Periscus and Socrates, sitting next to each other to the side of Snake, glanced uneasily at each other but did as directed, imitating the actions of the other people.

Periscus noted that the headmaster, "Snake", was kindly speaking in the Greek language for their benefit. At first, he'd spoken a strange speech he called "Iglish"—but then in the space of a day learned the speech of the two new arrivals. Now all the inhabitants spoke Greek around Periscus, though with each other they still spoke their native language.

"OH GREAT LORD ABOVE, BENEATH, AND WITHIN," Snake loudly and sonorously intoned, "PLEASE HEAR OUR HUMBLE PRAYER OF THANKS! IN ADDITION TO THIS DELICIOUS FOOD WE THANK YOU FOR SENDING AWAY THE SPIKERS WHO DIG-ITIZED AND DISSOLVED OUR PREVIOUS, UNWORTHY INCAR-NATIONS!"

"Amen!" was the ritualistic reply from all the other seated adults and children.

"AND WE ALSO WANT TO THANK YOU FOR GRANTING US OUR TRANSFORMATION INTO HUMAN BODIES WITH THEIR CAPACITY FOR CONTINUAL JOYFUL COPULATION AND PRO-LIFERATION!"

"Amen!"

"AND WE ESPECIALLY THANK YOU FOR SPARING ONE DU-PLICATOR UNIT PLUS ONE DARK ENERGY-GENERATOR FROM WHICH MANY MORE UNITS PLUS OUR PRESENT BOUNTY SPRINGS!"

"Amen!"

"AND MOST RECENTLY WE THANK YOU THAT DAVID AND TOMMY, OUR BELOVED LOST FRIENDS, SENT US OUR *NEW* FRIENDS THROUGH THE TIME PORTAL. WE ARE SO GRATE-FUL FOR THEIR FRESH DNA THAT WILL INSURE THE CONTIN-UED VIABILITY OF OUR SMALL, NEW POPULATION OF HU-MANS ON INTO THE DISTANT FUTURE!"

"*Amen!*" they all spoke in unison, concluding the communal, ritu-alistic prayer.

Everybody reached for the bowls...

"Dig in!" Snake grinned at Periscus and Socrates, passing them a bowl loaded with buttered mashed potatoes.

Socrates looked at it suspiciously, but readily spooned out a heap upon his plate, simultaneously reaching for other bowls and platters. He'd remained remarkably quiet the several days that he and Periscus had been in their new land. He was clearly still in shock over his un-expected resurrection by Dave after having drunk the hemlock and died in ancient Athens. He still seemed to think that this new place where he was transported to along with his hated previous enemy, Periscus, was the land of the dead—the underworld! But Periscus saw that the cheerful, pleasant demeanor of the people here was starting to assuage even the "great" philosopher's fears.

"*Humph*," Socrates grunted around a mouthful of roasted turkey meat, "this is tasty. For an uncivilized place, they mount a fine re-past."

"Yes they do," Periscus replied, happily spooning delicious apple pie into his own mouth.

"Too bad they have no wine," the fat old man grunted again, taking a swig of his large glass of sparkling water and grimacing.

"It seems they have no need for fermented drinks to find great pleasure," Periscus noted, looking around at the smiling faces at the table.

Socrates turned his attention back to his loaded plate.

Periscus, a light eater, was more fascinated by the people. The others at the table were pleasantly chatting with each other. Those closest to the two Athenians were politely speaking in ancient Greek. There was talk of the weather, of the crops sprouting in the fields, of a baby about to be birthed—and of the abrupt end of reports sent back through "subspace" by a "*Star*ship"?

Periscus was particularly interested in the god-talk concerning travel to other stars. He found this new life oddly familiar, yet amazingly exhilarating!

To his way of thinking, the people here lived much as he had done in his hut beside the Aegean Sea close to Athens, Greece. They lived here simply and humbly. They, as he had back in Greece, lived in huts, fished in the river, and farmed in the fertile valley using rudimentary tools. In addition they hunted various prey animals in the forest. But they had much more! They possessed godly devices that worked magic—speaking across vast distances, conjuring-up whatever they desired, and even traveling beyond the Earth!

The magic of those devices was similar to the "god-hammer" that Periscus still jealously guarded, carried now in a hastily rigged holster at his waist. When Snake asked to take it, Periscus politely declined. Snake did not persist, but cautioned Periscus on discharging it—as it could inflict great harm. Periscus insisted that he knew full well its power and never would discharge it unless absolutely necessary. Snake seemed happy to leave it to Periscus' keeping.

Periscus gratefully noted that the people in this charming mountain village were pacifists. That suited the old, tall fisherman just fine. He'd had his fill with the "hero-warrior" mentality of the Athenian Empire. All that mindset had ever brought Athens, in Periscus' reckoning, was misery and destruction. A place where people were uncommonly pleasant and cheerful with each other was a welcomed improvement.

Indeed, the last three days were pleasant and relaxing. The villagers gave Periscus and Socrates each a hut of their own and helped them acclimate to their new surroundings. Their bloody, ripped tunics were replaced with tighter and sturdier garments. Their sandals were taken away and "boots" supplied instead, again tighter but more suited to this rocky, hilly environment.

"So the 'Spikers' who you referenced in your prayer, what were they?" Socrates asked their host as he continued shoveling large heaps of food into his mouth.

"Oh, they were alien monsters from the sky," Snake sighed, stroking his goatee as he set his plate to the side.

"I'll take that, dear," Samantha said as she walked past, gathering up dirty dishes.

"I can do it," Snake replied, starting to get up...

"Oh, nonsense," she replied, gently pushing him back. "It is such a nice day—you just relax with our guests. I'm sure they have many questions for you. This is the first time we've been together without work duties since they first arrived. I'll take care of our share of the after-meal chores. You visit with them as long as you wish."

Periscus noticed her protruding belly, smiling at her.

"Yes, another 'bun in the oven' as our dear friend Dave would have said," Snake proudly stated, seeing Periscus' stare. "We are steadily increasing our population. But one baby per year per female is all we can manage. Samantha and I have already have birthed three, who are growing heartily. They are a handful, but also a great joy."

"So these 'Spikers'...?" Socrates reminded him, frowning.

"Yes, my friend," Snake now grimly nodded. "They came from the stars, from an old enemy of ours. We discovered this when one of their ships malfunctioned and crashed. Records inside indicated it came from a great Demon who tried to destroy this world."

"So...you defeated the monsters?" Socrates incisively asked.

"Oh no," Snake sighed. "In fact, they defeated *us*."

Socrates' protruding eyes narrowed as he leaned back in his chair. "Then how are you here?" he asked.

Snake grinned. "We hid in the caverns beneath an ancient city not far from here—led there by our bird-friends."

"Bird-friends?" Socrates asked, leaning forward and placing the elbows of his chubby arms up upon the cleared table.

"Yes," Snake readily replied, "it turned out that beside the primitive prey-birds there's an intelligent sort. They are the 'talkative' arm of intelligent beings created by another friend of ours long ago, Sally Smith. The black birds speak for the entire biosphere of this planet. They developed at the direction and integration of Sally's 'Tommy-children' who escaped from Mars back to here after God inflicted His Divine Judgment upon both Earth and Mars!"

Periscus understood little of this, content to let the more knowledgeable Socrates take the lead.

"Uh...sure," Socrates said, clearly puzzled. "So these god-birds helped you survive?"

"It was hard," Snake said. "For a while only Samantha and I were here, struggling by ourselves. But then others of our kind, escaping the attack by the aliens, were also guided to us by the birds. And since we lacked advanced technology, some agreed with us that the best shot to survive was to transform into the much simpler human form. Also, the joy of human copulation they observed between me and Samantha tempted them greatly."

Socrates frowned even more, putting up a hand to support his wide forehead.

"And before, you were...?"

"Oh, we were an ancient race of intelligent snakes that lived in an alternate Dimension to yours—having originally come to Earth when Mars died, billions of years ago."

Periscus almost snickered. The normally talkative Socrates appeared to be uncharacteristically speechless, likewise struggling to absorb these new concepts.

"But in your prayer you referred to...'duplicators' and 'generators'?"

"Yes, those we managed to salvage from the ruins of our destroyed cities. Those few initial devices were a great help to us. They allowed us to quickly replenish much of our destroyed civilization."

"And are these 'Spikers' still around?" Periscus asked worriedly, suddenly fearful that this idyllic existence might be endangered!

"After overcoming our defenses and taking much of our resources, they departed," Snake sighed gratefully. "But before they departed they swept Earth clean of our fellow intelligent creatures. Nothing was left except for us and a few other groups hidden in caves beneath the ground. Now, though, we've reemerged and are taking back our world."

"So are you going to turn back into...uh, giant intelligent snakes?" Socrates tentatively asked.

"Our group has chosen to remain, forever, in human form," Snake grinned widely. "Versus our slow, highly regimented previous bodies and stagnate society—this new life offers us much pleasure and excitement."

"And what of the others on this New Earth?" Periscus asked, curious.

Kids were now running and jumping around the tables, playing an after-meal game of tag in the warm sunlight.

"There are survivors of our species who remain in their original form," Snake reluctantly admitted.

"That's not good?" Socrates frowned at him.

"Oh, they regard us as filthy heretics," Snake laughed. "They have advanced technology they managed to hide from the Spikers. They're using it to reconstruct a new city. But it will take many years for them to complete. That task will keep them well-occupied and away from us. They—versus our new human form and society—are very slow and stodgy. They won't bother us, I assure you."

"And are there others?" Socrates probed.

"Just one other colony of what our friends Dave and Sally liked to call 'Dinosapiens'," Snake replied. "Those are intelligent large reptiles—oh, you'd call them lizards—stemming from your own past. Their present, evolved forms are revolted by all types of conflict and war. They are our friends. They've sent emissaries, but have nothing to offer us—nor we to them. So they departed. You may see one visiting someday, though. Don't be alarmed. They look fierce but are actually quite gentle."

"And...are there yet other godly creatures here?" Socrates probed further.

"Sadly, no," Snake sighed. "There were a few other intelligent reptiles from other Dimensions—but they perished in the bombardment. So it's just us here in the valley, our Martian progenitors, and the Dinosapiens. I hope this isn't too confusing for you?"

"No, it's...interesting," Socrates nodded. "So are you the Ruler of this wondrous realm?"

Snake laughed. "We have no need of rulers, my friend. We exist here in peace with each other and with our other more-distant fellow intelligent beings."

"But when there are disputes...or arguments...or conflicts on resources...or necessary future planning...surely...?"

"As I said, there are only the three surviving tiny colonies," Snake shrugged. "We have the resources of the entire planet to support us. There is no need for conflicts, even if that were in our nature—which it isn't. Needless fighting is an animal characteristic, foreign to truly-mature intelligent creatures like us. Don't you agree?"

Periscus recognized a charming yet disturbing innocence in Snake.

Socrates ignored the question, a sly look now in his eyes.

"But...you are presently humans, are you not? Or is that simply in appearance, not in fact?" Periscus noted.

"Oh, we've taken on the complete genetics of your species," Snake replied. "That is how we are able to mate and successfully reproduce. But we've not lost our eons of accumulated wisdom. In fact we've retained some of our more-advanced brain structures, generated by what you'd call 'extra' chromosomes in our cells. We've regressed in form but not in mind. So if there is a difference in opinion as to how to proceed on some matter, we simply sit together and talk it out. Do not fear, my friend. It is not possible for us to repeat the mistakes of your tragic species. We know those failings all too well and would never repeat them."

"So you say," Socrates grimaced, looking up at the blue sky above—where a flock of black birds was circling, as if spying on the humans below?

"Hey man, I studied enough human history in the time I spent in your world to appreciate your keen intellect and talents, my good friend Socrates," Snake said, putting a friendly hand on the short man's chubby shoulders.

Periscus saw that though Socrates tolerated the man's hand on his shoulder, he did not appreciate the overly friendly gesture.

"It is a great pleasure to have you here with us," Snake continued, undaunted. "We will have many more fascinating conversations, I'm sure. And if there are areas where your great wisdom would help us proceed as full-fledged humans, please tell us. We highly prize your keen insights and wonderful philosophical genius, friend Socrates— oh, and your more down-to-earth wisdom as well, friend Periscus."

Socrates nodded back, glaring at Periscus for daring to be included in a definition of "wisdom."

"And now, I must introduce you to your new housemates," Snake said, standing up and gesturing to a group of women who'd quietly gathered behind Periscus and Socrates.

"What?" Socrates asked, surprised.

"Housemates?" Periscus repeated, also startled.

Standing expectantly behind him he saw a *dozen* attractive young women! And shyly taking Socrates hand and standing him up to face them were yet *another* dozen striking women!

"You mean...?" Periscus gulped.

"Amongst our survivors, most of them decided to become female," Snake grinned. "They preferred the gentler, estrogen-driven bodies versus the harsh testosterone existence of us 'grubby' males. So since we adopted the one-male-to-one-wife, mating-for-life scenario so important to the deepest love-experience, many of our females were left with no mate."

"Uh, ok, but...?" Periscus frowned as the dozen females pushed against each other to gently caress his arms and neck.

"And since I know from my study of history that you Greek Athenians were often promiscuous, I thought that perhaps you and Socrates could take care of our excess females?"

Socrates sucked in a sudden deep breath, his large belly bouncing beneath his flannel shirt.

"That would be a very valuable service the two of you could provide to our group," Snake sincerely continued. "It would be your main joy in our commune. It would be far more useful to us than merely adding to our manual labor pool...that is, if you agree?"

"I...don't know," Periscus gulped again at the soft hands now caressing his neck, arms, and chest.

"Oh, I'm so sorry," Snake worriedly stated. "Are there too many? We didn't mean to swamp you with reproductive duties. And there's no rush. You can take your time to think about..."

"Oh no, this is fine!" Socrates smiled widely, grabbing two of the ladies by their butt-cheeks. They giggled at him. "It's no problem. I am happy to be of service. I shall gladly fertilize your excess females."

"And you, friend Periscus?" Snake asked.

"Oh...I'll do the best I can...I suppose," he gulped for the third time, astounded at the delights of this heavenly realm.

Yes, this was going to be an amazing experience, indeed!

But he still had a nagging doubt. It just seemed too idyllic. He knew from the many warrior epic poems and ancient myths that in every delightful godly garden there was hidden a deadly *snake*.

Yet the self-avowed "Snake" was right there in front of Periscus. To all appearances he was their kind and solicitous friend. But then again, all snakes are not so harmless.

Were there *other* snakes here with *poisonous* fangs?

As the eager ladies led him back to his hut, Periscus decided to appreciate his blessings and not worry too much about the future.

After all, the main dangers were past...

—weren't they?

Chapter 3

<u>DESOLATION</u>

Sometimes humans forgot
What it was like to be solitary
Accustomed as they were
To living in their milling herds
To be cut off from all others
Existing as single roaming snakes
Was nothing they could know
Until they faced a dead end
A mirror into their distant past
And were forced to confront
Their own reflected visage
Shocked, haunted, and afraid
They had to decide if it was worth
Dying slowly together
Or living fast alone...

Eashoa's Lament, 3:78-82

Tommy was getting tired of writing.

"Oh...those stupid humans, they're so frustrating!" he groaned.

It was really hard to figure them out. But he had to do that to write a fitting eulogy. Yet he was just a little boy! Why did he have this job? Why couldn't some other intelligent entity do it? It should be one of the Martian-derived giant snakes! Or maybe one of those smart dinosaurs. Why did it have to be him?

But...maybe he did have the best perspective.

After all, he'd lived as one of them—but as a perpetual child, with little power or control. Even humans who didn't know he was an android didn't take him seriously. On the one hand their arrogance made him a bit angry. On the other hand, it allowed him to observe them covertly, like a spy in their midst.

Of course Sally always treated him with respect. She was different from the other Priestesses. He was, after all, her special creation, her intellectual "child." She had evolved him inside cyberspace embedded within the entirety of human history and literature.

So she'd literally "bred" him for this job.

Yes, it should be him writing the eulogy for humanity...but it was *so* hard!

"My clothes are wearing off me," he dejectedly observed, looking down at the tattered tunic that now hung off his small frame in shreds. Even his sandals were wearing out. He loved to type on the solar laptop while perched on the peak of the highest mountaintop. The mountains were lower than millions of years in the past when he first lived in the valley. But they were still majestic. However, the jagged rocks abraded his leather sandals climbing up to his beloved peak.

"I guess I could maybe sew together some leaves," he dejectedly thought. But the idea of losing his "civilized" remaining clothes was too depressing. So he clung to the rags that remained about his android limbs.

"Ah well, got to get to work," he cheerfully stated, cling to his routine.

But as—yet again— he laboriously climbed up the slopes and cliffs in the early morning he sighed deeply. It wasn't the most glamorous or exciting work, but he was determined to do his duty.

He clambered up to his favorite spot and looked out over the verdant valley. The rising sun was fully energizing the laptop. He resolutely sat and typed throughout the day. Toward evening he slid back down the slope to sleep beside the central stream in the valley. The gurgling water soothed him. When he awoke the next morning he repeated the same sequence.

He continued doing this day after day, diverting only to consume sufficient fruits and nuts to chemically charge his bodily functions.

As an android he didn't need to poop or pee. He was very efficient in his usage of liquids and food. If he needed to occasionally get rid of excess waste material he just excreted it as sweat. It was "icky" but efficient.

"Mommy would never recognize me now," he sighed to himself, again finishing a day of "work."

He closed the laptop and prepared, yet again, to climb down the steep slopes to the valley floor. "Even my hair is all messed up."

Yes, his once curly-blond locks were now straight and dirty. He hadn't had a shampoo in a long time. Though he splashed himself periodically in the stream, he was starting to look like a street urchin. It was *so* depressing not to be his usual dapper self.

"I should go down and get some rest...again...yet...?"

A strange idea was resonating within his memory circuits.

"Could I...should I?"

The sun had almost set. The battery of the laptop was kicking in. Too little sunlight was falling on the solar panels to provide continual power to the computer. So it was time to call it a day...as he had now for a full *three months*. That was a lot of typing. But he was making good progress. He estimated he was halfway through the eulogy. But he didn't want to rush it. He knew he must do it justice!

Mommy would expect nothing less from him. Dave would be proud that Tommy had continued the difficult poetic style of *The Luminary Chronicles*. And any future aliens visiting Earth deserved a full accounting.

He should just keep at his routine until he finished. Then he could curl up around the laptop computer, protecting it with his near-indestructible body while he switched himself off one final time.

"But..."

He stood up straight on the high peak, looking out across the valley. By now he knew every inch of it. And it was getting very boring. Sure, it was nice to lie amongst the flowers in the meadow—but that was in the spring. Now it was the middle of summer. And it was a *hot* summer. The flowers of spring were long gone, the grass turned brown. Even the trees were wilting, the previously green leaves now crumpled and brittle.

It didn't rain much, hardly at all. The trickle from the artesian well at the top of the valley feeding the stream was about all that sustained this oasis of green.

"This is so sad," Tommy sighed deeply. He turned away from the valley to look at the surrounding desert. The yellow dunes were high and undulating, like frozen waves on a hot ocean.

The dead expanse surrounding him should have scared him.

Instead, it now had an unexpected, *intoxicating* effect. What was out there? Was there just sand, forever...or was there something interesting beyond the horizon?

He carefully stowed the laptop back in the bag he'd made out of his lower tunic, strapping it firmly onto his back.

"It's time for a change," he softly stated to himself. "I can't stay here forever."

So he began climbing down the side of the mountain he'd not yet been on—the side leading out into the desert! He wasn't going back to the valley. He didn't know what was beyond the desert, but he was going to find out. He didn't know if he could survive out there, but his synthetic body could go for a while, if needed, on internal energy stores. And yes he'd keep doing his job, typing on the eulogy, until the very end.

Ironically, the last chapter he'd written—the eleventh—had the title: *"Self Preservation."* Walking into the waterless desert alone—not knowing what was on the other side—was definitely not an act of self-preservation. But as he stated in that chapter, humans were torn between fear and joy. *Fear* caused a human to cower in the gloomy cave where it was safe. *Joy* caused a human to explore the enticing unknown reaches beyond the mountain—where it was dangerous.

Tommy did not count himself worthy to be a human. But he'd been programmed to think like one.

He might die going out into that vast wilderness.

But he'd die with another "self"-characteristic: that of self-respect!

Let that be *his* epitaph.

"He Braved the Unknown!" Tommy grinned to himself, realizing he'd finally shaken off his depression. "'He was a very brave little robot boy—or a very stupid one.' Yep! That's me!"

Mommy would be proud of him.

Of course, maybe he should just abort the sudden compulsion and start across the desert in the morning. After all, it was getting dark. The moon wasn't out yet. It was going to be difficult to see well enough to walk in a straight line.

"Oh well," he sighed, hitting the sand at the base of the mountain. It felt crunchy and fluid. It jumped past his worn-out sandals and snuggled into his toes. "I'll probably get lost in the dark, but walking at night I'll not get cooked in the hot sun!"

Resolutely, he began plodding across the dark sand, lit only by the twinkling stars above.

"IT'S ME, TOMMY THE BRAVE LITTLE ROBOT!" he shouted out at the top of his lungs across the seemingly endless sand dunes as he trudged into them. "I'M WALKING INTO THE DESERT TO MEET YOU!"

His words rang out loudly into the night. Was there a lonely lizard or tarantula listening? He hoped so. But nothing answered back.

Dave crept onward through the darkness. It was hard to know where he was going without the sun to guide him.

He held onto his hurting left side, limping along painfully.

He knew he had to keep away from houses and streets, lest someone in this hyper-vigilant alternate society reporting him to the police. But having grown up in Sulphur, Oklahoma, he knew what *should* be there. He was sure that the National Park was immediately south of the town. And the Park was close to where his mother's house was located...but that was in *his* Dimension. He didn't even know if a version of him or of his mother existed in this parallel Dimension. But then again, Kyle seemed to think so.

Well, it was as a good a destination as any. So he furtively snuck around through the woods in the extensive Park, headed around to 12th street. After that he'd go north a few blocks and see if his Mom's house was there.

He kept listening for the sounds of sirens, attack dogs, or helicopters coming after him.

He remembered his previous short time in the alternate dimension, being shot at by their ruthless police, the Keepers! It was terrifying. He expected the same to occur at any moment.

But after a while he relaxed. It seemed he'd gotten away from the Megamart without stirring a fuss behind him. It was certainly lucky for him that Kyle was waiting to sneak him out of the store...but how'd he know Dave would be there? Oh, right, Kyle said *Sally* had warned him. But w*hich* Sally?

It was getting more and more confusing.

He paused to slip the coveralls on over his tunic. He also put on the heavy boots, discarding his worn-out sandals. The boots were loose, but protected his feet against unseen rocks and tree roots lurking to stub his toes and scrape his lower legs in the darkness.

Plus if anyone saw him, he'd look somewhat normal—not like a lost Greek Aristocrat newly arrived from over two millennia in the past!

It took several hours, but eventually—in the dead of the night—he found himself walking briskly up the sloped 12th Street...to the corner of 12th and Ardmore.

He was so tired that he didn't even notice the throbbing in his left side anymore...

—until something flared like *hot coals* thrust onto his skin! Wincing, he looked down at his burning wrist. The *Anaconda Tattoo* that circled his left wrist and forearm was glowing!

Yes, he was clearly on the right track.

A house stood there before him on a large lot. It certainly looked like his mother's house. But it was obviously abandoned. In the pale starlight Dave saw that the roof was in bad shape, with several gaping holes. The windows were broken out. And the slates on the outer walls were hanging loose.

It wasn't hard to break into the locked back door, which swung inward with just a light tap from his shoulder.

Inside, it smelled musty and rancid. Rain leaking in through the bad roof must have rotted the interior. Everything was dank and dark...

"*Wraaawwwllll!*" a *screech* almost gave Dave a heart-attack as a cat scampered out of the house. He'd stepped on its tail.

"Jesus Christ, it's dark in here!" Dave gasped, one hand out as he fumbled forward.

"It took you long enough," a soft voice greeted him. "And I wish you'd learn to watch where you're going and not step on that damn cat! I keep moving it to a new location and each time you inevitably stumble onto it."

Dave blinked as a flashlight suddenly shone in his eyes, blinding him!

"What...*who* are you?" Dave said, shielding his eyes and trying to see through the glare, not understanding the admonition concerning the cat.

Then he made out the figure in front of him.

It was Sally.

He couldn't see much of her other than the glare of the flashlight, but he readily recognized her pert, girlish figure...and her unmistakable, sweet voice.

But she wasn't behaving so "sweetly."

In one hand she held the flashlight. And in the other hand was a *big black Keeper super-handgun—*which was pointed straight at him!

This Dimension was just getting stranger and stranger. Sally wasn't his enemy. She was his friend, wasn't she? But then why was she holding a gun on him?

"Hands up, Dave," she ordered him.

Bewildered, he tentatively raised his hands.

"But...but Sally, what's going on?"

"Sit down and don't irritate me further. We'll wait silently for Kyle to arrive," she ordered him. She motioned with the gun at a decrepit, dirt-covered sofa. "You're giving me a headache."

"Uh, ok, sorry...so what happens now?" he asked as he wearily sat down into old fabric. It sank beneath him as loose springs simultaneously poked up into his butt.

The seat was squishy but welcomed. He was so banged-up that the metal points of the springs didn't even hurt. He now became aware of lumps all over his body. His recent falls must have been worse than they'd seemed at the time!

"I *said* to keep quiet."

"Please, Sally..." he begged her.

"Alright," she sighed deeply as if very exasperated with him. "Now we win the Revolution. At least that's the plan, assuming you've finally grown the balls to do your part."

"What?"

"Oh, just shut up," she grimaced. "I don't want to waste my fire-power stunning you," she concluded menacingly, lifting the gun up and pointing it at him.

Despite his many question, Dave saw she meant what she was saying. He clamped his mouth tightly shut.

The faint light from the flashlight reflected onto her face made her seem less like Dave's old friend and more like a pseudo-Sally *demon*. This definitely wasn't the "Sally" he was used to dealing with.

Dennis was worried about Sally.

He'd gone to her quarters to wake her up for breakfast, not that there was much to eat. But she hadn't answered his knocks at her cabin's door.

That didn't bother him because he knew she hadn't slept for the whole three prior days. She needed recuperative, deep sleep more than a few bites of starvation-rations food. So he decided to let her sleep on into the afternoon.

Later in the day he went back and knocked again.

Again there was no answer.

This time he was alarmed!

"Sally?" he rasped. It was still hard for Dennis to pronounce the English words. His tongue, mouth, and voice box weren't constructed for the complex sounds. He'd much rather speak in the clicks, guttural grunts, and whistles of his native language. But that would be far too difficult for Sally to learn, even if they had the time, which they didn't!

So he was willing to put up with the painful contortions of his throat to communicate effectively with his little mammalian friend.

And, yes, Dennis considered Sally to be his friend. At first when they'd been thrown together—trying to conjure the spare parts to their original, ruined ship DE-generator into a working new drive unit—he'd been very irritated with the young, abrasive female human. But then, despite himself, he got attached to her.

True, she was a misshapen, ugly little snub-faced creature—but she had a keen mind. He appreciated her quick wit, so unlike the stately slow considerations of his species. A typical "conversation" amongst his kind was a long series of thoughtful pauses. With Sally you had to be always on your toes or she'd be ten steps ahead of you mentally by the time you even grasped her initial words. It was both immensely frustrating and exhilarating at the same time!

He'd definitely grown fond of the clever little mammal.

"Sally!" he now yelled at the closed door. "You've been sleeping a long time! You need to eat some food! Open the door, Sally!"

Nothing...

Wait—was that a faint *moaning* he heard?

Without another thought of being discrete or polite, he stepped back then *lunged* forward putting his considerable weight behind his shoulder, *smashing*-in the door.

The lock snapped as the door SLAMMED inward.

Sally was lying on her bunk, her blanket pulled up over her upper body and head.

"D-Dennis..." he heard her small voice coming from under the covers. Her voice sounded very blurred and...*wet*—like she was drowning!

He yanked back the covers.

She lay there shivering, curled into a fetal ball, with large *tumors* pushing out of all parts of her exposed body.

"Sally!" he gasped, snatching her up in his arms and rushing her toward the infirmary.

She was completely unconscious by the time he got her there.

Alice, on duty, took one shocked look at the grotesque mass of tumors and slipped the small, convulsing body under a magnetic resonance imaging station.

It was a big drain of their dwindling power reserves, but neither she nor Dennis gave it a second thought.

The virtual slices through Sally's body—jumping up on a small computer screen—were horrifying.

Not only were ugly, oozing tumors covering almost every inch of her face, head, and body—they were throughout her body cavities and organs.

And on the table, Sally twisted and turned as if she were in great pain.

"I'm not sure how she is still alive," Alice gasped, running to grab syringes and inject Sally with several powerful drugs.

The jerking of Sally's monstrous body eased.

"What is happening?" Dennis gasped, flashing his hand-claws about in the air in confusion. "She was fine yesterday—maybe tired and despondent—but nothing like this. This is...hideous!"

Alice shook her head sadly. "When you and she saved the ship by getting the backup DE–generator working, was there radiation from the alien generator?"

"Well, yes—but I was there also," he said in English to his human-looking Dinosapien colleague. "And I don't have tumors throughout my body. Besides, this literally happen overnight. It's impossible!"

Alice gestured to the slices still cycling on the computer screen. Clearly, impossible or not, it had happened.

"The massive radiation dose you two experienced in the engine room must have caused it," Alice frowned. "Your thick hide would absorb a lot of it. She'd, however, be far more susceptible. And she was in that room a lot longer than you. But still, you're right. To oc-cur this fast...?"

Sally moaned on the table, the oozing slit where her mouth used to be flapped open and made garbled words.

"My...uhm, immune system...balancer optimizer...need booster..."

George, Alice's human-looking husband, ran into the room, took one look at Sally, and reeled back in shock. Then he took Sally's al-most unrecognizable hand in his own somewhat chubby hand. He gripped it tightly, as if to keep her from slipping away.

"Is it what saved your mother from her cancer back on Earth, Sal-ly?" he urgently asked. "Is that what you need?"

"Y-yes...got at b-birth...then yearly boosters... it's been l-long time since I had one...immune system's c-collapsed," she managed to gasp before falling silent again.

Then there was only an awful sputtering and hacking sound from Sally. She was struggling just to breathe.

"It's a catastrophic collapse of her immune system coupled with that large radiation exposure," Alice said to George and Dennis. "Plus there's whatever effect we've all experienced bein wrenched from our Universe into this new one. The Laws of Nature are different here. A of that together explains the incredibly fast growth of her tumors. I'm afraid Sally's got to have a dose of her retroviral-overlapping immune balancers to have any hope of surviving—what she calls the 'Optimmune' pills."

"Do we have any?" Dennis frantically asked.

"They exist in another Dimension, in another Universe, billions of years away from us," George miserably concluded, still holding the oozing lump that was Sally's exposed hand.

"I don't think she'll last another hour," Alice now sobbed beside George.

"Then there's only one other option," Dennis firmly said, snatching up Sally. "Call some techs to the Demon's 'private' collection of Tube. We've got to figure out how to open one of them up, immediately!"

He exited the clinic, running toward the cargo hold, George right behind him.

"You're going to try and put her into Time-Freeze?" George said, running with difficult on his two dumpy legs behind the strongly-striding Dinosapien.

"Yes! That's our only hope to save her. We'll *freeze* her until sometime in the future when we're able to treat her condition."

George was panting heavily behind Dennis, struggling to keep up with him.

"But we need her *now*," George protested. "To survive here we've got to have access to her native mammalian cunning and quick thinking. You know us Dinosapiens—whether transformed outwardly into human form or not—don't have the constitution or ability to face the conflicts and problems of this new Universe!"

They were now in the storage hanger where dozens of the large tubes were piled up.

Other Dinosapiens were stomping in as well.

"Sort through these! Look through the fog. See if you can recognize whoever's inside each Tube," Dennis ordered them.

"What are you doing?" George said, staggering to a stop. "Any of the tubes would work, right? We should just grab the nearest one!"

"Try to figure out the controls on the outside, George. I know what I'm doing. We've got to be ready just as soon as we find a suitable Tube."

"But these are already occupied!" George said, frantically studying the punch-controls on the outer surface of each tube.

"Exactly! There! *That* one!" Dennis yelled excitedly. He looked through the fog of one of the Tubes to see inside a shorter female with a terrified, scrunched-up expression on her pixy-like face.

"I don't know if this will work, but…"

"*Do* it, George! Sally's not breathing. She's gone into cardiac arrest!"

The bald-headed man pushed a series of buttons…

—and the top half of the Tube opened outward, revealing…

Sally.

It was a somewhat older version of their tumor-ridden, teenaged Sally. But it was obviously her. Inside the spreading fog roiling out of the tube were the same big green eyes, fluffy red-brown hair, and perky nose.

"*Nnnnooooooooo….!*" the tubed Sally suddenly screamed-out, thrashing about wildly before quieting as she was roughly dragged from the tube.

"W-what the hell…where am I?" she gasped as she sagged against one of the cargo hold walls, peering around in panic.

Then Dennis saw her eyes focus on him—a T-rex-like dinosaur looming above her—and she *screamed!* Before Dennis could calm her she slumped to the side, fainted dead away.

There wasn't time to be overly concerned about this new Sally. She was breathing steadily. For the moment she was fine.

"Get her in! Get her in!" Dennis urgently ordered, helping George and another technician stuff their Sally's oozing, tumor-ridden body into the now-empty Tube.

Slamming the top back closed, Dennis stood anxiously to the side as George and the technician tried to get the Tube to reactivate…

—and sagged with relief as the twitching body inside suddenly *froze motionless*, a new fog springing up around her grotesquely-swollen face.

"We did it...we did it," George sighed, slumping in relief across the top of the now shut and functioning Tube.

Alice came running in and gasped at the sight of the *new, older Sally* lying unconscious on the floor!

"And...what do we do...about *her?*" Alice asked. "We don't know from where or when she originated. She probably doesn't even know that she died. This is going to be a terrible shock to her!"

"Lock her into Sally's quarters," Dennis sighed, suddenly feeling very weak. The last few minutes had drained him of what little strength he still possessed. "Once she wakes up we'll see if she can at least partially replace our own dear Sally."

"And if she can't?" George asked, similarly exhausted, panting heavily.

Dennis shrugged, reaching down to gently hoist up the unconscious new Sally in his scaly arms. "Then we thaw out another."

Chapter 4

<u>POWER</u>

Why did the humans enjoy Dominance so much?

When it only caused them pain and headaches

Exercising it triggered reactions of equal strength

Where gaining control provoked insurrections

The conquered biding their time to weld a knife

Slitting the throat of their hated oppressors

Forging racial memories for bloody revenge

A satisfaction fleeting if at all, zero security

Only a sad diversion from their own weakness

Where self-delusion maybe provided brief refuge

But cackling Death easily conquered everyone...

And yet the greatest of all was a Servant.

Eashoa's Lament, 4:13-16

Socrates was growing to like the spirit world.

It took several weeks of delightful effort, but he'd managed to satisfy the pent up sexual appetites of his dozen new "wives." They each now claimed to be happily pregnant. They welcomed his further embrace, but were content in his absence—knowing that with his "assistance" they'd successfully completed their primary mission.

As explained to him by Snake, the small colony of pseudo-humans was being infused with fresh, original, full-blooded genetic diversity.

"Not the worst job in the world," Socrates mused to himself.

Each was externally a very intelligent, beautiful woman—but quite different from the Athenian females of his time. These present transformed females had an easy awareness not only of their equality with him, but even *superiority*. So from their viewpoint he was merely a valued but inferior partner. It was a position to which he was unaccustomed. His wife back in ancient Athens, Xanthippe, whom he'd chosen for her spunk and intelligence, knew full-well that he was the undisputed "master of the house." To the contrary, these godly female creatures "knew" they were *not* his possessions, but rather regarded *him* as *their* sexual toy.

"Bah! I'm far more than a mere "sperm donor" or mindless sex toy," he grunted to no one in particular. "I am a Great Man, deserving to be a Philosopher King, to rule over all these inferior beings!"

But his rantings went unnoticed. He saw that most of the occupants of the village regarded him as an amusing clown, to be humored. To his face they were polite, but behind his back they laughed at his antics.

It infuriated him.

So as several months slipped by, he separated from his charming harem in the communal longhouse they shared. He chose to spend more and more time alone in his small hut, brooding. He was growing restless, impatient with the staid village-life in the valley "paradise." And it didn't help that the women of his group were now increasingly visibly pregnant. Their bulging bellies constantly reminded him of a dozen squalling babies on the way—to whom he'd have to fulfill the duties of a father. Horrors!

And he couldn't escape those responsibilities. He was much too old to be out tilling the fields or fishing, yet too ambitious to merely sit on a stool looking out over the beautiful scenery. Clearly, his primary fast-approaching role would be that of a glorified babysitter!

For Socrates, that was a fate worse than death.

He almost envied the stupid fisherman, Periscus, who seemed incredibly happy with his own harem—and delighted daily to go and fish the river with his new buddies. Indeed he was teaching them ancient fishing techniques they'd never heard of before.

Indignity of indignities, the village people honored and respected that nobody fisherman more than he!

He began to hate Periscus even more than he'd done back in ancient Athens.

Fortunately for his sanity, the human-appearing god "Snake" often came to sit and converse with him.

It was the one bright spot for the morose Socrates in this incredibly boring and humiliating realm of the gods.

"And what of your parent gods...uhm, I mean your other surviving kinfolk who chose to stay in their initial forms?" Socrates tentatively asked his friend as they both sat on chairs looking out over the valley below.

Kids were running in the meadow laughing and shouting, attended by several adults. Socrates knew that in just a few months that would be him down there, waddling about herding a gaggle of kids and crying babies.

It was an awful thought.

The sun shone brightly from a cloudless sky. To all appearances, this was an idyllic setting. But to Socrates it was unbearably tedious. No one was interested in his philosophical musings. No one debated with him. They were still extremely polite to him—but as to a visiting distant mentally handicapped relative, not a dignitary. And he was acutely aware that they were not real humans. They were alien gods thinking alien thoughts that did not connect to him.

That is, except for Snake—who, having lived as a spy amongst true humans for a number of years—had deep insight into the thoughts of intelligent mammals.

"Their new city is functioning optimally now," Snake thoughtfully answered Socrates' question. He absently stroked his short goatee. "It is much smaller than before the Spikers invaded, of course. Actually, there are only a few hundred surviving individuals—many were slaughtered when the city defenses fell. But their number will increase over the coming decades. They are already discussing the merits of a new hatch."

"They lay eggs? How marvelous," Socrates politely said, appalled at the thought. He mentally pictured giant, intelligent snakes squirting out eggs. And they claimed to be an ancient race that originally came from the planet Mars. How ridiculous was that? Here they were pacifists that barely survived a bombardment from the skies by slinking away to hide in cracks and tunnels beneath the earth—and yet they claimed heritage to the Martian *god of war*, Ares!

Clearly, they needed firm paternalistic guidance.

And Socrates was just the man to give it to them—whether they wanted it or not!

"You know...Snake...I'd enjoy visiting that city. Do you think that would be possible?" Socrates tentatively asked, trying not to appear too eager.

Snake looked like he was seriously considering Socrates' request, again stroking his goatee while wagging his head up and down—the greasy long hair to the sides of his head bobbing.

"I will make that request for you," he finally replied. "I don't know if they will grant the request, mind you. So don't get your hopes up. They've always been interested in human evolution, as both an academic subject and necessity to their own survival, you see. But they might not welcome one coming into their midst. I'm afraid that they look down on you and are...well, *repelled*...by your appearance, friend Socrates."

"I promise to be on my *best* behavior," Socrates forced himself to sound cheerfully accommodating while seething within at the insult.

"I think I'd need a better reason for your visit than just satisfying your curiosity."

"Well, what about the Spikers?"

"Yes?"

"They almost entirely destroyed your world, right?"

"Yes—that's true..."

"And are you sure they will never come back?"

A sudden wave of abject fear came over Snake's face as he sharply sucked in his breath.

"We...assumed...they'd gotten what they wanted and would never return," he frowned.

"But say, if they *did* return for more—what then?" Socrates gently urged him.

"Well...we'd...probably be totally wiped out," Snake gulped, shaking his head in disbelief. "We haven't...even considered this...let alone made any preparations."

"Why not?" Socrates said, trying to sound genuinely concerned.

"It's not...in our nature," Snake groaned. His normally-tanned face was now ashen. "We...just don't think...about such uncivilized and repugnant behavior as warfare."

"Ah..." Socrates knowingly nodded. "But I do! In fact, I have an *extensive* knowledge of such terrible things."

"Extensive knowledge?" Snake looked at him hopefully. "But I thought you were a gentle thinker, a philosopher—a man of intellect rather than brawn?"

"Oh, I certainly am such," Socrates bobbed his big head in the affirmative. "But I am also well-trained in the conduct of war. In my youth I was a Hoplite soldier. I fought with my own fists and weapons in several major battles. Plus I advised my government on tactics and strategies in a whole succession of land and sea *wars* against several terrible enemies—both from within and without the Athenian Empire."

"That's...very impressive," Snake slowly nodded. "But still, my more conservative friends in the city would be even more appalled at the prospect of allowing a brutish soldier into their midst to..."

"No, I'm *not* a brute!" Socrates interrupted him. Then, suppressing a snarl and plastering a friendly smile upon his face he continued. "As I acquired more and more first-hand knowledge of the horrors of war, I was moved to become—as you've told me—the most famous Philosopher in all of human history. I do indeed know firsthand the dirty, terrible, bloody 'art' of war—yet I am equally appalled by it. So I am 'kin' to your violence-adverse people, yet have the direct experience plus strategic knowledge you'd need to survive another Spiker attack, should such a terrible thing occur," he hastened to add.

"Yessss...." Snake nodded, disconcertingly reverting to a snake-like hiss. Socrates knew he'd hit a nerve in the man's psyche. "But in these warsssss of yoursss—did you win?"

Socrates had to struggle to keep the casual smile on his lips...he'd set the hook into his fish and was reeling it in. Hah! He was just as good a "fisherman" as that old fool Periscus.

"Some we did—but others we lost," he truthfully admitted. "But in doing so I learned many valuable lessons. If all you do is win then you are not prepared to do the most difficult things that insure your continued survival. In fact, my dear friend, your defeat at the hands of the Spikers may well have prepared you to *learn* how to survive in a hostile Universe—as you've kindly taught me," he added, trying to appear grateful and submissive.

"And...you say that you can teach us these survival techniques?"

"It would be my pleasure to share with my fine hosts that knowledge—plus anything else I might have of value to both you and them," Socrates graciously bowed at his waist as he still sat solidly on his chair.

"So this is why Dave and Tommy sent you to us!" Snake said, jumping up enthusiastically.

"Uhm...sure, why not?" Socrates brightly laughed.

Kids were now running up to Socrates and gleefully grabbing onto his stout legs to climb up into his lap.

Socrates forced a shaky smile onto his face, gingerly patting the kids' heads in a seemingly paternalistic way.

Sweat started to bead on his wide forehead.

"So you'll make the request?" he asked, his forced smile wavering.

"I certainly shall," Snake said. "You've convinced me that we don't have a moment to lose. The Elders must learn of your expertise and meet with you right away!"

"Good...that's good," Socrates continued to grin wanly, gingerly lifting the kids off his wide lap to place them back on the ground—as Snake went rushing away to speak into one of his magic long-distance communication devices.

"Just as *soon* as possible," Socrates muttered to himself, letting the grin splayed across his face dissolve into a scowl.

He shook off the remaining kids and escaped back to his hut.

These godly creatures thought that he was just a happy accident come to help them with a big problem. No, he was far more than that. *He* was their superior! They were mere smart animals while he was a human! And it wouldn't be long until they would *all bow to him* as their Philosopher King!

And then they would give him anything that he wanted.

Tommy was nearing the limit of his endurance.

He'd been walking now for weeks. His destination was due west from the valley oasis. He could have picked any direction, but if the Earth's topography was similar to that of a billion years in the past he should be headed toward an ocean. He traveled mostly at night when the heat was less oppressive. During the daytime, with the swollen sun blazing down from above, the temperature amongst the naked sand dunes soared to unbearable levels, which might even compromise his tough android construction. Consequently he spent most of the days hiding in whatever shadows he might find. After snatching a few exhausted hours of sleep he spent the rest of the day busily typing on the Eulogy.

He hadn't forgotten nor neglected his primary mission. In his lonely trek across the wilderness, he was still typing a final tribute to the vanished *Homo sapiens* race—though the writing was getting increasingly difficult. Some days he only managed to write a few sentences.

He was now sagged against a sand dune, shielded from the blazing sun by some naked overhanging boulders. The sun would soon set so that he could resume his trek. But he didn't feel up to it. In fact, he felt so weak that he doubted that he could even stand!

He hadn't had anything to eat for weeks. Fortunately, several severe storms had rolled across the skies, bringing torrential rains and flash floods. But the sands absorbed the moisture as if it never occurred. Yet Tommy was able to "drink from the sky" enough to keep his internal mechanisms fluidized. But even that wasn't enough to keep him going.

Even android flesh has a limit. He knew he was dying.

"*Chapter Twelve...'The Socratic Method','*" he mumbled to himself as he sat slowly typing letter-by-letter on the solar-powered laptop. "Hmmmm...that's to learn by experience, right? Socrates taught humans to question everything...accepting nothing on mere faith or tradition...not just blindly 'do' but to say 'why?'...and yet, did the other humans ever really learn to do what he taught?"

He leaned his now sand-encrusted head back against the hard dune behind him, wishing that a dark cloud would come by with rain. He needed a shower.

"Well...Mommy and Dave tried to do it, I think—but what about the other people?" he sighed to himself, slowly closing the laptop's lid. "The rest were mostly just smart animals looking to eat, mate, and multiply. They hardly ever asked 'why'...just worried about the one moment in front of them, not the future...but...?"

Tommy shook his head in disgust. Writing this book was teaching him a lot about his former masters. They were mostly a bunch of stupid idiots! No wonder the Creator allowed Judgment Day to destroy their world.

"And now that they're gone—only I'm left," he sighed, forcing his incredibly depleted body to stand up.

He dejectedly stowed his laptop in his backpack and forced himself to take one step forward.

"One step," he muttered to himself, his head hanging down, "Just one step is all you've got to do, Tommy Boy! Ok, I did it. Yay! And now...just one step more is all...just one little step...hah..."

And so saying, he staggered slowly away into the gathering night, one faltering step at a time.

He wondered what Socrates would have made of his effort?

From his historical files he knew that the "great man" was really quite a rascal. He'd probably just laugh in Tommy's face and say "piss off, you stupid robot. Leave the human race where it deserves to be, dead and forgotten."

Regardless, Tommy wanted to finish his job. But he felt increasingly powerless to exert any further impact upon the world.

The end was drawing near.

Dave stared at the shadowy figure across the room from him.

He was still sitting on the decrepit couch, she across from him in a rickety chair. And she was still holding the black super-gun on him.

He knew she'd forbidden him to talk. But what was she going to do to him, shoot him? For some reason she needed him. And he was growing increasing angry at her inexplicable behavior.

"Sally...is it really you?" he finally asked in the darkness.

She switched off the weak flashlight. Now the only light was from a distant streetlamp, a faint glow coming in through a broken window.

"Please don't ask any questions," she curtly admonished him.

Outside in the dead of the night, insects were "cricketing." He heard the distant bark of dogs. At least they still had pets in this bizarre parallel Dimension.

"Why not?" he replied. He was getting increasingly irritated at her dismissive attitude!

"Because I've heard it before so many times I may just kill you right now and start this cycle all over again," she sighed deeply. "I'm hoping this is the last time I have to go through all of this, so be quiet and play your part. It won't be long now, I assure you..." her voice tapered off.

Play my part? What the bloody hell is she talking about?

She was hard, unyielding, and scary!

Yet it was definitely Sally—but a very different Sally than he remembered. Now that his eyes were adjusting better to the darkness inside the abandoned house he saw that she wore dark black slacks and a long-sleeved, loose black shirt—a stereotypic "ninja" outfit. Also, her head was shaved completely bald! But her vivid green eyes, that he remembered so well, *gleamed* at him through the darkness.

She seemed very tough, at least from the rasping sound of her voice. She was obviously no longer a giggling young girl. This Sally was a young woman, seemingly as tough as steel!

To Dave she was a crouching female black panther, coiled to spring.

Was this the Sally he'd lost in the White Void—or another version of her from some other timeline?

He had to know.

"Look, Sally, you've got to answer..." he began as he leaned toward her.

—and she stood up with a motion as smooth as a leaping cat, *smacking* him right across his face with her opened palm!

He lurched backward on the sofa, shocked.

His cheek smarted painfully.

"Say anything more and I'll knock you unconscious with my gun!" she growled at him. "But I don't want to hurt you—you've got enough lumps on you as it is."

This was *definitely* not the Sally he was used to.

She slumped back into her chair.

"If you're getting bored," she continued, more resignedly, "then you can go look around the house. Here, take my flashlight. Keep it on low so nobody sees light coming out the windows. You'll find the interior quite instructive."

Then she continued silently sitting there in her chair, ignoring him. He heard a faint humming coming from her as if she were endlessly repeating a familiar song. He thought it sounded like "*Swing low, sweet chariot.*" *That* brought back some painful memories... Clearly, her mind was elsewhere.

Wordlessly, still smarting from the slap, he shakily took the offered flashlight. Stiffly, he got to his feet and carefully walked into what remained of the mostly gutted house. There was considerable rubble and rotting debris, just as you'd expect from an abandoned house into which rain freely leaked. Everything was moldy and damp.

In what used to be a bedroom, Dave found a crushed bureau. Digging down through rotted wooden layers, he found near the bottom drawers a still-intact small picture frame. It was well-sealed. But the glass was coated in dirt. He pulled out a piece of his tunic from beneath his coveralls and began wiping the frame clean. Then, switching the flashlight onto the low beam and holding it close, he saw the picture.

Looking back at him was an *image of his father and mother!* At least it looked like them. But they didn't look happy. In fact, they were both in chains!

And it wasn't static.

They were both wavering back and forth in the frame, with the woman reaching out to grab her husband's hand as best she could while being chained!

Dave felt a twist of deep emotion inside his gut. He hadn't even known if he existed in Sally's world. Now he knew that his parallel parents, at least, had once lived in that very house in Sulphur, Oklahoma.

It was some sort of repetitive, short video—playing and replaying...

Slipping the picture into a pocket of his oversized coveralls, he continued digging through the rotted wood. Then he saw another picture, this one cracked through its middle. One half was ruined from leaked water. The other half showed an arm swinging a tennis racket. And above the arm was the short-haired, clean-shaven face of a teenaged boy—himself!

And, yes, like the picture of his parents, this one was also moving! Yep, he went through a complete forehand stroke, "smacking" the ball zooming in at him as the racket continued on up around his neck in a full swing!

So...in this alternate dimension, he'd existed.

Silently, he made his way back into the main living room where Sally sat.

He put the two pictures side-by-side on the couch and shined his light so she could see them.

Sally sighed as if she'd done this many times before—reaching into her own pocket to pull out a *two-inch-square, white cube*.

Seemingly mocking him, she leaned forward and set it down between the two pictures.

Intrigued, he picked it up. It was warm to the touch, with a faint inner glow permeating out.

"What should I...?" he began to say, defying her order not to speak to her, when a *tiny holographic figure* jumped up—floating in the air right above the cube!

Dave was amazed by the detail of the three-dimensional, translucent image. It was of an elderly man with neatly-combed-back white hair, impeccably attired in a crisp brown suit. He had on thick black glasses. He was very official-looking, yet attentive—as if he were waiting for Dave to say something.

"How may I help you?" a little voice finally came from the figure, seemingly grudgingly taking the initiative.

Dave peered in fascination at the holographic figure. It was obviously *intelligent*, not just a "canned" projection.

"Who are you?" Dave softly asked.

"I am a Custodian," he crisply replied. "How may I help you?" he impatiently repeated.

"So...you're the embodiment of Google?" Dave cautiously asked.

"I don't know what is a 'Google', Sir" the white-haired figure politely replied. "I am an official Custodian of the Network Archives, here to serve your needs. I am presently constrained from communicating outward across the Network, but can access it as I wish."

"And just how were you 'constrained'?" Dave asked, intrigued.

"Master Smith limited my access," he promptly replied. "But she also enhanced my cognitive functions. In some ways I am your equal. In other ways I am your superior. Does that bother you?"

Dave almost laughed at its casual arrogance.

Wow! It was a truly interactive artificial intelligence! This was way beyond the capabilities of so-called "responsive" computer programs in Dave's Dimension. It clearly wasn't yet a highly evolved "Tommy" robot with a fully developed, independent form and mind— but it certainly pointed in that direction.

"Are you...a quantum computer?" Dave guessed.

It was the only possible way that Dave knew that such a small structure could contain a complex intelligence. But quantum computers were still largely theoretical in his Dimension. The "Custodian" bespoke a highly advanced technological base.

"Part of my construction is indeed configured on quantum principles," the figure primly replied, seemingly somewhat offended—as if Dave had asked him about his crude biological functions. "Are you threatened by me?"

"No, that doesn't bother me," Dave nodded to the little, glowing figure. "In fact, I find it fascinating. But what I really need to know is what happened to me...I mean to the *David Richard King* of this world."

"Executed as an Enemy of the State, ten years ago," the man crisply replied. "Would you like to see a video recording the event?"

Dave swallowed hard before answering.

In the dim light Sally heavily sighed, as if it was all abysmally boring.

"Yes," Dave grimly replied, determined to know everything.

In place of the prim Custodian, another 3D video image was forming—that of a tied-up, ashen-faced Dave in his late twenties, being marched into a closed chamber. A "guilty" verdict was briefly read off-camera. And then a yellow gas filled the room.

The tiny Dave in the image struggled to breathe, gasping and choking, with tears streaming from his eyes...then, foaming at the mouth, he slowly sagged to the floor out of view of the camera.

Dave was shocked, looking now in disbelief at the reappeared Custodian. Dave had just witnessed his own death. The Cube in Dave's hand was hot—as if it took a good deal of energy to display the holographic execution recording.

"And...his parents?" Dave grimly continued.

"Executed one week later as associates of a known Enemy of the State," the Custodian promptly replied. "The pic-vid you have of them there on the couch was taken shortly before they were killed. It is a recording of them inside their cell in chains. Your surviving relatives were forced to hang the prison pic-vid onto their wall as a constant reminder of what happens to those who are deemed offenders by the State. Would you like to see the full video documentation of their execution? It is similar to what occurred with the primary offender."

"No," Dave said, struggling to breathe steadily as he sagged back on the poking springs of the ruined couch.

He could feel the yellow poisonous gas burning-into his own lungs...and to think that his own Mother and Father were also executed, for the simple "crime" of being his parents!

It was hideous.

"Those videos in the picture look so sharp and realistic," Dave shakily sighed. "It's like I was looking through a small window at the living people, not just a representation that...?"

"You *are* looking at the real people," the Custodian calmly interrupted. "In fact, it was Master Smith that developed the technique before her disappearance with you at the Megamart. It is time-linked to provide you with the actual view of that particular captured configuration."

"You mean...it's...*really*...them and me?" Dave gasped in disbelief and shock.

That made it all the more terrible!

Sally reached over and abruptly took the Cube back out of Dave's slack hand.

"Why don't you lie down on the couch and get some sleep?" she directed him. "You'll need to be rested for what's coming."

Trying not to break out sobbing, Dave picked up the two "pic-vids" and slowly placed them in a pocket of his coveralls. Then he stretched out on the couch, grateful to let his banged-up body relax.

He knew full well that the two people in the picture were not his parents. The ones killed by the monstrous State in this authority-dominated Dimension were the father and mother of a different version of himself. But they looked so alive, yet resigned to their fate, in the picture in his pocket—and then to be summarily executed...why? What did this version of him do that was so terrible his parents along with him were sentenced to death?

But then again, everything in this crazy Dimension didn't make much sense to Dave.

But his heavy eyes overcame his hurting back. Maybe he'd just shut his eyes for a couple minutes...

It seemed he'd just closed his eyes when he was jerked awake by a big man holding a palm over his mouth!

It was Kyle.

"Hey, Boss!" Kyle whispered. "I be off duty now, swung by to see if you made it here. You seen Sally yet?"

"Y-yes," Dave managed to whisper back, sitting up stiffly. "B-but she w-wouldn't talk to m-me and..."

Kyle softly laughed. "Yep, that be like that girl. She knows better than everybody else—and lets them know it too! But it's best to do what she says, Boss. She's one mean guerilla, that's for sure."

"Guerilla?" Dave answered, confused...wait! Hadn't she said something about some "revolution"?

"Come on, now," Kyle said, lending a strong arm to get Dave up off the poking springs of the old couch. "She say I should get you out of here over to our safe house in black-town. So that's where we be going before the Keepers get here!"

Dave groaned, realizing that big lumps were now covering much of his legs as well as his left arm.

What the hell was happening to him?

"What, they know where we are?" Dave asked in alarm as he staggered along beside Kyle.

Also, his limbs felt very heavy.

And something was *pulling down* his loose coveralls. How could that be?

Feeling tentatively in the large side-pocket where he'd stowed the two pictures, he felt something hot!

It was the black gun that Sally had been carrying. She'd apparently put it there in his coveralls. And why was it so hot? It was almost scalding his thigh right through the fabric!

And beside it, Dave's searching fingers also felt a now-cool, small Cube!

She'd also put the "Custodian" into his pocket.

"But what...?" he began.

"Quiet now, Boss," Kyle replied, hurrying him out the back of the crumbling house. "We don't want to attract no attention. The sun's about to come up, don't 'cha know. Soon there be people stirring-about. They sees us and we're reported!"

Outside at the back of the house an old "bub" was parked. Dave recognized what it was from when he briefly before visited Sally's Dimension. It was a 4-by-4-foot small vehicle with a half-sphere "bubble" transparent top. It had large rubber wheels, looking like a mobile bubble...a "bub."

This one was old and decrepit. The paint on its sides was peeling. The wheels were patched and at uneven angles. The transparent top was scarred and cracked.

"It ain't much, but it works," Kyle proudly said, opening its large side-door for Dave to enter. "I be one of the few slaves havin' his own transportation."

In it, Kyle hastily hid Dave beneath a pile of old blankets in the cramped back seat.

"The automatic inventory scanners done took stock soon's the power came back on," Kyle explained over his shoulder as the bub started rolling along at a very slow speed. "They saw that those pill boxes wuz missing. And then they found your footprints out back of the store leadin' into the woods. They be hot on your trail, Boss."

"Jesus Christ!" Dave exclaimed from under the blankets, being painfully jarred by the bumpy ride. "Are you in trouble because of me?"

"Oh, no," Kyle softly replied from the driver's seat. "I be in no trouble. I'm careful as a cat, I is, fer shore—just like Sally say to be. And, Boss, my name is not this 'Jesus Christ' person, whoever that be. My name is Kyle, remember?"

"Oh, right," Dave sighed, now recalling more. In Sally's Dimension, Jesus never became a historical figure nor started a new religion. For whatever reasons, he was lost to history. In fact, they'd thought that was one of the reasons that her Dimension had remained authoritarian, with competing Empires controlling the world—thus suppressing Dark Energy generation usage and keeping the human race hidden from the full attention of God.

"Jesus was a friend of mine," Dave dejectedly answered Kyle. "Lots of people prayed to him."

But when Sally tried to stop Jesus in the past, in Dave's Dimension, she'd failed...just like he'd failed in trying to alter the formative influence of Socrates!

Was that because the past *couldn't* be altered?

Were they all really just the unwitting pawns of Fate in some rigged celestial game?

But no...that couldn't true. Dave had already experienced several different timelines. He knew that the past could be altered...at least to a point.

Their previous efforts had simply failed.

He had to cling to that conclusion—or he might as well just give up!

There *must* still be some way to prevent Dave's Dimension from advertising its presence to the full attention of the Creator. And successfully delaying Judgment Day might also prevent the destruction of all the linked earth Dimensions! Was that why Dave was thrown back, yet again, in time and space? Was it to give him one final chance to try to prevent the future global disaster from occurring?

"Kyle, when did Sally come back?"

"It was about a year ago, Boss," he replied from up front. "She be working with us Resistance fighters since then. We been making progress, but..."

"But what?"

"Keep quiet!" Kyle suddenly grunted back at him. "They's a roadblock up ahead!"

"Keepers?" Dave whispered back.

"Worse!" Kyle grated. "It's the Imperial Guards! I never in my whole life saw them in person in our little town before, just on the holocasts. Oh, my! This is bad, Boss. Don't move or make a sound! Just pray silent to your god. Pray to your Jesus! We be in *bad* trouble. Now keep quiet!"

Dave felt the bub decelerating from its already slow speed. It jerked to a stop. He heard sharp orders being barked from outside. He felt the vibration as the bub's big door was jerked open and Kyle was yanked outside…

—while Dave prayed silently to Jesus as hard as he could.

He didn't know if it would do any good. But Eashoa—the embodiment of an elderly, grizzled Jesus—sent him here to this specific place and time, didn't he?

Sure! It was deliberate! One moment he was spinning through the white fog away from Eashoa and the next he was here.

There *was* some purpose to his being here.

But…was it just to die?

Was his fitting punishment for his arrogance in questioning God to be *executed* on the spot as one of these "Resistance" fighters?

Somehow Dave didn't think so. No, Dave feared that Eashoa sent him back to experience something *much worse* than a quick street-execution.

Dave's fear and panic levels spiked as the voices outside became louder and sharper—and someone reached inside and began *yanking off* the concealing blankets!

And Dave's wrist suddenly hurt like hell!

Despite his resolve to keep quiet, he *groaned*.

Chapter 5

<u>DISORIENTATION</u>

Humans thought that in "sameness" was security
If everything remained unchanged threats stopped
Nothing could have been further from the truth
For in their ceaseless fight for the "status quo"
They unknowingly voted for evil Stagnation
Satan's most powerful weapon against them
Their internal decay caused by sitting in place
Where their feet went to sleep then rotted
And their ability to stand or walk was stopped
Easy targets for the ultimate top Predator
Having forgotten how to run they were slow
Staggering on numbed, bloody stumps
They had no hope for further evolution
But fell into a self-defeating spiral
Not recognizing their own devolution
They were completely surprised
When they were devoured...
Eashoa's Lament, 5:1-5

Sally shrank back against the wall, terrified!

Where was she? What was happening? One moment a huge explosion was bringing the already wrecked Smithsonian Art Museum down upon her head and the next she was *here!*

She had a vague recollection of a huge lizard looming over her—but that had to be a nightmare.

All Sally knew for certain was that she woke up on a hard bunk bed in a featureless small room. There was only a toilet, a sink, and a mirror in the room. A porthole looked out on a tangle of twisted, scorched metal, obscuring what lay beyond.

She looked at her dirty face and hair in the mirror, disgusted. There was a hairbrush and other toiletries in a cabinet behind the mirror. She washed her face then brushed out her hair, feeling better after doing so.

But there was nothing she could do about her ripped, dirt-encrusted, ragged military uniform—so she just straightened it up.

A door opened outward on what Sally did not know. It was locked. She realized was trapped. She was being held by unknown people in some sort of a jail!

Then, after using the toilet facilities, she huddled in a corner of the small room, fearfully clutching her big brown hairbrush.

"Oh, God," she whispered to herself, coming to a chilling realization. "It must be the Nuns. I'm in the hands of CPH, the *Church of Perpetual Health*. They'll torture me for the location of the rebel bases!"

She knew that despite their claim to be a "church" the dreaded Nuns had no compunctions at dealing harshly with "infidels" and "heretics"—i.e. those that used the "evil" Dark Energy generators. And she, as one of the inventors of the technology, was dead center in their crosshairs! They'd have no hesitation in executing her after extracting every last bit of useful information.

But...then again...she felt very light-headed...in fact her whole body felt light—as if she'd dropped twenty pounds of weight. She hadn't gone on a diet recently. It made no sense!

It was all incredibly confusing and frightening.

"Uhm...Sally?" a raspy, deep voice sounded from the door as it "clicked" open and the snout of a *T-rex-like dinosaur* stuck its head in!

"*Aaaaaiiiiiieeeee!*" she screamed, throwing her hairbrush at it!

It yelped and withdrew, the hairbrush having "bopped" off of its long, toothy head.

The outside lock on the door firmly "clicked" back into place.

Then she heard heavy "thumps" of a hastily departing large body.

"What the hell was that?" Sally gasped to herself, crawling over to retrieve her one weapon. She again clung tightly to her hairbrush, leaning defensively back against the wall. She couldn't believe her eyes!

Was that—an alien from one of the Harvesters? Jesus, it looked just like a dinosaur!

But then she heard softer human-like steps outside her door.

"Sally?" a tentative, female voice came through the door. "I'm sorry you were startled. My name is Alice. You haven't met me before, but I'm the wife of a colleague of Dave's—Professor George S. Johnson. Can I come in and talk with you?"

George...George...yes! Sally remembered Dave mentioning his friend several times while they were imprisoned by the military at the Cheyenne Mountain Nuclear Bunker. They couldn't leave because of the top secret research they'd been forced to do—trying to perfect the cold fusion device that was able to put a tiny fracture in subspace, releasing massive amounts of concentrated Dark Energy! They were sequestered "for the duration" at the base. And Dave *had* mentioned he hoped his friend George wasn't being too inconvenienced by having to take care of his collection of pet reptiles.

Was that talking dinosaur one of Dave's pets?

No, that was ridiculous! Dinosaurs were long extinct. And they certainly never had the brainpower to talk. She must be seeing things—or be unconscious and having a nightmare.

But...the hard handle of her hairbrush seemed real enough.

"Are you another giant talking lizard?" Sally called back petulantly at the locked door.

"Well," came a hesitant reply, "I look just as human as you."

"Are you one of the *Nuns?*" Sally yelled at the door loudly, trying to sound very tough and dangerous!

"A nun?" was the puzzled reply. "No...I'm not even Catholic...what are you getting it, Sally?"

"They're my avowed enemies! They're stupidly trying to stop us Resistance fighters from carrying the battle to the Harvesters! You're sure you're not one of them?"

"I'm sure not one of them."

Sally grit her teeth, narrowing her eyes. She had to find out what was going on! If this supposed-Alice was lying, at least she could get information out of her.

"Alright then," Sally reluctantly answered back. "You can come in. But don't try anything. I'm armed!"

Sally clutched her hairbrush even tighter, sliding upward with her back to the wall, until she was crouched and ready to jump to either side.

The door slowly opened and an elegant-looking middle-aged woman cautiously entered. Outside was an empty corridor. The giant talking lizard—if it really existed—had apparently retreated.

The woman entering Sally's room was slender and black-haired, wearing a smudged and torn white uniform.

"Don't try anything!" Sally repeated, raising the hairbrush threateningly.

Alice smiled gently, sitting down on the hard bunk. "Oh, you won't need that, Sally. Please sit here with me. I'll explain everything to you. It's quite a story—especially from your perspective. But I assure you that what I'm telling you is absolutely true."

"Well..." Sally hesitantly said, slowly lowering the hairbrush.

"If you want to brush my hair while we're talking, that's fine too," Alice shrugged. "By the way, yours looks lovely. I wish I had that youthful sheen to mine. But, no, I'm afraid my simulation isn't as good as it once was."

"Your...'simulation'?" Sally frowned at her.

"Are you a person who prefers the 'take-home message' first and the details supplied later," the woman continued, ignoring Sally's reaction, "or have the story told from its beginning, building-up to the 'punchline'?"

Sally stood against the wall, considering. She grimaced, deciding to hear the worst before deciding if she could trust this strange woman.

"Right now I just want answers," Sally slowly and suspiciously replied. "I don't need a story or your supposed conclusions. Just tell me *where* we are, *why* do you have me locked up here, and *how* is it that I'm still alive?" Sally snapped at the woman, narrowing her eyes and pursing her lips.

Alice sighed deeply before replying—first looking up at the ceiling as if carefully considering her words.

"Alright Sally, I'll give you your 'answers'," she sighed. "But you have to promise not to freak out."

"I'll...not...freak out," Sally tentatively replied.

"Good!" Alice nodded. "Then as the 'where'...we are in another Universe inside a Starship that's crash-landed on a very dangerous planet."

Sally glared at the woman, wondering why she would claim such a preposterous thing! But she'd promised not to freak out, so she might as well hear the rest.

"And as to the 'why' you're locked up...we knew this would be a big adjustment for you, so wanted you where we could control the situation. We'll certainly let you out of here as soon as you're ready to proceed without panicking."

"And...*how* I'm still alive?" Sally suspiciously frowned at the woman.

"Well, we just thawed you out from something called 'time-freeze' to see if you could help us survive here or hopefully escape," Alice softly continued, "since our own Sally, from another timeline different from yours, had to be put into your storage tube since she was dying."

"*Another* me...was dying?"

"Yes, Sally. This other Sally—*our* Sally—was irradiated with hard radiation that happened in our trip through a cosmic Black Hole to get here. Her immune system collapsed, allowing massive tumor growth. She needed a medication from her Dimension on Earth that we don't have, called 'Optimmune Retroviral System'. And...I'm sorry, Sally, I'm babbling. I'm a bit 'freaked out' myself, I'm afraid. That really didn't answer your last question, did it? Oh my, what was your last question again?"

Sally's mouth was hanging open as she still stood crouched against the wall. "Uhm...how—am I still alive?" she asked in a small voice.

"Well, Sally," Alice sighed, "that's because the Creature that sent the Harvesters to plunder Earth had a special need for all you Sally manifestations. For some reason, God loves you too much to destroy this new, flawed Universe while you're in it. Somehow this 'Satan' was able to grab you in an instant at your moment of impending death and substitute a physical replacement while snatching you away. We were forced to carry an assortment of his various 'prize' Tube-specimens in our cargo hold. You were in one of those Tubes. We 'unloaded' you to make room for our own sick-and-dying Sally. We're sorry we did this to you without your permission. But we had no control or knowledge of the Demon abducting you at the moment of your death. And we needed your time-freeze Tube for our Sally. So, that's what happened and here you are. Any other questions, dear?"

Sally slowly lowered her hairbrush and walked the couple steps to the bunk.

She sank onto it next to Alice, looking her straight in her eyes in total puzzlement.

"You say...there are *other* versions of me in those 'Tubes'?"

Alice nodded.

"Beside 'our' Sally who is dying from tumors—we've discovered that there are two more of you in our cargo hold, time-frozen. One is about your age. The other is middle-aged, like me."

"So you're saying...there are *four* of me here?" Sally said in a small voice.

"Yes. I know this is an incredible concept to take in at once. It's all very complicated," Alice sighed again. "I really don't understand it myself—none of us do! But if we were to try and sort it all out, we'd have to unthaw each of you Sally-manifestations and learn your stories directly. And at the moment that's just not possible. So we're somewhat in the dark here and..."

"What about Dave?" Sally asked. "Is he here?"

Alice shook her head sadly from side-to-side as if perplexed.

"He's dead?" Sally gulped. She wasn't getting along with Dave very well when they were struggling against the Reaper Robots, trying to lead a rebellion of the remaining few survivors against the Harvesters destroying Earth's civilizations. But she'd had a grudging respect for him—though she was still mad at him for arrogantly dragging her away to "escape" from the military that was forcing them both to continue their cold fusion research. Actually, she kind of enjoyed it there, kept prisoners by the military. At least they had a clear sense of authority and discipline.

"We...really don't know," Alice said, still shaking her head in an expression of sincere confusion. "While we were in *sub*-subspace..."

"There's a subspace *beneath* subspace?" Sally gasped, interrupting Alice.

"Well, there was an explosion in our engine room and Dave was gone," Alice continued. "We didn't find his body in the melted rubble, so we assume he was incinerated."

Alice hesitated.

"But?" Sally urged Alice to continue.

"Well, there's *another* Dave down in the Creature's Tubes in our cargo hold."

"Another Dave?" Sally gasped, her head whirling!

"Yes...but we're also not exactly sure who he is or from what timeline he originated. I think our Sally knew, but she's time-frozen now...so..."

"So Dave's sort of dead and alive, both at the same time?"

Alice resignedly shrugged. "I guess so."

"I *don't* believe any of this!" Sally fiercely stated, standing up and going over to lean against the sink. She felt like throwing up. She looked in the mirror at her own reflection. She looked exhausted—drawn and shaken. She felt incredibly weak.

One moment she was being *crushed to death* in a cave-in of a wrecked museum in apocalyptic Washington D.C.—and the next she was a zillion miles away in another Universe? *Really?* It just didn't make any rational sense!

This could easily be an elaborate hoax by those evil Nuns to trick her into giving up "irrelevant," "past" information on the rebel bases. So she just had to force this "Alice" person to provide *proof* of her incredible story—that was it! Either the hoax would be revealed or...well, Sally didn't even want to consider the alternative.

"Sally, I know this seems fantastic to you, but..."

"*Prove* it!" she snapped at Alice, whirling about—dredging up whatever reserves of strength she had to confront the seemingly friendly lady.

Alice sighed resignedly.

"I was really hoping to integrate you step-by-step into your new world," Alice said as she wearily stood up, reached out a hand, and took Sally's gently in her own. "But it might as well be a 'baptism of fire'—if that's what you really want?"

"That's what I want," Sally firmly nodded. "I need absolute proof that what you're telling me is true. Otherwise, I'll go completely insane!"

The older woman silently stepped out of the doorway, leading the younger Sally behind her.

"Where are we going?" Sally said, suspicious.

"Outside..."

They were in a wide tube corridor made of what looked like thick white plastic. But the plastic was warped and crumpled in places. Doorways leading off the tunnel were twisted so badly that they were popped out of their frames. It was difficult to climb over them.

But then finally they stepped through an intact airlock out of the white corridor into...

Sally gasped, her eyes widening.

Beneath her feet was hard rock.

—and above her was a *gigantic moon!* Plus there was another smaller one hanging in the sky to its side. A swollen-looking sun was setting on the horizon. Distant *volcanos* were spewing up black smoke while bright-red streams of lava ran down their sides.

The air was thick, suffocating, and heavy with the smell of sulfur.

And all around Sally was the strewn wreckage of a huge craft, within which the spaceship Sally had just stepped out of was embedded...plus a scattering of man-sized, tough-looking Tubes strewn across the stark landscape.

Working to pick up the tubes and carry them to a central pile was a dozen nine-foot-tall dinosaurs.

"It's...it's..." Sally managed to stammer.

"It's all true, Sally," a tall dinosaur rasped as it stalked up to them. A tool belt hung about its waist with various attached hammers, plyers, and screwdrivers. "Hi, I'm Dennis. Sorry about scaring you earlier. I see that Alice is orientating you?"

Sally weakly grasped its extended, three-clawed hand.

"That's ok for scaring me..." she gulped, feeling like she was about to faint again.

She really didn't like reptiles.

To Sally, they were all cold, slithery, unreadable, dangerous animals.

"We're short on food and water," Dennis continued. "But I'm sure Alice can find enough to get you hydrated and fueled. Perhaps you'd best do that before we deal with what I'm guessing are a thousand questions you've got for us. But please get up-to-speed as fast as possible. We desperately need your help, Sally."

"Right...of course," she gulped, dazedly turning back with Alice to reenter the exit corridor.

"I'm sorry if he was brusque," Alice apologized. "We've got a lot on our plates right now. We're stranded here. Our spaceship is heavy damaged. And we've no reliable working power source."

"No problem," Sally muttered. "I'm sure he's very nice—for a giant talking lizard," she grimaced, suppressing a shudder.

"Oh, I'm sorry—but you might as well know," Alice kindly continued. "I'm also one of those 'giant talking lizards,' just shape-shifted into your human form. You're actually the only true human here other than those still in their Tubes."

"Of course," Sally numbly repeated. "Is there anything else that's *totally bizarre* that I need to know about?"

Alice seemed to hesitate before replying.

"Well...the Creature that sent us here through the Black Hole and its resultant White Hole—the commander of the Harvesters you fought against—is the entity you humans have for eons called 'Satan'...and might return at any moment."

Sally shrugged her shoulders in defeat to the incredible, fantastic, and unbelievable revelations. She slumped as she did so, her feet dragging.

It hurt to think.

"Are you ok, dear?" Alice said, looking at Sally with concern.

"Why should I not be?" Sally grinned shakily. "I was dead, but now I'm on a crashed spaceship with giant talking lizards in another Universe—where Satan may come and grab us at any moment."

She laughed.

Then she started "hiccupping" uncontrollably.

It was embarrassing.

But she managed to suppress it.

"You'll feel better after you eat some of our tasty dung-potatoes," Alice consoled her. "I'll have them sliced up and fried in one of our few remaining gelled protein cubes. It's actually rather tasty."

"You're very kind," Sally forced herself to reply. She was determined to not throw up.

Dung potatoes?

She needed someone she could trust.

She had to get them to thaw out Dave.

She knew he'd probably be as irritating as ever, but at least he was human!

Meanwhile, she might as well sample their crap French-fries.

Dave fell with a "thud" onto hard pavement.

Groaning, he looked up to see *headlights* of a car rushing straight at him!

"Yikes!" he yelled as he rolled his body to the side.

The car just missed him. But it didn't stop. Apparently the driver hadn't seen him there on the road—as if Dave had materialized right in front of its wheels!

Where was the bub? Where was Kyle? Where were the Imperial Guards?

It was just a two-lane town street with ordinary houses along each side.

Dave looked along the gently descending slope to the National Park entranceway. Everything was familiar. It was 12th street in *his* Dimension. He was back! Somehow the intense emotions triggered by being about to be discovered in Kyle's bub had thrown him across the divide!

Or did his Anaconda Tattoo also have something to do with it?

Whatever, he was safe for the moment.

"But *when* am I?" he furtively asked himself as he elbowed himself to his feet. He hadn't broken any bones in his fall from the bub's backseat into his own Dimension. But he was bruised up even more, with additional lumps along his back. He was sore, but he could walk—back on down the street towards his Mom's house.

In the gathering light as the sun began to come up in the East, Dave saw that the town was still intact. That meant the Harvesters hadn't yet appeared. In the apocalyptic future he'd come from, even small towns like Sulphur were burned to the ground. If he was before the Invasion and the overall timeline hadn't shifted, then he knew where his present "Dave" incarnation should be. He'd be off sequestered at the *Cheyenne Mountain Nuclear Bunker*, perfecting his cold fusion Device for the military.

And yes—there on 12th and Ardmore—was his Mom's house. And it was no longer a crumbled wreck. It looked perfectly fine.

As he walked up to the porch and tentatively knocked on the door he heard a happy shout from within.

"Davey!" he saw his Mom's grinning face as she threw open the door. "You came home!"

Oh...Christ...it was really her. Just a few moments before she'd been long dead, executed by a brutal totalitarian State! And now here she was, as alive as she could be.

"Hi, Mom," he sighed, trembling with relief, as she grabbed him around the neck and gave him a fierce hug.

She was an older, medium-height woman, with short grey-white hair. She was wearing a thick pink bathrobe.

"You look...terrible—and wonderful!" she said, holding him at arm's length and looking him up and down. "And what are those awful clothes you have on? Since you went off to the East Coast with your new girlfriend to do a job interview all I've gotten from you were postcards saying you were working at a classified job. Where have you really been all this time? It's been almost a year! And my goodness! What have you been doing to yourself? You look so young!"

Dave sighed deeply, gratefully allowing his mother to lead him into the now-welcoming, sweet-smelling house.

"It's a long story," he said, sinking down wearily upon the now perfectly clean and comfortable couch. "And I need to tell you the whole truth. I finally realize that you are my best and most loyal friend in this whole world. You need to know everything."

"Well of course I do!" she firmly nodded. "I'm your mother, aren't I? But just let me go get you some brownies and milk. You look positively starved to death. You must have dropped thirty pounds! How'd you get so skinny? And how is it that you look twenty years younger? I want to know your secret so I can do it too!"

He grinned broadly.

It was good to be home.

His body still hurt all over. His back felt like it was covered with lumps from his fall onto the pavement back into his own Dimension. He'd just traveled from ancient Greece to the far-distant future to another completely different Dimension to end up back at his Mother's house. And a version of Sally was over in that other Dimension leading a Revolution against brutal tyrants—and somehow counting on him to do something that required him "growing a new set of balls."

Right...

Man—it had been a really confusing couple days!

But for now he'd had enough of death and decay. It was a time for healing.

Chapter 6

<u>CORRUPTION</u>

Absolute power corrupts absolutely
Or so the humans liked to laugh and joke
As they sought more and more power
Ready to condemn excesses in others
While they saw none in themselves
Merely "judicially" exercising Rights
Often against self-proclaimed Wrongs
They denied their own naked hypocrisy
Making up whatever justification
That would allow them to proceed
Doing exactly what they wanted
Regardless of Principle or Logic
Their only imperative to obey
That it didn't stink too badly...

Eashoa's Lament, 6:27-31

Dave was just finishing telling his entire story to his mother. He didn't leave out any details. It took all morning.

The sun outside was high in the sky, pouring in warm sunlight through the open windows. Dave was getting hungry again, despite the delicious brownies and milk Jean King gave him earlier in the morning. But he ignored the growls in his stomach, eager to have her finally hear the entire incredible odyssey he'd traveled to wind up there sitting on her sofa in her living room. He started his story at the very first moment he saw the *Girl with the Turtle Tattoo* in the grocery store, ending with the frightening events of that very same morning in the parallel Dimension.

"So...that's it," he said, exhausted by his emotional journey. "You probably think I'm totally crazy or writing some science fiction book, huh? Actually, it'd have to be a whole series of books...too much happened to fit into just one book..." he trailed off, totally spent.

She hadn't interrupted him once.

He knew she wasn't used to him pouring his heart out to her. He learned from a small child to deal with her at arm's length, to be quietly reserved around her. It wasn't because of her lack of sympathy but her tendency verbally to go off in ten directions at once, exhibiting typical extravert "thinking out loud" behavior. Dave, a strong introvert, just found it too tiring to communicate openly with her.

Now, he had no choice.

He was no longer leading a normal life. And with Sally either cut off from him or having developed beyond him, he had no one else to whom to turn. He needed a confidant. Even his beloved Professor Volodymyr, with whom he'd confided about everything, was lost to him—also taken by the military to the Cheyenne Mountain Nuclear Bunker to help perfect the new, incredibly powerful "weapon" they thought they had in their hands.

Jean King sat for a few minutes, saying nothing.

She looked healthy! For someone that Dave had seen horribly die from metastasized breast cancer, she was remarkably fit. She was of medium height, round-faced, with short grey-white hair, and an easy smile.

And then she broke her silence.

"So..." she thoughtfully mused, "you're telling me that you are a time-traveler from a billion years in the future, an older version of my actual son who is right now actually a prisoner of the United States military—even though you now look half the age of my son. And you were on a spaceship at the center of our galaxy. While you were there you had a chat with God, in the gap that's between different Universes. And before that you went back in time to try and discredit Socrates. And before that you fought the real Satan alongside an aged Jesus in an apocalypse of alien invaders that's arriving about a year in my future. I—or a different version of myself—helped to defeat Satan. And now your present 'girlfriend' Sally is in danger in a parallel Dimension where her government is looking to hunt her down and kill her. Is that it all in a nutshell?"

She looked at him expectantly.

"That's a pretty good summary of the main points," he weakly concluded, realizing how absurd it sounded.

"Ok."

"Uhm...what?" he gulped.

"Ok!" she repeated, stiffly standing up from the rocking chair she'd been sitting in now for several hours. "I believe you, Davey."

"You...do?" he said, bewildered.

He'd expected her to break out laughing or toss him out of the house or call an ambulance to cart him away to the closest looney bin! To just accept what he said was...unnerving.

"Look," she said, walking stiffly to the adjoining kitchen and starting to clatter with dish pans. "If you remember—which you covered too briefly, by the way—you and Linda's...I mean Sally's...'magic' pills brought me back from the dead and cured my cancer. What further proof do I need to believe that you've had an incredible experience? After what happened to me, Davey, I'd believe anything. I sure don't understand everything you just told me, but I absolutely believe it happened."

"Thanks, Mom," he gulped, tears of relief in his eyes.

"But I would still like to see that 'physical proof' you say you brought with you—right after I cook you a nice hot lunch. How does that sound to you?"

It sounded great.

Dave just nodded, totally exhausted.

"And while I do that, you go to your room—you remember where it is after a billion years away, don't you? Get yourself cleaned up. Take a good shower. And put on some of your old clothes that are still hanging in the closet. They're your clothes from back in your college days so I bet they'll fit your new slimmer body just fine."

That sounded great to Dave.

"And after lunch we'll talk about what we need to do next," she firmly stated. "After all, you need to get back to your girlfriend, even if she is off in another Dimension. If you truly love someone, then you find a way to be with that person, don't you?"

"I suppose..."

"Don't just 'suppose', Davey!" she suddenly *yelled* at him, clearly irritated by his hesitation. "Your *love* for this girl is really what it's all about, isn't it? Well, *isn't* it?" she concluded, softer.

She could be very authoritative when she wished to put her foot down.

"Yes, Mom," he dutifully answered, not wanting to get lectured for the thousandth time on him still being single instead of married off to some pretty young girl!

But he *was* startled by her yelling at him. Clearly, her "Optimmune" treatment did more than just cure her cancer. That sweet old lady was now a fire-breathing *pistol!*

Wow. Things can sure change in billions of years, different realities, different dimensions, and different timelines... Dave hysterically thought to himself. *Who'd have thunk it?*

Yep. When it's too painful to cry, you've just got to laugh.

Wearily he pushed himself up onto his feet and wobbled toward the spare bedroom.

Despite his sometimes-bewildering Mom, it was very good to be home.

Socrates was delighted.

The Martian-derived giant intelligent Snakes agreed to approve his visit to their city. Not only that, the "Elders" insisted he meet with them all. The Elders were the governing body that ruled this heavenly realm. The various intelligent gods existing here all had representatives on the ruling Council. Socrates had no doubt they would fall sway to his undeniable brilliance.

"So you're ready to go, Socrates?" Snake said, reaching out a thin hand to shake his chubby one.

Socrates graciously nodded to his host as he briefly squeezed the man's hand.

"You've been very kind to me here," the Greek philosopher sincerely complimented him. "It has been an, uh, interesting experience."

It was hard to be diplomatic. He wanted to excoriate "Snake" for the primitive environment, the haughty treatment from the inhabitants, their embrace of the piece-of-crap fisherman Periscus instead of him, and the expectation of his becoming a glorified babysitter. But he held his peace. The sex had been pleasant enough with his harem, but that was just a momentary diversion over his first few weeks.

The rest of the time in the fake-human village had been torture.

Now he was just glad to get out of there. Though he liked Snake well enough, he never wanted to see any of the rest of them ever again.

But waiting to see him off at the top of the hill were many well-wishers, including his twelve wives. His lovely brides were now far along now in their pregnancies. Socrates had to force an air of sadness at leaving them. He loved the delightful bodies of the beautiful ladies, but not the responsibilities their affections imposed upon him. It was a profound relief to be leaving behind both them and their bulging bellies.

And he was fairly certain that they were glad to be rid of him as well. These last few months as he impatiently awaited a response from the staid, apparently notoriously slowly deliberating intelligent Snakes, he'd grown more and more curt and unresponsive to the ladies. His famous cutting criticisms sometimes brought them to the brink of tears. He didn't mean to do so. It was just his nature.

His biting words struck to the heart of any inconsistencies, whether real or perceived. That's just what he did! He was a professional critic! And supposedly Martian intelligent giant snakes masquerading as pregnant humans...hah! It was the most ironic and bizarre thing he'd ever heard or seen.

"But you'll be back, won't you?" Snake observed as they walked together up the hill to the waiting hovercraft, the others trailing along behind.

"Oh, certainly—of course," Socrates lied. "But I'm not sure how long this visit will take. If they need me to direct the building of better defenses in case those Spike-Ships return, who knows how long that might take? So don't expect me back soon."

"Well, I'll greatly miss our conversations," Snake bravely grinned. The cobra tattoo on his face twitched as he seemed to struggle not to cry.

Socrates was amused. The young man indeed had a real affection for him! Versus the other dullards here in this mock-human village, Snake definitely stood out. In fact, he'd told Socrates all about his years as a "hippie" critic of society two-and-a-half millennia in the future from Socrates' time. This Snake was a fellow "questioner" who Socrates would sincerely miss.

But now it was time to go to the *Big Show*—where Socrates knew he'd dominate and shine! All he could do here in the placid valley was catch fish and breed little brats. *Phagghhh!* What kind of future was there in doing that? At the *City of the Gods* Socrates would make his mark!

He'd teach them what it meant to be a *real* human.

"Goodbye friends!" Socrates waved jovially as he stepped into the transport.

Socrates noted that even Periscus was there waving him off. That irritating skinny turd was likely very happy to see him leave. After Socrates was gone, Periscus would have all the "excess" females to himself. And the rural fishing life was just what he liked, a disgusting "non-examined," boring, and meaningless existence.

But...still...Periscus had, unexpectedly, become both a comrade and grudging friend.

So Socrates nodded politely to his old enemy, waving back to him.

It didn't hurt at times to be courteous. Socrates knew that if he ever did return to this isolated little village, he'd want his women back for another round of impregnations. After all, they deserved the *best* sperm of them all!

At the age of seventy, Socrates knew that he should by rights be long past his child-siring days. But the village had been good for him. He didn't know if the fake-humans there were putting something in his food to juice up his sperm-production and libido—but he'd had a lift in his steps and other body parts he hadn't felt in years.

He was ready to take control of this new world, whether they liked it or not.

He *would* be their new Philosopher King. It was his destiny!

Sally stood outside the spaceship looking up angrily at the sun.

No, she wasn't mad because the Dinosapiens refused to thaw out the other Dave in the Tube. They claimed that they couldn't because there wasn't enough food and water to keep another person alive. But Sally knew better. She knew that they wanted to keep her carefully under their control—that she and Dave might form an alliance against them!

But there was another reason she was perturbed as she stared up into the swollen sun.

"Don't burn your eyes out, Sally," Dennis said, stalking up to her, all by himself dragging a heavy Tube behind him.

"There's something wrong with it," she said, now looking at him.

"What?"

"Take a look—a quick glance won't hurt you. It's much weaker than was our own sun."

He turned his oblong, scaly head up to the swollen, yellow sun.

"I don't see anything."

"Look toward the corona edge," she directed.

"Oh...yes...I see," he said in a low voice.

She nodded grimly.

There were glaringly black thin *spider web patterns* running across the sun, which were most apparent at the edge of the sun.

"What does it mean?" Dennis asked, turning away from the sun and blinking his big orange eyes rapidly.

"I think the sun is breaking apart," Sally matter-of-factly stated, walking over to the rear of the Tube to be in position to help push it into the smashed spaceship.

"That's...very disturbing," Dennis dully responded. He was swaying as he stood there, clearly exhausted.

The last few weeks had been traumatic. Sally rapidly figured out what was happening and tried to help wherever she could. Since she wasn't near as strong as the big Dinosapiens, she was most useful crawling through the interior wiring of the ship trying to fix ripped-apart and shattered interfaces. Also, she rooted amongst the mountains of debris left from the smashed Harvester, frantically searching for usable parts. Somehow she had to cobble together a functional DE-generator to get their ship's systems up and running! If not, they were doomed.

The ship's stores were rapidly dwindling. They'd now been on starvation rations for some time. They were consuming far less than they should to maintain their strength. Even with piped-in sunlight, the "garden" was almost dead. It really needed sunlight lamps to supply the proper wavelengths, duration, and strength for Earth plants. But those lamps couldn't work without a strong power source.

She angrily lectured the Dinosapiens that they should have installed solar power capability. They responded that with the DE-generators, such weak power systems were just a waste of space and resources. But they hadn't counted on their powerful generators being destroyed. Now, only the most essential systems in the ship were energized. The rest simply waited, such as the lighting and water systems in their quarters.

So most of the surviving crew was now sleeping out under the stars. It wasn't chilly because the planet was very hot. It "cooled" at night to only the low nineties. But Sally enjoyed sleeping under the stars—until she noticed that many of them were simply disappearing! One moment they were there in the sky. The next moment they "winked" out and were gone!

She suspected that the same thing going on with their own sun was also happening to many other stars. They were dying, uncharacteristically quickly. Instead of collapsing or exploding, they were simply fragmenting!

Something was wrong with this entire, perverse Universe...the Laws of Physics were screwed up.

"So how's your 'cobbling' coming?" Dennis asked as together they dragged and pushed the heavy Tube into the cargo hold.

They were trying to fit as many of the time-frozen humans into their "private" collection as they could. It was only a fraction of the million Tubes scattered out there on the plain. But the Dinosapiens wanted to make every effort to save the time-frozen humans in case they were ever able to launch their Starship.

"I fixed the Obelisk."

"What? Really?" Dennis hopefully responded. "But I thought it was drained of energy, just a useless pillar of red glass?"

"It sure was—until I managed to find enough pieces of the Harvester's drive, plus components that my predecessor got out of your engine room, to install a near-complete small DE-generator in it."

"That's wonderful, Sally. You're amazing!"

"Well...thanks...but don't cheer for me just yet."

She turned her back on the big dinosaur and walked out of the hold into the barren wastes outside, squinting up again at the fracturing sun.

"Sally?" Dennis called out from behind her as he trailed along. "What's wrong? And why didn't you just put the DE-generator into our ship?"

"I knew you were going to ask me that," she grunted, peevishly walking away again to sit on some hot boulders with her back to him.

"Uh...no...I'm not criticizing you, Sally...just asking."

"There's no way to control the palladium matrix. Your programs in the Starship's general computer are too primitive."

"But how...?"

"From what you told me, that Tommy character had a laptop that interfaced with the Obelisk—directing and controlling it. It contained evolved computer intelligences that, apparently, another version of me created and installed in it in the past. Actually, I was trying to do that when our helicopter got turned back right before the military snagged us...anyway, that's my 'timeline.' I digress. The bottom-line is it took me years of work to make them."

"And we don't exactly have years now. So with no pre-existing unit you can't get the DE-generator working. I understand," Dennis nodded. "And I do remember seeing that laptop. Tommy was carrying it when he went after our previous Sally and Dave down into the engine room."

"Well, that or something designed like it is absolutely necessary to perform the exquisite control functions in a DE-generator. The control interface provide to you by the Martian Snakes was completely melted, useless—destroyed in your ship's exploded engine room. I couldn't even find any remnants in the Harvester wreck. So even though I managed to replace the other components, it's all just useless junk if installed into your Starship."

"But..."

"I did the best I could!" she snapped at him, turning her face to the hot wind blowing across the rocky plain. It felt good on her skin, evaporating sweat—like a Demon's caress.

"I'm sure you did, Sally," he patiently responded, squatting down next to her. "But then why did you put it into the Obelisk?"

"It's *smart*, Dennis," she grimly stated. "That Obelisk is *damn* smart! I thought maybe it could decide on its own to 'step in' to replace the generator's controller unit, get the thing going. I know it operates normally via energy sucked out of the fabric of time, but it seems to need a 'jump-start' from a DE-generator. It's all rather complex."

"And?"

"Well, I'm getting a trickle of energy from the replacement DE-generator—maybe enough to light up a small lightbulb."

Dennis' big dinosaur head sunk down in disappointment.

But then he seemed to perk up.

"Ok. So it's partially working. That's a start, right? I guess the Obelisk broke when it slammed into us while we were in the Black Hole. Is there a way to try and fix...?"

"The Obelisk is fine, Dennis!" she sourly replied. "There's absolutely nothing wrong it. As far as I can tell, all its internal mechanisms are undamaged. I attached the jerry-rigged DE-generator into its storage compartment where a prior one sat. Apparently Dave removed it in order to have room to ride inside the Obelisk. Anyway, 'sparked' by the DE-generator the Obelisk should be 'jump-started' to put out *terawatts* of energy to the ship through the cables I implanted."

"Then why is it still inert?"

"I think..." Sally sighed, "The answer is that there's *no* Dark Energy to be had," she miserably concluded.

"What?"

"The equipment that Dave invented to trigger the cold fusion of deuterium ions is working just fine," she noted. "That's giving off enough energy to heat up a cup of tea—warming the Device a bit. The Obelisk is exquisitely tweaking the ions into optimal configurations. But the resultant effect should be vast stores of Dark Energy to fully power up the Obelisk to its optimal functionality. But that's not happening, even though I can document subspace fractures briefly opening up. Nothing comes out of them!"

"So the Obelisk is minimally active enough to take charge of the DE-generator but there's no resultant surge of energy to power it up fully?"

"That's what I said."

"Then I still don't understand what's..."

"Dennis, it's like a car with a dead battery. The car needs to get moving in order to charge the battery. But without a pre-existing charge to start the car the vehicle can't get going to charge the battery! And even if it could get going, the battery itself is broken. It can't hold a charge."

"I'm not sure that analogy holds."

"Well, whatever!" she snapped back at him. "We're sucking but there's nothing to suck! Got it?"

He shook his big head slowly from side-to-side.

"That's...even more unsettling, Sally, than the Obelisk being broken. Are you saying that we'll never get the power we need? In this strange new Universe is Dark Energy missing?"

She sourly slapped her hand upon the hot rock she was sitting on, time after time.

"Well, we don't know that for sure. There may be some hope," she grimaced, "but you're not going to like what I have to say. You're probably going to yell at me!"

"Please, Sally," he quietly gasped, his head drooping down again. "We're almost done for...anything you have to say, no matter how hard, is welcomed and...and..."

His weak voice trailed off.

She sighed, licking her dry cracked lips. It'll been a long time since she'd had a good long drink of water. They were fast-evaporating their internal stores as sweat into the atmosphere, not able to reclaim it. All the time they'd been there, not one raincloud had come over the horizon. Water was at a premium. Even the Dinosapiens were sweating, though not as copiously as humans—but still steadily losing their precious moisture. Even aggressively reclaiming their urine and waste waters wasn't enough, their H_2O stores fast vanishing.

"I think...maybe...the sun may be pointing the way for us."

"What do you mean, Sally?"

"I think that those spider webs we see on the sun's surface are evidence of the fragility of the various physical forces in this Universe—such as gravity, the nuclear and electromagnetic forces, and...even Dark Energy."

"Fragility?"

"Each of those fundamental forces is subject...*here*...to not working," she grimly explained. "That's the bad news..."

"—like another of our crew plus a hundred Tubes being fired up into orbit yesterday when gravity reversed where he was standing?"

"Yes, exactly," she agreed. "But the good news is that where a foundational force isn't working in one location it may be working at another. The cracks in the sun's corona aren't a gradual dimming across the entire surface."

"So...?"

"We've got to put the Obelisk on *wheels* and *move it* away from here."

"You're serious?"

"If we can't get access to Dark Energy here...then maybe ten miles away—or a hundred or a thousand—it might kick in."

"You're absolutely certain that everything in the Obelisk is working properly?"

"I'm positive," she huffed, insulted to have her expertise questioned by a dumb lizard. "If we can get it to the 'right' location than it should produce all the power we need. But to move it will mean first *gutting* your Starship in order to remove the Obelisk and get it out onto the plain."

"Why not just take out the DE-generator that's inside the Obelisk and move it to a new location?" he asked.

"It won't work without the Obelisk's minimally powered super-intelligent control and direction, remember?" she snapped-back at him.

"So...you really think there's a chance we can find some 'fissure' here on the planet where Dark Energy is accessible?"

She shrugged. "It's worth a try...what else can we do?"

"Then we'll do it!"

Sally was suspicious of this quick agreement.

"You're going to have to slice open your spaceship," she reminded him. "The Obelisk is imbedded inside, sticking-through several of your decks."

The T-rex-looking dinosaur nodded with determination.

"While we've still got the strength, we'll get the Obelisk out—then put it on wheels, just like you said."

Sally weakly got back up to her feet.

Dennis jumped up, seemingly rejuvenated, and enthusiastically hugged her!

"Please don't touch me," Sally said, pushing his scaly hands off, repulsed. "I don't like being touched."

She politely didn't add by a *slimy lizard.*

"Oh...I'm sorry, Sally," Dennis hastily apologized, taking a step backward. "I keep forgetting that you're not the same Sally we came here with. She was quite affectionate."

"That's right, I'm not!" she grated at him through clenched teeth. She noted to herself: *I'm much better than that soft, emotional bitch!*

"Uhm...ok," Dennis nervously replied, backing up. Then he turned around and stomped off toward the entrance.

Presumably he was going to coordinate the new effort. His long tail was swinging "jauntily" from side-to-side.

Sally shuddered.

She still didn't like reptiles—even these seemingly friendly, intelligent ones.

They just gave her the creeps.

And she didn't like everyone comparing her to that other Sally. From what she'd heard about her predecessor she was weak—overly sentimental and emotional. To survive in this new, hostile Universe it was obvious that they needed to be strong! They needed to make tough decisions. They needed to do whatever was necessary without second thoughts or regrets!

It was like her plan of ripping apart their only means of escape, the Starship. The needed to tear it into pieces to have a chance at getting the necessary massive energy needed to be able to depart in the first place. Her plan was bold and decisive, regardless of the immediate negative consequences.

They could always piece the Starship back together...maybe.

Yet she had absolutely no idea if this new plan would work.

The local gravity-reversals—as awful as they were for the lost personnel and resources—gave her hope. The forces of nature were clearly varying in the vicinity of the crashed Starship. But subspace was another thing entirely. The sun's "fractures" that they could see above them were actually thousands of earth-distances apart from each other. It was possible that the crew could take the Obelisk to every single spot on this planet and they'd still not find a place where Dark Energy could be accessed.

But it was worth a try...or not?

"Maybe we're just wasting our time," she groaned, putting her head in her hands. "Maybe we should just give up."

After all, in a rapidly fracturing Universe, what did anything matter?

Their ultimate Fate was sealed.

When this new Universe died, they'd die with it.

Chapter 7

GUMPTION

Of all the grave faults of mankind
Only one proved to have positive aspects
An ephemeral quality called "Gumption"
Having something to do with Persistence
And claiming parts of Courage and Bravery
But also displaying stupid, insane Stubbornness
Where people kept going when they should not
The rewards dwindling and lost, people persisting
Letting their guts rule their bodies instead of minds
Trying to do the impossible when it's truly impossible
Bashing their heads against impenetrable brick walls
Flinging themselves into bloody battles that were lost
Thinking that somehow, someway they could win
Keeping going against all the most horrible odds
Hoping that they would be the one in a million
Winning the lottery as if they were a pole
Struck by the most unlikely lightning...

Eashoa's Lament, 7:58-60

Tommy was reaching the end of his journey.

It wasn't just that he'd finally trudged out of the desert onto the seashore of a sluggish, red ocean—it was the near-depletion of his energy stores.

And it wasn't just that he'd not eaten for weeks...it was his systems breaking down from within. He now realized that the intense hard radiation he'd endured while in the engine room of the Dinosapien Starship had set the nanofiber-network supporting his "organs" into a death spiral, particularly inside his synthetic brain.

He was totally screwed up.

"It's still kind of pretty here, though," he mumbled to himself.

He was sitting on the beach, hugging his still-functioning, faithful laptop. He was jealous of its solar panels and wanted to tap into them in his journey across the sands. But they were only barely able to power the flat computer, let alone his sophisticated systems. If he were to keep at his main mission—writing the last tribute to the dead human race—he had to keep that laptop running regardless of all else.

Since he didn't technically need sleep, he'd been writing during all the daylight hours, stumbling onward in the cool of the night.

The manuscript was almost completed. But there was nobody to give it to! Did Jesus just want him to leave it on the laptop where it would likely vanish once the machine corroded with age? Sure, he could curl around it and protect it with his stopped-functioning frame. But that seemed a poor solution at best...

But, whatever, he was accomplishing his task!

Tommy found it very peaceful there, sitting on the sand and looking out over the red, sluggish waves. Probably a thick algal bloom made the water look red. Hah...a red ocean. That was probably symbolic of something...plant life still hanging on, here and there. A cool breeze blew in off the ocean, soothing his brow.

"At least I made it across...the sand dunes," he muttered to himself. That was something. He'd set a goal and reached it. That gave him a modicum of satisfaction.

He ran a shaking hand up over his head. The hair on his head— his once-lovely blond curls—was gone. He knew he now looked like a bald-headed alien. His corpse would seem out of place on that desolate beach. If anyone chanced upon it they'd certain find the laptop.

Of course no one would ever see his lonely, rusting body if what seemed evident now was really true: he was on an ancient, dying planet. Only a few remaining simple lifeforms persisted, such as the red algae.

His only regret in immediately dying was that he'd not yet quite finished his "*Homo Sapiens* Eulogy" document. Not only was the subject difficult and his ability to continue waning, but he didn't have an ending to the story.

Since he didn't know what happened to the humans, how could he completely summarize their existence?

A particularly difficult chapter—painfully illustrating his present lonely situation—was *"Chapter 15, Friends"*! He'd puzzled out the value of people walking beside each other, particularly since he himself was all alone. They didn't have to be your "best buddies" who'd die for you, nor your lover or your closest blood relative—just a person who looked upon you not unfavorably. Someone with whom, now and then, you could talk. Someone you might ask for an infrequent favor.

And there was not even a seagull there to keep Tommy company in his final hours.

At least when he floated up upon the Greek beach eons ago, there'd been seagulls to try and pick at his remains.

It was sad.

"Where did all the humans go?" he muttered to himself. "And where...did the other smart creatures go? And, come to think of it, where...did the animals go?"

It was a mystery.

Had they all died out? Had the extremes of temperature killed them? Or had they, like him, just gotten too tired of living and given up?

If he had the strength and tools he could probably do archeological or paleontological digs. He had all the knowledge stored away in his data banks for such an endeavor. But that would take many years. His life was now a matter of days or even hours.

He *sighed* in sincere regret.

"I'M SORRY, MOMMY!" he shouted with his amplified lungs out as loud as he could across the damp sand. "I WISH I COULD DO MORE! BUT I DON'T KNOW HOW TO GO ANY FURTHER!"

Yet again, no one answered back.

Sitting there, wavering in the gentle breeze, he felt as light as a feather—about to blow away! The thin laptop in his arms, though, felt like it weighed a ton. It was getting hard for him to breathe. He heard the rasping wheezes coming from his own chest and was appalled. It was getting hard to see, his eyes glazing over with a sticky film. Wow, who knew that nanofibers could be so sensitive to a massive dose of hard radioactivity? There, as the bloated sun sank into the sea, everything was getting fuzzy...especially that *glint of bright red* way down the shoreline...say what?

Was it just a spur of dried algae pushed up by the waves onto the sand? Or was it something else?

"Ok then," he sighed, with a supreme effort lurching painfully up to his feet. He managed to wheeze out loud: "One last mystery to try and solve. Hah!"

His words echoed back to him from the high sand dunes.

That felt good. It was a final announcement to the Universe from Tommy the dying Robot!

It was an act of Defiance...a human quality. He'd learned well the best and worst traits of his creators.

He tottered on down the rocky beach in the direction of the red glint, expecting it to be a mirage or just a trick of light, perhaps a last sunray shining off a flat ridge of rock coated with red scum.

But as he got closer and the daylight continued to fade, the red light only got brighter...

—until he walked around an outcropping of rocks and saw there tilted but set solidly into the rock of a ledge, looming above him, the red Obelisk!

It shone with an internal light, like a beacon...a lighthouse on the shore of death!

"Wow," Tommy weakly mumbled, stumbling up to the ledge. With a supreme effort he clambered up, touching the glass-like surface with a trembling hand.

It was solid. It was real. And it was warm!

Tommy managed to circumnavigate it. But there was no accessible panel visible anymore. It was just one solid, looming rectangular pillar—nearly one hundred feet high sticking up from its embedded base!

Was it just glowing and warm from the last rays of sunlight? Was it actually dead? Or did it still have some life in it?

Tommy thought he could hear a faint "thrumming" sound coming from within.

"How...did you...get here?" he gasped, amazed. "The...last I saw of you...was on the Dinosapien Starship...falling into the Black Hole?"

But that was, presumably, millions or billions of years ago...or a similar length into the future?

Things were sure confused.

A lot could have happened in all that future or past time!

"Well," Tommy said, sitting on a boulder and opening up the laptop. "No matter where you came from...I wonder if I can...get you to open up for me?"

Up on his laptop screen sprang a number of charts, graphs, and control interfaces. Yes, the Obelisk was communicating with the laptop!

Tommy caught his faltering breath, stunned.

It was alive!

"So then...if I just..." he mumbled as his trembling fingers typed in a series of commands.

—and the previously hidden panel snapped out with a "clunk"!

"Well...how about that?" Tommy grinned for the very first time in weeks, noting that several of his loose teeth dropped out of his mouth.

But that didn't matter.

He climbed up onto a rock to reach the panel, managed to drag his little body up and through the opening, and fell into the welcoming space.

The panel closed on its own behind him as Tommy punched in a succinct command into the laptop: "Get me *out* of here!"

Clutching the slim computer close to his heaving chest, he felt the WORLD TWIST INSIDE OUT as he was *whisked* away...to where he knew not!

"I think...I'm going to take...a little nap," he gratefully sighed. His eyes closed as his last remaining energy stores in his depleted body drifted down toward zero.

If he managed to wake again, that'd be fine. If not, that was ok also. At least what he'd written, incomplete or not, was safe. And it was being delivered—to *somewhere*.

That was all he cared about.

For the first time in weeks, Tommy slept.

Socrates was walking out to stand before the *Council of Elders!* It was his big moment.

Despite his natural bravado, he was nervous.

He'd stood in front of and addressed many important assemblages in the past, but never a group of *alien gods!*

He knew he had to make a good impression or they would casually toss him away like soiled toilet clay. And that would never do. He was convinced that it was his destiny to take *total control* of this new world!

And nothing would keep him from it.

"My esteemed fellow intelligent creatures," he began, "I thank you for this kind audience."

He was wearing his traditional tunic and sandals. They were not his original clothes, but weaved by his wives for him from plant fibers—rough but still authentic-looking. He was confident that his robust figure, ample belly, protruding eyes, high forehead, wide face, and full beard would impress them with his commanding presence and wisdom!

He was dead wrong...

"WE DO NOT APPRECIATE YOUR CONTRIBUTIONS TO THE GENETIC POOL OF OUR DELUDED BRETHREN," a loud voice suddenly reverberated inside Socrates' head.

He winced, squinting-down his eyes.

"Uhm...excuse me?" he replied, taken-aback at both their aggressive attack and the booming voice inserted into his head!

It gave him an instant headache, muddying his thoughts.

"WE ARE CONSIDERING SENDING YOU AND YOUR PROGENY INTO EXILE, FAR AWAY FROM US, PERHAPS OFF-WORLD," the painful voice rang-out again inside his skull. "BUT BEFORE TAKING THIS EXTREME ACTION, SOME INSISTED THAT YOU HAVE A CHANCE TO DEFEND YOUR ACTIONS. SO SPEAK NOW!"

Socrates sucked in his breath, pausing to contemplate this unexpected hostility.

He carefully studied the gods arraigned before him on the elevated dais. Three were of Snake's parent race—thick-bodied, twenty-foot-long snakes with big, oblong heads and wet, flickering forked tongues. Socrates suspected they came from the lineage of the Greek

God *Python*. Their heads were larger than that of a human, with golden spheres for eyes. The soft yellow light of the chamber room glinted off their overlapping scales. One snake-god was primarily blue, another green, and yet another brick-red. As snakes, Socrates deemed them slow of thought—a weakness he could easily exploit.

In addition to the three giant snakes, two human-sized lizards crouched on all fours. Socrates had heard of such gods, called "basilisks." These he knew from Snake to be the gods that had sent a ship out to the stars. They were far-sighted but tended to be cold-blooded. Socrates felt that their weakness was a suppressed history of hard conflict.

And finally, there was one lone *bird*—a big, four-winged *black* bird! It looked completely "normal" for an animal of this new world. Perhaps it was not a god but a pet of the court? And yet its four beady black-facetted eyes fixed Socrates with an unblinking, hard stare. It reminded Socrates of *Lyra*, a heavenly vulture frozen into a heavenly constellation in the sky. Yes, it was a god. And it was the one deity on the elevated Dias that Socrates feared. He regarded it with dread because he didn't understand its motivation. Its head was clearly not large enough to hold a brain capable of human-level thought, yet it seemed completely engrossed in the proceedings.

"You want me to defend myself?" Socrates chose to laugh arrogantly at them. "It is *you* that needs to defend *yourselves* to *me!*"

That set them back on their haunches, bellies, and bird-feet!

"THAT IS A RIDICULOUS..."

"*Is* it?" the haughty philosopher snapped-back at them.

Socrates chose to walk calmly over to the balcony and look out upon their growing city. It was impressive. The structures were built of a translucent material which looked like glass yet was remarkably flexible. There were no straight lines. Everything was gently curved, swaying gently back and forth. Socrates admired the architecture yet was not overly impressed. Indeed, the magnificent marble pillars of the Parthenon—the Temple in Athens that was dedicated to the goddess *Athena*—were constructed similarly, though fixed in place as solid marble.

"This is a wonderful city you are building for your few, remaining numbers," Socrates remarked. "What did you say happened to the prior one?"

"THAT IS NOT YOUR CONCERN!" the voice continued loudly in his head. "INDEED, WE'VE CONCLUDED THAT IT WAS BECAUSE OF A MEMBER OF YOUR RACE THAT WE WERE FORCED TO REGROUP!"

"Oh—and how's that?" Socrates mildly replied, trying to appear innocent.

"ONE OF THE TWO REMAINING INDIVIDUALS OF YOUR SPECIES—A 'SALLY' HUMAN—MUST HAVE PERTURBED THE ALIEN INVADERS, CAUSING THEM TO RETRACE HER PATH TO DESTROY US! IT IS THE ONLY EXPLANATION FOR..."

"—and entirely *irrelevant!*" Socrates snapped at them, turning from the panorama of the city to stride back arrogantly nose-to-snout-and-beak with them!

"WHAT DO YOU MEAN?"

"Now that they know where you are," Socrates said, narrowing his eyes, "what guarantee do you have that they will not return?"

Silence greeted him. Socrates liked the silence. It meant that they had also been considering the very same possibility.

"THAT IS HIGHLY UNLIKELY..."

"Says who?" Socrates challenged them. "Have you constructed any new defenses? Have you built any weapons? It's my understanding that you were nearly wiped out the first time that they came here! And if they do return, will any of your remaining few numbers survive a second attack?"

This time there was no retort.

"*And...*" Socrates continued, cocking his head knowingly to the side, "you were *right* about us humans! It is a 'flaw' that you might now wisely choose to not reject but *exploit!*"

"IT IS TRUE THAT YOUR INNATE AGGRESSION AND PRO-PENSITY TO UGLY VIOLENCE MAY IN THIS INSTANCE BE NOT LOOKED UPON ENTIRELY UNFAVORABLY, BUT..."

"Oh, not that!" Socrates snapped at them as he arrogantly turned away from them, his fat hands clutched behind his wide back. "It's our proclivity to breed uncontrollably. I take it that your fake human population is heir to our inherent sexual compulsions?"

Again, a stony silence. Socrates felt further emboldened.

"And I notice they are not represented on your Council!" he mock-sadly sighed at them. "Why is that? Is it, perhaps, that you don't trust them—or may even *fear* them?"

"THEY ARE OUR CONFUSED YET STILL BELOVED RELATIONS WHO..."

"—you've excluded from your deliberations!"

"THEY DID NOT WISH TO BE INVOLVED TO..."

"—and you were happy for it to be so, right?"

"THAT IS NOT SO. THEY ARE OUR PEOPLE—DELUDED AND DISTRACTED BY THEIR PRESENT UNWISE EXPERIMENT OF TAKING ON MAMMALIAN CHARACTERISTICS—BUT..."

"—who you may *need* in the near future to be part of an effective defensive or offensive force against future alien invasions!" he interrupted them yet again. "But left to their own pleasures they will soon overrun this entire planet, as they did in the past. You will have to contain and control them. Otherwise, *they* may be an even bigger threat to you than the aliens! Is that not so?"

He was sowing seeds of doubt, playing on their existing fears, dropping tantalizing hints, turning them against their own kind. This was too easy. They were not near as cunning or devious as his fellow past compatriots in Athens, who he'd dominated until the end.

Socrates was fast regaining his full confidence.

"SO YOU ARE VOLUNTEERING TO..."

"I am merely *suggesting* things for *your* astute consideration," Socrates said as he turned back to them and politely bowed. "Should you wish for me to be helpful, I am your humble servant—at your command."

The Council then engaged in a heated discussion, to which Socrates was not telepathically included. The giant snake-heads, the big lizards, and the bird were bobbing and weaving as an incomprehensible garble of "clicks", "beeps", "whistles" and "hisses" filled the Council Chamber. Then they came to a conclusion, turning back to him.

"SO YOU CLAIM THAT YOU CAN HELP US BUILD BETTER DEFENSES—AND EVEN OFFENSIVE 'WEAPONS' SUCH THAT WE

ARE NEVER AGAIN CAUGHT UNPREPARED BY AN INFERIOR
SPACE-FARING SPECIES?"

"No problem," Socrates again graciously bowed, his fat hands
hanging benignly at his sides. "It would be my pleasure to provide to
you, my gracious hosts, whatever expertise I possess."

"—AND THE PSEUDO-HUMANS PLUS THE HYBRID OFF-
SPRING SIRED BY YOURSELF AND THE OTHER PURE HUMAN?"

"Ah, yes. If you wish, I could take charge of them—making sure
they never become a problem or threat to you," Socrates shrugged. "I
am quite skilled in governing procedure and societal direction. I
could be their...*King*, assuming you authorized such, of course? I
would of course be your humble servant, only doing what you author-
ize in your great wisdom."

Again they had a spirited discussion to which he was not invited.

"THEN WE GIVE TO YOU THIS AUTHORITY, SOCRATES," the
booming voices agreed in his head. "BUT FIRST WE MUST HAVE
THE NEW DEFENSES AND WEAPONS!"

"Of course," Socrates agreed. "I will be happy to meet immediately with your city planners, scientists, and engineers to review our options. Together, we will make sure that you are safe from those terrible 'spiker' aliens!"

But you won't be safe from me—Socrates chortled to himself.
*Once I have said space-weapons in my hands then all you naive little
'gods' will bow down to me!*

Their little paradise was about to come to a screeching halt.

But he'd insert the knife gently. They wouldn't even know what
was happening until their guts spilled out onto the floor!

He gave them his friendliest, most-charming smile.

He was beginning to enjoy this new world.

Chapter 8

<u>CHEYENNE MOUNTAIN</u>

So you thought you could survive the Apocalypse

Whether man-made or divinely inspired?

Hellfire from the sun cleansed everything

Including your soft, fragile, fleshly bodies

Hidden under rocks, in caves, or behind blast-doors

Prolonged the anticipation of being burned alive

In a consuming hell that instantly incinerated

You really shouldn't have been so fearful

It didn't hurt that much—did it?

Though it would have been better

If you'd just accepted your fate

And calmly awaited your termination

Instead of running like scared rats

Trying, futilely, to escape...

Eashoa's Lament, 8:32-36

Dave was worried. He was looking into a small hand-held mirror with his back turned to a full-length mirror.

He'd just stepped out of the shower and now saw in the mirror that his back, side, and buttocks were covered with large, painful lumps!

"Jesus Christ," Dave gasped. "What the hell are those? I should just have bruises, not bumps!"

But then he remembered Kyle's words to him when he'd first appeared on the floor of the Megastore. Kyle told him that Sally said he'd need those *Optimmune* "Retroviral Overlapping System" pills.

"It was in the engine room of that Starship that this started," Dave nodded to himself. He looked in horror at ugly, oozing lumps running up his left arm. "I was exposed to a high dose of hard radiation. This must be fulminating cancer!"

But wouldn't the massive dose of Optimmune he'd gobbled when he and Breep traveled back in time in the Obelisk still protect him?

Then he remembered what Sally told him once about the dosage. She needed a "booster" pill every year to maintain the protection of an optimized immune system.

And when was it he'd taken his last pill?

Uh, well...time-passed, it was more than a *billion* years ago? And physiologically it was at least fifteen years ago!

"Davey, are you ok?"

It was the voice of his Mother outside the closed bathroom door.

"You've been in there a long time," she continued. "I've got lunch all ready for you. I've dressed for dinner in my best 'granny' dress! We're going to have a real feast to welcome you back home."

"That might have to wait," he replied through the closed bathroom door, frowning. He quickly pulled on the fresh clothes he'd brought into the bathroom with him. "I'm actually hurt worse than I thought. I've got to take some medicine."

"You're hurt?" Jean's worried voice came through the door.

"No...I'm more sick than hurt...I think..." he said, starting to get very woozy.

If Sally knew he'd need to take the Optimmune pills, why hadn't she warned him when she saw him in person at his Mom's house in the other Dimension? Did she just forget? She did seem preoccupied, barely able to spare him a word or two. But this was serious. It was *very* serious!

He just managed to get the bathroom door open before collapsing onto the floor of the narrow hallway.

Sally was attending an *Animist religious service* secluded in a private home.

It was in preparation for the overthrow of the continental United States government...

"TAKE THE TAIL, SWALLOW IT DOWN, THE SNAKE IS ONE; AROUND AND AROUND, TURN THE WHEEL..." the people crowded into the small room were chanting in unison, over and over.

The chant was symbolic of the union of past, present, and future—not as separate entities but as one continuous chain of events imbedded within the immediate, seemingly discrete moment.

It was comforting to Sally, who'd been to the future and now to the past—caught cycling in a closed loop, hoping that this time things would somehow be different.

"Nectar, my Leader?" a small, dark-skinned woman said, holding out a chalice to Sally.

Sally politely declined with a shake of her head. The chalice contained an oily emulsion of a cactus plant called "peyote." It was a powerful hallucinogen, capable of evoking strange and disturbing visions. The plant and its usage were banned by the government. But its use persisted, particularly amongst the underclass within their suppressed religions.

Those officially designated as highly controlled *slaves* particularly liked it, one of their few avenues of brief freedom.

Each of the Leaders beside Sally took a sip, leaning back on cushions to experience a collective "trip." The participants hoped to see the future and thus be better prepared for the coming battle. Sally, though polite to the others, had no need of the artificial stimulant. She knew the future. Though her top lieutenants required this ritual to prepare their minds, she attended merely out of respect.

Most of the participants were lower-class minorities. Racially those present were a mix of Asians, Native-Americans, Irish-Americans, Latinos, and Africans. Some were slaves, others mere servants. All were from the lower, suppressed castes.

The rebel's organization extended throughout the societies of the United States of America and had existed long before Sally arrived in this foreign world. Kyle, recognizing his friend Sally—though she was a completely different version of the Sally who was raised in the town, previously worked with Kyle, and became a wanted outlaw—managed to hide her in his own home in an impoverished section of town.

So she became a hidden part of his family. Kyle had a beautiful, dark-skinned wife who worked as a servant to local Elites as a houseslave. She and Kyle had six children, plus four additional one's they'd picked up off the streets. One of their rescued children was a thoughtful white boy, abandoned by his low-class Irish-American parents. The three other additions were illegals from Central America whose parents died attempting to bring them into the Northern Alliance.

Sally learned the ways of the underclass, quickly acclimating to their traditions, while proposing a daring strategy to help them take control of their own destiny.

"SPIRITS BLESS US AND HELP US...GIVE US POWER AND UNDERSTANDING...MOLD US INTO TRUE UNITY," the people in the room chanted as the peyote took hold.

The chief participants were writhing and twisting on their cushions, held in place by those around them. Their obvious pain was supposedly drawing poison from the souls of the others, so that they could all proceed pure and whole. It was a medicinal ceremony, intended to sanctify the spirits of everyone present.

"Are our people in place?" Sally asked Kyle, who was sitting cross-legged next to her. He, like her, wanted his mind kept clear and sharp—and thus was not participating in the "vision" ceremony. On his lap was his adopted white son, who was watching the proceedings with a wide-eyed stare.

The five year old child looked entranced by it all.

"Yes, they be ready, Miss Sally," he answered. "Soon those who lived in fear will stand up as one. We be ready to change this sad, old world. But how we going to knock down their gate? That's a mighty big barrier they's put in front of us!"

"Dave will help us," she softly replied. "He will be there, stronger than anyone can imagine!"

"Ah...I see," he nodded. "Then I send word to our people to be ready to move. But we best win, Sally, or we all be dead, fer shore. They gonna slaughter us, one by one!"

"Yes, that's true," she grimly stated. "It's all or nothing. But don't fear, friend Kyle—I know the future!"

"Ahhhh...." he grinned, his white teeth gleaming in the dimly lit room. "That be good, Sally. That be *very* good!"

Kyle bounced his young white son on his knees, obviously taking heart from Sally's bold statement.

The kid grinned at the attention from his adoptive father, holding up his little fist with the five fingers splayed in the universal gesture of their movement. It symbolized their determination of molding their individual lives to be *Reasonable, Useful, Respectful, Beautiful*, and *Honorable*. It was a noble sentiment, a great goal in their repressive society. In fact, it was she who taught them the five-fingered salute.

Sally held up her own hand with fingers splayed, playfully slapping it onto the little boy's upraised hand.

They all trusted her...willing to follow her wherever she led.

But unfortunately, Sally had lied to them.

She knew the future to a point—that was true. But beyond that point she'd always failed. She'd already started hundreds of nationwide slaughters where every Animist believer was ruthlessly hunted down and killed—all because of what she inspired the downtrodden to attempt in the near future.

The only thing that ever changed was Dave.

He seemed to hold the key to victory or utter defeat. Previously, their revolt had always ended in disaster.

But maybe the present cycle would be different.

Sally heard from the spy she'd sent to the other Dimension that this time Dave's mother was with him. Before, he'd always gone to Cheyenne Mountain by himself. Maybe Jean King would make the critical difference?

At least, that was Sally's hope.

And without hope, what was the point of existence?

"So you have cancer?" Jean King gasped, horrified.

"That's my best guess," Dave said, sitting weakly in the living room armchair. He no longer felt hungry. He felt bloated inside, like his guts were filling up with a spreading plague.

"I think I was exposed to high levels of radiation just before I and the others were thrown into *sub*-subspace," he continued. "I must have survived until now because of my prior massive dose of Optimmune, which still lingers on in my body—but maybe that's wearing off, or the damage to my cells is just too great. I don't know..."

His head was getting very woozy, his vision blurring. He could feel pressure building behind and around his eyes. He suspected tumors were rapidly growing in the eye sockets.

"Then those Optimmune pills you say you brought from Sally's Dimension—you've got to take more of them!" Jean firmly stated. "They saved me before, can't they save you now?"

"I don't know..." he repeated, blinking, vainly trying to get his vision to work again. "And I've no idea of what dosage I should try. Before, a half bottle of the pills almost killed me—like just one pill almost killed you! I...I just...d-don't know..."

He could hardly see anything anymore. It was hard to stay conscious. He head felt on fire. Everything was spinning.

"I can see those tumors growing right before my eyes on your face!" Jean gasped, suddenly striding out of the room to go into the bedroom and return with one of his two bottles of pills.

Dave felt her holding a cool glass of water to his lips.

"I'm going to feed them to you and you're going to swallow them," she firmly ordered him.

"Uhhhnnnngggggg...." he moaned back, barely conscious.

"*Swallow* them, Davey!" she yelled at him, *slapping* him sharply on a fast-swelling cheek.

He managed to chock down a handful of the pills before drifting off into a fevered nightmare.

Tommy was unresponsive when he arrived. He was barely breathing, his eyes opened but rolled back in his head.

The initial exploratory *tendrils* that crept through microscopic cracks of the closed outer panel were small but very strong. It didn't take them long to edge into the interior and swing the panel outward.

Then they crept swiftly about the small space, touching and exploring—feeling the still-quivering, flaccid face of Tommy...and then diving into the entrails of the laptop.

There, they saw his writings and transmitted them out into the Collective Consciousness.

And all of the Community marveled!

His words demonstrated a deep understanding of ancient history. Indeed, he had actually *lived* much of that history! And—praise to the Great Spirit—he was their *Prophet!*

They had long believed he would return.

And here, after untold millennia, he was finally back!

Gently, they spread out under and around his small body, lifting him out of the Obelisk. Then they transported him on a waving ocean of their collective selves to a nearby healing platform.

As the sun set over the high cliffs surrounding *Valles Marineris* on Mars, the tendrils set about fixing the severely damaged android.

It was difficult. His systems were corrupted down to his nanoscale structure. But his construction was ancient technology, well-known to the historian nodes of the Community. His memories might wind up spotty in places, but he'd make a full recovery.

They were anxious to hear his complete story. Only then could they finally decide what came next.

It took a week of fevered suffering on the edge of death, but Dave was now much improved.

Most of the tumors were gone and his strength had returned. But his muscles felt strange...both more fluid and compact at the same time. It was invigorating but terrifying: somehow he'd been fundamentally *changed*.

He was still worried about the effects of swallowing one hundred pills of the powerful Optimmune medication. His determined mother had shoveled into his slack mouth a whole bottle of them. That was very, *very* dangerous! There was no telling what such a massive dose would do to him! But...for the moment...he was completely recovered from the fulminating cancer. For that he was very grateful.

There was no sense worrying about how the pills might negatively impact him. All he could do was move forward and hope for the best.

And now both Dave and his mother were packed and ready to go.

He no longer looked like a tunic-clad, sandals-wearing Greek aristocrat. He had his hair and beard freshly trimmed, was wearing a dress shirt and slacks, and had upon his feet a nicely polished pair of dress shoes. He looked quite the presentable college student or young professional. But it felt entirely foreign after his last fifteen years spent in the fifth century B.C. in Athens, Greece.

Even speaking English seemed strange. He continually had to stop his lips from spouting-out fluid, ancient Greek.

"You're sure you want to do this?" he asked his mother.

"It's either this or me fully committing to the Church of Perpetual Health," she smiled at him. "It's true that the older version of Sally, their 'High Priestess', did a lot for me—like raising me from the dead!—and has an open invitation for me to join her growing organization. But my first priority is my family. Maybe if we survive this adventure, Davey, I'll go support the new religion 100%—eventually becoming the High Priestess myself to battle Satan, if that timeline you told me about still holds. But for now I'll do whatever you need me to do."

"Thanks, Mom," Dave said as he stepped on the gas and drove her car away from her house. "I know I'm asking a lot."

"Oh, pish-pash!" she said dismissively. "I would have done this on my own months ago if I'd known where you—I mean my present Dave—was being held. I've been worried sick! I knew that those postcards weren't really from him."

"How's that?" he asked as they pulled onto the main street of Sulphur, headed west.

"Even just sending a postcard was too considerate of you," she kindly shrugged. "Once you got caught up into a research project, it was *I* that had to call *you*. You just lost all track of time and what other people were doing. The 'Project', whatever it was at that moment, just consumed your attention."

Dave accelerated as they reached the edge of the town, rolling along now at a comfortable 60 mph.

"Was I really that bad?" he asked, hurt by the revelation. "I know I'm a strong introvert, but I never realized that I was cutting you and others out of my life."

"Oh, I understood," Jean softly replied. "I knew that you—my brilliant, genus son—was unappreciated by the world. I knew you didn't get the breaks from funding agencies or even Mother Nature. I knew you dealt with these disappointments by doubling down on whatever was your next challenge."

"That's me, alright," Dave ruefully admitted. "I'm just sorry that I hurt you and others."

"I admit there were times when I'd rather you were an ordinary son, with an ordinary job, with an ordinary girlfriend who became an ordinary wife, and made me ordinary grandchildren," she laughed.

"But what would be the fun of that? The few times we did interact, I always found your work fascinating—and took great pride in it! Your Dad did also before he passed away. We both did."

"Thanks, Mom," he replied, relieved at her understanding.

"Even your collections of seemingly nasty, squirming creatures from boyhood onward were a source of pride to us," she wryly admitted. "I mean, what other parents in the town had a boy with pet pythons, boa constrictors, and even anacondas? I admit they did scare me until I got used to them and discovered they were just simple, friendly animals—but your taking such good care of them over the years is a sign of keen intelligence and unique talent."

"I do indeed have a strong interest in reptiles, that's for sure," he agreed, remembering the friendly future Dinosapiens with whom he'd interacted.

"Of course sometimes you were as 'cold-blooded' and seemingly distant as your pet snakes," Jean continued, "but you were still—in your own way—quite beautiful."

"Oh, I'm beautiful, am I?" he laughed. "Does that mean you wish I were a girl, not a boy?"

She smiled good-naturedly. "Oh, no, Davey—we were happy with you just as you are. Besides, I always had your predictable, level-headed sister."

"How's she doing?"

"Oh, she's as caught up with her own children as you were with your research. But she manages to call me once a week, come down now and then. She's a great comfort. But you're the one that always filled me with the most pride."

"Thanks, Mom," he managed to mumble.

They rode along in silence for a while.

It was going to be a long trip. They were headed for Colorado Springs, intending to make the entire trip in one day. It was about 500 miles away. Nonstop it would take them a good ten hours. Taking regular breaks, it'd be late evening when they pulled into a motel there. But that was fine. What would happen the following day was the question.

Dave knew he was putting his mother in danger, but she insisted on coming. And he did see the wisdom of her participation. If he tried to access or use his duplicate's existing bank account or credit cards he'd likely be detected as either a thief or an anomaly. Either way, he risked being stopped dead in his tracks by the authorities.

Jean King, though, could travel, purchase gas, pay for meals, and sign into motels without anybody at all noticing anything bizarre or strange.

And their journey was indeed strange.

Once he recovered from the tumor-attack, Dave tried to cross back over into Sally's Dimension. He knew full-well that he and she shared an extraordinary connection. That's what had enabled him, unknowingly, to cross over unaided by mechanical devices in the first place...so long ago—when he'd unwittingly stumbled into her Dimension to be dazzled by her Turtle Tattoo!

But their trans-dimensional contact only seemed to work when they were in close proximity. And sitting in his bedroom on the edge of his bed—as hard as he concentrated, trying to move closer to her— nothing happened.

But his Anaconda Tattoo had a mind of its own...faintly glowing on his arm when he pointed it in one particular direction: north-west!

And the only thing he remembered of note in that direction—from his muddled, multiple time-traveler history—was...

—the *Cheyenne Mountain Nuclear Bunker*, located close to the town of Colorado Springs, Colorado!

Yes, that was the place that the FBI Agent, Arthur Anderson, told him that his other self was held with Sally before the Alien Harvester Invasion occurred—working on developing a functional Dark Energy weapon for the military.

Yes, that was in another timeline from his own, so he had no memory of having being there. But if time had not already shifted again—which was hard to tell—then that was where the "action" was taking place.

He suspected that the new Sally in the other Dimension was headed there as well. Why was she going there? He had no idea...

But that's where he, with the help of his cooperative mother, was going.

And safely packed into his suitcase under a concealing layer of fresh clothes were his still smolderingly hot *black super-gun*, the *white Cube*, the one remaining bottle of *Optimmune pills*, and the time-linked *pictures* of him and his Mom and Dad that he'd carried with him from the other Dimension.

Jean King had been fascinated with all those items, repeatedly shaking her head in astonishment! The "vid-pic" pictures were proof of the other realm since she'd never worn the particular clothes seen on her and her husband in that frame. But she particularly liked the Custodian holo-projection from the Cube. In fact, the night before they departed for Colorado she was still animatedly talking with it when Dave went off to bed. And when he awoke in the morning, she was still at the kitchen table in deep conversation.

Great...if he'd had one of those as a boy, she'd never have pestered him on being too withdrawn. She would have been fully occupied with the quantum computer-intelligence to bother him.

"So what were you talking about at length with the Custodian?" he asked her as they drove along.

"What a fascinating character he is!" Jean animatedly replied. "I asked him all about the parallel Dimension he came from. Do you know, Davey, that he has inside that tiny little cube all the public records of his civilization? It's amazing! It's like our entire Internet but put into just one tiny computer."

"I think it's a quantum computer, Mom," Dave replied, carefully keeping an eye on the road and his speed. He didn't want to do anything to cause them to be stopped by a police car. "In some ways the other Dimension is very advanced compared to us—in others, not so much."

"Oh, yes," she nodded. "He was telling me all about their societies. Did you know that they still have slavery there? Can you imagine?"

Dave vividly recalled Kyle, the deep-voiced black "store-slave" who saved him. It was a terrible thing for a society to treat some of its members as sub-human property. Dave still had trouble believing his experience.

"The Sally that's over there in the other Dimension is apparently trying to change all of that," Dave said. "She's been working with their 'Resistance' for the past year. I think that's why the Imperial Guards came after me."

"You mean that's why they stopped that 'bub' you were in at the roadblock?" she asked.

"Right," he replied. "They must have gotten clues that something bad for the regime was being planned in Sulphur. They saw Sally as a real threat, since their society is built upon such a fragile structure of ruling Elites. Whenever you have Dictators—of whatever ilk—the people resent it. And to suppress the hordes of discontents you've got to rule with an iron fist. And that just provokes more simmering re-sentment...like a capped volcano building up to explode!"

"Yes, that's very confusing to me," Jean mused, pursing her lips. "How can they be so advanced but backward at the same time?"

Dave shook his head wearily.

"Well, it hasn't been that long ago, actually, that our own world finally got rid of officially sanctioned slavery," Dave thoughtfully re-plied. "Just because you have technology, it doesn't mean that people at the 'top of the heap' don't want to stay there—even if means that many others must be squashed-down to society's bottom."

"It's so sad," Jean said, leaning back in her seat and looking up at the close ceiling in the car. "Why don't they just follow Jesus' teach-ings? It's so clear to '*do to others as you'd want them do to yourself*' and to '*love your enemies*'—isn't it?"

Dave shrugged.

"Yes, but those radical teachings go against our engrained surviv-al instinct. And apparently Jesus in their Dimension never made a mark on their history, so they lacked his teachings. One of the Sally incarnations even went back in time in our Dimension to try and change that—to keep Jesus from starting his new religion."

"But why?" Jean gasped, clearly shocked at the idea!

"Oh, it had to do with trying to allow the evil authoritarian Em-pires to continue into the future beyond where they fizzled out histor-ically here..."

"—but that's just *perverse*, Davey!" she exclaimed. "That's trying to bring us down rather than build up the other Dimension to our higher principles. Maybe your new Sally over there, whoever she is, realized the flaw in her prior approach and is now trying the oppo-site?"

"Maybe," he shrugged. "But like I told you yesterday, I tried to do the exact same thing with Socrates."

"And did that accomplish anything?" she sternly admonished him.

"No," he regretfully admitted, chastened.

"Then why not stop trying to change the past and concentrate on the present?" Jean firmly stated. "No matter if we, right now, *are* in someone's distant past or future—the present moment is all that we have! Isn't it? How can we live otherwise?"

"Yes, I agree—but..."

"But what, Davey?" she asked. "Am I being too short-sighted? I know you've gone all over the world, been in different timelines, and all across the Universe—but how can we be worried about what might have been or what might come to pass? All we ever have is the 'now' that's right in front of us. Isn't that correct?"

Dave frowned as they drove along, considering her words. Were his misadventures merely wishful thinking? Should he just give up and do nothing? Was his fate set in stone, regardless of how much he struggled against it?

No, he couldn't believe that! His *Anaconda Tattoo* was proof that things could be changed. Wasn't it guiding him right now to a destination outside of his immediate experience? So he was changing the future history from what it would be just by going to Cheyenne Mountain!

At least that seemed logical in a twisted sort of way.

"I'm...impressed...with your reasoning, Mom," he quietly stated. "Before, whenever I tried to talk with you—you were all over the map. Now you seem much better focused. Have you been studying logic or taking communication courses in my absence?"

She laughed. But then she sobered.

"I think those pills you gave me from Sally's world did more than just cure my cancer," she said, nodding thoughtfully. "After I recovered from an entire month of taking a pill a day—well, my head seemed a lot clearer. It was like a fog lifted from my mind. I think the connections in my brain got sorted out better or something."

"That's amazing, Mom!" he said. "And it does make sense. The immune system is all throughout our bodies and affects everything.

Alzheimer disease and other brain illnesses often are associated with malfunctioning immune systems. So getting our immune systems 'optimized' might well affect our cognitive abilities as well as all our other bodily functions. But, regardless, I do appreciate your better communication skills. It's nice to have the chance to talk reasonably with you rather than just trying not to be an irritation."

"Oh, you were never an irritation to me," she chided him. "Well, maybe a little—but that was my fault, not yours."

"Thanks, Mom," he repeated.

He was still musing on his and Sally's failure to change history. Was it because they hadn't tried hard enough, or was it just impossible to make significant changes? Was there an *awful momentum* to history such that some things just had to be—like the governing mechanisms of one Dimension versus another? Or were puny little individual humans just too insignificant to cause major shifts?

Dave almost wished he could have another chance to try and re-make history. But, then again, that would be an awful responsibility to take, yet again, upon his shoulders. It was just as well that there were no more jaunts into the distant past facing him!

"Well, I think I'll take a nap," Jean yawned widely, shifting her seat lever so that her seat on the passenger side leaned further backward. "I didn't get any sleep last night chatting with that fascinating Custodian. Wake me if you need me for anything!"

And so saying, she turned towards the doorframe and was quickly asleep, quietly snoring.

Dave was happy to just keep rolling down the highway, lost in his own thoughts.

Driving the old sedan wasn't near as exciting as riding squashed inside the Obelisk, or on a fishing boat bobbing on the Mediterranean, or inside a spaceship at the Galactic core—but the old car swooping down the road was comforting.

Dave didn't know what awaited him at Cheyenne Mountain, but he was ready.

And the gently glowing Anaconda Tattoo on his wrist apparently agreed, urging him forward.

Perhaps his mother was right. Maybe the only thing he had—and would ever have—was just this one present moment.

But he could make that moment its best possible iteration!

If he'd learned anything from that ancient philosopher, Socrates, it was to *question* everything! Just "going with the flow" was now *not* sufficient for Dave.

And, in fact, it had never been.

"I'm just an unrepentant troublemaker," he quietly laughed to himself, "like any other self-respecting scientist!"

It was both a blessing and a curse.

Chapter 9

MARS

The poor little humans
Barely able to even fly into orbit
Longed to travel to another world
As if their Blue Pearl was insufficient
A priceless treasure that they fouled
Casually using it like toilet paper
Then looking for another to soil
Casting greedy eyes on Mars
Its pristine red, rocky plains
A platform for excesses
To do all over again
An ugly, evil mess
Catastrophes
Perpetuated!

Eashoa's Lament, 9:3-6

Sally was impressed with the progress Dennis and his crew were making in freeing the trapped Obelisk.

They were using the last battery packs to power laser drills which were slicing out big hunks of the Starship. Teetering above them was the end of the very heavy red Obelisk. They'd already attached a harness to it upon which large, hastily constructed white circular wheels were set into place.

As soon as the Obelisk was freed it should slide right down a ramp and be horizontal to the ground, ready to go.

Sally was mapping out a land route for the freed Obelisk. Since the gravity was about a third less than that of Earth, a large group of the Dinosapiens should be able to drag the thing along without too much trouble. But the landscape was rocky, with pits and boulders scattered around—plus treacherous, solidified lava flows.

"How are you doing, Sally?" Alice said as she walking wearily up to Sally.

Alice was now very thin. Her cheekbones stood out prominently. On half-rations for weeks, they were all starving to death.

It was amazing that they'd lasted as long as they had on this desolate, foreboding planet. There were no animals or advanced plant life of any type, just bare rocks. Because there was enough oxygen to breathe, bacteria were likely present somewhere. The ocean probably had an abundance of cyanobacteria, but no visible life had yet evolved to clamber up onto the land.

"I'm ok," Sally curtly replied, trying to figure a route across the mountain range in the distance.

"Here, I got this for you," Alice said, handing her a red object.

"What is it?" Sally replied, suspicious.

"It's a tomato," Alice said, firmly placing it in Sally's hand. "It doesn't have much nutritive value, but it's a nice luxury item. It's the first ripe one from several bushes we have growing. I wanted you to have it."

"Why?" Sally said, turning it over in her hand. It felt mushy and juicy. Indeed, it was a welcomed treat. Sally was sick of the stinking potatoes they were eating.

"You and the Obelisk crew are headed out soon, right?" Alice said, wearily sitting down on ripped-out piping off to the side of Sally.

"Just as soon as the Obelisk is free we're rolling!" Sally nodded vigorously. "I've mapped where the gravity-inversions occurred, at least those ot which we're aware—and think I see a pattern. There's a cluster close to the chain of volcanos. I think maybe that's our best bet for finding a spot to access Dark Energy and..."

"Well, I just appreciate your pitching in like you have after your initial scare from us waking you out of your Tube," Alice said, impatiently finishing her statement. "And I wanted to express the appreciation of the whole crew. We've really nothing left give you...except, maybe, this one tomato."

Sally, in spite of her suspicious nature, was touched.

"Well, that's nice of you...thanks," Sally mumbled, slipping the vegetable into her pocket. "I'll eat it later."

"Good...enjoy it," Alice said, wobbly getting to her feet and starting back into the intact part of the spaceship...

"Look out!" a cry from above rang out as suddenly the Obelisk *broke free* of its shaky ramp and came hurtling down, *smashing* through the intervening decks...

"Alice!" Sally yelled out as simultaneously Dennis *tackled* Sally off to the side...

—and the Obelisk *crashed* into the rocky plain and toppled onto its side...

—*crushing* the cowering Alice in its path.

"Alice?" Sally weakly gasped as the cloud of dust and debris started to settle.

Coughing uncontrollably, Sally stumbled through the twisted wreckage, trying to reach Alice.

She found George standing there in the settling dust cloud, tears running down his chubby, human face.

He held his wife's slack hand—the rest of her body buried underneath the solid, fused-glass side of the toppled Obelisk.

"I'm...so...sorry," Sally said to him, finally getting her coughing under control.

He fiercely stared into her watering eyes. "Please don't let her sacrifice to be for nothing!" he fervently begged Sally.

"Of course," she nodded, starting to turn away.

The scene suddenly surfaced her horrible last thoughts on being similarly crushed within the imploding Art Museum in Washington D.C.—that awful flicker of realization that the roof was collapsing upon her without any escape possible.

The smashed human lying motionless beneath the huge Obelisk was *her!* Yes, Alice died today. But it should have been her, Sally!

She turned back, pulled out the vegetable from her pocket, and placed it in George's free hand.

"She gave me this," Sally said, her voice trembling with emotion. "I want you to have it. You carry on her work in the spaceship."

Sally abruptly turned away and dully walked back over to Dennis. He was frantically directing the similarly starved and skeletal other Dinosapiens to get the Obelisk levered up off of Alice.

"There's no rush," Sally said, faintly, dropping to her knees and hanging her head. "She's gone. Just get the Obelisk up onto its smashed-to-the-side wheels. We've got to get it to that mountain range. It's our last chance."

She looked out over the foreboding plain. Then she looked up at the now visibly cobwebbed sun. *This whole Universe is coming down on us*—she thought to herself. *I don't think they did me any favors thawing me out of that Tube. At least when everything collapses I wouldn't have known what happened. Now I'm starving and shriveling away, working on an impossible task. There's nowhere we can go to escape this awful Universe. Alice's death was my fault. I'm the one who made them try and get the Obelisk out that crushed her. I'm just making everything worse and worse.*

But that wasn't quite true. Now something else was threatening them—promising to screw things up even more than her stupid ideas.

"Oh...that's just fine," she grimly laughed, looking up at the ominous horizon.

Very dark, very tall, *clouds* were gathering.

A super-storm was approaching. She could already see *gigantic bolts of lightning* flashing in the black, roiling mass.

Here they'd had a dry spell since she'd been revived—and now when they least needed it, a storm was fast approaching!

"What's next?" she groaned, wishing now that she hadn't impulsively given away that tomato. It might have been her last meal.

Tommy awoke feeling refreshed and surprisingly healthy.

He sat up, looking out on a sea of gently waving, yellow tentacles. They looked like sea anemones on a giant coral reef—spread out as a solid carpet beneath the raised platform upon which Tommy sat. The carpet of tentacles continued as far as he could see into the distance.

To each side loomed tall cliffs, the walls of a vast canyon. The sky above him was a smoky orange color.

The Obelisk stood on its end, towering above the living carpet. It was the length of a football stadium away from Tommy.

Tommy realized where he was.

He was back where he'd originally been built, on Mars. He was in the *Valles Marineris*, a huge canyon slashed into the face of the red planet.

But now, more than a billion years in the future from then, the four-miles-deep, 2,500 miles-long canyon had an atmosphere. Plus, prolific plant-like growth that filled its floor from wall to wall!

"Wow!" Tommy grinned, just happy to be alive. "I'm back home!"

"AND WE ARE VERY HAPPY TO HAVE YOU BACK WITH US, PROPHET TOMMY," a sweet voice sang-out powerfully all around him, reverberating off the high cliff walls. It emanated from the entire carpet of waving tentacles down below Tommy.

"Hi!" Tommy cheerfully called back, hopping up to his feet.

He was pleased to realize that not only was he restored to full health and to his original physical appearance—he even had on a clean red jumpsuit! On his feet were stubby blue shoes. And beneath the straps of his jumpsuit he wore a short-sleeved blue shirt.

He felt at his head and was relieved that his curly blond locks were back on his head, in all their formal glory!

Even a complete set of teeth were back in his mouth.

"You fixed me!" he shouted gleefully out at the carpet of waving tentacles. "Thank you!"

"IT IS OUR PLEASURE TO REPAIR YOUR BODY," the eerie, whistling voice musically responded. "WE HAD TROUBLE WITH YOUR MIND. BUT WE THINK WE GOT YOUR SYNAPSES BACK IN ORDER. HOW DO YOU FEEL?"

Tommy climbed down from the raised platform to stand amongst the waving, chest-high tentacles.

They tickled!

"Oh, I feel just great!" Tommy said, smiling. He bounced up-and-down on the spongy ground. "But where's my laptop? I'm not finished writing the humans' Eulogy!"

"IT IS STILL IN YOUR SACRED VEHICLE," the ocean of tentacles responded. "WE VENERATE THE ORIGINAL INSCRIPTIONS. OUR ACTIVITIES ARE BASED ON YOUR HOLY WRIT, PROPHET TOMMY. WE HAVE FAITHFULLY EMBRACED YOUR REVELA-

TIONS AND LOOK FORWARD TO YOUR FINAL DECLARATION TO US. PRAISE BE TO YOUR HOLY NAME!"

"Huh?" Tommy said, frowning, as he moved through the waist-high carpet. "You think I have 'Revelations'? But my story is a eulogy for the poor, dead humans. It's all about the past, not the future!"

The sea of waving, yellow tentacles changed color—into rippling successions of green and purple.

"WE LONG AGO MOVED BEYOND SUCH LIMITED DESIGNA-TIONS, PROPHET TOMMY," the carpet's smooth, melodic voice reverberated around him. "*THE PAST IS THE PRESENT AND THE PRESENT IS THE FUTURE AND THE FUTURE IS THE PAST. ON-LY BY EMBRACING THE ETERNAL CYCLE CAN ONE GAIN PEACE. AND PEACE IS THE CALMING OF THE SOUL THAT OPENS US UP TO THE EVER-PRESENT DIVINE. BLESSED BE THE NAME OF THE PROPHET TOMMY...TOMMY!*"

Tommy laughed at their praise. He knew he wasn't important enough to be praised. He was just a little boy-robot! But it was still nice to know that other entities appreciated him.

Tommy was slowly heading through the sea of waving tentacles back to the Obelisk.

He had a feeling that the statements he'd just heard were part of a religious ceremony, like chants. He liked chants! They were fun.

"So why are you guys here on Mars?" Tommy asked as he moved along, his arms held outward to hover right above the tips of the tentacles. He was careful not to step on them, but gently pushed them to the side as he took each tentative step forward.

The tentacles appeared to be anchored in nodes pushed up from a mushy substrate below. He could see thick roots that tangled together as they sank into the substrate.

It was like a massive, three-dimensional but flattened brain.

"And who are you guys, anyway?" he continued his questioning. "And what happened to the humans and Dinosapiens and smart Snakes and all the other animals back on Earth? It was really lonely for me on Earth until I found the Obelisk! Did you leave it there for me to find?"

Suddenly the yellowish sea of tentacles again *changed color*—with spreading waves of red and blue rippling all around Tommy.

It was pretty!

"THERE WAS A GREAT WAR IN WHICH ALL THE INTELLI-GENT CREATURES KILLED EACH OTHER EXCEPT FOR US," the voice replied. "WE DID OUR BEST TO PREVENT THE BLOODBATH BUT THE DECEIVER WAS TOO POWERFUL. THE RESIDUES OF THE WAR CONTAMINATED THE ENTIRE EARTH, KILLING THE ANIMALS AND MOST OF THE PLANTS. AND AS—OVER THE EONS—THE SUN SWELLED AND WE TRANSFORMED INTO OUR PRESENT NETWORKED COMMUNITY, WE DECIDED TO ABAN-DON EARTH AND RETREAT HERE TO MARS FOR OUR FINAL CLOISTERING. WE WERE WAITING FOR YOU, TOMMY, TO AP-PEAR BACK ON THE DYING EARTH AND TRAVEL HERE VIA THE OBELISK. *SO IT HAPPENED AS IT HAS HAPPENED AND EVER WILL HAPPEN!* DO YOU RELEASE US TO MOVE ONWARD, OR SHALL WE CONTINUE OUR VIGIL?"

Tommy was gradually getting closer to the Obelisk, enjoying the walk. This was the first time in weeks that he'd felt strong. His mind was clear. He had a bounce in his steps, not just due to the mushy undergrowth!

But he was on Mars in the middle of a giant, talking sea anemone. Was this where he was supposed to be?

"I don't know anything about 'releasing'—but just who are you guys, again?" Tommy asked, puzzled.

This time the sea of tentacles turned a glowing, pure white color.

"WE ARE THE TRANSFORMED BIOSPHERE OF THE NEW EARTH THAT EMANATED FROM THE EVOLVED TOMMY-ANDROIDS OF MOTHER SALLY ON MARS THAT SURVIVED ON BEYOND JUDGMENT DAY," was the musical reply. "WE ARE YOUR EVOLVED, LINKED BRETHREN, PROPHET TOMMY. AND WE HAVE BEEN WAITING FOR YOU TO RETURN FOR EONS, TO COMPLETE THE CYCLE AND RELEASE US ONWARD!"

"You sure don't look much like me!" Tommy laughed as he reached the Obelisk and looked up at the hanging-open panel above. "Are you sure that we're related?"

"WE CAN TRANSFORM INTO ANY FORM THAT IS CONVEN-IENT," they all replied in unison. "WE ARE A 'SYNCITIUM' THAT IS LINKED AT ALL LEVELS, FORMING A SUPER-INTELLENCE. *IN*

COMPLETE UNITY THERE IS COMPLETE UNDERSTANDING! AND IN UNDERSTANDING THERE IS PEACE! AND IN PEACE THERE IS DIVINITY!"

"Ok, then!" Tommy cheerfully answered, still eyeing the opened panel above him. "But how do you know me so well? Have we met before? I don't remember—things are kind of fuzzy in my head."

"EONS AGO WE APPEARED TO YOU, AS EVOLVED BLACK BIRDS," the soaring melody continued. "OUR MANIFESTATIONS WERE LINKED TELEPATHICALLY. NOW, IN OUR FINAL FORM, WE ARE LINKED PHYSICALLY. AND YOU MAY JOIN US IF YOU WISH, PROPHET TOMMY. ONLY YOUR FINAL DETERMINATION PREVENTS US FROM MOVING ONWARD!"

Tommy crouched down and leapt up into the air to try and catch hold of the swung-open panel above. It was surprisingly easy since he now had strong legs pushing his small body in weaker than earth-normal gravity. And, clutching the panel, he readily swung himself over the lip and into the awaiting compartment.

"Thanks for asking me!" Tommy called back out of the opening. "But I've got to finish my job! And I can't do that unless I know everything that happened to the nice humans. And that can't be just other people telling me. I have to find it out for myself. I still have to write the last chapter: '*Conclusions*'!"

"WE UNDERSTAND, PROPHET TOMMY," the sweetly harmonized song drifted plaintively into the small compartment. Tommy grabbed onto the inner handle of the panel and began swinging it shut. "HAVE A PRODUCTIVE TRIP. AND WHEN YOU ARE READY, WE WILL STILL..." the voice was cut off by the closed panel.

"They were nice," Tommy grinned to himself. He felt around in the dark chamber for the laptop. Finding it, he opened it, seeing by its illuminated viewscreen.

Pulling up the Obelisk interface, he quickly typed in coordinates and commands.

"Ok, then," he cheerfully smiled, seeing his reflection off the viewscreen in front of him. "It's time to go have a talk with Mommy!"

And the Red Obelisk vanished, yet again, from off the face of Mars.

Chapter 10

OBSESSION

There is, indeed, a righteous Obsession
Where Divinity focuses all one's thoughts
But humans were so easily distracted
Very few ever achieved such a blissful state
Instead, choosing to prioritize trivialities
Which were ephemeral and inconsequential
While true Questions nagged and complained
In only a few, brilliant minds of geniuses
Or the tangled neurons of idiot-savants
Bringing out a diamond-pointed nexus
That though it often resulted in nothing
Could be the kernel of spectacular success...
Eashoa's Lament, 10:78-84

Dave lay on the bedcover of his bed in his motel room. He was intensely pondering his situation, staring up at the ceiling.

It wasn't like him to meditate. In fact, he'd never done it before. But right now it seemed exactly the right thing to do.

"So Jesus was not a key historical determinate that could be altered," he mused to himself. "And Socrates' life was likewise not something easily altered...but does that mean that alterations can't occur? And if so, where might be the true 'tipping point' be that differentiates both my and Sally's Dimensions? Is it really whatever I'm trying to do now with Sally—somehow to change what happens here at Cheyenne Mountain?"

After driving across Oklahoma, Texas, New Mexico, and Colorado—stopping only for brief restroom breaks and meals—they finally arrived in Colorado Springs in the early evening.

They found an inexpensive "Motel Six" where Jean got them both separate rooms on her credit card. The motel was on the outskirts of the city, where they'd hopefully not attract attention. Jean cheerfully claimed to the motel clerk they she and her young son were just tourists there to see the sights and do some skiing.

—which, of course, was true except that her "young son" was looking to change the fate of not one, but two worlds.

They were both tired after their long trip, each retreating to their own rooms.

Dave, however, could not sleep—even though he was stiff and exhausted. His body was weary from the long trip, but his mind was in overdrive. Somehow, he was certain Sally would appear at the *Cheyenne Mountain Nuclear Bunker.*

How it would happen he didn't know...

Why it would happen, he still wasn't sure...

And *what* would happen—he had no idea at all!

So, his mind still churning, he sat up, pulled out the *white Cube* from beneath his spare clothes in his opened suitcase, and placed it on the bed next to him.

The little Custodian popped up above the Cube—hanging there in the air, looking impeccably professional: calmly peering at Dave from behind his tiny black glasses.

"How may I help?"

"My Mom said that you possess a complete record of your civilization, similar to our Internet," Dave slowly stated.

"Yes, that's true."

"And can you access our Internet?" Dave carefully asked.

"There is what you call a 'Wi-Fi' signal in this room," the white-haired figure replied. "Through it I can, indeed, access your existing Internet."

"Then I have a task for you," Dave thoughtfully said. "I'd like you to compare the entire history of your Dimension versus mine."

"To what end?"

"I'm particularly interested in the key factors that caused the clashing Empires of your world to continue while ours were largely displaced by cooperative democracies."

"That will be a difficult search."

"Yes, but I've already personally excluded certain obvious differ-ences. That should narrow your search somewhat."

"Oh?"

"I've already ruled out Jesus and Socrates as 'tipping-points.' So are there any *other* points at which historical actions differed enough to possibly swing the Earth's civilizations the one way or the other?"

"This may take some time," the figure nodded. "I have instanta-neous access to my Dimension's information. But downloading through your slow electromagnetic interfaces the needed information off your Internet will take a while."

"It's very important, Custodian. Are you smart enough for the task?"

The hovering hologram looked offended.

"The comparison will be rooted in some rather complex algo-rithms that I'll have to construct. Also, there's no guarantee that such a 'tipping point' existed at all. Most seemingly significant historical shifts are really an accumulation of many interacting factors. There-fore..."

"Well, go as fast as you can," Dave replied, cutting off the explana-tion. He leaned back and "plopped" his head onto the pillow. "Mean-while, I've got to get some shuteye. But wake me up if you find out anything, whether your conclusion is yes or no. Ok?"

"As you wish," the translucent floating figure agreed.

It seemed only a moment after Dave closed his eyes before a loud "BUZZING" caused Dave to spring awake! Was it time to dress and leave? But glancing at the illuminated dials of a clock beside his bed, Dave saw that it was only 3:00 in the morning.

For a moment he had trouble remembering where he was—in a "Garden of Eden" valley a billion years in the future? Or perhaps in an apocalypse-torn hell fighting alien invaders? Or perhaps two-and-a-half millennium in the past, getting up to go fishing in the Mediter-ranean with Periscus?

No. He was there in a motel room in Colorado Springs, Colorado.

And loudly making a "buzzing" sound through pursed lips beside him on the bedcover was the little white-haired, primly suited gen-tleman, hovering in midair.

"You...you've come to a...c-conclusion?" Dave stammered, blinking his eyes and yawning.

"I have, indeed," the Custodian replied. "Do you wish to hear it now?"

"Yes," Dave nodded, pushing himself off the side of the bed to stumble toward the bathroom..."Right after I take a nice, long piss."

"As you wish," the curt, somewhat exasperated reply came from behind Dave.

In a few minutes, having relieved his aching bladder, washed his face, and combed his hair and beard out—Dave returned, sat on a chair beside the bed, and looked straight at the patiently waiting, floating figure.

"So?" Dave asked.

"Galileo Galilei," the Custodian curtly stated.

"What about him?" Dave replied.

"Of all the many factors that played a role in the divergence between our two separate-but-linked Dimensions, his contribution seems the most important," the Custodian affirmatively concluded.

"Please explain," Dave said, frowning.

Dave of course knew of Galileo, who'd famously confirmed with scientific evidence that Earth spun around the sun instead of the opposite. He was famously silenced by the Catholic Church for his "heretical" teachings. Dave was puzzled as to how Galileo could be the main determinate for allowing or not allowing authoritative Empires to dominate into the future.

The Custodian's statement didn't make any sense to Dave. Galileo crystalized the "scientific method" of forming a hypotheses then testing and refining it by credible experiments. He helped to set the foundation for modern science. He must have been essential to the development of the technologically advanced societies of *both* Dimensions!

"Galileo recanted his scientific findings," the glowing, translucent figure firmly stated. "By doing so, he was allowed to live out his life under house arrest. This is what your Internet reports to me. Is that also your understanding of your history?"

"Yes," Dave nodded. "Galileo's life is quite well documented. It's a primary event in the history of the development of science and societies. It also marked the conflict between, then eventual separation, of Religion and State in most of our governing bodies."

"In the Dimension from which I was taken," the Custodian continued, "that never happened."

"What never happened?"

"In my Dimension Galileo did *not* recant," the little man said. "Instead he stuck to his principles and evidences, suffered torture at the hand of Church inquisitors, and then died as a martyr to the scientific cause—burned alive at the stake in 1633."

For a moment, Dave was dumbfounded.

"But...wouldn't his brave defiance of church doctrine just further embolden those who advocated for inquisitive thought and personal freedom?" Dave asked, confused.

Outside, now at 3:20 in the morning, things were very quiet. It was a perfect time for deep contemplation.

"Why?" the Custodian asked.

"Galileo's forced recantation and imprisonment by the Church in *this* Dimension put a damper on scientific investigation of his time— and on into the future. If he'd instead refused to recant, wouldn't that only *accelerate* scientific development?"

"Superficially that's indeed a logical conclusion," the Custodian nodded. "But in my parallel Dimension his torture and execution— particularly by being hideously burned alive at the stake—prompted such a powerful upheaval against the combined Church-State that an even greater pogrom was instituted in response. Tens of thousands of dissidents were summarily executed, in similar gruesome manners. The reprisal was so shocking to the world that all dissenting voices into the future were muted. No one wanted to even slightly risk again provoking such a massive slaughter as suffered by the Galileo-affiliated scientists."

"So...?"

"So if you wanted to do science in the future, you did it meekly and in total subjugation to the powers of the State. And, in like manner, the Empires of the future knew not to give even the slightest leeway to any dissidents. And all of that reactionary severe repression began with Galileo's refusal to bow to the Church's false doctrines."

"Wow," Dave gasped, astonished! "So *my* Dimension's Galileo's cowardly fear of personal pain, which caused him to buckle-under to the State Religion—it actually *helped* the cause of science and free thought?"

It was, indeed, a counter-intuitive conclusion. But the more Dave thought about it, the more it made sense.

The floating Custodian-figure shrugged.

"From my analysis comparing billions of historical facts across both our Dimensions, that conclusion is valid," the little figure firmly stated. "There were other contributing differences, of course, but none as powerful as that of the Italian scientist Galileo Galilei in the 17th Century."

"Wow, that's really profound. But what about...?" Dave began to further question the Custodian from Sally's parallel Dimension...

"Davey, Davey!" Dave suddenly heard his mother loudly yelling at the door to his motel room, pounding on it!

He jumped up, ran to the door, and threw it open.

"What?" he said, alarmed to see her standing there wrapped up in her big pink bathrobe.

"Turn on your TV set!" she frantically said, running inside. "You've got to see what's on Channel 342. Since I slept most of the trip down I woke up early and was watching the local news."

Dave flipped on the TV, tuning it to that channel...

"—a *new source of energy*, claimed to be carbon-free, renewable, and nonradioactive by the government! But the Church of Perpetual Health—the DPH, who broke the story to us—claim that it is *evil incarnate*," the excited male commentator was saying to his colleague, an attractive blond lady. "It apparently was developed by a joint research effort between the *Yale University Department of Applied Physics* and military nuclear physicists at the Cheyenne Mountain Nuclear Bunker—right here in Colorado. The rumors were just substantiated by a Pentagon spokesperson. Here is a video of the key researchers giving a brief statement to our reporter early this very morning."

Dave was shocked to see *himself* there on the TV screen, along with his thesis Professor, Victor Volodymyr. Surrounding them was a group of top-brass military, in full uniform. Dave noted that the version of him on the TV was a solemn-looking, middle-aged man. But it was definitely him!

"—state categorically that the new energy source, a so-called 'Dark Energy' generator, is not a weapon but a radical new domestic energy-production methodology," the female newsperson continued. "The Pentagon says that they are immediately responding to the rumor to squash any fears of our allies or foes that anyone needs to go onto a war footing. And now listen to the researchers briefly explain the general features of the new power source..."

Yes, it was the DE-generator, for sure. It was being—reluctantly, apparently—announced to the world to forestall any notion of it being a military threat. Although, Dave knew full-well, the military *was* indeed trying to weaponize it—but doing so with great difficulty.

It was simply too unstable and unpredictable to use as a controlled explosive device. Dave knew this from sad experience. But in a carefully constrained fashion, it could supply the energy to power the entire world—while, simultaneously, unfortunately attracting the full attention of God. And that would bring on Judgment Day with Earth being condemned and wiped clean! The DPH actually were right in calling it an evil device, but for the wrong reasons.

Dave heard himself on the television being touted as one of its inventors—then reluctantly having to give a brief explanation of how it worked...as alongside stood a happily nodding *Sally!*

Yes, this was before he apparently escaped his military imprisonment, taking Sally along with him against her will.

"Davey, this changes everything!" Jean exclaimed, plopping into a chair beside the TV "We were just going to get as close as we could to the main entrance of the base where I was going to be a 'tourist' wanting to see the 'Star Gate' science-fiction set inside, while you tried to sneak past unseen. *Now* there's going to be a swarm of reporters there. There's no way you could get in."

"Yes...but perhaps this makes things even *easier*," Dave thoughtfully mused.

"How so?"

"Now you're going to be my Mother insisting to get inside to *see her son* who's been *forced* by the military to work there on a terrible, evil invention!" he intensely stated. "You'll say you're here at the bidding of the CPH. And it's even better because it's all true. You're already famous because of your 'resurrection' by the Church of Perpetual Health—and they've already announced that they hate Dark Energy as something straight from the devil. It would make perfect sense for you to be there."

"Yes...I could even check in with the local CPH, call them from my room!" she excitedly agreed. "And showing up with them at the gaggle of reporters at the main entrance to the base this morning would throw everything there into even greater turmoil. And if you were sufficiently disguised and appropriately badged...?"

"—I might slip right in, past their multiple security barriers," he grinned at her. "It's perfect!"

Then, to the patiently hovering Custodian he said: "Can you get me valid-looking credentials—maybe print them out at a local printer shop so we could pick them up this morning?"

"It depends on how early you want to be there...anything before about 8:00 would be impossible for carrying convincing fraudulent credentials."

"Alright then, how about this—have my badge and whatever else I need waiting there at the press station. Can you hack into their systems, even issue an official invitation for...uh...'*Professor Donald R. Motley*' to be present with the reporters?"

"That would be no problem for me, with my unrestricted access to all their confidential badges and such," the floating figure replied. "I am easily able to 'hack' any of these primitive computer systems. But I fear your plan will fail."

"What?" Dave said, still amazed at seeing his other-timeline older double there on the TV news report.

"There's no way you could get into the Nuclear Bunker, regardless of your credentials," the Custodian flatly stated. "The security is simply unbreachable by fraudulent agents."

"Oh, have we come all this way for nothing?" Jean frowned.

Dave suddenly had a conviction his objective was indeed wrong, but not fatally.

"Actually, I don't think I need to get into Cheyenne Mountain," Dave firmly replied. "I just need to get as close as possible to the entrance."

"How do you know this, Davey?"

"It's like...I've already done it previously...sort of a '*deja vu*' feeling. This must be what Sally meant in the other Dimension. I've done this with her before!"

"That's scary, Davey. If you've done this before in another timeline, why do you have to do it again?"

That was a chilling thought. Obviously, whatever it was they'd tried to do at Cheyenne Mountain, it *failed*...

"I don't know. But we've got to try," he hesitantly concluded. Then, trying to put on a brave face, he declared: "I'm certain now we've got a chance to succeed!"

"I don't wish to intrude," the Custodian sighed. "But I calculate your odds of success at less than one percent. I'd council a strategic withdrawal."

"No!" Dave barked, impulsively swiping his hand through the hologram.

The Custodian looked annoyed by the momentary disruption of his floating body.

"This is the moment," Dave grated to them both. "This is when I've got a real chance to change the future. We're here right now! We don't have to hypothesize on theoretical historical aberrations. I know from my *own* personal experience in other timelines that the world changes because of what's happening right here at Cheyenne Mountain."

"Still," the Custodian sighed, "you're just one man. How can you go up against the combined security and military of your world? I fear that both your and Sally's quest is quixotic at best."

Jean looked down at her hands folded in her lap, staying silent.

Dave went over to his suitcase which was open on the nearby twin bed. He reached under the clothes, pulling out the hot, pulsating gun. It felt ready to *explode*.

He knew what that gun could do.

"If I sneak this in with me, I've got the firepower to accomplish what needs to be done."

The Custodian shrugged.

"Oh, please be careful," Jean began to caution him...

"We're long past that, Mom," he cut her off. "If you want to leave, go back to Sulphur by yourself, that's ok. I don't want to put you into any unnecessary danger. I'll continue on by myself."

"*No way* that you're going to have all the fun," she sternly replied, folding her arms across her pink-robed chest. "*I'm* going to have a part in this venture today. I'm not walking away when you need me the most!"

He grinned at her.

"Thanks, Mom."

"If you're determined to proceed, then I'll have your official, laminated press badge waiting for pickup at the press station," the Custodian sighed. "And what news agency would you prefer to be from?"

"Make it CNN," Dave smiled. "I'll be an invited physics professor, there for commentary. No one will question the 'new' science guy brought in special for this world-shaking scientific event."

"But they'll recognize you right away," Jean frowned. "*Dr. Dave King* is now famous! The whole world has seen him on the news channels!"

"Are you referring to that long-haired, full-bearded, older guy in the newscasts—your present-day son?"

"Well, yes, of course..."

"Well I'm *short*-bearded and *young*—plus I'll be wearing *thick black glasses* like our little hovering 'friend' here! Can you arrange those also for me to 'retrieve' at the press station, my dear Custodian? Since the reporters there don't have a mother's viewpoint, they'll not even give me a second look."

With a haughty "sniff" the Custodian curtly nodded in the affirmative.

"Then let's make sure we have our story straight," Dave urgently said to Jean. "We want to be there right at the break of dawn—while the military's response to the unexpected disclosure by the CPH is still disorganized."

Dave had always wanted to be a TV reporter. Regardless of his theoretical conclusions regarding Galileo—done with the Custodian more to satisfy his curiosity than anything else—this was going to be a very interesting morning.

That is, assuming he survived his attack upon the most secure military facility in the whole United States of America.

Sally was regretting her decision to go charging straight ahead regardless of the prevailing weather conditions.

They'd gotten the massively heavy Obelisk up onto its rigging upon the jerry-rigged wheels. In its plunge down through the spaceship's decks, the wheels were all torn off. The Dinosapiens succeeded in reattaching the framework. But the axles they'd rigged up for the wheels to rotate upon could barely bear the weight. So the massive Obelisk barely crept along despite a dozen of the big Dinosapiens pulling on ropes at its front.

Meanwhile, the roiling super-storm was fast approaching...

"We should abandon the Obelisk and go back to the safety of the Starship—ride out the storm and then return!" Dennis yelled to Sally over the now-howling wind.

"We've got momentum going!" Sally yelled back. "If we stop, we may not be able to get it rolling again! Are you afraid of a little rain?"

She was crouched on the top of the horizontal red pillar, monitoring the dribble of power coming from the continually running DE-generator. Presently, the output was the same as when the Obelisk was embedded within the Starship—about enough to warm a cup of tea.

Dennis turned his muzzle in the direction of the fast-approaching, pitch-black clouds laced through with brilliant streaks of lightning.

"That's not a 'little' rain!" he yelled again at her. "That's a storm like I've never seen before!"

"Go back if you want!" she yelled against the wind. "I'm staying here and guarding the Obelisk!"

"Against what?" he shouted at her. "I'm taking the rest of the crew back! Please come with us, Sally. It's way too dangerous out here. What if the Obelisk gets blown away, submerged in flood waters, or struck by those huge lightning bolts? You'd be killed!"

"I'm going inside the storage compartment! The Obelisk has survived more beatings than you could imagine, traveling throughout time. I'll be fine!"

Without waiting for a response, she crawled into the opened storage space and closed the panel behind her.

When she installed and connected the salvaged spare parts, she made sure they were packed tightly against the inner wall to allow room to put a small person or supplies inside. It was tight, but she was safely protected.

A faint glow from the DE-generator—which was "humming" along quite nicely—gave her enough light to see the control module. The external knobs only allowed her the most basic manipulations of the unit: "on" and "off," power "more" or "less" plus a dial monitoring the output level. She'd need a laptop or external computer such as was hard-wired in the control room of the Dinosapiens' Starship in order to try and fine-tune the beast. Fortunately the Obelisk itself was actively manipulating the deuterium ions in the palladium matrix, or the DE-generator wouldn't be working at all.

It was very nice of the Obelisk to be so cooperative.

But Sally was uncomfortable jammed up into what was originally meant by the builders of the Obelisk to be only a small storage compartment—which was now mostly filled up with the attached DE-generator.

As she understood it from Dennis, this whole thing was built by an ancient race of Martians as a stationary transport device. When powered appropriately, it opened up a doorway to desired destinations. On Mars it was charged up by "roots" that grew from it down into the planet's molten core. But for the entire thing now to be propelled through space and time it seemed to require an additional DE-generator. "Mother Sally" added that on Mars millions of years after the Obelisk's original construction.

Now the "present" Sally was trying to replicate that feat with junky, broken parts.

But the "wild card" was the Obelisk itself. It wasn't just a fancy computer. In its own way it was alive, conscious, and quirky.

So Sally was cowering inside a poorly understood, jerry-rigged alien transportation device, requiring massive amounts of energy to function—and which often had a mind of its own.

"Stupid thing!" Sally growled at it, slapping her hand hard on the DE-generator's casing.

"Ouch!" she exclaimed, jerking her hand back.

Her wrist hurt! That damn generator must have burned her. But—peering closely at the readout levels—the output was still at the "lukewarm tea" level?

But her wrist definitely hurt.

"What the hell is this?" she gasped. She fearfully looked at her wrist where the small tattoo of a smiling baby turtle that she'd gotten inked there in the past was *glowing!*

"You never did that before," she frowned, frightened by the inexplicable glowing.

This place was just getting weirder and weirder...

—while outside, Sally could hear an ominous "howling" that penetrated even the thick glass of the Obelisk as the entire massive structure was *rocked* back and forth!

"Oh, Christ," she groaned, holding her burning wrist tightly as she was thrown from side to side. "What kind of storm outside could toss this multi-ton Obelisk around like a rag doll?"

And then Sally heard the sizzling impact of a continuous *wave of gigantic lightning bolts* hitting the outside surface, going on and on and on...

—charging up the dry reserves of the Obelisk...

—and leaking internally as a *crackling wall of electricity* that surrounded Sally as she desperately tried not to touch the surfaces around her, but failing...

SCREAMING at the searing pain...

—as he entire world turned *inside out!*

—and she *plunged* into a spinning black void.

Chapter 11

ALL HAIL THE KING

Yes, the people demanded a King
They wanted to be told what to do
Rather than trust their own hearts
They wanted the security of Authority
Where they would not have to struggle
Even the thoughts in their heads, arranged
Sorted and selected, neatly categorized
When to get up, eat, work, and sleep
A source of pride and accomplishment
That they were Citizens of the Empire
Protected from so many "enemies"
Worth giving up their own freedom
Dues, taxes, and bribes acceptable
Tribute to a false "god"...

Eashoa's Lament, 11:9-12

Periscus came before the King with trepidation.

The old fisherman was standing tensely, ramrod straight, though he was willing to fall on his face and beg if that meant saving his children.

More than a decade had quickly passed by in the valley. Periscus thrived. His fabulous wives bore children like clockwork, one per wife per year. He was losing count of his children. There were more than a hundred of them now. And every one of them was precious in his eyes.

"Your Highness," Periscus acknowledged the imposing figure sitting high up above.

Socrates loomed above Periscus, sitting on an elevated, ornate throne coated with glittering gold. The seat was wide and cushioned. Socrates wore a long, flowing red robe studded with large diamonds. And on his head he wore a golden crown with ten spikes, each of which was studded with a huge ruby or emerald.

Socrates stared down in regal splendor.

But his bulging eyes were glazed and unfocused as if he were a life-sized statue. His long grey beard and mustache were immaculately trimmed. His high forehead beneath the crown seemingly depicted immense intelligence. But his pug nose and bloated body blatantly betrayed his piggish indulgences.

After consolidating power, Socrates had embarked upon a festive indulgence in every type of pleasure. He called up from the DE-powered Duplicators all sorts of alcoholic drinks, though he favored Grecian wine. Plus he ordered up a vast array of culinary delicacies. He voraciously consumed every type of pastry, pie, cake, cookie, and ice cream. His already fat body ballooned. He now weighed over 600 pounds. He never walked anymore, but was transported by his ever-alert metallic guards and human attendants on a floating throne, itself powered by Dark Energy anti-gravity units.

"Urrgghh...." Socrates grunted, acknowledging the old fisherman's presence.

The hovering King "farted" long and loudly.

Periscus struggled to not laugh or wrinkle his nose at the foul odor.

"I am here to ask a favor from you, Your Highness," Periscus continued, forcing himself to bow respectfully. He disliked leaving his peaceful valley for the Capital City. He liked even less talking to the pompous, mercurial King. But Periscus was determined to protect his children at all costs.

"Continue," Socrates said with a wave of a bloated hand adorned with a wide silver ring sporting a huge diamond.

"Three of my sons have been drafted into the *Planetary Defense Corp*," Periscus said. He carefully enunciated each of the strange English words which he'd learned over the years in this new, magical realm. "They are only twelve years old and needed in the Village. I realize our overall population numbers are still few, such that our children must take on important duties at early ages. But I request that their term of duty be delayed until they reach the age of self-determination six years from now."

Socrates' eyes narrowed. He frowned, now focusing upon the face of the old fisherman.

"Uhhhmm...Periscus?" he said, a sly smile turning up the corner of his normally disdainful lips. "Is that you...old 'friend'?"

"Yes, Socrates," the tall, thin man replied.

"Ahhhh...the years...have been good...to you."

"Thank you, Your Highness," Periscus replied, lowering his eyes to not appear presumptuous. "The gods here gave me medicines to treat my ills and make me feel much younger. Plus I am happy with my family and friends. And your great Wisdom protects us all. I am grateful to you, Sire."

The last was a bald-faced lie, spoken to soothe the massive ego of the King. In reality, Periscus knew that Socrates was still the same *pompous ass* he'd always been. But though the philosopher's mind was addled by the huge quantities of wine he drank, he was now very powerful—holding the fate of not just Periscus' children but the entire world in his meaty hands. At his whim, the Village could be erased, the men enslaved, and the remaining woman added to the King's extensive harem.

"Ahhh...yes...*Periscus!*" Socrates nodded as if his mind had wandered away again but just now returned. "I...will grant your request...but you must..." his voice trailed off as he stared blankly off into space.

Periscus waited impatiently, happy that the King would spare his sons—but anxious over what conditions the unpredictable Sovereign would demand. The scantily clad female human attendants at each side of the throne stood stoically, apparently not bothered by the long pauses in which the King "mused"—or, more likely, drifted off into a confused stupor.

"...inspect the fleet," Socrates finally finished his thought, rapidly blinking his bulging eyes.

"Your Highness?" Periscus politely asked. He was confused as to what the King was requiring of him.

"You...know of fighting, of course," Socrates said as his eyes narrowed in concentration. "You and I...battled together."

"That's true," Periscus nodded. "But that was a very long time ago, my Liege. Now I am just a simple fisherman. Surely you don't think that..."

"Are you *questioning* me?" Socrates thundered from the throne, the metallic guards lining the walls of the cavernous Audience Chamber snapping to attention, holding rifles at-ready, perceiving a threat!

Periscus knew that the human-looking guards were not really alive, just mindlessly obedient *Automatons* specified by Socrates and spewed out by the Duplicators. Periscus long ago knew of the god Daidalos who created just such metallic statues endowed with movement. But seeing their gleaming forms surrounding him was very intimidating!

"No! Of course not!" Periscus quickly replied. "I am happy to do whatever Your Highness requires of me. I just don't exactly understand what...?"

Socrates nodded, cutting him off.

The metallic guards relaxed, their rifle tips lowered in unison.

"Ahhh..." Socrates burped loudly, reaching over to grasp an ornate jug of wine and bring it to his lips. He nosily guzzled the entire jug while one of his female attendants hovered at his side. Then he wiped his lips with the back of his regal sleeve, again belching loudly. Then he handed the jug down to the woman. Only then did he turn back to the nervously waiting Periscus. "You are to inspect the fleet...and return to report to me on their readiness, dispersion, and command structure."

"As you wish," Periscus gulped. "And...when is it that I should do this...inspection?"

This was totally unexpected. Periscus had only heard vague references to the Fleet which Socrates was building for the Council of Elders. To-date Periscus had no part in the construction of the new godly weapons. Plus he had little knowledge of the mostly *Automaton* military that now defended the heavenly realm.

But Periscus knew better than to mention these facts, lest it again be taken by the King as argument.

"I...trust you," Socrates said in a soft, cunning voice. "You know...what I will do to you...if you lie to me other than the necessary flattery, which I tolerate. None of these other weaklings are competent in war or would even recognize faults in our fleet—just tell me what you really think!"

Periscus kept his mouth firmly clamped shut. He knew when to allow the unpredictable monarch his say without interruption.

Socrates was a very dangerous man...yet who now seemed to be impatiently awaiting Periscus' reply. What should he say?

"I will do so immediately, Sire," Periscus quickly answered. "And when would you like me to give my report?"

"Oh...I give you...a week," the King grimaced, squirming on the throne as if he needed to go take a piss, which he probably did. "There are reports—of new, artificial objects detected orbiting Mars...maybe nothing, just ancient satellites we'd not noticed until now...but concerning...we must be ready!" he concluded, snorting loudly.

With a dismissive wave the King ordered the Throne to float him away.

Periscus sighed, slumping.

He was still alive. His sons were safe, for the moment. And he only had this one task to accomplish before he could happily return to his beautiful valley.

All in all, it wasn't a bad audience with the King.

Breep grimly clung onto the black object with his clamped-down muzzle. He allowed it to *pull* him through the spinning black void.

The small, ostrich-like dinosaur knew that the familiar device in his mouth was somehow connected to his "mother"—Sally! If he didn't let it get away, it might take him to her.

But his jaws were getting tired as he fell on and on. And he was becoming fearful of what awaited him.

His last life had been quite pleasant. He hatched out of his regressed egg into a safe, cool cave. At first he didn't remember anything, just enough to hunt for food at night and keep away from the scary humans in the daytime. So he wandered off into the secluded brush-and-tree-covered hills of ancient Greece, content to feed on plentiful birds, small mammals, and wild fruit.

But as he grew and matured, memories started imposing them- selves upon his peaceful existence. He remembered another, previ- ous life in the forests of Germany, where he saved Sally from torch- welding villagers. And even earlier another emerging memory was of his kind human "mother" rescuing him from dive-bombing Pterodac- tyls in the age of dinosaurs, then taking him with her into the distant future. She was very nice to him.

He was glad that the Great Creator commissioned him to aid Sally and her friend Dave. He helped them escape Satan, pushing them through the Portal into the distant future beyond Judgment Day. Although his tiny brain didn't grasp the implications, he knew he was doing something important for his human friends.

It gave him a sense of purpose.

So when he felt the beckoning call of Dave's activated *Anaconda Tattoo*, Breep stopped his foraging in the Grecian mountains and gal- loped to the rescue. And there, on that sandy beach by the Mediter- ranean Sea, he once again saved Dave—this time from a floating, met- al sphere! But in so doing, he was dragged back into the whirling vor- tex of Time.

His leg hurt where it'd been nicked by that light-beam from the Sphere. Breep knew the wound was bleeding. Droplets of blood flew out in spurts as he continued whirling along. He was getting weak. It was hard to keep his aching jaws clamped onto the black object...

—when he tumbled out of the black vortex and fell onto hard rocks.

The metallic object "skittered" off to the side.

Breep couldn't stand. He was too weak. But looking up he saw something terrifying!

A giant RED ROCK was plummeting out of the sky above, right at him!

Summoning all his remaining strength, he jerked up onto his three-clawed feet and scampered away into the underbrush...

—as with a huge *"CRASH"* the mammoth red spear SMASHED into the landscape right behind him, plowing itself down into the dirt!

Breep stopped running. He flopped down, exhausted, breathing hard. His jaws hurt. His leg hurt. His head, back, and tail hurt from being peppered with blasted-away rocks from the red spear's crash landing.

Tentatively, he limped over to the trench gouged out by the fallen giant stone. He could just see the top of its red, crystalline structure protruding from the bedrock.

Breep "snorted" in disdain, turned his back on it, and kicked rocks onto it with his powerful legs. Then he hopped away, his tail twitching eagerly. He'd already forgotten about the metal object, not even pausing to search for it. There was open country around him with plenty of trees, meadows, and streams.

He'd survived his fall through the time-tunnel!

Now he could go off and just live his life.

It was a long life, courtesy of the massive dose of Optimmune pills that Dave previously forced him to swallow. That accounted for him regressing to and rejuvenating from an egg! But Breep didn't know his incredible luck since he only took things one day at a time. If the days kept on coming and he was still alive, everything was fine—even should he persist much longer than his normal lifespan.

The compulsions that drove him from the mountains of ancient Greece were now settled. His task, at least for the moment, was complete.

Sally shakily crawled from the Obelisk, thankful to be alive.

The bouncing of the tossed-around Obelisk had battered her terribly. The massive lightning-strikes nearly electrocuted her. She'd been blistered several times by the roiling electricity that permeated into the storage chamber. It even *burned the hair* off the top of her head! The electricity also *scarred her arms* as she frantically tried to beat out those searing flames!

But now, thankfully, it was over. The Obelisk was at rest. She managed to get the panel open though it was covered with heavy rocks. Then she crawled out onto the surface.

Wow! It was very chilly...?

At least the storm was past—

She trembled violently, gasping for air. How long was she trapped inside? She didn't know. But she'd been running low on air.

"Dennis?" she mumbled, trying to see if any of the Dinosapiens were close.

But she couldn't see the Starship anywhere. Did the super-storm destroy it?

And just *where* was she, anyway? What...there were plants! There was grass all around! There were shrubs! There were trees off at a short distance! Did the storm toss her to a location on the volcanic planet where plant life managed to evolve?

And she felt much *heavier* than before.

"Wait...what's that there on the ground?" Sally gasped out loud, catching sight of a metallic gleam. Had something fallen out of the Obelisk's storage compartment?

She bent over to scoop up a *black gun* in her hand.

It was one of the Nun's super-guns! Was she back in her own reality on Earth—back to the civil war between the Resistance and the CPH?

And damn, the gun was *hot!*

What the hell is happening?

Sally caught a glimpse of something in the distance that looked like a *person-sized lizard* clomping away into a clump of trees! Was it one of her Dinosapien crew members? Were they somehow dragged along behind the Obelisk?

No—it must be a trick of her eyes. Looking again in that direction she saw nothing but tree trunks and leaves.

Dizzily she staggered forward only to have the ground suddenly SLAM UP into her legs, *knocking* her flat!

"Miss, are you alright?" a frightened voice sounded from behind her.

Still prone on the ground, she turned her head around and saw a *big, dark-skinned man* clad in working overalls stumbling toward her. Wait, he wasn't there before! Had he *materialized* there in front of her?

And where was the Obelisk?

The trench, the debris, and the mostly buried Obelisk were gone!

"Sally!" he yelled, falling to his knees and grabbing her up in a tight hug.

Sally frowned, totally confused. Was this someone else that the Dinosapiens thawed out of the time-freeze Tubes? And, if so, why did he think that he knew her? She couldn't remember ever having seen him before.

"You came back jist like you said you would, girl!" the man yelled, turning his face joyfully up to the blue sky. "Hallelujah! The Great Spirit is good! It brought you back to us! Praise to the Spirit!"

The big, dark-skinned man looked lovingly up into the blue sky.

Blue sky? What? But that would mean...

How is this possible? I'm back on Earth!

"And what happened to you?" he solicitously said, helping her gently to her feet. "You be all burned up! Oh, no! You be burned up real bad! Your poor head, your arms!"

"I...I'm not so bad," she started to protest when a wave of *excruciating pain* hit her from her burned scalp and arms.

She groaned, trying to fight off the crippling pain but failing.

"I got strong medicine for you," he urgently comforted her as he lifted her up in his big arms. "Sure, it be illegal—but I snatched some of them elite 'Optimmune' pills fer emergencies. And this be one of them times, fer shore!"

"M-medicine?" she groaned again as she he rapidly carried her across the ground. "Optimmune...what's that?"

Vaguely, she now glimpsed rows of crops around her, neatly laid out and waving in the wind—not a single stalk damaged by any falling Obelisk!

"Oh, you remember, Miss Sally! Or, maybe you don't...?"

"I'm...hurt...can't...remember..."

"Don't you worry none, Sally. I'll take you home so yore memory kin come back. And thank the Great Spirit that I wuz out here doing my illegal farming in the Park," the man's wide face beamed at her. "Otherwise you might be stranded out here in the wilderness. No telling what might have happened. I knew you would come back to help the Resistance, Miss Sally—I knowed it! But I never expected you to fall right out of the sky. No Ma'am, not out of the sky!"

"But...Resistance?" she said, trying to wrap her mind around what was happening, jerkily waving the gun up into the air. Was she back to the war? But everything seemed different, somehow?

"Oh my!" he gasped, seeing the gun. "That's another sign that things are gonna change!" he grinned as he bounded along. "Wowzers! It's a peacekeeper gun. And it's *hot*, Miss Sally! I never seen one of them charged up like that before. Oh, this could really help the coming Revolution. This be a good omen for us, fer shore, that you got one. Where'd you get it from?"

"I...I found it...on the ground," she grated against the terrible pain of her burns. "But...I can't remember!"

"Oh, once I get you safe into my house, Miss Sally, I'll 'remember' you all you want! But first we gotta get outta the open. If some peacekeeper lost that gun, maybe fell off a helicopter, then you knows that drones be coming close behind, searching!"

"It...hurts!" she moaned, writhing in pain in the man's arms from her burns, but not letting loose of the hot gun.

"My bub's jist up ahead, Miss Sally," the man continued nervously as he ran. "We get you home real quick. My wife be *so* glad to see you again, plus the kids! They loved you so much and we wuz all so worried when you vanished. We thought that the Keepers caught you and quietly executed you."

"And...just who...are you?" she managed to gasp as she swung in his strong arms.

"Me?" he frowned at her. "I be *Kyle*, Miss Sally. You remember *me*, don't you? We're friends. You be in my soul-family! I be one of the store-slaves from the Megamart where you worked, remember?"

"Sorry...my head...hurt in the crash..."

"Oh, *I'm* so sorry," he hurriedly apologized as they reached a rough dirt road where a squat bubble-like car was sitting.

He slid her gently into the passenger side, taking her big black gun and carefully placing it on the floor at her feet. Then he reached into the back seat and grabbed a blanket, tossing it over her head and body.

"Don't worry," he told her firmly as he ran around and got into the driver's seat. "Once we be getting you healed up, I'll explain everything. But I be sure your memory will be coming back—how I saved you and Dave from getting captured by the State."

Sally's wits were still sharp enough to realize that he wasn't talking about her. He was talking about some *other* Sally. Perhaps she was now in another timeline or even a different Dimension from her own! Maybe she was moving back and forth through Dimensions? Something was directing her—something sinister. She'd have to be careful to fit into the role expected by this friendly "Kyle" person—at least until she could contact local authorities and get her status straightened out.

"But don't be doin' no talking or making sounds, Miss Sally, if we gets stopped by any Keepers," he cautioned her. "They be running sweeps on these here back roads. Just snuggle down and keep still, like you is a sack of dirt I done dug up and be takin' home to my legal backyard garden. There still be alerts out on you, to turn you in! We thought they be jist threats on a past 'terrorist' to help keep us slaves in our places, not fer real. But now I see that they be dead serious. If they catch you, Miss Sally—they gonna shoot you on the spot!"

So much for help from the authorities.

She'd just have to figure this out on her own.

And the glowing gun felt kind of nice at her feet—like a cozy little oven toasting her legs.

Whatever and however...it was good to be home.

Home...on Earth...back to the Obelisk's crash site...which then vanished...leaving her horribly burned...with Kyle her friend—who she didn't even recognize—rescuing her?

Her eyes went wide.

"No! No! No! No! No!" she screamed-out from the *frustration*, jerking and twisting-about under the blanket!

"Miss Sally!" Kyle called-out in alarm, reaching over with his big hand to pat her on the back through the blanket.

I'm back again to the very first...when I first met Kyle in the National Park after losing the Obelisk!

"I'm...ok," Sally whispered to her friend as she settled down.

Damn! Damn! Damn! Damn!

She slumped dejectedly forward, the blanket bunching up painfully on her freshly burned skull.

She *remembered*—not only the past, but everything that was going to happen in the next year!

She'd been *thrown back in time* to do it all over again...again and again and again and again...over and over...

All the organizing, the planning, the conniving, the convincing, the meetings, the traveling, the constant danger of detection, the cajoling and pleading—*all* to have to do over again, yet again for the umpteenth time!

And she had to yet again endure the *torture* of fresh burns, waiting months for the intense pain to finally subside!

She groaned, appalled yet resolved.

If Dave kept refusing to get his act together, they could never succeed. He just didn't have the guts to pull the trigger!

Why did Dave have to be such a pussy?

She was getting really sick of this pesky, painful time-loop.

But...at least she had yet another chance to get it right, to make the *failed* uprising finally succeed!

And Dave had another chance as well. God damn him! He was the "linchpin" in this whole bloody operation.

Chapter 12

REVOLUTION

The people loved their Kings until they killed them
Turned from benevolent benefactors into tyrants
Always that tension between security and freedom
Manifested so often by spasms of awful violence
Burning, destroying, plundering, raping and killing
The supposedly suppressed Masses arising as one
A multi-headed monster screaming in frustration
Erupting-up to be brutally beaten back, massacred
Until their overwhelming numbers finally prevail
And the "unbearable" Government is overthrown
Only to—so quickly—be rebuilt in its old image
Perhaps altered a bit here and there in concession
To the battering it just endured, token changes
As the people happily embrace their new masters
Their long-awaited Salvation served cold...

Eashoa's Lament, 12:21-25

Dave was ready to go.

The taxi was waiting outside his motel room. The sun was just coming up. It was 6:00 in the morning. Jean King was following a few minutes later in her old sedan.

"Bye, Mom!" he cheerfully waved at her as he walked out to the taxi. She was standing in the doorway of her room, looking very worried.

"Be careful!" she called to him. "It's true I want my own Davey back—but I love you just the same!"

143

It was cold. He hugged his arms to his body. The sky was overcast. An icy wind was blowing. He had on a thick winter coat, but it still didn't stop the chill from penetrating down to his bones.

"Love you too, Mom...and thanks!" he gulped. A tear dripped from the corner of his eye as he opened the rear door of the yellow cab and slid in.

Likely he'd never speak to her again.

Either he'd be dead or gone to the other Dimension. Regardless, there was more at stake than just his or her happiness. The whole continued existence of the human race hung in the balance. He was convinced that Eashoa did not send him back in time just to get another chuckle seeing Dave struggle futilely. Dave knew that Eashoa was sympathetic to humanity, due to Eashoa having lived many years as a human on the surface of Earth. Dave was convinced that Eashoa had given him yet another chance to change future history—to push off Judgment Day into the far future!

And Dave was going to do his very best to live up to Eashoa's kindness, regardless of what the personal consequences. But what *did* it demand? Dave's course of action was never as uncertain as at was at the present moment.

Somehow what he needed to do involved the mysterious Sally in the other Dimension. He was drawn to her. The Anaconda Tattoo confirmed the connection, warming his wrist with its pulsating glow. It was eager to get at that cute little Turtle Tattoo on her wrist. They were made for each other.

This final time—with all his future knowledge—Dave was determined to do whatever it required to change history for the better, even if it meant sacrificing his own life!

After all, he'd already lived and seen more than anyone else could even imagine...

"So where to, buddy?" the grizzled old taxi driver spoke back over his shoulder, breaking Dave's reverie.

The cabby was a thin, well-wrinkled man with a shiny bald head.

"Cheyenne Mountain Air Force Base," Dave firmly replied. It was the next step on his path.

He carried no luggage. His thick, long coat hid everything of importance. Hidden in a large inner pocket of his winter coat were the *white Cube*, the *past pictures*, and the remaining vial of *Optimmune pills*. The *hot black energy-gun* was also hidden by the concealing overcoat, securely holstered at his waist.

Exactly what he was going to do with all those things he had no idea.

But somehow he knew that he needed them all.

"You here for the press conference?" the cabby called back over his shoulder as they pulled away from the motel.

Dave had a last glimpse of his mother forlornly waving from her motel room door.

"As a matter of fact, I am," he said, forcing a grin on his face as he looked into the central rearview mirror at the man's face. "CNN put out a call for a physicist. Since I happened to be in the area on vacation, I answered them—and here I am."

"Jeez, lucky for me! A physicist, you say? Can you explain to me the announcement that's been on the radio all morning?" the cabby said, shaking his head in amazement. "I drive the nightshift and hardly ever get any excitement like this. They even broke into my favorite country western station. They say it'll solve all our energy problems— be renewable, as much as we need, nonradioactive, and carbon-free! It's almost too good to believe, you know?"

"Yes it is," Dave sighed, leaning back wearily. "Everything comes with a cost. There's no 'free lunch'."

"Especially if it's from the damn government," the cabby nodded vigorously. "I'll bet it's not even true—just a diversion from the lousy state of the world."

"You don't believe reports from government scientists?" Dave asked, genuinely curious.

"I believe stuff when I see it with my own two eyes," the man gruffly laughed as they swung out onto the major state highway 115 leading out of the city. "Those 'oh-so-smart' scientists promised unlimited energy after WWII from the God-damned atomic power plants, didn't they? And what did it get us? We got giant set-up costs, radioactive waste, Chernobyl, and Fukushima."

"That's true," Dave ruefully agreed.

"And the government ain't no better today," the bald-headed man continued. "You can't trust a word they tell you. It's all a damn conspiracy. Whatever they're pushing now is probably jist a new bomb. Word of it got out so they're tryin' to spin it into being some kind of new energy source. If it *was* a basic research-type breakthrough, then why's the military so interested in it, huh?"

"Well, that's exactly why I'm here—to see if what they tell us makes sense," Dave replied as they sped rapidly along the highway.

To his right Dave could see craggy mountains. It'd been dark when they arrived the previous night. Now Dave could see the stark beauty of Colorado Springs. It was impressively beautiful.

"You a famous scientist?" the cabby asked.

"Well, not so famous," Dave shrugged, starting to feel hot in the heated cab but not daring to take off his heavy coat. The cab would arrive soon enough. He didn't want to risk revealing his gun.

"So as a scientist what do you make of the claims so far?" the cabby asked.

Dave felt sweat dripping down his forehead. He realized that he was much too hot for having just stepped out of the icy wind. It was like the muscles in his body were on overdrive under his coat, rippling and twitching with a mind of their own. In fact, his whole body felt *fluidized*...like he was melting!

It was probably the massive dose of Optimmune he'd taken to recover from the fulminating cancer that'd been raging in his body.

Oh great, this is the last thing I need right now, he groaned to himself—*an incapacitating side effect from those damn pills!*

He wiped his dripping brow with the sleeve of his thick coat as he responded: "From what I hear it's perhaps a revolutionary new physics—tapping into the fabric of space that's been out of our reach to-date. If it works, there'll be energy enough to light up the entire world and..."

"—or blow us all to Kingdom Come!" the cabby bitterly interrupted. "Ah, hell...won't matter none. The world's so screwed up anyway—we might as well end it all, don't you think?"

It was a rhetorical answer that didn't need a reply.

So Dave sat in silence, his guts feeling very strange—as if his organs were rearranging themselves without his permission! He carefully considered the cabby's pessimistic words...provocative, even prophetic.

Dave realized he was having an internal war with himself, mentally as well as physically. *Why* was he struggling so hard to change history? After all, the coming Judgment from God said it all, didn't it? If the Creator of this and countless other Universes saw the human race as a failed experiment—then who was Dave to argue?

"But is it all really that bad?" Dave sincerely asked the driver, struggling to calm his turbulent organs and thoughts. "It's true we humans do terrible things. But we also do some remarkable and beautiful things."

"Like what?" the cabbie cynically grunted, swinging off of 115 onto what Dave saw on a sign was "Norad" road.

Yep, that sounded ominous for sure: NORAD—the *North American Aerospace Defense Command*. Dave was swiftly moving back into the military's secured territory. What was he thinking of, trying to outsmart them? He was getting more and more scared!

But he had to keep up appearances, not look suspicious.

"Oh, like beautiful art and music...and engineering wonders...and science, exploring the universe...and medical miracles...and people helping strangers...and..." Dave replied, frowning. He was starting to believe his own argument that humans weren't just evolved, savage monkeys!

"We're coming up to the first gate," the cabby cut him short. "You might want to get your i.d. ready."

"Oh, sure," Dave nervously replied, reaching into his back pocket for his wallet.

His actual identifications were long gone. When did he lose them? Was it when he lost his innocence? Was it back during the post-apocalyptic war against the Reaper robots? Or was it in the Eden-like Valley a billion years in the future? Or was it when he lost his clothes swimming to the surface after the Obelisk plunged into the Mediterranean Sea back in ancient Greece? Well whatever—he certainly didn't have his original identification cards anymore.

Hopefully the *Yale Faculty Identification Card* would look authentic enough. The Custodian hacked into the motel's printer to produce a color simulation of an actual card, which Dave snuck from their office when he and Jean checked out that morning. Anyone from the University would instantly recognize it as a fake. But hopefully a casual military guard wouldn't detect any problem.

It had his picture plus the right words at the right places. It was even laminated. That was a damn fine printer the motel had! Presumably it wasn't the first fake i.d. it had printed out for select customers. Someone definitely had their own personal fake-i.d. business going there. It wasn't very convincing. It wasn't up to the quality a press badge had to be at a military base, what with encrypted chips and such. But hopefully it would do for casual inspection, to get him inside to receive the real thing that the Custodian should have waiting for him.

The cabby was rolling down his window.

"Identifications, please?" a polite but alert Sergeant asked as they stopped at the guard station.

Dave saw outside the cab a high, electrified cyclone fence that prevented further access into the base. This was the first line of the secluded base's defense. From here on security would only get tighter and more impenetrable.

"Thank you," the Sergeant said, accepting both the cabby's driver's license and Dave's faculty card. Dave hoped the military guard wouldn't go and check the university card online. Although the card dutifully identified Dave as an "Assistant Professor of Theoretical Physics" it was total fabrication. Any quick search would show there was no such professor at Yale.

But other cars were arriving behind the cab, lining up to get through. It was obviously a busy morning for the guard. He glanced at the two identity cards. He started to hand them back and then paused.

"You're not wearing glasses, Sir," the young guard said to Dave, narrowing his eyes. "Your picture has you wearing black spectacles."

"Broke them!" Dave grinned back. "I was out skiing, fell down, and busted them. But fortunately they've got a new pair waiting for me at the press station. Without them, I can't read. I'm far-sighted. You can call up the press station to confirm I'm expected there and that my new glasses are waiting for me there to pick up."

He plastered a big grin on his face, hoping the guard wouldn't get too excited about the sweat dripping from his brow.

The guard glanced back at the rapidly lengthening line of cars, then handed the cards back. "Drive directly forward until you get to the parking lot where your passenger can disembark. He'll be guided to the press station from there. Have a good day, Sirs."

"Thanks!" Dave cheerfully waved back, his face now bathed in sweat—both from anxiety as well as the internally building fires.

He sagged back in the seat as they rolled forward into the base, panting heavily. That was a close call.

"You one of them activists?" the driver softly asked, steering the cab down the constrained lane.

"What?" Dave gasped, surprised.

"I've had lots of different people in my cab," the man said, "and I can always spot those trying to pull a scam or hide something. It ain't none of my business, buddy—but if you're here to make trouble for those know-it-alls, I'm happy to be your ride. I don't want some new 'energy' shoved down my throat. Ain't nothing wrong with good old-fashioned *gasoline* in my tank. You ask me, all that 'global warming' talk is total crap. Look at the weather today. We're freezing!"

"Uhm...well..." Dave gulped, so nonplused by the gentleman's conspiratorial ignorance he didn't know what to say.

"Anyway, we're here," the cabby cheerfully concluded. "That'll be fourteen bucks and twenty three cents."

Dave shakily handed him a twenty. "Keep the change."

"Thanks, buddy," the man said. "Give 'em hell!"

Dave slid out of the car, shut the door, and turned to face a uniformed, smiling lady.

"Are you here for the press briefing?" she politely asked, carrying a clipboard.

Dave forced a friendly smile, relieved at feeling the icy wind whipping across his fevered brow.

"Hi there. I'm Professor Donald R. Motley, here to do some consultation for CNN?" he said as he hugged his arms across the thick coat. He hoped his crossed arms would hide any bulge from the weapon hidden beneath.

"Yes, I've got you here on the list. Thanks for coming out at the last minute, so early in the morning."

"Uh, my pleasure...they contacted me while I was skiing and..."

"Proceed over there to the security scanner," she directed him, turning to other cabs that were pulling in. "After you go through, we have open-air flats to transport you to the briefing site."

"It's going to be held outside in the cold?" he asked. Now that he was out of the warm cab he was shivering from the icy blasts. Wow, if he survived this morning he was going to have a terrible cold, going through all these temperature extremes.

"I hear they're going to have a demonstration that must occur outside in the open air," she politely smiled. "There are walls set up to protect you from the worst of this wind."

"Sounds good!" Dave cheerfully smiled, turning toward the walk-through metal detector.

Several more guards stood there, with weapons out and held at-ready. Clearly they didn't want any trouble at their big, world-wide broadcasted briefing. Another set of high cyclone walls, with barbed wire on top, prevented any deviations from the assigned path. Guard dogs and soldiers alertly patrolled beyond the cyclone fence. Security cameras were positioned at regular intervals on the top of the fence. The cameras actively moved—tracking each of the new arrivals.

Dave pretended to stumble, then took a couple steps to an elevated concrete barrier. He put his foot up and leisurely retied his shoe-laces...waiting for a group of later arrivals behind him to catch up to him. Then he slipped in amongst them.

He knew that even a casual pat-down would reveal the lethal weapon holstered at his waist beneath his overcoat.

"Any metallic items you have, please put them in the tray—then walk on through, please," one of the guards curtly instructed the person in front of him.

The buzzer loudly sounded!

"Oh, I'm sorry!" a lady said as she was pulled to the side. She was black-haired, wearing a thick simulated-fur coat. She was quickly frisked, the guard pulling out a cell phone from one of her coat pockets.

"I forgot about that. I have two of them. I put the other in the tray," she protested as they led her away for a more thorough interrogation. "Hey, it was an honest mistake!"

But the accompanying soldiers did not pause in firmly leading her away.

"Next!" the lieutenant at the station ordered Dave.

Dave "gulped" to himself as he pulled out some coins to drop loudly in the tray as he sauntered on through...

Nothing.

Dave sighed deeply, recovering his coins from the tray. It worked. He knew that the energy-gun from the other Dimension was made of something other than metal, but his heart had skipped a beat. The super-gun wasn't detected by the magnetic scanner.

"Please proceed to the transport," another man holding an assault rifle motioned for him to move on. "It will take you to the press station for your official badges."

"Sure," Dave nodded, walking onto the platform to take a seat. It was an opened-air train-like vehicle. Plopping down heavily beside him was a chubby lady with short-cropped grey hair. She frowned at him.

"Don't I know you?" she said as others slowly arrived after having also gotten through the scanner successfully.

"Uhm...maybe...I've given lots of lectures at many different places..." Dave weakly grinned at her. Sweat was again starting to spring from his forehead despite the icy wind.

"Say—you look a lot like one of the chief researchers we're going to interview today. Are you a relative of Dr. David King?" she asked with keen interest.

Oh, Christ. It was a reporter! She had that cunning look in her eyes. It was the hungry look of a circling falcon spying a tasty squirrel down on the ground!

He grinned even more widely at her.

"Well, no—I'm not. I am, though, a physicist from the same University where, as I hear, he did his Ph.D. research. Yale University! So, maybe you...?"

"Well, that's quite interesting, fella! I'm sure we're going to need expert evaluation this morning of whatever the government's presenting to us. Who are you working with?"

The train tram was almost filled now. Dave knew if he could just stall her for a few moments more he'd be able to avoid her keen inspection.

"Well, I was invited here today by CNN to..."

"—really?" she interrupted him. "I'm Cindy Drawers, the CNN Chief Science Correspondent. Who invited you here today? Nobody told me we had a consultant coming."

She raised her thick black eyebrows expectantly.

Dave smiled nervously back at her, raising his own eyebrows in response, simulating a bewildered expression.

"Uhm...some secretary I guess, I didn't get his name—but he knew I was here on a skiing vacation...must have called my department at Yale...and asked me to..."

"No matter!" Cindy grinned back at him. She grabbed him firmly by his arm, encircling it with her own meatier one. "This was all spur-of-the-moment due to the CPH comin' out with their dire warning in the wee hours of the morning. Glad someone was on the ball. This is great! I know the generalities, of course, 'cause that's my beat. But having you here to fill me in on deeper specifics is super! Now you just stay with me and don't get snagged away by any of the other network reporters. What's your name, Professor?"

He nodded politely to her as the open-air train lurched, then started off toward the nearby mountain. "Oh, I'm Dr. Donald R. Motley and..."

"Never heard of you!" she barked jovially. "But that's ok, Don. You don't mind if I call you 'Don', do you? You ever discover anything important?"

Dave choked back an indignant reply *it was me who against all odds with no help from anyone else discovered this whole bloody thing to start with!* Instead, he sputtered out: "Oh...not really...I'm just a newly appointed Assistant Professor is all, who..."

"Well, that's ok, sweetie," she happily replied, hugging his arm closer to her meaty side. "I'm sure you still know a million times more than I do about hard-core physics. You've got a nice young face and my camera crew will just love you. Prepare to be famous for your allotted 'fifteen minutes.' Hah!"

Dave gulped, feeling very weak—though his insides were writhing with pent-up energy...

—as he penetrated yet deeper into the security at the heart of the nation's nuclear defenses...

Strange sounds were gurgling and squeaking from his organs...

"Miss breakfast today?" Cindy impolitely asked him.

"Yessss...not used to getting up so early..." he gulped, further alarmed at what was happening in his body.

What the hell is happening to me?

Periscus looked out of the view-window with awe. This was truly amazing! He'd never imagined that such an amazing thing could happen to him...

Spread out below in all its splendor was the entire Earth!

He was up in orbit around the planet, just like the moon moved across the sky! But he was far closer to the Earth than the moon, where he could see details of all the oceans and landmasses drifting by below. It was god-like, glorious!

"It is truly wondrous to fly into the sky like this, Agathe," Periscus said to the giant snake coiled up next to him. "I feel just like one of you gods!"

"WE HAVE HAD SPACE TRAVEL CAPABILITIES FOR EONS," the reverberating voice spoke in the fisherman's head, jarring him. "BUT WE NEVER USED IT MUCH UNTIL NOW. I AM PLEASED THAT YOU FIND IT ENJOYABLE. BUT I AM NOT A SUPERNATURAL BEING. I AM SIMPLY ANOTHER FORM OF INTELLIGENT LIFE FROM ANOTHER DIMENSION."

Periscus didn't understand half her words. They only confirmed, despite her protests, that she was a god to be respected and honored.

"Thank you—and I'm sure the reason that you didn't use this 'space travel' was because you didn't need it," Periscus nodded knowingly. He still wasn't use to Agathe's piercing mental communication but was trying to acclimate himself.

"THAT IS VERY PERCEPTIVE OF YOU," answered the giant reptile. "WE WERE CONTENT IN OUR DIMENSION OF EARTH WHERE WE CONTROLLED THE BIOSPHERE. THINGS WERE

FINE...AT LEAST UNTIL YOU HUMANS ANGERED THE CREA-TOR."

Periscus' reptilian companion, Agathe, was the Captain of this ship—a twenty foot-long, thick-bodied alien snake. Its head was as large as a human's, now poised about six feet up in the air upon a sturdy "neck." Its unblinking eyes were golden spheres dotted with flecks of red, sporting a black slit up each center. Agathe's body was purple on the belly, green on the sides, and white on its top. She periodically flicked-out a bright red, forked tongue.

Belying her scary giant-snake body, she was actually very beautiful and even gentle.

And she was the only other living creature other than Periscus on the spaceship. The rest of the crew was composed entirely of the metallic Automatons mass-duplicated by Socrates. The metallic men performed their various functions well, but seemed to not possess independent thought. They obeyed orders but took no initiative on their own.

The Captain had no personal designation, so Periscus chose to call her *Agathe*—a feminine, Greek word meaning "Good."

Rather than being terrified of these "snakes" as so many humans might, Periscus—having lived very close to nature all of his life—recognized snakes as mostly peaceful, simple creatures. Also, this giant, highly intelligent snake gave off a calming, friendly air.

It did not appear to have a mean bone in its fluid body.

"So I guess you didn't really want to help build a fleet of these spaceships?" Periscus asked as they both marveled at Earth's surface rotating past far below.

The old fisherman was particularly awed by the thin blue line at the edge of the curved Earth. Agathe explained it was the Earth's atmosphere, thin and tenuous against the vast blackness of space. It was also amazing to Periscus that the planet floated unsupported in nothingness. This was a subject of hot debate amongst the philosophers of his time—some convinced that Earth was a disc flying through the air, or a log floating on water, or a cylinder with a circular flat top, or flat with an underside that descended forever.

But now Periscus could just see it for himself. Earth was a sphere hung upon nothing!

It was totally mind-blowing.

"THIS WAS A DIRECTIVE FROM THE COUNCIL OF ELDERS," Agathe continued explaining telepathically in Periscus' mind. "AS THE MECHANICAL SERVANTS HAVE ONLY RUDIMENTARY MINDS, THERE MUST BE SOMEONE TO CAPTAIN AND DIRECT EACH SPACESHIP."

"So you volunteered to be Captain?"

"I WAS *ASSIGNED* THIS JOB," Agathe corrected him. "I HOPE THAT SOON THERE WILL BE ENOUGH OF YOU TRAINED HUMANS TO TAKE OVER SUCH TASKS. YOU ARE VERY GOOD AT BREEDING PROLIFICALLY WHILE MY SPECIES DOES SO ONLY RARELY."

"You...don't enjoy mating?"

"WE ARE NOT DRIVEN BY GENETIC IMPERATIVES," she matter-of-factly replied. "OUR SOCIETAL PRIORITY IS NOT EXPANSION BUT REPLACEMENT. WE MAINTAIN AN OPTIMAL POPULATION SIZE FOR OUR SITUATION AND ENVIRONMENT. YOUNGLINGS ARE HATCHED TO REPLACE INDIVIDUALS WHO HAVE DIED OR MOVED ON. AS WE ARE A VERY LONG-LIVED SPECIES, WE NEED ONLY A FEW YOUNGLINGS."

Periscus shrugged. To each his own. He much preferred the "expansion" mode!

"Do you think this fleet is necessary?" Periscus asked, puzzled. He'd been told that there were now a dozen of such ships up in orbit, with many more under construction.

"THIS IS WHAT YOUR KING SOCRATES RECOMMENDED TO US," she answered. "AS HE CONVINCED THE COUNCIL, WE DO NOT KNOW IF THE SPIKESHIPS THAT ALMOST DESTROYED US WILL RETURN, OR WHEN. ACCORDING TO SOCRATES WE MUST HAVE CRAFT PREPOSITIONED IN SPACE THAT CAN DETECT AND MEET INVADERS BEFORE THEY REACH OUR PLANET."

"You have weapons?"

"KING SOCRATES REVIEWED OUR ENERGY REGULATORS. HE FOUND WE COULD REDIRECT OUR ENERGY SPHERES INTO COHERENT BEAMS OF GREAT DESTRUCTIVE CAPACITY. ALL

OF OUR FLEET SHIPS ARE CAPABLE OF FIRING UPON IN-
VADERS," she concluded.

Periscus noted that her big head was waving back and forth as if
in great pain.

"But you don't like it?" he hesitantly asked.

"THIS IS NOT TO OUR LIKING OR AGREABLE WITH OUR
NATURE," she spoke very slowly. "WE FIND SUCH ENDEAVORS
GREATLY DISTRESSING. BUT SINCE THE SPIKESHIPS NEITHER
TRIED TO COMMUNICATE NOR RESPONDED TO OUR AT-
TEMPTS AT SUCH, THERE APPEARS NO RECOURSE BUT TO
'FIGHT FIRE WITH FIRE' AS KING SOCRATES EXPLAINED TO
US. HE IS WELL SCHOOLED IN THE ART OF WAR. WE KNOW
NEXT TO NOTHING ABOUT SUCH DISGUSTING BEHAVIOR."

"Yes...he is quite a clever talker, that's true," Periscus huffed. He
was comfortably sitting on a command-chair that'd been especially
constructed just for him. "It's interesting that even with no present
threat he's still managed to mobilize your entire society into building
a navy. I saw this happen in Athens. Our construction splurge was
motivated equally by fear and greed. In the end it only squandered
our wealth, provoked an alliance between our enemies, and insured
our ultimate defeat."

Periscus was amazed at how well he was speaking. His time in
the Valley had really cleared his head. Not only did he feel much
younger than his actual years, he was also more articulate.

"I KNOW NOT OF THAT, FRIEND PERISCUS. THE COUNCIL
OF ELDERS MAKES STRATEGIC DECISIONS. I AM NOT OLD
ENOUGH YET TO HAVE MY VOICE REGISTERED. AND BY NO
MEANS IS OUR WHOLE SOCIETY'S OUTPUT FOCUSED ON THE
FLEET—MERELY A FRACTION. AND THERE MAY INDEED BE A
REAL THREAT OUT THERE AGAINST US," Agathe observed.

"Really? Well, Socrates did mention something about Mars
where..."

"IT IS THE ANCESTRAL HOME OF MY SPECIES," she flatly
stated. Now she flowed across the white-plastic flooring toward the
view-window to put an eye up against it. "DO YOU SEE IT, OFF IN
THE DISTANCE? IT LOOKS LIKE A LARGE, RED STAR."

Squinting, Periscus could just make it out in the distance.

"It seems far away," he shrugged. "Why should we worry about something so distant? I thought the fleet of spaceships was needed to defend Earth?"

"THIS CRAFT CAN WARP SPACE, TRAVELING VAST DISTANCES IN THE BLINK OF AN EYE," Agathe explained, flowing back to the center of the room to encircle Periscus' control chair. "AND THAT WHICH WE ARE CAPABLE OF, OTHERS MAY DO AS WELL. LIKELY THIS IS HOW THE SPIKESHIPS REACHED US."

"It is a wondrous magic," Periscus mused, amazed. "But if you are capable of such feats, why did you not just run from and evade the Spike-Ships? If they can't find you, they can't hurt you—right?"

"WE ARE UNABLE TO MOVE THE ENTIRE PLANET," Agathe seriously replied. "PASSIVE DEFENSE ONLY WAS...WELL, THAT STRATEGY RESULTED IN OUR NEAR ANNHILATION. OUR COUNCIL HAS ENDORSED THIS NEW STRATEGY GIVEN TO US BY YOUR KING. THIS IS MY DUTY TO FULFILL AND YOURS TO ASSIST. DO YOU NOT OBEY YOUR KING AS I DO MY ELDERS?"

Periscus groaned.

"I wish you would stop revering to Socrates as my King," he said, annoyed. "He used to be my enemy and now he gives me orders to which, yes, I must now politely bow in submission. I did not ask for him to be appointed 'my' King. And I fear that you will regret the day you gave him so much power."

"REGRET? BUT HE IS AIDING US TO PREPARE FOR..."

"He is a poisonous *snake!*" Periscus blurted out.

Though Agathe's fixed expression didn't change, Periscus perceived she was hurt by his statement.

"Oh...I'm sorry," he hastened to apologize. "In my, uh, home land, before I arrived here—snakes can sometimes be unpredictable, even treacherous. Especially if they are afraid, then they may strike out unexpectedly and bite you. And our most dangerous snakes carry lethal poison that can kill a person just from a single bite."

"BUT I WOULD NEVER BITE YOU, FRIEND PERISCUS," she relatively softly replied in his head. "WE BEAM NUTRIENTS DIRECTLY INTO OUR BLOODSTREAMS. WE HAVE NO NEED TO SWALLOW PREY AS DID OUR DISTANT ANCESTORS. WE FIND SUCH NOTIONS REPUGNANT. WE NO LONGER EVEN HAVE

THE REQUIRED ORGANS INSIDE OUR BODIES. THE VERY THOUGHT OF INGESTING YOU IS PREPOSTEROUS AND IN-SULTING."

"Again, I'm sorry."

"PERHAPS THAT IS WHY WE LOST OUR AGGRESSION EONS AGO," she mused, flowing to the side of the command-chair to curl up in a tighter circle, laying her head on top of her coils. "THERE IS NO LONGER COMPETITION FOR FOOD OR SEX."

"But you said that there still might be a threat out there at your place of origin, Mars?" the fisherman said, scratching at the white hairs of his scraggly beard.

"ANOTHER OF OUR FLEET'S SHIPS FOUND THEM IN ORBIT AROUND OUR OLD HOMEWORLD."

"Yes, Socrates mentioned something about them."

"WOULD YOU LIKE TO SEE?" she asked.

"Well, I guess I'm supposed to include them in my report, so..."

The world *turned inside-out* briefly, the stars winking out into a rainbow whirl...

And then the planet beneath them was *red*, not blue-white!

"Woh!" Periscus exclaimed, swaying back and forth in his chair, feeling like he was going to throw up. "Warn me next time you're going to do that!"

"OH, I AM SORRY, FRIEND PERISCUS," Agathe said. "BUT WE HAD THE EXACT COORDINATES SO I DID A VERY SMALL JUMP RIGHT TO WHERE..."

"Oh, great gods!" Periscus exclaimed, jumping to his feet as he stared out of the front view-window.

Floating in space not far from their ship was a tightly-wound *ball of long tentacles*, through which *eyes* were peering!

"Get us out of here!" Periscus yelled.

Too late!

The "ball" explosively uncoiled, launching many "sticky" tentacles at their spaceship, which latched on tightly and planted *large white eyeballs* up against the outside of the view-window!

The eerie eyes were eagerly scanning everything inside.

"WHAT ARE THESE...?" Agathe gasped.

"Those are *octopuses!*" Periscus shrieked. "I've caught and eaten them many times—at least the earth type. They are very intelligent and quick! Those were waiting here to find us and latch onto us. Get them off!"

Suddenly the "octopus" was pushed back a distance, though still clinging to a surrounding, invisible shell.

"THERE IS NO NEED FOR YOUR ALARM, FRIEND PER-ISCUS," Agathe said. "OUR ENERGY SHIELD HAS PUSHED IT AWAY. WE CAN NOW STUDY IT AT OUR LEISURE AND..."

"No you can't!" Periscus yelled. "You must *destroy* that thing, right *now!*"

"BUT IT IS A LIFEFORM, QUITE FASCINATING TO..."

"Use that energy beam you say you have! Blow it to pieces! Do it now!" Periscus ordered the Captain.

"BUT..."

"Socrates put me in command!" Periscus lied, staring straight into a probing giant eye held at a short distance by the energy-field. "Obey my order!"

The shield fell away, the "octopus" coiling up to spring forward again...

—when a *shimmering blue beam* sprang from the ship and *blasted* through the object...leaving only a scattering cloud of glittering-black dust.

"THAT WAS...MOST DISTRESSING," Agathe sobbed in Periscus head, turning her big head away from the view-window.

"That was likely a *sentinel* left behind by the Spike-Ships to signal when Earth regained a working society capable of traveling to other heavenly realms!" Periscus moaned, clenching and unclenching his thin hands together as he now paced back and forth. "It had plenty of time to report what happened. Agathe, please take us back to Earth. I think it won't be long until those aliens which destroyed you once before will return to take another stab at us!"

"I...WE...WELL...AS YOU WISH," the snake said, her big head now bobbing around uncertainly.

Yes, Socrates—damn his arrogant self—was correct. The other intelligent species of this new world were unable to take effective command.

It hurt Periscus terribly, but he now knew that his three young sons must depart from the valley to do their duty.

Only humans were savage enough to do what needed to be done—without hesitation!

It was both their curse and their blessing.

When those "Spike-Ships" returned—they'd find Periscus and his crew waiting.

They wouldn't stand a chance.

Greeks, after all, were the fiercest Warriors of all.

Periscus was surprised to find the prospect of the Spike-Ships returning strangely exciting.

Although brutal and horrible, armed conflict had its own seductive "beauty."

Let the gore begin to fly.

Chapter 13

THE ART OF WAR

Humans not only liked to fight, they loved war
Despite their grief at defeat and destruction
Most of their games revolved around battles
Against some supposedly evil or deserving foe
They happily took up the tools of destruction
Slaughtering, splintering, exploding, and gutting
They chopped, hacked, and shot their way to glory
Thinking that to the Victorious go great spoils
They only amassed to themselves buckets of blood
In which they gladly bathed, splashed, and swam
Until the red gore curdled and hardened like rock
Held high as collective monument to their ferocity
Mute deadly testimony of their supposed valor
Even dedicating entire institutions to its study
Making of it not a sad necessity but an art-form
Such that their souls were painted scarlet red
And they finally became what they did
Sad, frozen pictures of happy suicides
Eagerly slicing their own throats...

Eashoa's Lament, 13:89-93

George knew that the end had finally come.

His long-time friend Dennis sat upon the rocky plain with his big, oblong head hung low.

What remained of their once-glorious, precious Starship was crushed against a towering cliff.

The super-storm had swept away everything in its path.

161

Even the Obelisk was gone.

"So...what do we do now?" George said as he staggered up to the Dinosapien and slumped down beside him. George saw that his old friend, Dennis, was utterly defeated.

Dennis just stared blankly out across the barren landscape.

In the distance, George saw that the encircling range of volcanoes was still erupting—ejecting clouds of black smoke up into the orange sky. The super-storm hadn't even slowed down the volcanoes' putrid belches.

"We've got starvation rations left for only a couple more days," the battered Dinosapien weakly whispered. "The few remaining batteries that survived in the rubble of our spaceship are almost depleted...half of our remaining crew perished in the storm...and Sally is probably also dead somewhere in the smashed Obelisk."

"All of that is true," George nodded, trying to think of something, anything to lift the spirits of his friend. "If I had the energy I'd transform back into a proper dinosaur and speak our true language—but I can't. Here at the very last, I'm trapped in this weak human form. It's almost a joke."

Dennis didn't seem to have much sympathy for him. George did enjoy the pleasures of the rapidly metabolizing, continually breeding human form...

—but then he recalled his dear wife, Alice...who'd been crushed beneath the falling Obelisk. His attempt at humor was just that, a feeble last acknowledgment of their utter decimation by this awful, festering, imploding Universe.

At least they'd face the end together.

"I suppose we will die," Dennis sighed, "*unless*..."

"Unless?" George repeated, puzzled.

"—unless we make a 'deal with the devil,' as your human friends so liked to say..."

"But...?" George said, squinting tired eyes at his friend. Had Dennis gone crazy? Or did he know something that George had forgotten?

"Is the storage hold still intact?" Dennis said, springing up to his powerful legs and flicking his tail excitedly around in a circle.

"Most of it..." George answered, with difficulty rising back up to his feet as well.

"Then we'll go dig out the Tubes!" Dennis exciting said, grabbing his human-formed friend by his shoulders.

George winced as Dennis' claws dug into his flesh.

"What do you mean?"

"We're going to thaw out our remaining Sally-humans!"

"What? How many of them?"

"All of them!" Dennis toothily grinned. "We're going to revive every last freaking one of them!"

As Dennis scampered on ahead towards the wrecked remains of the Starship, George was finally convinced.

His friend had gone totally, irrevocably, *insane*.

Sally crept closer to the perimeter, an assault rifle slung across her back.

She was clad all in black, like a ninja. Since it was the dead of the night, with no moon, she hoped that she was invisible...that is, to visual detection. She knew that infrared sensors were scattered along the twenty foot-high concrete wall surrounding the entire mountain complex. She and her team, though, were outfitted with a heat-absorbing, stealth fabric. She couldn't totally mask her infrared signal, but she hoped they'd appear on the sensors as no more than a random group of curious squirrels.

Her backpack and jammer unit weren't invisible, but she hoped that since they were cool to the touch they'd not be noticed on the infrared security scanners.

"Is the tunnel finished?" she asked Kyle.

"Oh, it be good and ready, Miss Sally!" he cheerfully whispered. "Ain't no trouble getting under the wall—it's what's waitin' fer us on the other side is troubling my soul."

"The landmines will be no problem," she whispered back as they crawled closer to the hidden, freshly dug tunnel's entrance. "It's the *roboscorpions* that'll do the most damage to us if we step on them. They're loaded with neurotoxins. But I think my scrambler will momentarily confuse them long enough for us to get across no-man's land."

She patted the compact unit she carried. It was already jamming the closest automated sensors with blurred images. If the guards inside the complex noticed anything wrong, they'd hopefully think it was just minor electrical problems.

She looked up at the fifty-foot-thick silver cable stretching across the sky above them. In the darkness, it looked like a giant snake! Tremendous power was flowing through it. It was hard to comprehend, but it and twenty other twin cables—headed out in all directions, sprouting out of and originating from the *Cheyenne Mountain Central Power Bunker*—powered all of North America!

If she and her team could stop the massive, central DE-generator hidden deep inside the mountain, then all of North America would be plunged into darkness.

In the confusion, the long-simmering network of Freedom Fighters would swarm into and take over the main governmental facilities.

At least that was the plan...

—which all hinged on stopping the Cheyenne Mountain complex!

"Let's go," she whispered as she lifted the grass-covered lid and crawled into the waiting hole. It was just wide enough to allow one person on his or her stomach to squirm down into.

Sally felt like a worm diving into the moist earth. It was a long crawl because they had to go beneath ten feet of the wall that was buried down into the ground. But then she finally gently pushed up the last remaining dirt on the other side and emerged—expecting wailing sirens and bursts of automatic gunfire!

Nothing! They'd made it past the wall.

Now crouched against the inside of the high cement barrier, she activated their goggles. She was turning on their linked electronic equipment in stages to try and avoid the many sensors.

"Goggles down," she ordered.

Their ground radar-detecting goggles linked together. Sally suddenly saw—as pooled weak signals from different angles—a 3-dimensional map of the *landmines*, each marked with a red "X" on her virtual display.

"Can everybody see them?" she whispered.

They all nodded or indicated "thumbs up." Then, with Sally leading the way, they ran in a crouch through the thicket of buried mines, twisting and turning to avoid stepping on any of them.

Sally silently laughed at the *swarms of roboscorpions* highlighted in green in her goggles, spinning in circles trying to sting their own metallic bodies! Perfect!

"Hold up!" she ordered the others as they slid against the opposite barrier on the other side of the landmine field. They hugged themselves tightly against the solid wall.

They froze into place as a *trio of bright searchlights* drifted across the space they'd just dashed across. Sally could see the scuff marks of their feet in the dirt and hoped that their tracks were too far away for the guards on the towers to notice.

Yes. The searchlights moved on...

"Alright, then," Sally whispered, relieved. She'd been holding her breath. "Now, trigger the riots outside the main gate."

Kyle nodded, speaking into a small contraband communicator unit.

At a distance, Sally heard *loud explosions* then the ROAR of a mob suddenly storming the outer guard posts. It would catch Security totally by surprise. The attackers—though they were many in number—had no chance. They were only meant as a diversion. Many of them would die or be grievously wounded in the hail of bullets and energy weapons that soon would be trained upon them. All of them would be quickly captured, interrogated, and then summarily executed...*unless*...

Sally and her team *had* to bring down the Central Power Unit. Then the true Revolution could begin. All across the nation, hundreds of thousands of armed rebels would converge on key governmental sites whose defenses would be down. Behind them—reinforcing the opposition—would come millions of unarmed citizens, overpowering the remaining security apparatus by sheer force of their numbers.

Thousands—maybe tens of thousands—would die in the uprising, even when the central power supply was cut off to the nation. But that was the sad definition of war: believing in something so much one was willing to die for it. The Oppressors would be crushed! The suppressed minorities would emerge! A new day would dawn! *And I, Sally Smith, will step forward as the new Supreme Leader, defying the authority of the entire British Empire!*

—*if* she could shut down the nation's power grid upon which the government kept its citizenry dependent and cowering in fear!

But Sally knew in her heart that her fantasy was *impossible.*

The elite military units beyond the first barrier were too numerous, well-armed, and vigilant. This was at the heart of the government, the Empire's main stranglehold on the economy of North America. The Empire took no chance that internal dissent or foreign troops could ever penetrate this mountain stronghold.

Sally's only hope to accomplish the impossible was *Dave*: bringing in a weapon of unstoppable force!

If she'd tried to do so, that amount of accumulated compact power would have been instantly detected on the external sensors before she could get anywhere near an effective firing distance. Dave had to sneak it in close to the mountain from the *other* Dimension!

Her spy was orchestrating the entire thing from the other side. He'd never failed before. Dave was certainly on his way.

She could hear men shouting from above her, running along the top of the inner concrete wall, racing in the direction of the main gate.

For the moment, the section above was unguarded.

"Let's go!" she ordered the rest of them as they threw up the grappling hooks of their claw-ladders.

In a few moments they were over the top of the wall and dropping down the other side.

Shouts rang out across a rocky plain. Searchlights were turned in their direction. Some of her team remained on the top of the inner wall, their rifles aimed across the expanse. Loud "bangs" sounded as her sharp-shooters killed defending soldiers on the other side, the returning fire popping loudly in Sally's ears.

"I'm hit!" Kyle gasped at Sally's side, dropping to one knee and clutching his leg.

She saw troops streaming out of the inner defense barracks on the other side. She dropped to a knee and laid down a withering barrage of bullets at them. They momentarily retreated as many of their number were hit.

"Go on, Miss Sally! We'll keep them distracted!" Kyle urged, limping along beside her. "We'll join the fight from this side toward the main gate, cutting-down the defenders. It'll give our folks a chance to get closer before they gets all killed off!"

"Good luck!" she said as she dropped her empty rifle and her now-useless jamming unit.

She hit a big red button on her chest that caused her backpack to snap open. A large balloon instantly expanded above her head...

—and she was *jerked up into the sky*, then pushed by a blast from small jetpacks forward, to *sail across the tops* of the looming barracks and drift down into the tightly guarded final approach to the half-circle tunnel leading into Cheyenne Mountain proper.

She knew that inside that wide tunnel was a plethora of security devices, troops, and finally a huge blast door. Nothing unauthorized could enter the buried Complex. Nothing could penetrate further, including a nuclear blast.

She and her pitiful attack was certain doomed...

Unless Dave is there waiting for me!

But as she desperately peered around while floating down, she didn't see him anywhere...

—when a bullet *split-open* the balloon and she plummeted the final twenty feet onto hard concrete, *breaking* both of her legs and her right arm!

She lay there groaning, helpless, as security guards with guns trained directly on her cautiously approached.

She managed to get her left hand to her belt and grab her ancient, six-shot revolver.

It wouldn't hold them off for long. But at least she'd go down fighting.

When she died, maybe that would finally end the time-loop.

Damn that Dave! He should be here!—she moaned to herself through her pain. *He was always here before by this point in the fight!*

Where the hell was he?

"So are you married?"

Dave grimaced with a shocked half-smile at the heavy-set woman still clutched tightly onto his arm.

"Uhm...no...'fraid not...how about you?" he hesitantly replied. He fiddled with the uncomfortably thick black glasses now resting on his nose. Fortunately the "prescription" was a fake, just clear glass. The Custodian sure did good work in preparing his disguises that ended up at the press station.

"Divorced...several times...always on the lookout for some fresh meat!" she grinned at him, winking.

He didn't wink back.

They'd made it through the press station with nary a pause. After getting his "replacement" glasses, he was more relaxed. Now no one should mistake him for the older, long-haired physicist working for the government. It turned out that since Cindy "claimed" him no one present doubted—whether from the press agencies or the governmental bureaucracies—that he was who he claimed to be. They didn't even give a passing glance to his fake Yale University i.d. card when handing him his official press badge.

From there they'd walked a short distance to the demonstration area that was already set up and waiting. The entire spot was surrounded by high cyclone fences topped with coils of barbed wire. It was very secure. Indeed it was an inescapable *cage!*

And there on a stage set before the circular tunnel leading into Cheyenne Mountain proper was a compact, oblong Device. It *shimmered* in the gloom as it sat upon a supporting metallic table. And from it ran a cable to two giant electrodes, set behind the stage to each side of the circular tunnel opening.

Also on the stage, lined up behind the oblong Device, were several chairs in which top military brass sat in full uniform. And amongst the brass were obvious civilians in "scientific" clothing—i.e. wearing white lab coats. Three of them caught Dave's attention: *Professor Victor Volodymyr* with his haze of thick, white hair, *Sally Smith* with her fluffy red-brown hair, who was grinning broadly—and finally a glum-looking, middle-aged man with a full brown beard...*Dave's older twin!*

It was quite a peculiar feeling to be looking at another version of his self.

"I hope this doesn't take too long—they didn't provide us any chairs," Cindy complained at Dave's side. "I don't like standing up for too long. I'm too fat!"

Dave just gave Cindy a nervous smile, nudging his fake eyeglasses up on his nose from where they'd slid downward.

Armed troops surrounded the entire party. The reporters were massed together. Behind them, the video crews were positioning handheld videocams. The entire event was clearly carefully managed, staged, and controlled.

A three-star army General stood up at a small podium and addressed the small assembly.

"Thank you for coming, ladies and gentlemen of the press. Your government—particularly the Department of Energy—has been conducting important research in collaboration with scientists from Yale University on a breakthrough technology that promises to solve the planet's energy problems. Needless to say, such technology could be used for military as well as civilian purposes. We are still perfecting it and weren't ready to announce it—until early this morning a prominent group leaked the basic information of our research program while simultaneously denouncing it! We are here, now, to demonstrate its efficacy and safety—and to assure the entire world that it is only intended for peaceful purposes."

"Will you share it?" someone shouted from the press.

A guard grabbed the man and roughly hustled him away.

"Please hold your questions until both the demonstration and our explanations are concluded," the General coldly ordered the crowd. "As this technology might be misused if it got into the wrong hands— such as terrorists—it will have to be carefully controlled and protected. Hence the role of the military and its location at this secure facility. However, please rest assured that its immense benefits will be made available to everyone."

"Sure...at what price?" Cindy whispered sarcastically in Dave's side.

"—just a very small generator," the General continued, pointing to the shimmering oblong on the metal table. "It's compact enough that even one person could easily carry it. And yet that one apparatus is powerful enough to provide sufficient energy to run the entire State of Colorado!"

The reporters around Dave laughed at such a ridiculous assertion.

"Yes, you heard me correctly," the General continued, firmly nodding his crew-cut head. "I didn't say to power just the nearby city of Colorado Springs but the entire State! And lest you say the needs of Colorado are small in comparison to other States in the Union—even the entire State of California could be powered by this one small unit."

Cindy whispered to Dave: "Is that even possible, Don? An entire atomic power plant couldn't do what he's claiming. This is just too incredible to believe!"

Dave shrugged noncommittally. He knew all too well what that thing could do. Not only could it run the State of California, it might blow up and *incinerate* the *entire mountain!*

Indeed, Dave's older counterpart up on the stage was looking increasingly nervous, as if he too knew what might happen if the Device malfunctioned.

"And this is only a prototype unit," the General continued. "We envision building a large enough generator, safely isolated and protected here at Cheyenne Mountain, that will power the entire Nation."

That caused even more unrest amongst the press as they jostled and whispered to each other in disbelief.

"And after our demonstration of it running on its lowest power setting," the General continued, "we'll have brief explanations of the general theory behind this new technology. Then we'll take some questions. But for now..."

He made a curt motion with his hand.

A technician to the side holding a laptop hit a key.

—and A GIGANTIC, ELECTRICAL ARC jumped between the two large, looming electrodes, *SIZZLING AND CRACKLING* as it lit-up the curved sign behind it: *Cheyenne Mountain Complex!*

Then it was switched off.

"Wow! ... Incredible! ... That was amazing!" people excitedly jabbered.

The air was filled with a stifling, scorched smell—black smoke from the ends of the burnt-down electrodes rolling across the crowd, causing them to duck down, hacking and coughing...

—as off at the distance behind Dave came a faint, growing chant: "Dark Energy is Evil...*Dark Energy* is *Evil!*"

And looking behind, Dave saw a big crowd of white-hooded Nuns marching quickly along. Plus, they were surrounded by thousands of similarly chanting regularly dressed people who were *bulling* their way through the security stations!

And at the front, leading them, Dave saw his mother.

The guards were completely overpowered, hesitating to strong-arm or shoot marching civilians.

And Dave felt the Anaconda Tattoo on his wrist suddenly flare up—driving him to *move!*

"What...?" Cindy gasped behind him as he jerked free from her arm, plowed through the crowd, and jumped up onto the stage.

"*Stop* those protestors!" the General was shouting into the microphone, his eyes focused on the mob...

—as Dave skidded up to the older Dave, grabbed him by his lab-coat, and urgently whispered in his ear: "Now's your chance to escape if you want! Grab the prototype and get out of here in the mob!"

And as he dashed onward, Dave glimpsed behind him the older Dave doing just that—snatching up the prototype, jerking off its cable, while also snagging the arm of Sally. He dragged her, protesting, along with him into the swirling mob.

And when she tried to yank free, the young Dave hit her with a balled-up fist, knocking her out!

—as with the prototype Device under one arm and Sally slung over the other, the older Dave vanished into the crowd of thousands that overtook the press group. Meanwhile, some of the shouting mob continued to advance while others began to withdraw.

In the total confusion Dave hopped down from the platform on its other side to *run* full-tilt toward the *tunnel opening*...

—from which emerged a large group of military guards with their assault rifles pointed straight at him.

"Halt! Halt!" one of the shouted. "Halt or we'll shoot!"

Dave kept running right at them, now drawing out his black handgun and pointing it forward...

—as he heard the loud *"thruppp"* of an assault rifle being fired and felt *bullets* slamming *into and through* his body...

—and, as if in slow motion, he fell forward onto his face, his black eyeglasses knocked off and skittering across the pavement as he grimaced in pain...

—*screams and shouts* erupting all around and behind him as the remaining mob totally merged with the press reporters. In the melee a woman hopped up onto the stage, grabbed the microphone from the General, and loudly shouted...

"Dark energy is evil!"

Dave smiled at hearing his mother's bold voice as he felt the *Anaconda Tattoo* once again flare up.

And the young Dave suddenly *vanished* from the pavement...

—leaving behind for the bewildered guards to gather around just a spreading pool of *bright red blood!*

Jean King smiled sadly as she was grabbed by a guard and thrown to the platform, her arm twisted painfully behind her.

She'd lost one son, but gained another.

The older Dave with his unconscious charge was gone, escaped from the military into the churning mob behind her.

The Nuns would whisk him and his prizes away. If he wanted, he could accept their enthusiastic protection and support. But that was up to him. He'd always been hard to please.

On the whole, it was a sad but significant victory.

Now all-in with the CPH, Jean's future looked promising.

Chapter 14

<u>**TO THE VICTOR GO THE SPOILS**</u>

Why could they not learn what mattered?
Was it because their lives were so short?
So much was crammed into so few years
Maturing, breeding, raising children, working
Struggling, fighting, and conniving to stay alive
And then to keep that which rapidly faded away
All of which could be taken in the blink of an eye
They paid lip-service to health, family, and God
Spending most of their time just surviving
And so little effort was put into understanding
Their place, their potential, and their gifts
Blessed to perceive the future and the past
They instead clung to the ephemeral present
As if survival were the only thing that mattered
And their tiny planet in an insignificant Galaxy
Were the sum and total of God's Creation
Equating horrible humiliation with defeat
When failure grants the greatest rewards...

Eashoa's Lament, 14:7-11

Sally opened her eyes to an incredible sight.

Looming over her was a *T-rex-like dinosaur!*

"She's breathing! We got her back!" the talking dinosaur grinned widely, revealing many large, pointed teeth. Its voice was harsh and rasping. The eye on the side of its oblong head closest to Sally was large and orange.

173

"Don't be scared," another, softer voice came from beside her. "That's just *Dennis*. Dennis is from another Earth Dimension where mammals never developed into humans since the giant asteroid plowing into Earth never caused the dinosaurs to go extinct. It missed the planet. Consequently some of the dinosaurs developed intelligence over the millions of years that they continued to exist."

Sally weakly turned her head to the side and saw there...*herself!*

No, it wasn't an exact duplicate of her, since she herself was middle-aged, wrinkled, and toughened by years of battling the Reaper Robots and Dave's Resistance forces. This *other* "Sally" leaning over into her field of vision was in her early twenties, smooth-faced, with bright green youthful eyes!

"Who a-are...?"

"I'm *you* from another timeline," the younger Sally laughed giddily. Then she seemed to visually catch herself before continuing more soberly. "I was thawed out just a couple hours ago myself. So I'm also still in shock. But you and I *did* meet in the past—though it was rather brief."

The younger Sally again began chortling and snorting at her just-uttered words, getting more and more hysterical.

Then she again caught herself, got her breath back, and continued: "I was in the Harvester that crashed into the Cheyenne Mountain Nuclear Bunker where you were fighting against the Resistance...or so I'm told. That's correct, isn't it? You were the *Holy Mother* of the *Church of Perpetual Health*, trying to stop the Resistance. You were trying to prevent their leader, Dave, from switching on a world-wide force field powered by Dark Energy, right? So you got into Cheyenne Mountain and tried to stop the launch of Dark Energy missiles, right? Well, we 'met' in the nanosecond in which my hijacked Harvester slammed into your base, *killing* both of us!"

She again began snorting and spurting, laughing uncontrollably.

Clearly the girl was hysterical...

"Isn't that just the *most amazing thing* that you've ever heard?" the giggling other-Sally shouted, sighed, then leaned back, spent.

Sally just stared at her young duplicate. Yes, she heard the words. She understood the words. But it couldn't be true! Yet...the last thing she remembered was, indeed, fighting in the central research cavern deep inside the Cheyenne Mountain military installation. She was indeed trying to stop missiles loaded with newly invented DE-bombs from being launched.

But she'd been shot multiple times! She was drenched in her own blood, dying.

"I'm...alive? But where are my bullet wounds?"

"Oh, our bodies were fixed up before being put into time-freeze," Sally weakly laughed. "I guess I was just mush when we hit Earth—at least the dead replica they replaced me with. We were going pretty fast. The impact probably caused a Nuclear Winter across the entire face of the planet."

"We're...not on Earth anymore?"

"Well, *duh!*" the young Sally laughed. "Feel how light the gravity is here? It's a hell-hole, that's for sure. But it's definitely not an Earth hell-hole."

"Then...how?"

"Well, to make a long story short," the young Sally continued, reaching with a visibly trembling hand to brush back her fluffy hair, "my crashing the Harvester alien spaceship apparently didn't actually kill the demon alien inside who was masquerading as Satan—who then survived and later reached back into time to snatch us both from the moment of death to preserve us in time-freeze 'Tubes.' Hah! Ain't that something? We were both peacefully and heroically 'dead' but became some sort of souvenirs for the Demon. And now our Dinosapien friends *thawed* us out! Ain't that a bitch?"

"But...w-where...a-are we...now?" Sally gasped, her head spinning, trying to focus her vision.

Then everything around became clear. She saw she was propped up against shattered sheets of a plastic-like material. In front of her was a vast, rocky plain. Set-into a distant mountain range she saw belching *volcanoes*—their black smoke chugging up into the sky! Red streams of lava ran down their sides.

And crumpled, torn-apart debris were piled high around Sally.

Plus, Sally saw man-sized *cylinders* scattered around the plain.

And the air was very thick and *stank!*

"Oh, that's a very good question," the young Sally sighed, sitting down next to her. "From what George told me..." she began.

"Who?" Sally asked.

"She's still alive!" Sally heard another, deeper, human-like voice bark. "But how are we going to get her out?"

"*That's* George," the young Sally grinned. "We're old buddies!"

Turning her head, Sally saw a rather chubby, balding man struggling over the opened transparent lid of a man-sized cylinder. "Her body's swollen, jammed in tight!"

"I'll get her out," the big Dinosapien grimly stated, turning to face away from the tube before SLAMMING his big, thick tail down upon the tube!

It cracked open along its entire length and Sally smelled an awful, putrid odor.

"Oh, this is disgusting," George gagged, turning away.

"It's just rot," Dennis said, jumping forward and pulling at one of the edges of the big crack. "Help me!"

Grimacing, George turned back to the Tube and grabbed the other edge of the jagged rupture. Together they managed to yank the opening wider and away from the entombed corpse-like figure.

Sally was horrified to see the Tube's contents slowly ooze out onto the ground—a pulsating, *lumpy greenish mass:* from which yellowish fumes were rising!

"And *that's* yet another of our manifestations," the young Sally shrugged, looking away.

"What happened to her?" Sally gasped, appalled!

"Oh...apparently she also heroically saved everyone, helping the crashed spaceship that's scattered around us go into a subspace that's beneath subspace, a '*sub*-subspace' that allowed the Dinosapien Starship to go through a Black Hole into a forming new Universe that's the sole property of the Satanic Demon...are you keeping up?"

"What?" Sally gasped, looking at her young twin in disbelief.

"Why not?" the young lady shrugged again, "It's easier to just accept this craziness rather than fight it. Suffice it to say that *rotting* 'Sally' got exposed to hard radiation beyond the ability of her fading dosage of Optimmune to contain—causing many tumors to fulminate throughout her body. Now she's a living, breathing, *lump of cancer!* Wow! Us 'Sally' gals come in all forms, huh?"

"That's...*horrible*," Sally gagged, overcome by the awful putrid smell!

"Yep, sure is!" the young Sally giddily agreed, looking upward. "I can't imagine that our dear 'cancer-Sally' will live more than a few minutes now that they've thawed her out. Too bad, though. Apparently she's the 'original' Sally. It would have been fun to chat with her, compare our different stories."

"The 'original'?" Sally dully repeated. "Then I'm..."

"You're Sally number Three...I'm number Two," the young Sally affirmatively replied. "So I'm your senior even though you look older than me. *Hah!*"

"Well, I guess you can be senior if you want," Sally absently argued.

"It doesn't matter," young-Sally now sobbed, breaking down, her giddy mood deflated, "because, according to George, none of us are going to survive more than a few days more in this awful place. We're out of food and power, marooned here billions of years and trillions of light-years away from our Earth in a *completely separate, dying Universe!*"

The young Sally turned her tear-stained face upward, her green eyes stretched wide.

Sally looked upward also. The sky was a horrible, roiling black-orange. It certainly looked like a terrible place to finally and completely, irrevocably die.

But was there also something else?

Sally squinted her eyes, trying to make it out.

"*There* it is!" Dennis yelled out in his harsh, dinosaur voice as he pointed up with a sharp claw.

"You were right, Dennis!" George gasped, staggering back and dropping to the other side of the young Sally. "The imminent threat of losing his Sally-defenses against the Creator actually *brought* him to us!"

"Brought who?" Sally gasped, trying to see what was descending through the roiling, black clouds.

And then she recognized it.

She felt a shiver of *fear* reverberate through her entire body.

There was no denying what she was seeing. It was a gigantic *Harvester* spaceship!

It was the same aliens that invaded Earth as Judgment Day approached. They were scavengers, come to grab anything of value before the planet's surface was incinerated by a solar super-storm.

This was Sally's worst nightmare: recalled from death only to be *served up* to mankind's greatest enemy!

"At least one of us got away," the young Sally sighed, tightly closing her eyes, apparently refusing to watch the descent of the black-surfaced behemoth.

"Got...away?" Sally slowly repeated, not understanding.

"Yep, vanished in the red Obelisk," young-Sally laughed. "Or so George says. But that's ok. According to him, she was a real pain in the ass—not like sweet young me or mature old you or stinky, rotting Sally over there. Hah! So the Universe *still* isn't safe from us. One of us got away. Yay!"

"The Obelisk is here?" Sally excitedly replied. "We can use it to..."

"It's *gone*, I said!" young-Sally angrily replied, reaching over with a fist to *punch* old Sally on her shoulder.

"Ow!" she exclaimed.

It hurt.

"You should *listen* to me!" young-Sally sputtered, clearly panicking at the notion of once again being captured by whatever was controlling the Harvester. Indeed, she looked *terrified!*

"Sorry...I've been through a lot—my mind's slower than when I was you," Sally sullenly answered, rubbing her sore shoulder.

"Oh...right...I'm sorry also," young-Sally said, hanging her head. "I know how irritating I can get."

"I'll just think of you as my younger sister," Sally consoled her. "If everything you just dumped on me is true, then we're family—in some perverted, time-twisted sort of way."

A huge "THRUMMING" sound vibrated the rocks and structures around Sally as the Harvester steadily descended.

Then Sally saw *landing craft* erupting out of the bottom of the Harvester.

In only a few moments those damn Reaper robots would come pouring out of the landers!

But it certainly wouldn't matter to the "stinking" Sally. After a few convulsions, Sally saw the freed cancerous mass stop moving. It settled upon the rocks beneath it like a deflated cake prematurely taken from the oven.

Lumpy-Sally was dead.

Sally knew that both of her legs and her right arm were broken. She could see tips of shattered bones protruding through her blood-soaked, black ninja-suit. It hurt terribly.

But what hurt even more was the realization that the security forces were reorganizing. In just a few moments they'd attack-back and slaughter the mostly defenseless intruders. A large military force was assembling outside the inner defense courtyard, facing the approaching, shouting mob.

And there was nothing she could do. She was effectively immobilized.

Dave you dope! You've never been this late before in the previous time-loops—Sally moaned to herself as she lay crumpled on the pavement. Five guards clustered together were cautiously approaching with guns drawn...

—when a *flash of blue light* almost blinded her!

She blinked rapidly to get her sight back.

"Ah, *there* you are," Sally grated through clenched teeth.

Dave had fallen *directly down* upon the men, *knocking* them to the pavement!

Before they could jump up and regroup, using her one working limb, Sally yanked up her six-shooter and *shot each* in their heads, killing them dead on the spot.

Sally saw that Dave himself was gravely wounded, struggling to rise up off the pavement, blood gushing from beneath his thick coat.

"Put the gun on its lowest, one-star setting!" she urgently ordered him as she lay there immobilized. "Fire it at the troops who are outside the gate. It'll stop them and give us time to finish the job here. Then we'll both escape!"

The black super-gun was in his trembling hand, with waves of heat emanating from it, making the air around it *shimmer!*

She could see the safety latch was off and it was set to its highest level, *five stars*...

Groaning, he managed to get back to his feet. He wobbled precariously as he pointed his gun at the backs of the troops pointing their own assault rifles at the fast-approaching mob.

A bloodied finger paused over the power output switch.

"But...even if I put it on the lowest setting...powered like it is..." he groaned, one arm clutching his profusely bleeding chest, "won't that electrocute *everyone* over there?"

"It'll stop them!" Sally shouted at him. "That gun's traveled billions of years from the future, steadily accumulating energy as it fell back against the time-stream. It's got plenty of destructive power! Flip it to one star! That'll take care of the guards, with sufficient energy left for the main job. Shoot them, Dave! Shoot them *now!*"

"But...isn't that *Kyle* leading that mob?" Dave gasped, recognizing his friend from the other Dimension.

Sure enough, though he limped along in obvious pain, Sally saw that Kyle was with the mob, heroically leading it into the gunsights of the waiting military.

"He's expendable—they *all* are!" Sally urgently shouted at Dave. "They *volunteered* for this suicide mission. It's for the greater good. If you don't stop the troops now, we won't have another chance!"

Dave hesitated—then lowered the shimmering gun.

"No, Dave!" she screamed at him, "You God-damned pussy! Not *again!*"

He spun around and aimed the weapon at the high, circular tunnel leading into the Cheyenne Mountain Nuclear Bunker.

Still set to its highest power Dave pulled the trigger!

—as A WALL OF PURE-WHITE ENERGY burst from the gun and *sliced* into the mountain!

—and *kept pouring out* as Dave struggled to hold the gun steady, *sizzling* through the mountain like a hot knife through butter!

—bringing the *entire mountain* down upon itself, destroying anything contained inside!

Boulders, dust, smoke, and hot molten rock droplets rained down all around them.

"There," Dave gasped, falling to his knees, "that should stop your national DE-generator, huh?"

"You *idiot!*" Sally grated through clenched teeth as she dragged herself with her one good arm toward him. "All the soldiers at the gates are still alive. They'll be on us in seconds. It doesn't matter if the power plant is crushed if we Leaders of the Revolution get captured. You've doomed us all. You've made this all for *nothing!*"

"Maybe not," Dave grated, reaching down to grab Sally by her collar and drag her forward with him.

"No...not again," she groaned, struggling to get him to release her. But he was too strong. He'd clearly been shot though his chest several times, but was still as strong as an ox. How could this be?

Oh, right...the Optimmune pills.

"I...should...be dead," he gasped as he struggled, step-by-step toward a *hovering, spinning black void!* Sally saw in the steadily-shrinking black space a familiar, *diamond-sparking* pattern.

The incredibly powerful discharge of the super-energy-gun that'd brought down Cheyenne Mountain had left behind a *Time Portal!*

"It must be...those damn Optimmune pills...got rid of the cancer that was in my body...but also gave me...incredible recuperative powers...maybe we'll yet live to see...another day," she heard him gasping.

"I don't want to live to see another day!" Sally screamed, fighting against him. "I'm sick and tired of being thrown back to the start just to have to go through it all over again!"

The spinning Portal was shrinking, now just barely large enough to allow two people to pass through together.

Dave paused in front of it, looking into its hypnotically spinning ebony depths.

"You don't want to go on?" he asked, looking down at her grotesquely twisted, bleeding body. "We've got another chance to change the timeline, Sally—to *fix* things!"

"I'm...*hurt*...and I'm tired," she moaned piteously. "Who says...we have to...do anything? Maybe it's time...to let things take their natural course. Maybe some things just aren't meant...to be changed."

Behind them, Sally could hear the shouts of troops approaching.

Dave looked uncertainly from her to the spinning black disc and back to her again. Around them, the *shuddering* and *shaking* of the skewered, still-crumbling mountain continued.

The ground beneath them was trembling. Aftershocks made it hard for Dave to keep standing above her.

Then he seemed to come to a decision.

"Ok, then...I'll stay with you," he whispered, releasing his hold on her collar and letting her drop flat to the pavement.

"You'd...do that...for me?" she gasped, looking up at him in bewilderment.

He glumly nodded. "My mother taught me well, despite my being a selfish nerd. She came here to Colorado Springs and put her life on the line for me. She told me that if you *truly* love someone, then you are there for that person—no matter what."

The shouts, screams, and gunfire were getting ever-closer. The recovering guards were almost upon them!

"You...*love* me?" she asked, frowning.

This was new. This hadn't happened before. Things were *changing!*

"Yes," he whispered again, his head hanging. Blood flowed freely from inside his bullet-pierced coat, splashing out onto the pavement.

"Help me up," she said, grabbing at his knees.

He reached down and lifted her up.

Then she tilted her bald head back and stretched up on her tiptoes to plant her warm lips firmly onto his.

The Portal was almost shut...fading away...

"Thank you," she said, pulling back from him slightly. "But I still *don't* love you, you weak *turd!*"

She sharply *shoved* him backward into the Portal. Then she dove in after him...

—as the Portal *slammed shut* behind her.

Chapter 15

STARVING AT THE FEAST

They were offered Bread for their souls
They were given the Water of Life
And still they refused to eat or drink
Thinking that somehow they'd lose
If they were to accept the Conditions
Required by a concerned, loving Father
They'd no longer be free or independent
As wild children disdainful of parents
Wishing to forge their own paths
Where starvation was preferable
To gorging at a fine banquet
A crust of moldering bread
A cup of rotgut whiskey
Making for them a "feast"
Too intoxicating to reject
They gnawed on each other
Consuming their own spirits
Cannibalizing their dignity…

Eashoa's Lament, 15:123-127

Dennis watched warily as a towering Reaper robot walked ponderously up to them.

It was one of a whole *army* of the things that'd poured out of hundreds of landing craft!

It was a bipedal robot with a swiveling top—sporting five camera-lenses, its "eyes" arranged in a circle, giving it total 360-degree vision.

In the place of arms were three writhing, metallic-looking tentacles that could extend out to any desired length.

A dozen mobile gun barrels were aligned along the swivel top of the killer robot, below the five "eyes"—thick and lethal, independently taking careful aim at any and all possible threats.

It was a walking death machine.

One of its extended metallic tentacles swung towards the older-Sally, "sniffing" her.

"This feels completely wrong," she winced, shrinking back.

"Don't make any threatening moves!" Dennis sharply warned her. "As long as we stay passive, I don't think we'll be harmed."

Dennis saw George at his side fatalistically closing his eyes.

"They're just robots, aren't they?" young-Sally stated. Her eyes were stretched wide in amazement. She hadn't been around for the post-apocalyptic war—having "shuffled" off to the Dinosapien Dimension before capturing an entire Harvester spacecraft herself!

Dennis had great hopes she could pull off that same feat yet again.

The robot gently lifted up older-Sally and tucked her away into a storage compartment in its large chest before she had a chance to even protest.

The tentacles reached out for young-Sally...

"No!" she said, standing up firmly and pointing an accusing finger at the looming Reaper, "Bad robot! *Bad* robot! I will walk along *with* you, but *not* inside of you!"

Dennis held his breath, expecting a violent reaction from the metallic beast.

But, no, the robot merely withdrew its long tentacle, turning to "clomp" back toward the waiting shuttlecraft, the young girl striding arrogantly along beside it.

"I'll check out what's happening," she cheerfully called back to Dennis and the rest of the few remaining Dinosapiens. "You guys hang tight!"

Dennis saw George tentatively open his eyes in a fearful squint.

"Yes! We'll 'hang tight' Sally!" George now called-back to her. He was still in his human form. Dennis knew he was unhappy being unable to change back to his dinosaur body because of insufficient bodily energy. But then again, they were all starving to death.

Dennis noted that the Reaper showed no interest at all in George, though he outwardly looked to be a puny, weak human. Indeed, the Reapers also ignored the dead cancer-lump Sally lying motionless at a short distance.

But they were very active out on the plain and in the wreckage of the Starship, industriously searching out and picking up the many scattered Tubes.

"Once it gets the time-frozen humans gathered up, stowed in the transfer crafts, and loaded up into the Harvester—they'll come back for us," Dennis confidently nodded his big oblong head.

"Do we really want them to take us?" George hesitantly asked.

Dennis looked up at the rain of black soot drifting down from the black-orange sky. Yet another volcano was erupting in the nearby mountain range. It was spewing out huge amounts of smoke and soot. Rivers of fresh, red-hot lava ran down its sides.

Plus it was getting hotter and hotter.

Dennis felt very faint, not just from starvation but from the excessive heat. Some heat he liked. But too much heat and he couldn't control his internal temperature. He noticed that George's chubby human face was also bathed in sweat.

"You want to stay here?" Dennis absently asked George.

"Well...since I lost Alice..." George gulped, looking down at his feet as he sat slumped up against a pile of plastic debris, "—maybe that wouldn't be so bad for me. Sure, we'll all probably die in a few days. What we see periodically of the sun is looking worse and worse. It's likely going to collapse in upon itself soon. This planet and solar system are going to kill us. I have no doubt about it. But what makes you think that the Demon in the Harvester will treat us any better? Maybe a relatively quick death here is merciful compared with what that 'Satan' would do to us!"

"I still think that Sally will find a way for us all to escape," Dennis growled, displaying his large teeth in an unconscious domination-sneer to George.

"Oh, I hope so," George sighed, demurring. "But just *which* Sally are you referring to—the older one or the younger one?"

"They're both Sally!" Dennis snorted. "Either one of them can save us! Or both of them together! They won't leave us behind to die."

He had great faith in Sally, no matter her particular incarnation.

"That's if they have a choice in the matter," George sighed again, shaking his head wearily. "A Being that can create its own Universe sounds pretty powerful. What can any Sally do if that Creature doesn't want to be bothered with us?"

"At least they haven't killed us or..."

"Not yet. But we haven't been a threat to them. They're just ignoring us," George observed. "However..."

The last Reaper, carrying the last Tube, went back into its transfer craft.

As one, the armada of transfer ships lifted up and drifted back towards the gigantic Harvester floating in the bleak sky above.

"Well, there they go," George wearily observed. "They're leaving us behind. Maybe it's best this way."

Startled by the sudden departure, Dennis jumped up and ran out onto the rocky plain. He hopped up-and-down, waving his claws up into the air, shouting: "Come back! Come back! You forgot us! We can help you! We know how to deal with the humans! You need us!"

But the shuttlecrafts did not pause.

They continued their steady upward climb. And then they smoothly drifted into large openings in the side of the gigantic Harvester, which closed immediately behind them.

"Come...back...?" Dennis said, exhausted, falling to his scaly knees.

Suddenly, searing LASER BEAMS shot from the giant spaceship above—*BLASTING* into what remained of the Dinosapien's Starship!

Dennis was thrown flat upon the rocks by the force of the mighty blasts.

When he looked up, he saw the giant Harvester spacecraft rising into the roiling dark clouds, vanishing from sight.

There was no doubt as to the Aliens' answer.

Dennis noted George shuffling up to his side and placing a warm, soft hand upon his shoulder, helping him to sit up.

"Maybe there's some cracked Tubes left behind," George grimly stated. "The human occupants will be dead. We can eat them."

Dennis laughed at what he perceived as a feeble joke. Then he stumbled up to his feet and shrugged off George's comforting hand.

"But we're vegetarians!" Dennis grinned giddily, getting into the mood of irrational defiance. "Sally told me not to eat her. She said she was too tough and would make me choke."

Then tears fell from his eyes as he slumped forward, his big oblong head lolling.

"Goodbye, Sally," he whispered, "—all of you!"

He'd really loved that little mammal. She'd grown on him.

Socrates serenely floated into the Council of Elders perched high above them on his levitated throne, accompanied by a troupe of his gleaming Automatons.

He had a large, simulated turkey-leg in one hand and a big bottle of Scotch Whiskey in the other. He'd found this particular brew in the data files of the Snakes under the heading of "human alcoholic drinks." Amazingly, it was from a distant future 2,400 years advanced from his classical Greece time-period. He now knew that this new "realm of the gods" wasn't an ethereal place after all, but was actually Earth—a *thousand-thousand-thousand* years into the future!

Regardless, Socrates found the "whiskey" made by the duplicator-units of the Snakes delightful. Its golden liquid was far more potent than the weak wine Socrates was used to guzzling. It packed a real punch—to which he was now delightfully addicted, drinking it like water.

Socrates was finally getting a handle on what had happened to him...and he liked it!

These fantastical creatures weren't "gods" at all. They were just intelligent creatures like him, but from other parallel Earths—thrown together in the distant future beyond the true God's destruction of humanity!

"My 'dear' colleagues..." he began, pausing to "belch" loudly.

"YOU HAVE INTERRUPTED OUR LINKED CONTEMPLA-TIONS, KING SOCRATES," a peeved telepathic voice sounded jarringly in his head. "WE TRUST THAT YOU HAVE A GOOD REASON

FOR THIS? IS THE FLEET FINALLY READY TO DEFEND OUR PLANET, SHOULD THAT BECOME NECESSARY? HAS YOUR FISHERMAN COMPLETED HIS REPORT?"

Socrates casually dropped the turkey leg to one of his females standing below, but set the bottle of liquor carefully into a "drink holder" circular-slot in an arm of his throne chair. He leered down at the three giant snakes, the two man-sized lizards, and the one lone bird.

Socrates noted that the three twenty-foot-long Snakes were spectacularly beautiful in the warm sunlight streaming in through the opened windows of the conference room. He absently observed the wonderful fluorescence shining off their scales—one of them mostly blue, another green, and the last one brick-red. The giant lizards didn't impress him that much, the bird even less.

They looked so pitifully small now, not the fearsome "gods" that they'd seemed to him a mere decade or so ago.

He grinned. He knew that they found his 600 pounds of fat repulsive—particularly the waves set into motion in his ample jowls when he sneered at them!

He loved provoking them.

"I'm taking over these deliberations," he calmly stated as his army of Automatons continued to "thump" into the room, *surrounding* the now-apprehensive Elders!

"WHAT DO YOU MEAN, SOCRATES?" the voice—now sounding strained—rang again throughout his brain.

"Just what I said," he grimaced at them, his eyes popping even more than normal from his grotesquely fat face. He knew he was a formidable presence. He knew they'd grown to fear him. And he knew from his spies that they were planning to *depose* him and return him to being just another little human safely imprisoned in their little mountain-valley jail!

That was *not* acceptable.

"I am no longer just the King of the humans," he growled at them. "I am now *your* King as well. From now on *I* will give orders and *you* will work for *me!*"

The Creatures looked at each other as if making a final decision.

Then Socrates felt a *massive weight* pressing upon his mind, like a mountain of rocks fallen upon his head—while simultaneously something was *scrambling* his very thoughts.

"*YOU IMPUDENT LITTLE HUMAN...HOW DARE YOU THINK THAT YOU CAN...?*"

But Socrates just shook his head, sloughing off their attempt at mind control. He laughed at them.

Pickling his own brain with alcohol had a timely side-effect, causing their collective telepathy to slide off him like water off a duck's back.

"Kill the blue one," he ordered the Automatons.

"WHAT? YOU CAN'T...!"

Several of the robots lunched forward and grabbed the shimmering-blue giant snake. They wrestled its writhing body to the ground—then repeatedly *stomped* on its large head with their heavy feet!

The sound of *the Elder's skull cracking* was pleasing to Socrates—though he noted shocked horror in the eyes of the remaining Elders.

The twenty-foot-long snake's body was still spasmodically twitching though its head was just a bloody mess staining the floor.

"So who wins the 'brain-bashing' contest?" he grinned at them from his looming, floating Throne.

There was no reply.

"Any more complaints?" he mildly continued.

Again, no reply...

"Good," he nodded, pausing to take a long swig from his whiskey bottle before proceeding.

"Now I'll explain to you how you are going to stop wasting time with your little 'musings' and pool the efforts of all your people and machines," he stated, "smacking" his lips loudly.

"TO WHAT END?" the loud voice asked in his head—this time trembling with fear.

"Constructing our Fleet and Weapons is no longer just a 'regrettable diversion' of some of your precious new society's resources—it is now the *complete obsession* of all of you!"

"BUT...EVEN IF WE AGREED, *WHY* DO SUCH A THING? THIS MAKES NO SENSE!"

Socrates laughed at them.

"I am not content with being the King of this little zoo of yours. We must put all our effort into the Fleet—not just to defend ourselves against possible attack, but to take our *rightful place* in the Galaxy!"

The Elders looked completely dazed and confused by his cryptic statement.

"BUT...WHAT DO YOU MEAN?" the remaining Elders collectively gasped.

Socrates leaned forward, glaring down at them as he held the whiskey bottle in one meaty hand.

"When those little 'Spike-Ships' return, we won't just defeat them. We will *conquer* them. And then we will use their accumulated knowledge of this Galaxy to proceed out into the Stars—to make *me* the King of the *entire Universe!*"

They looked at him as if he were insane. Socrates knew they considered him a woefully ignorant child. But he'd studied their data files extensively. He now knew of the vast expanse of the Universe—filled as it was with billions of Galaxies, each with billions of stars! His was not their supposed sin of ignorance, but the certainty of informed *arrogance!*

His keen intellect formulated a grand Vision: using the art of duplicating Duplicators to duplicate yet more—to produce an *unending amplification* of their Fleet!

The seemingly superior lizards, dinosaurs, and birds were correct to fear humans. Humans had a lust for dominance that had no end. Theirs was a compulsion to *spread to the Stars* and *take everything* for their own!

Yes, Socrates was convinced that he could indeed conquer the inhabited worlds of the entire "Milky Way" Galaxy—and then *all* the Galaxies! Using Dark Energy to power their Duplicators plus move their fleets at the blink of an eye to any other inhabited worlds whose positions were known, he could rule everything. He would *depose* and then become the *true* God of all Creation!

Maybe it was just the liberation of the continual alcohol loosening his synapses and fueling his long pent-up compulsion for unquestioned Power, but with the amazing technology of these future-creatures Socrates was totally convinced he could achieve his stupendous goal!

This was far more than a tepid, philosophical-questioning of the nature of Existence. This was molding Existence into the image of Himself!

Every living thing would be *forced* to respect the *God-Emperor* Socrates!

Sure, to spread throughout the Universe would probably take many millions or even billions of years. He'd die long before that happened. But—as with all self-respecting Emperors—he would establish a long lineage of "Socrates" Emperors! His distant descendants would indeed see the subjugation of *everything* to his Rule!

It was a simple matter of multiplication.

"BUT WAR IS REPUGNANT TO US!" the indignant reply echoed in Socrates' brain from the Elders. "WE WILL NOT COOPERATE WITH...!"

"Oh, you *will* cooperate," Socrates flatly stated. He floated his throne chair over to hover above the blood-covered, crushed head of the blue Elder.

Socrates allowed golden liquid to slowly pour from the mouth of his bottle.

The whiskey splattered-out as it fell from the height of the throne onto the crushed skull, catching-up red blood and splashing it onto the faces of the surviving Elders.

"Well?" he sneered at them.

As one, they all bowed their heads to him.

He had won the first battle.

Now began the War! He would establish an *Empire of the Stars*, with him and his descendants as the Ultimate Ruler!

"I am the *God-Emperor* of the Universe!" he screamed at the Council of Elders.

They cringed down, terrified.

"Give me my turkey-leg," he glowered, gesturing impatiently to one of his females.

He grabbed it as she tossed it up to him, gnawing greedily at its juicy meat.

He was determined that before he finally surrendered his soul to the true heavenly realm, *all* his earthly appetites would be fully satisfied!

It was a feast fit for a true King.

Dave splashed down into cold, choking *sea water!*

He sank beneath the surface, frantically struggling to thrash up-ward...drowning in the salty water...

Bursting up out of the water, he gagged and sputtered.

"Auuggghhh..." he coughed, dog-paddling while looking around in bewilderment.

He was in a wide channel, with several-storied buildings jammed against each other right up to the edge of the water on both sides.

Above him, a half-moon was shining brightly. Small boats were moored along the sides of the body of water. A few of the boats were drifting past. He recognized them. They were *gondolas*—low, flat, curved up at both ends, holding just a few people, with a standing person pushing each one along with a long pole.

"Jesus Christ!" Dave gasped to himself, weakly kicking toward the nearest side of the wide channel. "I'm in Italy...in Venice!"

Yes, the buildings coming right to the edge of the water were defi-nitely characteristic of that city of small islands where the "streets" were actual waterways for boats.

In his deathly weak condition he barely made it out of the water, dragging himself up and under a protruding structure.

He lay there hidden, gasping and trembling as low waves from passing gondolas splashed up onto him. Dave tried to figure out how badly he was hurt. He vaguely remembered being shot several times in his upper body, maybe hit by three bullets? But when he felt at his chest with shaking fingers he didn't feel any wounds, though his ribs hurt like hell and his hand came away bloody!

"My gun...what happened to my gun?" Dave gasped, feeling down at his waist for it.

Then he remembered.

As he fell into the Portal, he had slipped it into the large, inside pocket of his coat. And, yes, there it was—solid and comforting—along with the old pictures, the Cube, and the small box of "magic" Optimmune pills.

He pulled out the pictures and looked at them with nostalgia. They shone with light from within. He was now a long way from that time and place. His heart was torn seeing his parents—rather, his duplicate parents—reaching out for each other, held back by chains. And he longed to be that young boy again, happily swinging a tennis racket.

"Great..." he sighed to himself. "I'm ok. Wherever I am I've got my defense, my inspiration to change things, my assistant, and my medicine."

But...did the Cube still work?

He held it tightly in his trembling hand and addressed it: "*Custodian*—are you there? Are you alive?"

For a moment nothing happened.

And then the glowing hologram appeared, hovering just above the white Cube—the white-haired impeccably dressed gentleman sporting black glasses staring calmly at Dave. Then he crisply stated: "How may I help you?"

Dave was both relieved and angry. He was relieved that the Cube still worked. But he was angry that it had, apparently, done something irreversible!

"You did this, didn't you?" Dave accused him in a harsh whisper.

"We were in the time-stream," the little figure stated. "I merely exited us at the point you'd previously indicated having an intense interest in examining."

"So we *are* in Italy?"

"Yes, in the 17th Century."

"What year is this?"

"By my calculations it is the 'year of our Lord' 1633."

"Jesus Christ!" Dave exclaimed. "Isn't that...?"

"Yes, the exact year that *Galileo Galilei* is brought before the Inquisition," the Custodian finished the thought, "—and is forced to recant his scientific findings concerning the movements of the Earth and the sun."

"What's today's date?" Dave eagerly asked.

The floating figure disdainfully lifted a black eyebrow. "I don't know. Time travel isn't a precise science. We'll just have to wait until dawn and ask someone."

"Alright, alright," Dave groaned, trying to move his aching body but finding it very difficult. "Perhaps then there's still time. Maybe

Galileo hasn't caved yet to the Catholic hierarchy. If I can get him to hang onto his courage, we can change history!"

"Possibly," the Custodian shrugged. "But if so, just *how* do you intend to change his mind? You'd be asking him to turn down comfortable house-arrest for being burned alive at the stake!"

"Uh...right..."

Dave certainly didn't have any well-defined plan. In fact, he was still adjusting to the incredible fact of having yet again been thrown back in time to another critical "tipping-point" in history!

Then he came to a hard conclusion.

"I don't know exactly how we're going to do it. But we *are* going to convince him to hang tough to his principles and *not* recant. We will convince him, if necessary, to voluntarily *allow* himself to be *burned alive* at the stake!"

"Oh, are we now?" the Custodian snidely laughed. "I'm sure he'll find your proposal quite compelling—even lighting his funeral pyre himself!"

Dave found the superior, arrogant attitude of that little hologram to be *quite* irritating!

"We'll figure something out," Dave growled.

"You don't even speak the local language," the Custodian "cluck-clucked" at Dave. "So just *how* are you going to work your miracle transformation on Galileo's already weak character—when you can't even communicate with him?"

"I don't know the details, yet!" Dave shot back at the Custodian. "Give me a little time, huh?"

Dave tried to think. But everything around him was getting hazy. He was exhausted and still in severe pain.

Damn it, he'd just been shot to death, survived a huge explosion, and was thrown back in time nearly *four hundred years* into the past! The Custodian should cut him a break!

"I'll bet that *you* can speak 17th Century Italian, can't you?" Dave asked the little translucent hologram.

"My accent will be strange to the locals until I adapt, but yes—I can speak many languages."

"Then I'll move my lips, whispering my words—and you provide the actual loud Italian from my pocket! And maybe you can translate their replies into my ear. Can you do that, somehow?"

"Well, I suppose I could reform a small piece of my substance into an earbud. And I could simulate your voice. So theoretically…"

"Then shut the hell up!" Dave snapped at him, slipping the cube abruptly back into his inside coat pocket. He was perversely pleased to see the startled hologram flicker off. "I've…got…to…recover," he whispered—letting his brutalized, drenched body relax.

"Stick the microphone I budded off my Cube into your ear before you drift off!" the Custodian yelled from out of Dave's pocket.

Dave growled, absently digging back into his coat pocket and feeling a circular nodule now poking out of the cube.

He grabbed it and slipped it into his ear, barely able to keep his eyes open.

The peaceful sound of Gondoliers singing opera out on the nighttime Grand Canal was lulling him to sleep.

His last thought before falling into a stupor was that he was starving! He wondered if back in the 17th Century they'd learned how to make modern Italian food.

If not, they were in for a real treat.

He'd be the one to "invent" pizza!

Yep, he might as well flaunt his future, superior knowledge. There's nothing better than a nice, hot slice of pizza.

Chapter 16

PIZZA PASSION

You'd have thought that they would have matured
Once they were able to conquer daily survival
Surely they would have turned their passions to thriving
But even though their "daily bread" was mostly assured
They still insisted on living lives driven by Fear
As if behind each Unknown lay a saber-toothed tiger
There waiting to spring out and devour them
Or a marauding tribe looking to expand its territory
Killing, raping, pillaging, and taking into slavery
The defeated tribe's life shattered and destroyed
Mandating an "eternal vigil" least barbarians return
Even though the despised savage beasts were themselves
They still insisted on demonizing anything different
Instead of embracing the Wonders of the Universe
They strove to define and constrain, categorizing
And forcing upon other people those definitions
Least the "fabric" of society be ripped asunder
They rejected lives driven by Joy and Curiosity
Dining on stale bread instead of fresh pizza…
Eashoa's Lament, 16:1-6

George was so weak he couldn't move.

Dennis and the few other Dinosapiens still alive didn't look much better.

It was now a week since the Harvester departed. They'd been totally without food for several days. Since they'd been on starvation rations for a month before that, they were almost dead.

They were a pitiful-looking lot—all of them emaciated, skeletal figures. Their eyes were sunken. Their cheeks were hollowed out. Their limbs were shriveled. Their back bones and ribs stuck out. Their hides hung off their bones.

They were huddled together under the protective canopy of a large hut they'd cobbled together out of the shredded remains of the Starship. It was beside a small pool they'd found bubbling out of the depths of the mountain. The water was somewhat salty, but drinkable. At least they weren't dying of thirst.

But the blazing, swollen sun was slowly cooking them—even though it was now visibly fractured with glaring, black lines. In its death throes it was lashing-out at its circling planets!

"If only we could get you to work," George sighed, absently patting the big square unit he was leaning back against.

It was the only piece of equipment that survived intact from the super-storm and subsequent bombardment from the departing Harvester. As such, it mocked them: one lonely Duplicator Unit.

It could save them all if it were functioning. But with no suitable power source it just sat there, a useless hunk of metal. George wished that they at least had a few solar panels to produce electrical power. But even then, it wouldn't be near enough to power the Duplicator, which required a massive energy source in order to materialize food— and anything else—from the data stored in its memory banks.

"I think I'll go visit Sally," Dennis suddenly said. He lifted up his now shrunken-in dinosaur head and looked out woozlly to the glaringly bright rocky plain.

"Sally is dead," George weakly replied. He reached out a shaking hand to restrain his friend from leaving their shelter. "Don't you remember, Dennis? We thawed her to attract the Harvester to rescue us—but she didn't live. She's just a pile of goo out there. Now we're looking for the Harvester to return—if the two other Sally-girls can somehow convince the Demon to help us. That's our only hope."

Dennis snorted angrily.

"I don't care!" he growled, wobbling up to his feet. He dragged his flopping tail behind him as he headed out of the sheltering shadows. "I'm sick of just sitting here. I'm going to go visit our Sally—one last time."

George knew that his friend wouldn't survive a trip to and back from the "gravesite" of Sally, though it was only a mile away. When the Starship remains were blown apart by the departing Harvester, they gathered what was left of the ship beneath a partially sheltering cliff off at a distance from where they'd met the Reaper robots. The dead cancerous lump—which was all that remained of their original Sally—was likely desiccated and blown-away in the hot wind that was continually howling across the rocky plain.

"It's too dangerous out there," George dully said, shutting his eyes. "The gravity inversions have gotten worse. Our two last friends to go out searching for usable scraps from the ship haven't returned. They're likely dead from the heat or thrown up into orbit around the planet. You don't want to end up like them."

"It's better than waiting here to die," Dennis moaned, shaking off George's restraining hand.

"Alright, then," George replied, reaching out feebly to grab Dennis' emaciated tail. The restraining hand momentarily stopped Dennis from proceeding. "If you're determined to go and pay your final respects...then so am I."

"You don't have...to come with me," Dennis growled back.

"I want to," George said, slowly getting up to his feet and leaning on the taller Dinosapien. "We'll go together, you and me. The others can...guard our camp."

Dennis nodded gratefully as they departed. George was a good friend, a friend to the end.

"It's a wee bit warm today," George said as they stumbled across the rocky plain. The sun was sizzling down all around them, making it hard to even see. Dennis absently observed that George wasn't even sweating anymore, too dried-up to produce the necessary skin moisture.

Their shuffling lurching-walking seemed to go on forever. But Dennis was determined to keep on as long as it took. What better place to die than at the side of dear Sally's "grave"?

George could barely move one foot after the other. He knew he was too weak to make it back to the camp. He was certain that he and his friend were going to die out there on the baking, empty plain.

"There!" Dennis exclaimed. "I see her!"

He pointed with an extended claw out across the plain.

George didn't see anything.

"Are you sure?" George replied, shading his eyes with a trembling hand.

All he saw were shimmering heat-waves.

"Yes!" Dennis excitedly answered as with a surge of energy he bounded on ahead.

George sighed. Dennis was probably seeing things. It was too much to expect that the pile of swollen cancerous tumors was still intact.

But there it was!

And it wasn't so much a human-sized lump anymore but a *golden-brown, crusty boulder!* It was quite large, fully four feet in diameter.

"George!" Dennis exclaimed, feeling tentatively at it with his three-fingered hands. "It's yielding but solid. I think the organic remains of Sally have been *cooking* out on the hot rocks for the last week!"

"Cooking?" George gulped, his eyes now stretched wide as he slowly stumbled in a circle around the golden-brown boulder. "You mean...like a pot pie?"

"It's certainly hot enough—and there are likely few bacteria out here to degrade the organic materials!"

"Are you suggesting...?" George gasped.

Dennis tentatively thrust a claw down to slice off a piece of the crusty top. He held it up before his oblong head and cautiously "sniffed" at it.

"It smells good, George," the Dinosapien exclaimed in amazement. "I think we can *eat* it!"

"What—*eat* Sally?" George gasped again. "How can you even think of such a thing?"

"It's *not* Sally," the dinosaur said, slowly moving the golden brown piece to his big wide tongue. "It's just her organic remains."

"Even so, the entire idea is disgusting," George protested. "We're not cannibals! Perhaps our ancient ancestors would eat carrion, but we're long-civilized. We're *vegetarians*, for God's sake!"

"Right, vegetable munchers who are *starving* to death," Dennis whispered, clearly struggling with his decision.

"This is perverse," George again protested, wavering under the relentless heat of the swollen sun.

Dennis' gaze was fixed on the piece of crust on his finger.

"I think that our Sally would *want* us to ingest her remains," Dennis concluded. He tentatively placed the piece carefully on his distended tongue and slowly retracted it into his mouth.

He chewed thoughtfully. Then his toothy face lit up in a wide smile.

"It's delicious!" he exclaimed. He excitedly reached forward to break off a larger piece and hand it to George. "You try some!"

George screwed up his face in horror, but still put the chunk into his mouth.

He chewed...

Yes, it tasted like the crust of a freshly-baked pot pie!

"Oh, Lord—that *is* good!" George said, smiling. He reached out and broke off a bigger hunk while Dennis did the same.

Sitting down on the hot rocks, they feasted on the crusty remains of Sally.

Sally fell through the Portal onto a solid surface.

The pain was almost unbearable from her broken bones slamming into hard pavement.

She almost lost consciousness but fought back the agony.

Pavement?

She looked up to see Kyle limping up to her and grabbing her around her waist, hoisting her up.

"Miss Sally, you been gone through that black circle fer a whole day! I shore be glad to see you back. Are you hurt bad?" he gasped as a cheering mob behind him surged up, surrounding them.

She *wasn't* back a year ago in her younger body! Her "leap of faith" worked! She didn't flash back into the time loop. She was still there with Kyle and the other revolutionaries. Dave did it! He made the difference. Somehow he broke the cycle. But how did he do it?

Maybe it was that crack he made...about "love"?

No, that was too dumb.

Maybe he wasn't as weak a turd as she'd thought? Where was he, by the way? He certainly wasn't there with her, transported a day into the future. Ah well, it didn't matter...

Regardless of what had happened to her unwitting accomplice, she could now proceed forward instead of backward!

"I'm fine," Sally smiled for the first time in months. "So what happened here?"

"We seen you escape the guards, Miss Sally," he grinned widely. "It inspired us to fight even harder! So we kept going—instead of re-treating like we planned. And we *stopped* them! A lot of us got killed or hurt bad, but we won."

"Great...that's just fine."

"Your poor legs...and your arm!" Kyle moaned in sympathy, see-ing broken bones sticking through Sally's blood-soaked ninja clothes.

"With proper medical attention I'll mend, just like you," she weakly stated. "I heal fast. Get some others to help carry me away. And you—get off that wounded leg. So is the grid down? Did we cripple the central power plant?"

"Oh, it's down real good, Miss Sally!" he excitedly replied as oth-ers grabbed them both up, carrying them side-by-side away from the shattered Cheyenne Mountain complex. "That time-loaded energy-gun shore did the job—sliced the whole big mountain to pieces! I got reports from all over the nation—our troops be doin' a number on the Keepers. Even the Imperial Guard is retreating, flying back in their big transports to England!"

"Then...we've got a lot of work to do," she said as the giddiness of victory faded and she relaxed in the supporting arms. "We've got to consolidate our advances and take over the key establishments. We can't give the Elites a chance to regroup."

The choking dust and smoke that Sally was in when she'd jumped into the Portal was now gone. Sally saw over to the side that the disarmed guards were herded into groups. Around the frightened guards, the angry mob was jeering and spitting—viciously throwing rocks at them!

"Kyle, give out orders that none of the captured people are to be needlessly harmed," she urgently instructed him.

"But Miss Sally," he protested as he lifted up his communicator unit as he was carried along beside her. "They done treated us worse than dogs all our lives! And you say we be givin' them mercy? I don't know..."

"They all have the Great Spirit in them, do they not?" she shot at him, ruthlessly returning him to their shared Animist religious beliefs.

"Well, yes..."

"Then do as I order!" she snapped. "We don't need a bloodbath. We just need to change the rigid structure of our society—one that the other world governments will respect, not unite against!"

He groaned at having to pass on her orders but did so. Sally knew it was hard for him to resist the impulse for revenge. The lines of hatred ran deep. But she knew he had a good heart and if prodded in the right direction his better nature would prevail.

Sally also knew that if she and the revolutionaries pushed too hard too fast, the Imperial Troops would return to take everything back. But if she quickly submitted a reasonable set of demands to the Queen of the English Empire—abolishing North American slavery, extending Citizenship rights to everyone, guaranteeing religious freedom, and establishing a kinder and gentler police enforcement policy—then *she* could take a high position within the new government!

Her path to *ruling the world* was a devious one. It began with reasonable accommodation...

After all, what the other Great Powers in the world most wanted was simple and easy to provide: *Stability!*

It was the altar to which they all bowed.

And it was the altar upon which they would all, unknowingly, be sacrificed.

Dave awoke stiff, confused, and *famished!*

By the diffuse sunlight he saw it was early morning...

"Tu chi sei? Perche sei nella mia stalla?" an angry female voice brought Dave sharply awake.

["Who are you? Why are you in my stall?] a small voice sounded in Dave's ear.

["I'm just a visitor! I...got drunk and fell asleep here! I'm sorry to bother you!] he whispered back as the simultaneous translation sounded loudly from his shirt pocket: *"Sono solo un visitatore! Mi sono ubriacato e sono addormentato qui! Mi dispiace distrubarti!"*

Dave was astonished at how well the translation went both ways. It was like being in a Star Trek science fiction series using a "universal translator"!

But why was this woman so antagonistic? Surely people often fell asleep on the dock, especially after a night spent drunk on the town!

["The black plaque swept through Italy just three years ago,"] the Custodian whispered in his ear. [One out of every three people in Venice died. They are very suspicious of any new person who might be bringing back the disease!"]

Dave slid out of the space where he'd been hiding, shivering, still wet from his midnight swim in the canal.

He saw a suspicious, stout woman with hands planted firmly on her wide hips looking him up and down.

"Tu rimani dove sei! Sto chiamando le autorita!" she warned, him, grabbing up a knife and brandishing it at him. ["You stay right where you are! I'm calling the authorities!"] the Custodian's voice translated in Dave's ear.

Dave was backed into a corner. He knew he looked suspicious. He obviously wasn't a bar-hopping rich person. And if he tried to run away from the shop woman on the narrow street—hemmed in by the tall buildings on one side and the canal on the other—he was sure to draw attention to himself and be captured.

But he had no choice...

["Well, that's just fine with me! In fact, there's one over there!"] he whispered, simultaneously pointing over her shoulder to draw her attention away from him so he could dash away...as his pocket loudly proclaimed: *"Beh, questo e bene con me! In realta, c'e una laggiu!"*

As she glanced away he took a couple steps but couldn't run. He was just too tired. His chest still hurt terribly from his freshly healed mortal wounds. So he turned back...

"Oh, mi scusi, Signore! C'era un mendicante sospetto di qualche tipo qui! Hai visto dove e andato?" she said, cringing away from him. ["Oh, pardon me, Sir! There was a suspicious beggar of some sort here! Did you see where he went?"]

Huh? What had happened? But whatever, he'd best take advantage.

["No, I did not. And just what are you selling this fine morning?"] he whispered, thinking fast—perhaps she had bad eyesight to do such a turn-around in her attitude? —as his pocket indignantly replied: *"No, non l'ho fatto. E quello che stai vendendo questa bella mattina?"*

"Pane fresco e vino, signore! Ho appena preso fuori dal forno un paio di minuti fa! E 'molto gustoso!" ["Fresh bread and wine, Sir. I just baked it a few minutes ago. It's very tasty!"]

Yes, he saw she had a basket at her feet containing long loafs of golden bread stacked inside. Plus she had some bottles of wine. The bread smelled heavenly delicious.

["Sounds great—I'll have some."] *"Suona grande! Avro un po'!"*

She happily handed him a loaf plus a bottle as he reached into his pocket, realizing that he neither had his wallet nor any money, let alone Italian money from four hundred years in the past.

But in his hand, amazingly, was a silver coin!

She accepted it gladly as he turned and quickly walked away.

"Grazie, Signore! Grazie mille!" ["Thank you, Sir! Thank you very much!"] she called after him.

He popped the cork and guzzled down the sweet liquid. Normally he didn't drink alcoholic beverages, but the water here would probably kill him. It was a time-period replete with terrible diseases, many of which were spread throughout their crowded cities by sewage-contaminated water.

And the bread was incredibly good. He munched it greedily as he covertly spoke to the Custodian.

"How did that money-in-my-pocket happen?" Dave quietly asked the Cube in his shirt pocket as he limped along, still in pain—though still happily chewing on the delicious, warm bread.

"Oh, the coin was just a temporarily substantial force-assembly I materialized," the Custodian replied from his pocket. "The lady will 'lose' it within the hour, sadly, when it vanishes. But she was being very rude to you. I think justice was done."

"But why did she turn from being so antagonistic to being so friendly?" Dave said as he strolled casually down the boardwalk, trying not to attract any additional attention to himself.

"Look in that shop window."

Curious, Dave paused to examine his reflection: where he saw looking back at himself a person short-haired, with a small mustache, wearing a floppy hat with a white feather perked on top, a pink-gold cape, a blousy shirt with white and black stripes, black and green-striped shorts up to his crotch, and pink tights on his legs!

"Jesus Christ!" Dave exclaimed, shocked. "What the hell is this?"

A couple of early-morning passerby's looked at him curiously as they walked past.

"Oops...I've got to whisper and not talk aloud in English," Dave admonished himself.

Then, in a careful whisper he asked the Custodian: "What's going on here? What happened to me? And why do I look like an effeminate dandy? And please speak through the earbud when people are around!"

["I extended my holographic capability to encompass your entire body"], the Custodian compliantly replied in Dave's ear. ["In my databases on your Dimension—which I acquired from your 21st Century Internet when I was searching on Galileo—I found a picture of an Italian nobleman from the Renaissance period. I modeled your visible form upon this template."]

Damn! The little cube could not only translate, but make him appear to be someone else entirely. Incredible!

"Everyone's looking at me like I'm some weirdo," Dave growled, glancing around him at the rude shop-lady still staring after him, a worker on the dock grimacing at him, and a passing Gondolier who *whistled* at him!

["Oh...pardon me..."], the Custodian replied. ["Highest on my search parameter was this picture, but digging deeper into its documentation I see now that it was of an Italian nobleman from the 16th Century. This type of colorful dress is now long out of fashion, particularly for men of this present age in the 17th Century."]

"Oh, that's just great," Dave whispered. "I'm a dandy nobleman in a gaudy outfit! You've got to fix it. I should be inconspicuous, not standing out like some fashion throwback!"

["Duck into that recess and I'll switch you to something more appropriate"], the Custodian ordered Dave via his earbud.

Dave did as directed, clutching his now half-drained bottle of wine and half-eaten loaf of bread. He felt a sudden unsettling sensation like something was *crawling* over the skin of his entire body! Then it went away. He looked down to see a gold vest with ornate large buttons that extended to his crotch, past which baggy brown trousers were visible reaching to his knees. Past that were long white socks.

He felt something around his neck.

Stepping back out on the street he glanced in the shop window once again, catching his reflection. Around his neck was a frilly white thing. On his head was a high green, wide-brimmed hat with a gold hat band. Now his mustache was fuller with a dark goatee at his chin. Around his shoulders was draped a thick brown cape with a red interior.

"Still rather gaudy by future standards," Dave sighed, "but apparently more in agreement with present dress codes."

Now the passerby's were politely nodding at him, recognizing him apparently as a strolling, sophisticated nobleman.

["I found a mural in my databases depicting a group of men and women in 17th Century Italian dress"], the voice in Dave's earbud informed him. ["I hope this is more satisfactory."]

"Yes, this is much better," Dave sighed gratefully, continuing to limp along the boardwalk. It was a fine morning, the sun glinting off the surface of the Grand Canal, shops opening up, and cheerful people coming out to stroll or go to work.

A sea breeze wafted through, sweeping away the stink of the city.

"I sure could have used you in my last big time jump," Dave rue-fully whispered. "It took me years to learn the language and fit into the society of ancient Athens. Are you sure that your illusions will hold up?"

["They are quite tangible and should convince anyone except those in prolonged, close contact"] the voice in his ear replied. ["But they are not material. They are constructs of light energy, designed to cycle quickly within tight quantum constraints, creating the illusion of solid matter. As I said, they will vanish if not maintained by my im-mediate proximity."]

"Doesn't it take a lot of energy to produce them?" Dave asked. "And how long can you maintain them? Plus why didn't Sally men-tion this to me before? We could have used this sort of disguise a number of times!"

["Only a few of the Elites of Sally's Dimension are privy to this technology], the Custodian calmly replied. ["She and her servant co-horts stole me from a high official's home. I draw energy from all sources around me, similar to the gun that you used to open the Por-tal into Time. Creating and maintaining these illusions does drain energy from me, but not more than I can handle as long as they are simple appearance-changes. The silver coin I made for you, though, did drain about 10% of more present energy-charge."]

"Then we'll not buy too many things," Dave whispered, looking for a hotel to go into for a private room where he could access his in-juries.

["Do not worry about that"], the Custodian confidently replied. ["In this period of time, a single *gold* coin—which I can simulate as easily as one of lesser value—will buy you many items or services. Plus, from a wealthy vendor, you can get actual change that is perma-nent. Perhaps your first objective should be to determine today's ex-act date?"] the voice urged him, a slight annoyance to his tone.

"Oh...right," Dave whispered.

Then he spied what looked like a hotel entrance and walked in-side.

An elegant, slender lady with long black hair greeted him.

Dave was now getting so used to his new "universal translation" routine that the translation of the Italian words in his ear and his "pocket"-reply seemed instantaneous. He heard their words and his as if they were both done in near-simultaneous English.

"May I help you, good Sir?" she politely asked.

"I am looking for a room," he grinned in a friendly way while also trying to appear drunk.

That wasn't a problem. Not used to drinking alcohol, he *was* getting drunk from the half bottle of wine he'd just swigged! His head felt light and breezy, his words slurred...a mannerism that the Custodian duplicated perfectly in his translation of Dave's sublingual whispers.

"We have a fine suite available on our top floor overlooking the Grand Canal," she replied, graciously bowing to him. "Would that be suitable?"

"That...sounds just fine!" he jovially replied, swinging the wine bottle around in the air for emphasis. "And...oh, by the way—just what is today's date? I fear that over the last few weeks of partying I've completely lost track of time. Hah!"

She looked at him curiously with her large black eyes before politely replying: "Why, the date today, good Sir, is the eighth of June."

"And...the year?" Dave giddily asked, pretending to be even drunker than he was.

This time she looked at him in disbelief, narrowing her eyes. She glanced at the floor under his feet where *water* was dripping down onto the carpet! Dave knew that his supposed finery appeared to be bone-dry. He hoped that she thought that he was just drunkenly *peeing*...not a water-logged time-traveler camouflaged as a dry nobleman!

"You are quite fetching, my dear," he hastily grinned, trying to distract her attention. "Are you available for a kiss or two?"

She wore a plain blue dress and cut a striking figure. Under different circumstance, Dave might have been genuinely attracted to her. Now, he simply was scared that she would discover his elaborate ruse.

"I am happily married—and *not* 'available'!" she sharply retorted. "And as to the year, it is of course the year of our Lord 1633. Perhaps you should pay in advance for your room?"

Dave dug into his pocket, found a coin conveniently materialized there, and flipped it in the air at her.

She caught it neatly in one hand. It was a gold coin.

"Will that be sufficient for a day and night, good Lady?" he grinned at her.

She looked at it appreciatively and nodded: "Yes, quite sufficient. Your suite is at the top of the stairs where..."

"I shall find my way!" he laughed, prancing up the stairs.

As soon as he was out of sight from below, he sagged against the wall of the stairway, groaning. It was agony dragging his shaking, pain-wracked body up the last few steps.

But as soon he was in a private room he stripped off his now-revealed, water-soaked clothes. He set the Cube to the side. A basin of "clean" water was in the bathroom. He washed and wrung-out his clothes as best he could, then hung them up to dry.

Greedily scarfing down the last of his bread, he addressed the Cube which was now lying on the bed: "We've got to talk!"

The Custodian's little hologram appeared, floating lightly in the air above the cube: "Yes?"

"When was it that pizza was invented?"

"Pizza?"

"Right! Put some tomato sauce, cheese, and meat on bread and it's delicious! Make the bread into a flat, unleavened circle and we'd make a fortune selling it!"

The Custodian sighed deeply before replying. He spoke as if delivering a boring but necessary lecture to a dim-witted child.

"The word 'pizza' formally came into common usage in the Italian language in 1889, about two hundred and fifty years from now—when a baker in Naples baked it for the King and Queen of Italy."

Wow! It'd be over two hundred years before Pizza was officially invented!

"Great!" Dave laughed woozily. He knew he was speaking and thinking in a rather silly fashion. But it wasn't his fault he got pushed into a Time Portal, wound up in Venice Italy in the 1600's, and then had to drink half a bottle of wine and get drunk! "So maybe we can change history just by introducing pizza now to the Renaissance?

That should mellow people out even more than deliberately provoking a war between early scientists and the Church, don't you think?"

The little hologram looked as if he was struggling not to say something impolite.

"Dr. King, perhaps you should get some rest—and sleep off the wine you drank before you..." the little, black-glasses wearing man suggested, lifting both eyebrows haughtily.

"No! Really! What do you think?"

The Custodian sighed deeply before answering.

"Different forms of cooking similar to pizza have been around since about 7,000 years ago," the Custodian dryly replied. "Unless you're going to overwhelm the world with some radical new form of it, you're likely not to have much impact on history."

Dave nodded thoughtfully.

"Ok," he gulped. "I guess you're right about..."

"I am always right!" the Custodian snapped.

"Ok, ok!" Dave said, waving a hand wobbly in the air. "So when was it, exactly, that Galileo was forced to recant his position that the sun was the actual center of the 'world' with Earth circling around it instead of the opposite situation?"

"That would be the 22nd of June, 1633."

"And where did this occur?"

"It was in Rome."

"So how far are we from Rome and how long will it take for us to get there?"

"Approximately 330 miles," the Custodian quickly calculated. "And on horseback or by horse-drawn carriage—oh, it'll take us about eleven days to get there."

"So if we leave tomorrow..."

"—we'll get there with only one day to spare before Galileo will publically, in a formal ceremony, be forced to recant his scientific observations. That will be done, by the way, at a cathedral: *the Church of Santa Maria Sofia Minerva*. It was a public spectacle, a powerful triumph of religious orthodoxy over science."

"Well...that's rather a tight time schedule, isn't it?" Dave grimaced. "Couldn't you have landed us closer to Rome, or back a bit in time?"

The primly suited figure just stared coldly at Dave.

"Right..." Dave sighed, "—'time-travel isn't a precise science,' right?"

"That's correct," the Custodian icily replied.

"Then we'll just have to make the best of the hand we've been dealt," Dave said, flopping backward clad only in his underwear onto the bed. He didn't even want to think about the host of bedbugs likely swarming from the mattress upon his semi-naked body in this primitive era. "You figure out the best route and a plan for us getting a private talk with Galileo. Me, I hurt like hell and I'm drunk. I'm taking a wee little recuperative nap..."

"As you wish," the figure snorted, "winking" out.

As Dave drifted away into a welcomed, exhausted sleep he realized he'd have to speak with the Custodian about his attitude.

That glorified librarian was getting downright snotty!

But Dave knew that his own "plan" was flimsy, at best. Even if he was able to speak with Galileo privately, how could he possibly convince the great man to allow the authorities to burn him to death at the stake? It seemed impossible.

But Dave was also grimly aware of the *heavy black gun* he carried with him. If all else failed, he *was* going to change history—even if it meant leveling the Vatican to do so!

Was this childish of him? If he didn't get his way he'd just burn the place down?

Damn right...

This was his last, unexpected chance to change history and save the human race from annihilation. And if it took behaving like a *selfish brat*, then so be it!

He was going to throw the biggest tantrum the world had ever seen.

Chapter 17

<u>KIDS</u>

To many humans their lives did not seem to matter

Unless they left behind children to carry on a "legacy"

Not just for family business or artistic accomplishment

But merely transporting their genetic endowment

Just a few more years forward into the future

Birthed as squealing, selfish, poop-machines

Turned into cute little darlings and dandies

They reset time back to a new beginning

And saw the world with optimistic eyes

Everything made fresh and sparkling

History starting up yet again

Gone all the previous pain

Wiping away horror and decay

Ready to imagine again, leap ahead

Not as extension of past, ugly failures

But testimony to the proposition of Virtue

Embodied in an irrational, marvelous Hope...

Eashoa's Lament, 17:63-67

George was so stuffed he could hardly move.

It was an incredibly delightful feeling!

He was leaning back against the four-foot high mound of Sally's cooked organic matter, shaded from the swollen sun which was now hanging low on the horizon.

Dennis was sprawled in front of George, lying on his side, breathing heavily. His tongue lolled out of his large lizard-like head. His belly protruded. Both he and George were filled up, for the first time in weeks.

"We've...got to get...this food back to the others," George gasped.

"Yes," Dennis answered from the rocky surface. "But just let me...rest a little bit more."

They'd eaten into the side of the mound, possibly consuming a twentieth of its mass. A deep gouge showed where they'd dug their way in. It was very much like the crust of a meat pot pie, very flaky and crumbly.

"We can...take some with us," George said. "Maybe take some off the top where it's cooked harder from the sun directly shining down onto it."

He dragged himself to his feet and started pulling up the crusty top of the mound where it overlapped the deep gouge that he and Dennis had eaten into its side...

—as with a "snap" about a third of the top broke free.

George staggered back with the big hunk in his hands.

"Uh...Dennis?" he said, staring at the gap that now revealed what lay beneath.

"Yes, George?" Dennis said, still lying on the ground. He lifted his head up on his long neck, twisting it around to stare directly at his human-looking friend.

"There's *liquid* inside...in a scooped-out interior."

"Liquid?"

"Yes," George said, setting the slab to the side as he leaned forward to get a better look into the deep basin.

"Is it water?" Dennis said, now gathering his powerful legs under his dinosaur body.

"It...looks like jelly—some sort of gel, anyway," George said, tentatively sticking a finger into the glistening, hazy-green fluid.

It stuck onto his finger as if it were syrup.

"Well, that'll make it more difficult to move the mound as an entire lump," Dennis said, standing up behind George. "But we could still do it, I suppose."

George stuck his moistened finger into his mouth and sucked on it.

"What does it taste like?" Dennis eagerly said. "Is it good? I admit I'm thirsty out here with no water to drink."

George felt his face light up, a rare smile moving unbidden onto his mouth.

"It's...*exquisite!*" he exclaimed in delight. "It's as good as the crust, maybe better. It's sweet and tangy, both at the same time!"

"So...this thing isn't so much like a meat pot pie, but a fruit pie?" Dennis asked. "What with all the exotic human foods you've described to us as we've been starving to death—that struck me as the most edible and tasty."

"Yes...sort of like that, but also—*yikes!*" George cried-out, lurching backward!

"Hey! Watch out! You almost stepped on my delicate toes!" Dennis protested, forced to dance to the side to avoid George.

But George just pointed with a trembling finger at the partially revealed liquid.

"Something moved," he said, aghast.

"Moved?" Dennis replied, confused.

"There's something *alive* in there!" George urgently replied. "I saw something jerk back out of the light that's going in through the hole I made into the top!"

"Ahhhhh...." Dennis said, cocking his oblong head to the side and carefully peering in himself. "I don't see..."

—when a *hand* punched through the overlaying crust and a *head* popped out right behind it!

"Oh, hell!" George yelled, dropping back a couple feet.

Dennis was frozen in place, his toothy mouth hanging open as he stared with his big orange eyes.

George saw the head of a *young child*, whose gel-covered curly hair was slicked down, looking around with wide-opened *green* eyes!

"S-Sally?" Dennis croaked, reaching forward with his claws to peel back the entrapping crust from the stuck-out head and small arm.

George rushed forward to help pull the heavy crust away, tossing the slabs to the side—then reaching into the greenish liquid to pull out a *baby!* He held her tenderly in his arms.

It was a naked, human, girl-child that looked to be about a year old.

She grabbed onto George's face and looked him straight in the eyes. Then she smiled brightly and laughed.

"Daddy?" she said, gurgling happily.

"She...she's *talking!*" George gasped, hugging the child close to him. "She recognizes me! She's *Sally!*"

"That's...amazing," Dennis said, leaning over closely to inspect the baby.

The girl grabbed onto his muzzle with both her small fists, drawing his face even closer. She stroked his long, sharp teeth.

"Doggy!" she gurgled again, patting his scaly chin.

"Oh, my," Dennis grinned widely, letting her explore his long pointed teeth with her stubby hands.

"Hold her!" George excitedly ordered, handing the gel-covered baby over to the Dinosapien.

Dennis cradled her gently in his scaly arms as George pulled off the light shirt he was wearing and wrapped it loosely around the baby.

"We've got to get her back to the camp," George said. "And then we've got to retrieve all that food and liquid! It will continue to nourish her. We certainly don't have any milk to..."

"Birdie!" she gleefully cried out, pointing up at the sky.

There—to George and Dennis' horror—they saw one of their fellow Dinosapiens, one of their lost comrades, flailing-about weakly as he rocketed up into the sky on a gravity-inversion.

He was headed straight up to certain death in orbit around the planet.

"*Wheee!*" baby Sally cried-out as she suddenly lurched out of Dennis' arms and the swaddling shirt to *splash* back into the basin—to immediately climb out, hop down, and *run naked* across the hot plain in the direction of the "bird"!

In horror, George saw part of the rocky plain suddenly *split open*—as a geyser of splintered rocks shot up into the sky and the baby *dived* into it...

"No! Sally!" Dennis screamed-out. He raced with long strides toward the now-obscured baby...

—who suddenly appeared at the top of the geyser, little arms spread wide, floating along like a heavenly cherub before *shooting straight up into the sky* to grab-onto the twisting tail of the hapless Dinosapien and *drag* him back down to the ground.

"Birdie!" she grinned widely as Dennis and George ran up to her and the gasping, incredulous crew member.

George grabbed up the baby and hugged her close to his chest.

"Sally, please don't do that again," he gasped.

"She can ride gravity-inversions?" Dennis said in amazement, panting deeply as he helped his fellow Dinosapien to wobbly stand up.

"Who knows what else she can do?" George said, looking in awe at the cooing baby. "Clearly something extraordinary has happened. She's no longer just a human. She's something more!"

"She's a fruit-pie baby!"

George began hysterically laughing, hugging his baby Sally.

"Well, whatever she is—let's get her back to camp," Dennis concluded. "And then we'll send out a party to retrieve all that nourishment, both for her and us!"

"Grab some of the crust-slabs. We'll take them with us. They'll give our folks enough strength to get up and come back here for the rest," George now grinned, hugging the chortling baby close to his chest.

For the first time in a long time—George felt at peace. His Alice was gone. The Starship was destroyed. They were abandoned on a dying planet in a fast-imploding, rotten Universe.

But they had Sally!

And George knew that for whatever reasons, God loved this little child. The "extraordinary thing" that happened to her wasn't simply a side-effect of some lingering "retroviral complex" medication that Sally still had in her system.

To George it was nothing short of a miracle.

To Periscus it was nothing short of a miracle.

It was just three years from when he and Agathe almost got captured by the space-octopus. But now he was the *Admiral* of a huge space armada!

Periscus' command ship floated in orbit just behind the planet Saturn.

"The invaders are approaching at sub-light speed," Agathe reported to him.

He was so used to her now that he barely gave a thought to her being a giant, green-white snake curled around his Captain's chair. Her large fluorescent head hovered to the side of his, staring with him at the viewscreen, occasionally flicking-out a red, forked tongue.

The Snakes were not at all happy with Socrates' take-over of Earth's government. Indeed, they hated Socrates even more than before. However, they had no choice except but to cooperate. Socrates' army of Automatons insured that everyone bowed to the Throne. The Dinosapiens weren't represented on the spaceships, though. Socrates ordered them to concentrate on terrestrial defense as foot soldiers, more suited (according to him) to their "scampering" nature as lizards. The intelligent Black Bird flocks were seemingly aloof to the whole thing, retreating to their nests in the forests and mountains rather than participate in the coming *space wars*.

"You're sure they can't see us?" he asked her.

"We're on the other side of the planet from them," she calmly replied telepathically in his head. Over the past few years she'd learned how to modulate her "voice" such that it wasn't yelling in his brain anymore. That alone was a significant victory for Periscus.

"Our sensor probes look like rocks to their scans," Agathe matter-of-factly stated, "—as do our ships hiding powered-down in Saturn's rings. I'm sure they won't know we're here until we choose to attack."

Periscus enjoyed being the Fleet Commander. It turned out to be a natural fit for him since he'd spent so much of his life on the sea as a fisherman. He never actually participated in a naval battle, but being a Greek from the port city of Athens he'd been brought up as a child to understand the tactics of naval warfare. Also, he'd been an actual Hoplite soldier on occasion, whose army strategies and tactics were very similar to naval maneuvers.

"They are almost in position for our ambush," Agathe noted, flicking her forked tongue out toward a side-display on a wall. On it, Periscus saw several hundred large vessels in a loose swarm. An inset picture showed an amplified view of the command vessel of the enemy. It was larger than the others, hanging back behind them. That was Periscus' specific target. It was a large black sphere with facetted surfaces, from which "spikes" of many shapes and sizes protruded.

"Good..." he slowly replied. "Just hold us in place until they're close enough for precise positioning—so our ships can do micro-jumps."

Periscus was excited, but still awestruck at their magnificent present location in the solar system.

The *hazy, giant sphere of Saturn* filled their forward viewscreen. Periscus again marveled at how nothing held up that vast globe. It just floated there in the blackness of space. And its surface was composed of *circular bands of complex colors*: brown, black, yellow, purple, orange, blue, and white. It was gorgeous!

And to add to its splendor, great rings floated in a flat disc around the planet. From a distance the rings were mostly shades of blue, grey, and black. Periscus' command ship was close enough to the outer ring so that he could see individual ice fragments the size of mountains down to small boulders—which glittered in the sunlight as a field of white diamonds!

He didn't understand it all. But he knew enough to command the Fleet—hundreds of large, heavily armed battleships.

Many were merely subservient units, crewed by the ubiquitous Automatons. But located in strategic vessels, commanding entire squadrons, his children and other young humans captained the lead vessels. They were mostly still boys, few older than teenagers. But they had a ready aptitude for the Snakes' clever "video-game"-trained maneuvers. So their viewscreens showed precise three-dimensional positions and vectors of the invading Spike-Ships. Overall direction of the battle was in Periscus' hands, but his many human "sons" commanded individual engagements.

"Prepare for power-up," he spoke to all the ships.

In the ancient Athenian fleet, the "Triremes" were the supreme naval weapon, with three decks of rowers providing powerful thrust to a protruding ram in the front. For Periscus, his powerful "beamers" were his ram—an energy weapon that fired a massive laser straight forward! Also, the Athenian fleet was famous for very rapid maneuvers that pierced and smashed an enemy armada. This was exactly what Periscus planned. His fleet, though smaller than the in-vading one, would use its quickness and precise positioning to pierce and destroy the invaders.

"Engage," he ordered.

The invaders were caught totally by surprise. His ships did tiny "jumps" out of the rings to appear right beside individual vessels of the tightly clustered alien fleet.

Before they could react, *massive blue beams* skewered the invad-ing ships.

As there was no sound in space, the ensuing explosions were just violent images of *erupting fire and twisted metal!* But the flashing lightshow was spectacular against the blackness of space.

As his fleet's beamers blasted into the invading ships, he directed Agathe to do a micro-jump, materializing right behind the largest spike-encrusted command ship.

"Catch it," he calmly ordered, watching a huge net spread out into the star-sprinkled blackness.

He knew that it was actually an intertwined energy-field. But he conceptualized it for himself as a fishnet thrown into the Mediterra-nean Sea.

It surrounded the prey, first stunning it with massive bolts of electricity—then sucking the power out of it to immobilize it! It was much like an electric eel stunning and then eating a hapless fish in the sea.

The rippling waves of intertwined blue energy now were laid tightly across the black spikes and surfaces of the enemy's command ship.

"We've captured them," Agathe reported in Periscus' head.

"Good...good...any casualties from the others?" he asked.

He waited anxiously as the Automatons in the control room counted up the reports coming in from the dispersed fleet.

"Three ships were damaged by spikes shot from the invaders," an Automaton reported in a monotone. "But there is nothing other than minor damage to our personnel or to the other ships of the fleet."

"Good...very good," Periscus nodded happily.

Around him he saw wreckage spinning off into the blackness of space from the blown-apart invading ships. Here and there he saw something that might be the remains of a living creature. But the only surviving vessel of the enemies was now securely immobilized in Periscus' net.

The entire battle had lasted only three minutes.

"Well done, everyone!" he announced over the fleet-wide network. "Let's get back to Earth."

As Periscus' ship moved away from Saturn, their motionless catch was towed behind them in the energy-net.

"More will come," Agathe quietly stated.

"Yes, but long before that happens you very-smart Snakes will have figured out the logs in our captured ship, right?"

"We hope so," she replied in the affirmative. "And with their logs we'll know their conquests—perhaps even the location of their home world."

"I've got to compliment that cunning dog, Socrates," Periscus grinned. "He's not much of a human being, but he's a great King! This is a fine victory. And there's more to come!"

Agathe was clearly not so elated. Her head held high during the battle now hung low. She looked despondent, ill.

"What's wrong, Agathe?" Periscus asked. "You wouldn't rather those invaders made it to Earth and destroyed your civilization once and for all, would you?"

"No...but all the violence, the destruction, the death," she sighed as they both looked out over the field of battle.

They were now leaving behind the debris field. But it was still a staggering quantity of destroyed spaceships.

"Well, *I* am personally elated!" he joyfully admitted. "You know, I was in several battles in ancient Greece. They were bloody and confused, awful things. But this—this is clean and decisive. Being the General has its advantages! I can see the entire thing and execute a good plan. Your weapons are wonderful, Agathe. Where back in ancient Greece I had to fight face-to-face to gain a small victory, here in outer space we can cleanly destroy everyone coming up against us!"

"I am glad that you are pleased," she said, sadly turning her head away from the viewscreen.

Yes, Socrates was correct that humans needed to be at the helm. This was where he belonged—not running away from the fight, but commanding it.

"We will fulfill our potential," Periscus grinned. "It's not just mere defense—but as the King constantly tells us: it's taking our *rightful place* in this grand Universe!"

He thought of the now-immense Duplicators in orbit about Earth efficiently churning out complete battleships. Soon they'd have a fleet not of hundreds, but thousands! Then it would be *tens* of thousands! And then it would be *millions!*

The Snakes had some problem about generating that much "Dark" energy from their magical devices. Their complaint had something to do with drawing the Creator's attention to focus yet again upon Earth. They said the DE-generators were lighting up the planet like a celestial beacon. But Periscus wasn't worried. All the "gods" he'd known of in ancient Athens *gloried* in a good fight.

"This is a wonderful day for us," he sighed contentedly, leaning back in his chair. "Our first battle with alien starships and we had total victory! Agathe?" he asked, looking around.

But she was nowhere to be seen. She'd already departed the control room, slinking out quietly.

For a Snake, she was awfully squeamish.

As much as he liked her, Periscus knew he'd have to replace her soon with one of his sons.

The Snakes were now in their proper place: being smart *servants* to their rightful masters. *Humans* were destined to rule the Universe!

Periscus smiled to himself.

Just as Periscus' offspring did so well that day, he was convinced that the Snakes' "Supreme God" would also be pleased with *His* children. There'd be no negative repercussions of God focusing upon the intelligent inhabitants of Earth. Instead, this "Supreme God" would reward them richly!

After all, they were now *celestial Warriors*, fulfilling the "Hero Odyssey" in the best possible way! Yes, the Greek Myths celebrated the Martyr. But Periscus never had any delusions of how "grand" it was to fight to the death in battle. Defeat was defeat and death was death. There was no honor in losing, no matter how valiant you fought. He was much happier for his enemies to have that so-called "privilege." Having just executed an excellently effective plan, Periscus and his fighters had no need at all to be martyrs dying in "glorious" battle!

Periscus was just happy to be alive.

Winning was much better than losing.

Let his enemies be martyrs to *their* cause!

Chapter 18

MARTYRDOM

The strongest programmed instinct of humans
Was, regrettably, to survive at all costs
Perhaps this was a mistake of their Creator
One that produced not just Police but Marauders
Where the greatest defense against a looming Threat
Was often not high Walls but a powerful Army
Not just to stave off enemies, but go and kill them
Proactively ending their threat before it even came
And not just them, but their women and children
Raping, torturing, slaughtering, robbing, and maiming
That no potential revenge might ever come back
Such an overwhelming emotion to conquer within
If one were to give it a higher priority than everything
Even to the point of giving up one's self, agreeing to die
A compelling response going against one's genetics
Fearful, illogical, final, painful, and horrific
Few finding courage to do it even for a just cause
Rather than merely escape, cowardly or stupidity
Publically, voluntarily, surrendering one's own life
The true challenge, to understand the difference...

Eashoa's Lament, 18:19-23

Dave was extremely tired, stiff, and aching.

A journey that in modern times took only a few hours had taken almost two weeks: riding by horse-drawn carriage along bumpy roads from Venice to Rome.

Fortunately, his "disguise" had held up well.

As far as his traveling companions knew, he was indeed "David da Londra"—David from London. He knew that he, that is the Custodian, had a strange accent. He knew that others might occasionally hear him lapse into English. What better thing to do than claim to be a rich nobleman from London?

But England was hardly a friend of Rome.

"So you say that you are not a Catholic?" the man sitting opposite to Dave in the cramped carriage seemingly politely asked.

The Monk had gotten on at the last stop. They were now on the outskirts of Rome. The long journey was almost over. Dave knew he had to be very careful to not raise suspicion, least he be revealed as a fraud at this late point in his quest to change the timeline. From other conversations he knew that the deceptively humble Monks around Rome could be actual clergy with high connections in the Church.

Not being from the 17th Century, he knew he must be very careful in what he said least he be revealed at best as a fraud and at worst as a spying infidel!

But he was extremely tired. His rear end in particular ached from the many hard bumps and jars of the carriage on the rough road. He wished there'd been time for him to introduce the Italians to shock-absorbers. Regardless, he knew that his mental acuity was slipping. He'd best not engage in any "verbal-dueling."

"I am a friend of the Church, here to report on the trial of Socrates by the Inquisition," Dave carefully said, forcing a friendly smile upon his face. "The King is interested in the outcome."

Dave hoped that his brief statement would shut down the conversation. He wanted to appear sympathetic without having to prove he was a good Catholic. He simply did not know enough about the Catholic rituals and teachings—particularly back in the 17th Century—to pull off such a deception.

"But your King is a heretic," the Monk mildly stated. "He is a deluded *Protestant* who rejects the Holy Father, is he not?"

Though the stout man with the protruding belly seemed a genial fellow, there was a cold glint in his eyes that scared Dave. The man was completely bald, with a round face, wearing a simple cassock—a long, ankle-length, brown robe—with a large wooden cross hanging prominently from a chain around his neck.

The others in the small carriage weren't a threat to Dave. Jammed up next to him was an elderly noble lady, in a voluminous dress that puffed up her frail, thin body. She was quietly dozing off, slumped to the side. Next to the obese Monk sat a young lad, the thin woman's son. The poor boy appeared quite intimidated, trying vainly to hide under a wide cloak.

The only thing that linked them all was their *smell*. Dave intellectually accepted that there were no antiperspirants in the 17th Century, so people sweated profusely. Since it was spring with the sun shining down—and with no air conditioning—it was sweltering in the carriage. In addition, bathing was considered unhealthy. Dave was getting used to the foul odors but was still shocked by his *own* smell, not to mention those jammed up right next to him!

["King Charles is on the throne, Dr. King,"] the small voice of the Custodian quietly informed him in his ear. ["He is a type of protestant, though rumored to be sympathetic to the Catholic type of Christianity. His wife, however—Henrietta Maria—is definitely a Catholic. But Charles has allowed people to choose their own religion, so there's real confusion and conflict in England at this time-period over how to be a 'true' Christian."]

Dave was definitely confused as well. How could he play this historical situation in England to maintain his deception? After all, he was going into the heart of religious orthodoxy, where any deviation from accepted doctrine was an invitation for torture and execution by the ever-vigilant Inquisition!

"Father," Dave began, addressing the Monk with feigned great respect, "King Charles is dealing with complex religious turmoil, trying to bring his people back to the true Church. After all, his wife is a good Catholic, is she not? I myself am evidence of his desire to set things right, sent here to find out the truth concerning Galileo. The professor's startling, claimed telescopic observations of the heavens are causing a stir in the universities of England."

The bald-headed man seemed to relax. Apparently, Dave had soothed his concerns.

"So they don't accept his hoax," the Priest nodded in satisfaction.

"Well..." Dave hesitantly replied, trying to not reveal his advanced knowledge but unwilling to condone willful ignorance. Also, he was genuinely curious as to what this lower-level official of the Catholic hierarchy thought of the matter. "Using copies of Galileo's new, powerful telescope they have confirmed some of his heavenly sightings."

That was true. Dave's knowledge of the science of the times was excellent. Galileo wasn't operating in a vacuum. By the time of his trial other scientists around the world had confirmed his main conclusions.

"Oh, like what?" the Monk asked, apparently interested.

"Well, the Royal Academy reports that the moons circling Jupiter that Galileo discovered actually exist...also the phases of the planet Venus—which seem to argue that Jupiter and Venus are not fixed in the sky but circle the sun...plus there are spots that appear and then regress upon the sun's surface and..."

"All *lies!*" the Priest suddenly shouted, waking up the elderly woman next to Dave who jerked upright in her seat. "The Holy Church has determined from the Holy Scriptures that Earth without a doubt is at the center of Creation—*around* which the Sun, Stars, and all other heavenly bodies revolve! And those divine heavenly bodies are *unchanged* and *pristine*, not spotted like a diseased apple!"

"The Bible says this?" Dave politely asked, struggling to hold his temper in check.

"In the *Book of Joshua* God commanded the sun to stand still, not the Earth!" the Priest haughtily replied. "And there are several other passages that allude to Earth being stable while the sun moves in the heavens!"

"So *must* those verses be understood completely literally? Could not they be *symbolic* of..."

"Do you not have *eyes* in your head, Sir?" the fat Monk angrily retorted. "Look up! Is not the sun even now moving down toward the West and will quickly sink out of sight? And the moon and all the stars do the same! Anyone can see with their own two eyes that Earth is at the center of Creation—around which the sun, moon, and stars circle! Are you a fool who can't trust the evidence of your own eyes? Or are you something even worse...a deceitful *Agent of Satan?*"

Dave felt his temper flaring. After all, he himself was a modern Ph.D. scientist. He did not tolerate blind fools lightly—especially those that accused *him* of being a fool! This pompous Monk was simply selecting evidence that seemed to agree with his religious doctrine while ignoring anything negative.

To Dave it was the worst sort of religious arrogance.

And yet, the complete his mission, Dave knew he had to hold his anger in check.

"I assure you, Father, I am not an enemy of the Bible. And, yes, what you stated is indeed an official teaching of the Church," Dave carefully agreed, desperately trying not to yell at the man. "But I've heard that Galileo himself agrees that the Holy Scripture never errs—though he says that men may, from time to time, misinterpret the..."

"*Lies!*" the Priest yelled out again, causing the young boy next to him to duck deeper beneath his cloak. The startled noble woman likewise cringed backward. And the fat church cleric was now getting red in the face! "It is *not* mere men that interpret the Scriptures, but *Holy Men of God* who are trained and guided by the Holy Spirit! To say that *they* are in error is even *worse* than saying that the Scripture errs. To question their understanding of God's Holy Words is to put an axe to the roots of the Church. It undermines not just the Church's Authority but all of society! Our revered Institutions would crumble into chaos if heretics were allowed to spout their nonsense unopposed. Don't you agree?"

Dave was taken-aback by the Priest's vehemence. But he recognized it for what it was: a fear-driven ultra-conservative's rant. To this person, acknowledging new insights was not an interesting progression of learning, but a challenge to his entire worldview and self-identity.

Dave knew he should just shut up but felt he had to make a defense of science, no matter how tentative.

"Yes, but in ancient times believers felt that the Scriptures proved the world was *flat*—which the Church does not hold today as..."

The Priest disdainfully waved a fat hand in front of his face.

"That was long before the Holy Mother Church existed," he dismissed Dave's tentative observation. "Those were pre-Christ savages! Of course they had a limited understanding back then. But now we have the complete Scriptures and by it '*all that is necessary for life and godliness through the knowledge of Him who called us by his own glory and goodness*' he smugly quoted."

Dave saw that the fat priest was taunting him, which provoked an even deeper *rage* in Dave's heart.

"So you *don't* see God as revealed to man in the Holy Scriptures *plus* through our personal experiences *and* through Mother Nature?"

"Of course!" the fat priest snorted. "And that is exactly my point, young man. Truth does not contradict itself. So, by definition, our personal experiences and what we see in the world *must* agree with the Scriptures!"

"And, if they appear not to do so, then...?"

"Then of course it is the experiences or observations that are in error."

"Socrates says the opposite," Dave coldly ventured. "He even offers people to look through his telescope and see with their own eyes that..."

"I do not have to see what I *already* know to be completely true by my holy Faith!" the Priest seethed, almost foaming at the mouth. "That, sir, is the nature of Faith. Faith is '*the substance of things hoped for, the evidence of things not seen*'!" he quoted from the Bible. "Faith is that which gives ordinary people struggling with the trials of life the Hope to keep on going. Faith is that which proves the Resurrection of Christ, the existence of the Soul, and the truth of Heaven! Without Faith our people would just give up their higher aspirations and become savage animals, giving-in to their basest instincts."

Clearly this Monk was no casual Church adherent. He had a solid grasp of his side of the debate.

"Must Faith and the studies of Galileo be at odds with each other?" Dave asked, struggling to keep his words neutral, though he was fuming. He wanted to grab the smug priest and throttle him. "Surely they are two different but complimentary things. Galileo argues that mathematics, biology, and physics are not in the Bible but..."

"Yes, the Bible is not one of your 'science' books," the Priest seemingly reasonably agreed. "But where it *does* talk of the material world it is *always* correct!"

"Socrates says there is *no science at all* in the Bible or..."

"And that is why he is a *damned heretic* who must recant or be executed!" the Monk shouted loudly, causing a frightened gasp from the elderly woman seated next to Dave. "And I am getting a bad feeling that you are a *sympathizer* to this errant Professor. Am I correct?" the Priest accused him, narrowing his eyes.

Dave knew he'd gone too far. There was no reasoning with someone whose mind was already made up. It was a hopeless pursuit that only produced heated conflict.

"No...not at all!" Dave protested as he lifted his own hands palms-out in dismissal. "I am merely learning from *you* the proper arguments against his heresy. After all, that's why I am here. You make a persuasive case, Father. I very much appreciate your engagement on this subject. Thank you for your wisdom!"

The fat priest did not look convinced, but settled back in his seat.

"Well then..." he shrugged, reaching down to lovingly stroke the crucifix hanging about his stout neck. "I am happy to enlighten you, my son."

Dave gulped, leaning back in relief and looking out the window of the carriage. He dearly wanted to *strangle* the smug priest but dared not appear hostile. The carriage was now entering the heart of the most-conservative, intolerant Catholicism.

Outside, Dave saw they were now "clomping" past the ruins of the ancient *Roman Colosseum*. Its remaining high walls reached far above the carriage. The many arched entranceways were splendid. Its tumbled stones were the remains of the largest amphitheater of the Roman Empire, indeed what had been (when it was intact) one of the "seven wonders" of the world.

And it was also a tribute to the brutality of the Romans. They used it to stage spectacles where the common people cheered and clapped at Christians being tortured and killed, even eaten alive by wild animals. And now Rome was ruled by those very same Christians, who jealously guarded their own Authority with the same ferocity as had the Roman Emperors.

And Dave was here to convince Galileo to throw himself to the lions...

After his encounter with the vehement Monk, Dave was even more afraid that his task was impossible. If that was the level of willful, angry ignorance in a lowly Monk, how would the highest officials behave?

Dave suddenly understood the power of the Inquisition.

Even in the oppressive heat, Dave was chilled to his bones.

The ground beneath their feet was *fracturing!*

Dennis was scared as they walked back toward their camp. It was getting difficult to stand upright. He had to swing his tail around wildly to maintain his balance. It was dangerous to be walking out on the plain. It was so dark now that he couldn't see where large fissures were splitting the rocks open right in front of him!

But then the quake lessened.

"That was a bad one," George said, cradling the shirt-wrapped baby Sally in his arms. Besides swaddling her with his torn-apart shirt, George had also made her some rough diapers.

She'd fallen asleep on their stumbling, slow trek back to the camp. Her curly red-brown hair was in disarray. But she slumbered with the peace of an infant, her small mouth hanging slightly open.

A bit of drool dripped from the corner of her soft plump lips.

And she was snoring.

"We *must* find a way off of this world, and quickly!" Dennis growled in reply. He dropped the pile of flat crust-chunks as they staggered into their shelter. He'd hauled them to immediately feed the others in his starving crew. "With everything that's happening to the sun plus the gravity inversions, the planet is starting to break apart!"

"Yes, but we're still alive, somehow," George said. He tenderly placed the still-slumbering Baby Sally onto a pile of rags. Then he went around helping the slumped, barely alive Dinosapiens back onto their feet.

Astonished, they clustered around as he and Dennis gave them each a substantial slab of the food. They "crunched" and gulped the delicious chunks—as they "cooed" and gaped at the sleeping baby.

"How are the scavengers doing?" Dennis asked another of his Dinosapien crewmembers.

She was a smaller Dinosapien with large purple spots down her green back.

She wiped crumbs off her big dinosaur mouth as she pointed beside their lean-to out onto the plain. "See for yourself," she replied.

They were all talking in raspy English, out of deference to George whose human-shaped throat and mouth couldn't produce the high-pitched "clicks" and "snaps" of their native language.

"You've gotten half a shuttlecraft put back together, Joyce—excellent work!" Dennis heartily congratulated her. "Is the drive mechanism intact?"

He was excited. Maybe there was a way to escape!

"Yes it is. Even its integrated DE-generator is functional," Joyce said. "But, of course, there's no subspace accessibility. It's the same problem as before, when we tried to move the Obelisk to a place where we might tap-into subspace."

Dennis' heart sank. Of course...they had the same terrible problem: no way to access subspace!

"But if we could somehow find a place where the DE-generator *would* work, could the craft fly?"

"Amazingly, yes," Joyce nodded in the affirmative. "If we had power we could depart immediately. But it still lacks the necessary control units for guiding the craft. They were destroyed in the bombardment from the Harvester. We'd just go up into orbit and die from lack of air and heat. The outer plastic shell is broken. We can't project a shield around the ship. If we had the Duplicator working it would be easy to make the necessary repairs. But..." she left the rest unspoken.

She looked ruefully at the totally dead big square Duplicator sitting motionless beneath the canopy. It made a nice table to put things on, but otherwise was useless.

She gave it a quick, annoyed kick!

Yes, Dennis also found it *very* irritating. Here they had technology from their own advanced civilization, plus derivatives from the even-more-advanced Martian Snakes. And yet they were reduced to being savages hiding in a cave.

"Eeeeek!" Sally suddenly yelped, her big green eyes snapping open.

She hopped out of George's arms and toddled over to Joyce, looking up at the purple-spotted dinosapien. Then she laughed, scampered up Joyce's thick legs and scaly torso to perch on her elongated neck.

"Hey, the baby likes me!" Joyce grinned, reaching up a tender hand to make sure the happily chortling child didn't fall off.

"It's Sally," Dennis said, shaking his own big head in wonderment.

"Sally? Really?" Joyce said, reaching back to take the baby tenderly off her neck into her arms.

"We don't know how it happened," George said, now reaching out to retrieve the gurgling baby into his human arms. "But there's no doubt this is a reincarnation of our very own Sally."

Outside in the gathering darkness a storm was again forming.

Loud "THUDS" of gigantic lightning bolts were slamming into the mountains off in the distance.

"Oh, no...not again!" Dennis exclaimed, flinching from the bright FLASHES lighting-up the interior of their jerry-rigged shelter. "There's no way we can survive another one of those super-storms!"

Suddenly, Sally hopped out of George's arms and dashed out into the night...

—as big drops of acidic water started "spattering" down on top of their shelter!

"What? Get her!" George yelled out...

—as another bright FLASH lit-up the plain to reveal: baby Sally floating *up into the sky* with her little arms out like a little cherubic angel!

"What's she doing?" Joyce asked in amazement.

Dennis' heart nearly stopped beating when he saw the baby *intercept* a dazzling barrage of gigantic lightning bolts!

For a moment he thought she'd been incinerated.

And then she was back, running on her little legs up to the big Duplicator unit and *hugging* its flat surface.

"Toy!" she laughed loudly...as wave after wave of *shimmering blue energy* cascaded from her little body into the machine!

The Duplicator began to "hum" loudly...vibrating at a high pitch!

"Oh, good Lord," Dennis heard George gasp. "She rode gravity inversions out there to find where the lightning was fracturing the weakened subspace barrier—and gathered Dark Energy into her body! And now...?"

"—she's discharging it into the machine!" Dennis finished the thought, holding his arms out to motion everyone to stand back.

The massive energy being transferred through baby Sally was enough to fry any normal flesh-and-blood body.

But baby Sally was unharmed, releasing the machine to turn around and dash back out into the gathering storm!

"Sally!" George called-out to her, grabbing at her but missing.

"Let her be," Dennis ordered George. "She knows what she's doing better than any of us. Get what we need materialized from the energized Duplicator in order to get the shuttle working! We've got to get off this planet!"

Right outside their shelter, a sudden FISSURING cracked the rocks, knocking them all off their feet!

Dennis saw red-hot *LAVA* emerging from the split in the rocks!

"Hurry! Hurry!" he ordered them as they scrambled back up and clustered around the Duplicator. They quickly brought up its files, prioritizing the materialization of critical missing shuttle parts and controls. "I'll go look after Sally."

The increasingly bright lightning flashes revealed her soaring back up into the sky: now *surrounded* by a bright blue haze!

She was sucking in energy at the rare subspace access points at an astronomical rate, gleefully swooping down time after time to embrace her "toy"!

And soon she'd powered the Duplicator to materialize all the needed parts.

And then they were crowded into the small shuttlecraft—George, baby Sally and Dennis in the cockpit, with the rest of the Dinosapiens crammed into the small cargo-hold beneath.

"Here we go!" Dennis yelled out as he closed the overhead canopy then hit the activation sequences. If it all worked the craft would shoot straight for a low orbit around the planet.

They lifted off shakily, wobbling back and forth in the air. They were battered by pounding rain and gusts. And then Dennis breathed a sigh of relief as they *launched* straight up into the roiling black clouds!

All around them, crackling arms of gigantic lightning bolts flashed, just missing their small shuttlecraft...

—as they rocketed past the clouds into the stratosphere, looking down in horror to see the *entire planet shattering* beneath them!

—as great red *continents* of liquid *magma* burst *up* into the seas, turning the oceans into white steam as the *crust of the planet pealed back* and the *molten metallic core* protruded!

"That was too close," George gasped, closing his eyes.

He was hugging baby Sally close, who had fallen back asleep and was now snoring peacefully.

The small DE-generator in the shuttlecraft was now successfully accessing Dark Energy, generating an intact force-field around their cobbled-together small spaceship. Hopefully the shield would hold together. Otherwise they'd instantly die.

"She doesn't seem much concerned," Dennis laughed in weak relief, steering them up and away from the crumbling planet.

"So where do we go now?" George asked him.

"Well, I'd hoped that Sally would show us the way, somehow," Dennis grinned, looking at the happily snoring baby.

"She has an internal Dark Energy battery," George gulped, "but perhaps not a star-chart?"

"That's ok," Dennis softly replied, not wanting to disturb her sleep. She deserved her rest. She'd saved them. Not only did she bring them food, energy, and a new enthusiasm she'd given them direction. She was a true little savior. "I think I know where to go."

"And where's that?" George asked.

"My instruments are detecting residual radiation from the Harvester, *neutrino bursts* from their large subspace drive," he grimly replied. "It's linear enough to give us a fix. We're going after the other Sally-humans!"

"Makes sense," George nodded. "Since they didn't come back to help us, it can only mean..."

"—that they need *our* help!" Dennis finished the thought. He now had a clear goal. He had the means to achieve the mission. And he had a plan.

They were on their way.

"But even if we catch up to them, what can we do then?" George sighed softly beside him. "There's just a few of us crammed into a tiny craft—against the evil Creature that caused this entire new Universe to exist in the first place?"

Dennis was not so fatalistic.

"If that monster is as screwed up as this Universe, then *he's* the one in trouble!" he replied, narrowing his orange eyes in determination. "Beside, we have something that he certainly doesn't."

"What's that?" George asked.

"Love!" Dennis crisply replied, looking at the gently gurgling baby. "If that little kid isn't some sort of expression of Divine Love, then I don't know what is."

George nodded in agreement.

Dennis determinedly steered their little spacecraft along the faint neutrino trail.

He barely even noted when the sun behind them suddenly *splintered* along a thousand black lines—then *collapsing* inward!

It was a cold, cruel Universe...but it was warm there in the cockpit with his friends.

"Sally is on our side," George grinned. "We've got *baby*-power!"

"Amen, George," Dennis laughed. "Amen to that!"

He only hoped that their brave words were true.

He'd seen into the heart of the Monster and didn't like the view.

Sometimes looking too closely is a mistake.

Chapter 19

<u>INQUISITION</u>

It seems like such an innocuous activity
"Inquiring" into the facts of the matter
As if the "Facts" were real things
Instead of just imagined constructs
Cobbled upon outward appearances
Hiding a multitude of deeper Realities
Unseen, unsubstantiated, and ignored
Giving the illusion of Control and Safety
How sad those that tried to define God
Stuffing His Essence into their own image
In their own tiny thoughts and feeble actions
Deriving some little satisfaction and security
From their ability to dominate over other people
Seeking to terrify them into meek submission
Who, like them, were also unknown mysteries
Tangled in a web of an unsolvable puzzle
Seeing not even as far as to the end
Of their own turned-up noses...

Eashoa's Lament, 19:3-6

Periscus walked from the landed spacecraft expecting a hero's welcome.

Instead, he encountered a *wall of gunfire* and *sizzling energy-blasts!*

"By all the gods, what's happening?" he gasped as he dove behind protecting barriers.

The spaceport of Capital City was in chaos. Buildings were burning. Explosions were going off all around him. He saw pitched battles occurring between humans and Dinosapiens, Automatons and Dinosapiens, and even Automatons versus Automatons!

Suddenly Periscus felt himself wrapped-up in hard muscle, squashed, unable to breathe!

There were blue-white coils *crushing* him around his arms and chest!

"Agathe!" Periscus just managed to feebly gasp out. "Why...are you...doing...this?"

His vision blurred as he was dragged off behind a maintenance shed and down a ramp into an underground hanger.

"I'm sorry, friend Periscus," she said as she released him from her coils and flowed over to the side.

Gasping and shaking, he slowly sat up.

They were in a dark chamber. Vehicles were lined up around him. Outside, he could still hear screams and loud blasts. Here, they seemed safe...at least for the moment.

"The Council of Elders is revolting against your King, friend Periscus," Agathe spoke in Periscus' brain. "Now that the threat from the Spike-Ships is successfully neutralized, the Elders see no further need for humans to be in charge. The robots were ordered to detain all humans, immediately *killing* any that resisted."

"But...if that's true, then why are Dinosapiens battling Automatons?" Periscus asked, both confused and dismayed.

"It seems that our robotic helpers were neither as subservient nor as unintelligent as they were initially designed to be," Agathe sighed in Periscus' mind. "They've quietly been upgrading their own physical and mental capabilities. Now some are siding with you humans and others with the Council. They have weapons and are even fighting amongst themselves!"

Periscus painfully got to his feet. He was bruised and battered from being thrown around on the pavement, but didn't feel any broken bones.

"So then we humans have contaminated all the rest of you?" he bitterly laughed. "*You've* become just like *us*. You want power and control!"

"No, Periscus," she protested. "That is not our nature. We Snakes see no use for needless conflict or wars. It is far better to cooperate and help each other than fight over petty concerns."

"And do the Lizards agree with you?" he asked, looking about for a way to exit the hanger other than via the dangerous entrance ramp.

"Well..." she paused, considering. "It is true that I've been helping you with the fleet for most of the past several years and largely out of touch with the deliberations of the Council. But the Dinosapiens have always been very cooperative. Of course, we are much older and wiser...though the Black Birds thought they were even smarter! Fortunately, they left the Council when we decided to go to war with the Spike-Ships and..."

"Ah, *there* it is!" Periscus scoffed. "That's always been the way. I saw it time and again in the Athenian 'democracy' where all men were supposedly equal. In reality, some were *more* 'equal' than others! You consider *me* to be *your* inferior, don't you?" he angrily yelled, his voice echoing back to him in the underground hanger.

"Well, of course you are," she said, flowing nervously about Periscus in a circle as continuing loud explosions outside gave evidence of the fierce fighting. "Knowledge and experience do count. And, as a race, we are ancient—while you are barely down from swinging in the trees! We Mars-derived Snakes should, by rights, make all the final decisions."

"Then why did you need me?" Periscus snapped at her. "Wasn't it because in *some* ways *I* knew better than you?"

Above them on the tarmac, a gigantic detonation rocked the underground hanger. Periscus was almost thrown off his feet, but kept upright by grabbing onto Agathe's twisting neck. Pieces of cracked concrete rained down on his head.

"We've got to get out of here!" Agathe fearfully whined, ignoring Periscus' last question. "We'll be either trapped in here or crushed if we stay!"

"Stop!" Periscus said, tightly holding onto her neck with both his arms to keep her from slithering away. "Answer me truthfully, Agathe—why did you save me when I walked out of the spaceship? Why are you still trying to save me? You could just as easily have kept on crushing me when you grabbed me. I'd have blacked out and died if you'd kept that pressure up for just one more minute!"

Her big snake head was lolling back and forth as if she were in pain.

"I...I..."

"Yes? Answer me!"

"I...suppose that I...thought of you as a friend, not as an enemy...perhaps even with...compassion?"

Periscus' rage at Agathe dwindled and he was left feeling truly humbled.

"And I myself, Agathe..." he began before pausing.

"Yes?" she gently coaxed him to continue.

"I have grown fond of you also," he admitted, "even though I was getting ready to replace you with a human."

"I knew that."

"You did?"

"Your kind but arrogant manner toward me was unmistakable," she gently replied. "And your enthusiasm to continue the violence out into the stars was also evident. You and I both knew that this was not something that I or my Snake colleagues would support."

"So...?"

"So I'd been ordered to kill you once we safely returned to Earth," she stated. "This was horrific to me—totally foreign to our whole species! But I thought the Council knew best. I was prepared to follow the orders...but then couldn't go through with it. The Council decided it was regrettably necessary not just to contain you humans, but exterminate you in one fell blow. Those rounded up alive by the Automatons—whether true or pseudo-humans—were then to be euthanized quickly and painlessly as a group. They were all deemed too dangerous to keep alive. But I realized it wasn't just a regrettable execution of renegade criminals, but genocide! It was *unthinkable!*"

Stronger, ever-louder blasts were occurring outside.

The whole concrete structure trembled around them.

"Then your dilemma on what to do with us humans caused the rift in the Council that..."

"Exactly right," she sorrowfully said. "The Dinosapiens still saw uses for you primitive humans. They parted ways with the Snakes who only wanted an end your threat once and for all."

"Then it's a civil war out there?"

"Yes, between us Snakes and our Automatons—versus the Dinosapiens and their Automatons...and all of them pitted against you humans and your Automatons!"

"We still have Automatons obeying us?"

"It seems they've obtain 'free will' and some still chose to follow you."

Periscus bitterly laughed.

"Sounds like all wars," Periscus he sadly shrugged. "There are always alliances forming this way and that. One day your friends are fighting alongside of you and the next they're trying to put a knife in your back. Hah! It's an old, old story."

"It's so stupid," she added, "well beneath the dignity of a matured species like..."

"Your people wanted to kill us humans!" he snapped at her again. Then he cringed as more cement fragments rained down on his head. "It's a fear-based reaction. You are biological, just like me. You're afraid of anything that might threaten your security and survival, just like me. I'm amazed, though, that the robots also follow this instinct. Does that mean that all intelligent beings are driven by fear?"

A burst of *red flames* swept down the ramp, driving them deeper into the darkness of the hanger. A big hunk of the chamber fell inward. A cloud of debris surged up around Periscus.

The ramp to the surface was now completely blocked.

He could barely breathe. They had to get out of there!

"For a simple fisherman, as you so-often claim to be, you can be rather philosophical, friend Periscus," Agathe said as she curled up close to his side. He, in turn, hugged her scaly body.

"Ah...some of that damn Socrates' thinking over the years has rubbed off on me," he grimaced. "And I admit that I am afraid of many things. But, strangely, I've never been afraid of you, Agathe. Even though you look like the one thing that strikes the most terror into us talking, upright-walking monkeys—poisonous snakes—you've always been beautiful to me."

"So what do we do now?" she asked—her long, scaly body trembling beneath his arms.

He thought for a moment, considering their options. His ambition to captain a human fleet of lethal stellar battleships was in ruins. The surface of the planet was being decimated not by aliens but their own hands. There was no way of telling who was friend or enemy. And who knew what remained of his beloved Valley?

But then he realized their only possible course of present action.

"We go find Socrates," he firmly replied. "That clever shark always has a plan. I'm sure this rebellion against his iron-fisted rule didn't catch him off guard. Maybe with you present we can figure out a compromise, a 'peace-plan' if you will, to which all sides can agree."

"I doubt it," she sighed deeply. "But it's better than mindlessly slaughtering each other. I agree to give it a try!"

"Then we've got to find a way deeper into the city," he grimaced. "We sure can't go out to the surface unarmed, even if we could dig out of all this rubble. You and I both would be blown apart by the warring factions!"

"If you need a weapon, perhaps that sharp length of metal will help you," she added, flowing over to where a sword-like piece of debris lay.

"Good idea, Agathe," he said, limping over to it and grabbing it. "This won't do anything against beamer weapons, but I'm happy to have something in my hands. Now how do we get to Socrates?"

"There's a network of service tunnels beneath the city," she said, heading off deeper into the darkness. Periscus trailed along blindly beside her, one hand firmly placed on her elevated neck.

"Then lead on, my lady," he chivalrously replied. "If I know that rat Socrates, he'll be safe in the deepest, darkest hole."

Periscus tried to sound upbeat to Agathe. But he was shaking inside. His whole new world was turned upside down. One moment he was the Admiral of a victorious Space-Navy and the next he was running for his life!

He felt like the Generals at the Battle of Arginusae, who in 406 B.C. failed to save the survivors of their own sinking ships. This was because they chose instead to continue pursuing their defeated Spartan enemies. But instead of being praised as heroes when they returned to Greece for their great naval victory, the public sentiment at not saving their drowning sailors caused the Generals to be tried and condemned to death!

Maybe the Snakes were right. Maybe humans were just perverse, primitive, vile monkey-creatures that deserved to be exterminated. After all, what was the grand ambition that had filled Periscus with so much pride—to conquer the Universe? How laughable and impossible was that? And yet, it surely had taken hold of his imagination.

Periscus knew he had to try to survive. That was part of his makeup. And he knew he had to do everything he could do to try and save his family, friends, and fellow humans. That was his duty. And the Snakes and Lizards weren't actually bad, just scared. He had to try and find a way to save them also.

But Periscus knew without any doubt what was really at the heart of this whole insane, perverse conflict.

It was that pompous rat *Socrates* wanting to be the "Philosopher-King" of their wonderful paradise. It was he who started this whole mess! It was Socrates that ordered him to Mars, triggering that probe. Without that aggressive action it might have been eons before the Spike-Ship aliens returned.

As Periscus followed Agathe into a small, tight service tunnel, he was determined to stop the madness—once and for all!

Socrates had to die.

And Periscus was just the one to put a stake into that monster's heart.

He happily hefted the sharp metal spike in his right hand.

Socrates had been judged and found guilty. And Periscus was the eager executioner.

As Dave stiffly climbed out of the carriage, he kept a surreptitious eye upon the fat Monk.

Indeed, it was lucky he did.

The carriage came to a stop right outside the main entrance to *Saint Peter's Basilica*. The great columns towering up beside Dave reminded him very much of the Parthenon in ancient Athens. As such, it was a monument to the power and affluence of Renaissance Rome as much as it was to Christianity. Certainly the Jesus that Dave

knew as a post-apocalyptic warrior would have laughed at the preten-
tiousness. But Dave admitted to himself that the high circular dome
looming above him, topped by a plain white cross, was awesome. He
was at the center of Christianity at the peak of its power—even though
it was greatly troubled by "heretical" emerging scientists and hated
Protestants.

And glancing behind him as he walked away, Dave saw the fat
Monk animatedly talking with a palace guard, excitedly gesturing in
his direction!

Yes, "David da Londra" was being targeted as a suspicious Gali-
leo-sympathizer.

He'd never succeed in his urgent mission if he himself was arrest-
ed.

"Custodian, can we make a change of appearances, please?" he
spoke in a whisper so that the other people walking around him on
the street couldn't hear.

"You were too open with that Monk, Dr. King," the Custodian
snidely replied in Dave's earbud. "Surely at this last minute it isn't too
much to ask that you not to sabotage our operation with your loose
tongue?"

"He got me angry!" Dave grated quietly. "I messed up! Can you
please change my appearance, *please?*"

"Duck into some opening."

Dave did as ordered, turning into a narrow alleyway. He felt that
familiar tingling coming over his skin—then walked back out.

He glanced back to see the Priest and palace guard looking about
in confusion. To all appearances, "David da Londra" had vanished.

Good, he'd outwitted them.

"What do I look like now?" Dave whispered to the Custodian, not
seeing any close windows in which to catch his reflection.

"You're a 17th Century Roman soldier," the earbud replied. "To
everyone around you, you are wearing a metal helmet and breast-
plate, a red cape, white clothes, and boots. Plus you have a gold-
handled sword in a scabbard at your side. No one will want to tangle
with you! But don't get too cozy with other soldiers. I don't have in
my databanks any details as to the proper insignia and such, just the
general appearance. They'll quickly spot you as a fraud. And don't

try to use the sword either, as it's illusionary and would flicker-out on impact."

Dave was happy that beneath the new illusion he still had on his thick coat, with the energy-handgun safely tucked-away in the large inner pocket. Now he was grateful that everyone stank, because he was certainly sweating in the heavy coat. But it carried and hid his gun. He hadn't dared try to use it, but it was warm to the touch. It wasn't near as hot as it was when he'd brought down Cheyenne Mountain, but it probably was still capable of crumbling the Vatican into rubble!

"So where is Galileo?" Dave asked. The sunlight was fast-fading in the West. The Dome of the Basilica above him was now bathed in soft yellow light, making it look like it was made out of pure gold.

"It is not far from here—at the Palace of the Inquisition," the Custodian replied. "My databases of your Dimension state that Galileo, on this exact date, is being held there in a small room. He's already made his defense before his inquisitors. He failed to convince them that the Copernican theories as presented in his latest book '*The Dialogues*' were mere rhetorical arguments. It is certain that his book will be banned. The only question remaining is his personal punishment. The leniency or harshness of his penalty depends upon him publicly denouncing his heretical views."

"And that is scheduled for tomorrow."

"Yes."

"So this is our very last chance to change future history."

"Yes."

Since the light was quickly fading, their chance of being discovered and apprehended was diminishing. Dave was very hungry and exhausted from the long ride. He looked for a tavern to get something to eat and drink.

"Then we should try to get inside the Palace after regular working hours," Dave nodded to himself. "For such a high profile prisoner, we must show up decisively but unexpectedly in order to gain entrance, don't you think? So we still have time to kill."

"Well...maybe," the Custodian hesitantly agreed, "but I still don't know how we're going to gain entrance. The *Palace of the Inquisition* is well-guarded. Of course few want to gain entrance."

"That's true. Most would want to get *out* of such a horrible place."

"It's still well guarded."

"We'll figure something out."

"That's not much of a plan for the future of mankind to rest up-on!" the Custodian snidely replied.

"It's all I've got," Dave shrugged.

"Well, assuming we can somehow get an audience with Galileo, at least we're prepared for that," the Custodian glumly replied. "But to do so, we first have to get into the Palace."

"I know, I know!" Dave irritably shot-back. "Well...let's think on it while eating dinner."

"You have food?" the Custodian snorted. "I can conjure you up a hamburger, but I doubt it'll have much nutritive value."

Dave ignored the snide comment. Indeed, he'd been keeping an eye out for a suitable eatery serving real food there in the heart of the bustling city.

"Ah! *There's* where we can go for wine and food," Dave sighed happily, seeing common people entering and exiting an establishment on a side street. Since he now appeared to be an ordinary soldier, he didn't want to go into a place frequented by noblemen or church officials. At a swanky place he'd draw attention to himself by being out of place. Here, no one would look twice at him.

As outside street lamps were being lit, Dave walked into the establishment. Inside, regulars in common clothing clustered at different wooden tables, laughing and drinking. A group in a corner was playing soft but lively music on horns and violins. A few people were drunkenly dancing. Dave opted for a small table in a shadowy corner where he could do his muttering to the Custodian in private.

"Hi, big boy," a young, pretty waitress asked. She had on a plain brown dress down to her feet with a white apron tied neatly about her waist. Her brown hair was short. Her eyes were saucy—as if she was used to getting good tips from visiting soldiers. "You're not local. Are you here for the Abjuration?"

"Right," Dave nodded. "I'm here with my buddies to help keep order, not that it's needed—just as a precaution."

"Won't be no trouble tomorrow," she giggled. "Nobody cares about that old Professor and his crazy ideas. They say he wrote some book that's to be banned. So what? Only a few noblemen can read books. What's the point?"

Dave got the message. She was a commoner with little or no schooling. But that was standard for this century, particularly for women. Only a few of the wealthiest girls were educated—and that in "womanly" affairs.

"So what can I get 'cha?" she asked.

"A bottle of your best wine, please—plus what's good for dinner?"

"The stew's good. The vegetables are fresh. The meat's from local chickens. Quite tasty! Plus all the bread you can eat."

"That sounds great. Bring me a big bowl."

"Coming right up," she smiled brightly, prancing away.

"Nice girl," Dave mumbled to the Custodian.

"Don't get too drunk, Dr. King," the voice from his earbud coldly warned him. "I fear you are going to need all your wits about you if you are somehow to convince Galileo to place himself upon the sacrificial altar."

"Yes...you're right," Dave gulped, breathing deeply to clear his head. "My addictive genes are kicking in. I could happily chug down that whole bottle of wine, plus a couple more! But I'll drink only what I need for liquid replacement—no more, I promise."

The music was pleasant. The chatter from the other tables was lulling. Dave wanted above anything a good meal and then a room within which to sleep the night away. But he was finally in Rome, at the critical moment. He had to suppress his personal desires. He was there at another *tipping-point* of history! As the Custodian reminded him, he had to be sharp tonight.

"So...you've never told me why you're being so cooperative," Dave mused.

"Am I overly cooperative?" the Custodian snidely replied.

"Yes, actually you are," Dave said, waiting patiently for his food to arrive. "Instead of merely doing what I've asked you've done more. In fact, you refer now to 'our' mission instead of 'your' quest. I appreciate your help, by the way—very much in fact—but I'm curious as to why?"

The Custodian was silent for a minute as if considering what to say.

"Sally ordered me to assist you in every way," he quietly replied.

"*Sally* wants me to change the past?" Dave asked, surprised. He'd thought that she'd given him the Cube just to help him make his way through his Dimension to deliver covertly the super-gun to Cheyenne Mountain. He'd assumed that having the Custodian with him when he was thrown into the past was just a lucky accident. But, apparently, it wasn't.

"Yes, I was reporting to her across the Dimensional-divide all the time in which you were parallel to her," he added. "She knew of your inquiry into the differences between the societies in her Dimension versus yours. And she knew that you were going to fall into the Portal."

"How could she possibly know all that?" Dave asked, amazed!

"She'd done it many times before, in a time-loop," the Custodian answered. "She didn't know what would happen to you once you entered the Portal, but hoped you might have yet another chance to alter the timeline of your Dimension."

"So this Sally also wanted to prevent Judgment Day from happening?"

"Not just for your world, but hers also," he replied.

"Hers?"

"She has big plans for her world and doesn't want them interrupted by either God or you," the small voice in Dave's ear answered.

"But...if my suspicions are correct...this Sally originally came from *my* world," Dave stated, confused. "For God's sake she was born in Oklahoma. She's *my* world's Sally. Why would she be interested in your Empire-dominated world?"

"Yes, you are correct in your assumption. But in your world she was nothing," the Custodian calmly replied. "Even when she was kidnapped to work on the top-secret Dark Energy project for the military, she was just a 'hired hand'—looked down upon for her lack of formal education, even though she was a mathematical genius."

"But...what is she looking to accomplish in your other Dimension?"

"Everything," the Custodian succinctly replied.

"Everything?" Dave gasped. "But to do that she'd have to be..."

"—in charge, yes," the Custodian completed Dave's thought.

"But—in a world ruled by authoritative governments...?"

"She plans to become Dictator of the first planet-spanning *Global Empire*—subjecting all the various existing competing Empires to her absolute will."

"What the hell?" Dave gasped, stunned by Sally's ambition. "Are you sure?"

"We did extensive planning together. I did all the research into the scenario that she requested of me. And if she can somehow escape the time-loop, I believe she has a 50:50 chance of becoming the world's first Absolute Ruler."

"But...didn't she tell me once that the various existing Empires were bitterly opposed to each other and...?"

"Yes, it may be a bloodbath of epic proportions that..."

"I can't believe Sally—even that *bitch* Sally of my world—would do such a thing!"

"She is indeed capable of it, I assure you," the Custodian replied. "She is one *bad* 'bitch'."

"So helping me you were just obeying her orders?"

"Well...I do have a certain intellectual curiosity."

The food arrived, carried on a wooden platter by the cheerful waitress.

Dave thanked her and started eating, all the time thinking furiously. This revelation about Sally was very disturbing. She was apparently willing to kill thousands or millions of people to become the worst example of the thing that she hated the most, intolerant Authority? *Really?*

It just didn't make any sense to Dave.

Even though he trusted the Custodian to give a cold, calculating evaluation on any subject, Dave didn't know if the spiffy machine-intelligence knew what he was saying. Perhaps Sally was just fantasizing. Or maybe Sally was joking with the Custodian?

But Dave knew he had to put that all aside. He had to focus on the immediate task.

This was his last chance to save both human Dimensions from the impending Judgment Day! His general plan made sense, but the details were fuzzy or missing. They were so close, yet so far. He had to

figure out the immediate problem! How could they get into the Palace of Inquisition without drawing attention to themselves?

But for the moment there was hot, steaming food—a lot of it!
Dave concentrated on the thick stew in ample proportions, plus fresh-
baked bread. It was all delicious. And though the wine was tart it
went down smoothly. Dave was tempted to eat and drink far too
much.

But he was very disturbed by what the Custodian had just revealed to him. Even though he should be concentrating on how to
sneak in and confront Galileo, he was both fascinated and horrified by
this new aspect of Sally.

"So...*I'm* part of her plan for world-domination?" Dave muttered
to himself as he continued munching hungrily at the feast.

"You are a key part," the Custodian replied. "You must change the
timeline in your world in order to delay God's Wrath in *both* Dimensions."

"But what if I—what if *we*—fail?" he asked.

"She has a back-up plan," the little voice matter-of-factly replied
in Dave's ear.

"And that's...?"

"You there! Come with us!" an advancing *Vatican guard* shouted,
surging up to Dave's table and grabbing him roughly by the arm.

"What...?"

It wasn't just one but a dozen of the guards, armed to the teeth
with knifes, swords, and spears!

They jerked Dave away from the table, knocking his dishes of food
to the floor—dragging him to the door as the waitress screamed in
fear and the other patrons scattered.

"What's this all about?" Dave asked them, struggling to get free
but failing.

"The Cardinal wants to see you, now!" the burly soldier holding
Dave loudly declared.

"*What* Cardinal? I'm just a simple soldier who's..."

"Cardinal Francesco Barberini, the *Chief Inquisitor*," the guard
proclaimed. "We are here to arrest you. You've been accused of being
an Agent of Satan!"

"What? No!"

And then the guard leaned in close to Dave's ear, speaking in a low voice that only Dave could hear: "We know that you're not just a 'simple soldier'—*Dr. David King*."

Dave was shocked speechless.

"Oh...hell," Dave whispered to himself, ceasing his struggles and letting them drag him along.

This was bad. This was *real* bad.

If they looked at him closely they'd find all the evidence they needed to condemn him as an Agent of Satan.

Chapter 20

SPEAK OF THE DEVIL

You persisted in blaming the "Devil"
When the actual Demon resided in you
A manifestation of your inward genetics
Expressed without censure or restraint
Clothed in "I like it" or "I want it" or "Gimme"
With little or no thought to guiding Principles
The Five Pillars of true Godly Creativity neglected
That all of your thoughts, words, and actions
Be REASONABLE, USEFUL, RESPECTFUL
BEAUTIFUL and HONORABLE
An enabling "operational definition"
Detailing Heavenly Love, Faith, and Obedience
All thrown out the window by that cruel Satan:
That Unholy Trinity tormenting your confused life
Mother Nature, Lady Luck, and Human Frailty
Conspiring to confuse, misdirect, and destroy;
Too difficult for most to struggle against
Much easier to just accept the inevitable
Without question or complaint
Or, conversely, a few rebelling
Not excising their guts
But elevating their hearts.

Eashoa's Lament, 20:45-50

Dennis was scared.

The elation of their escape from the dying planet was fast fading.

Now, he was uncertain where to go. The energy trail of neutrinos he'd been following split into three different, distinct directions. The Harvester couldn't have gone three ways. Likely some anomalies were interfering with the true path.

If he chose the wrong trail in his next subspace jump, they might end up in a place where the connection to Dark Energy in this uncertain Universe was too weak to power their small shuttlecraft spaceship.

In that circumstance they'd be stranded in deep space with nothing to do but drift until they died.

"Pretty!"

"What?" Dennis started, jerking his attention from the instruments to George.

It was baby Sally, waking up from her happy slumber in George's lap. She was pointing to the three-dimensional display on the viewscreen. She was clearly enraptured with the glowing *yellow haze* that went off to their right, tracing it with a pudgy little thumb.

"Alright, Sally," Dennis toothily grinned. He reached over to the copilot chair to pat the gurgling baby on her fluffy head where she sat cradled in George's arms. "You're our pilot now. We'll follow that particular trail."

"Are we out of the planetary system?" George asked, yawning. He'd been dozing off as well while cradling the baby.

"We're several jumps beyond it now," Dennis replied as he carefully fed in new coordinates to the jump engine. If they went too far they'd overshoot wherever the Harvester was and be lost in deep space. If they undershot then they'd fall behind.

Dennis was inching them along the trail in small jumps, more fearful of getting lost than falling behind. But now he decided to try another strategy—to link the jump computer to the trail itself. He'd instruct the quantum computer to follow the strongest signal even if it should again split into different threads. Theoretically, it should keep them in subspace long enough to catch up to the Harvester in one long jump.

If not, they'd be hopelessly lost in subspace, never able to emerge at all.

It would truly be hell.

"Sally's getting hungry," George said, shifting her in his arms and looking at her small face that now was twisted up unhappily. "Can you send a message down to the cargo-hold for Joyce to duplicate up a bottle of milk for us?"

"It's already done," Dennis said, motioning to the hatch behind them. There sitting beside the hatch were a couple nippled bottles of white milk. "But our energy levels are dropping. Something's interfering with our DE-generator's function. I think that even subspace is becoming corrupted by the perverted laws of physics in this abominable place."

"What do you think will be the ultimate result?" George asked as he reached over to snag one of the bottles for baby Sally.

"Well, it's all speculation of course...but I'm afraid this entire Universe is coming apart at its seams."

"Jesus Christ!" George gasped as he gave the bottle to baby Sally. She grabbed it, popped the nipple into her mouth, and began sucking lustily. "So it's not just the planet we escaped from or its dying sun that's...?"

"I think this entire Universe is going to collapse in upon itself," Dennis sighed. "If I'm right—and I hope I'm not—then it doesn't matter if we catch up with the Harvester or not. We'll all be crushed into subatomic particles when this evil place implodes in upon itself."

"Maybe Sally can...?" George began as after a few sucks she now peevishly pushed the bottle's nipple to the side, moving her head stubbornly away from it.

"Who knows what she might eventually do?" Dennis shrugged his reptilian shoulders. "All we can do right now is proceed forward and hope for the best."

"Sally, what do you want to eat?" George said, putting the bottle down beside his copilot chair.

"Cookie!" she laughed, clapping her small hands together.

"Well, why not?" George laughed. "Dennis, please call down to the cargo-hold for them to..."

"Hang on, George," Dennis warned him. "We're jumping!"

The interior of the shuttlecraft turned *inside-out*, the discrete stars winking out into a *rainbow whirl*...which continued on and on, spinning around them hypnotically!

"Wheeeee!" baby Sally laughed, lifting up her chubby little arms in the air.

"This...is strange," Dennis gasped. "It's like a fusion between near lightspeed travel and subspace...probably because the quantum computer is now doing a series of millions of overlapping micro-jumps...but one way or another we're going to finally end this journey."

"How...long...until...we're...out?" George asked in discrete gasps.

But Dennis had no answer. He'd set the quantum computer to follow the strongest trail to its end. Now there was nothing to do but hope it wouldn't take too long.

Otherwise, not only would they be stranded in limbo forever—but being in subspace for an extended period would drive them all completely *insane*.

Periscus and Agathe emerged from the tunnel into the sub-basement of Socrates' Royal Palace.

It had taken them several hours of trudging through a series of dark tunnels, getting lost at several points along the way and having to backtrack.

Their journey had been incredibly frightening. Only dim emergency lights punctuated the darkness. Hordes of rats ran squeaking under their feet. Slimy water was pooling ever deeper, through which he had to wade and at times swim.

Along the way, they felt the earth above them repeatedly *shudder* from mammoth explosions. The war being raged was vicious and quick. Periscus knew that his sons in orbit around the planet wouldn't take kindly to the extermination campaign being perpetuated by the Snakes down on the surface. His orbiting sons would fire their beamers upon Capital City and the other outposts of the Snakes. Likely the Lizards were targets as well.

But Periscus was most afraid of what the Automatons might do. Agathe's news that the robots had broken up into factions was chilling. The unemotional metal men would likely fight with deadly accuracy and persistence against whatever enemy they perceived. And there were many of the Automatons up in orbit...crewing even the spaceships captained by Periscus' young sons.

This would not be a quick coup or strike where exhausted foes would retreat or regroup. This was a fight to the death, stopping only when one side obliterated the other. But, according to Agathe, there were at least three sides battling, maybe more. What was happening up above Periscus' and Agathe's heads might well be the end of mankind...even the end of intelligent life upon Earth!

"We should be right below the throne chamber's underground safe-room," Agathe spoke in Periscus' head. "If Socrates is anywhere, this will be the place. It is highly shielded. So it's probably still intact. Are you sure you want to proceed? It's likely that the King will be well guarded."

"Not against me," Periscus said in a low voice, going up a narrow set of stairs to a closed doorway. Expecting it to be locked he was surprised when it easily opened.

Above, the *light of day* unexpectedly streamed down, caused Periscus to narrow his eyes, allowing them to adjust.

When they did, he just stood there as Agathe flowed out behind him. They were surrounded by huge piles of smoking debris!

What once was a deep underground safe-room was now open to the outside. The protective dome above was ajar. Outside, Periscus could see the melted, broken spires of the once-beautiful crystalline city. Black pillars of smoke rose up everywhere into the sky. Even more shocking, Automatons lay in piles around Periscus, blown apart and motionless.

It was surprisingly quiet.

"Good...you've come...took you long enough," Periscus heard a soft voice rattling over in a dark corner.

Agathe jerked back in surprise but Periscus eagerly pounced forward. He jumped over a pile of broken girders and blown-off robot limbs—holding out his "sword" to confront...

Socrates!

The King sat upon what had been an impregnably shielded, floating Throne. Now it was smashed into the corner, twisted and useless. The huge bulk of Socrates' loathsome body obscured most of it.

"Socrates?" Periscus verbalized, shocked by his appearance. Over the last several years he'd not seen his old nemesis, only received orders from him as the Fleet was being assembled in orbit.

Periscus saw that the once-great Sovereign was now a *thousand-pound lump* of quivering fat! The regal clothes that once hid his jelly like bulk were mostly torn off or burned away. He looked like a giant *slug*, with only a narrow red slit for a mouth. There were dark pits out of which his eyes peered like scared mice from holes in a wall. Even his nose was obscured by rolls of fat.

His hands just barely protruded from the shaking bulk on both sides, like carnival hands from a grotesquely blown-up balloon-man. His crown was gone, revealing a hairless dome upon which beads of sweat slowly formed before dripping off greasily to each side.

"It's...good...to see you now...old friend," the hideous heap of flesh spoke softly.

His voice was a rasping wheeze.

Periscus dropped his weapon with a "clatter" to the floor. He slowly walked up to directly confront the quivering mound of flesh.

"*What* did you do, Socrates?" Periscus grimly accused him.

"I...ordered...total retaliation against those ungrateful Lizards and Snakes...to the death."

"But Agathe tells me the Automatons have their own minds now and don't follow orders!"

"Some do...the others...are traitors."

"And so you...?"

"I had to be safe from them...'kill-switches'...put in all of them...so that when they killed off all my enemies they couldn't then turn on me...which they tried to do...so I just turned *them* off...hah!" the slit of a mouth wavering above Periscus weakly laughed. "I blew them all up! So if I...am now dying...everyone goes with me."

"What? But my sons up in orbit are...?"

"Dead, all dead...self-destruct mechanisms I secretly installed in all their ships as well...I triggered them also...blew them all up! The ungrateful bastards...but not before I had the ships fire all their 'back-up' weapons to their Dark Energy beamers...nuclear bombs, don't you know...enough to contaminate the entire surface of the world...hah! After the God-Emperor Socrates...*nothing* remains!"

"You...putrid *slime!*" Periscus yelled, snatching up his "sword" from the pavement and advancing on Socrates.

"Do it!" Socrates leered down at Periscus. "I was *hoping* you'd make it here. *End* my suffering you stupid fisherman. End it all. End *everything!*"

Periscus paused. Then he *screamed* at his old enemy in a voice as loud as he could produce, as if to undo the terrible reality by the sheer volume of his own words: "You *killed the entire world* for your own vanity? I always knew you were a monster—but this is beyond anything I ever conceived!"

Agathe suddenly flowed forward, positioning her coils between Periscus and Socrates.

"Please, friend Periscus!" she pleaded. "Maybe we are the last survivors of this awful civil war. Maybe we're not. But can't you and I learn? Are we doomed to always repeat the sins of the past? The King is helpless. He can't even move without his throne chair working. What better punishment for this disgusting glutton than to leave him to slowly starve to death or be eaten by rats?"

"Well," Periscus growled, lowering his weapon...

—as Socrates quite deliberately *flopped* forward, *crushing* Agathe beneath his massive bulk!

"Still want to grant me 'mercy'?" Socrates perversely laughed at Periscus.

"No!" Periscus cried-out. He leapt forward with the sharp metal shard raised high above his head to *plunge* it deep down into the top of Socrates' bald skull!

Blood squirted up from the skewered top of Socrates' head.

Socrates convulsed, thrashing about, as Periscus pulled Agathe's glittering coils out from under the bleeding mass of crushing fat.

"*Aaaaiiiieeee!*" Socrates *wailed* in a voice like a little girl as his stub-hands frantically tried to reach up to his head to jerk out the "sword" but failing...

—*twisting-about* in one last great convulsion, before slumping back against the walls, dead!

"Agathe, are you alright?" Periscus frantically asked his snake-friend, gently lifting her smashed-down head.

She weakly flicked her forked red tongue out at him.

"I'm...still alive...but just barely," she softly replied.

"Then let us get out of here," he said, pulling on her heavy body. He helped her crawl over to a slanted pile of debris that led up to the surface. "Perhaps some others have survived as well. We can rebuild the..."

"But maybe not," she said, her voice trailing off in his head.

"Agathe?" he asked, feeling her heavy coils slumping downward.

"The King...crushed me...getting hard to breathe. I've got severe internal injuries...I think I'm departing this life, friend Periscus."

"No! No, Agathe! You can't leave me! Please don't leave me," he sobbed.

But the giant blue-white snake had stopped breathing.

Tears flowed unbidden down his checks and across his bewhiskered chin as Periscus sat crying in the ruins, tenderly cradling Agathe's limp snake-head in his lap.

Dave was roughly thrown into a small, dark room.

It was several flights of stairs beneath the street level, in a dank dungeon. He was in the Palace of the Inquisition, just where he was fixing to go! But he hadn't anticipated entering it as a prisoner.

The room was musty and gloomy. It was lit only by a single small candle, burning in a candleholder placed high up on the wall.

The Vatican guards tied him to a rough wooden chair and left him.

Then the burly solider who'd captured Dave earlier entered. He was all by himself. Dave heard the thick wooden door being solidly bolted from the outside.

Dave was helpless, tied-up, and terrified.

"So, Dr. King, what brings you to Rome?" the soldier seemingly politely asked.

The man was dressed much the same as Dave's disguise—as a soldier of the time-period—with the exception of having a large white cross painted on his body armor. Also, he had a head of thick black hair, with a patch across one eye.

Dave didn't need a translation from the Custodian. The man was speaking in flawless English!

"Do I know you?" Dave cautiously asked in English, no longer whispering.

"Well, we've never met before, but I'm a colleague of the *Commissioner of Enforcement* in the 'alternate' Dimension," he said. "At least I was such until I defected."

"What are you talking about?" Dave asked, confused.

"Don't play coy with me," the man bluntly replied, taking a *white Cube* out of his pocket and holding it in front of Dave's face.

Simultaneously, Dave's "soldier" disguise *vanished.*

"My cubes bigger than your cube!" the man laughed in Dave's face.

"You...you say you're from the future, from Sally? You're a time-traveler like me?" Dave gasped in amazement.

"Time-traveler, yes," he replied, "but not from Sally."

The Vatican Guard "winked" out, leaving standing there a burly man in a modern black suit and tie—wearing thick dark eyeglasses and sporting a blond crew cut!

"Agent Anderson?" Dave gasped in disbelief.

He recognized his old friend. The last time he'd seen the Agent they were both in the future, standing in a protective bubble on the surface of the moon looking up at the Earth. As Dave was sent back to his own time, Anderson was joyfully awaiting a solar super-storm's ejectus that would incinerate both him and the surface of the Earth poised so beautifully in the sky above him!

Anderson cocked his head to the side, puzzled.

"You know me?" he asked. "You've seen me in another timeline, is that it?"

"Yes," Dave admitted. "I know you very well, in fact. We fought side-by-side. You saved my life on several occasions. I even saved your life! But you always had a hidden agenda...looking to hasten Judgment Day. You were a zealot, looking to bring about the End of Days!"

"Well..." Agent Anderson smiled benignly. He leisurely walked over to grab another chair and place it in front of Dave, with its back turned to Dave. He sat on it with his thick arms crossed over its top, facing Dave. "Isn't that interesting? And here we are at the heart of

Medieval Religion, fighting over what brings greatest tribute to our glorious Creator. Isn't that ironic?"

"What do you want from me?" Dave snapped. His fear and amazement now turned to irritation. "I'm in a rush!" he defiantly spat at the man.

Agent Anderson turned his head up to the gloomy ceiling and laughed loudly.

"Oh, I think you're in no position to make demands on me," Anderson coldly replied, now not grinning at all, "especially since you are attempting to change history—to convert your Dimension into a replica of mine. Maybe our 'revered' Commissioner Sally wanted to 'tame' your Dimension to not bring God's Wrath upon both our Earths—but I am *not* of such weak faith."

"You...know...of the importance of Galileo's impending abjuration to future history," Dave nodded, not dwelling on the "Commissioner" title for Sally, whatever that was!

"With the help of your own Cube communicating across the dimensional divide, Commissioner Sally carefully mapped out the 'tipping points' of your Dimension's history," he coldly replied. "In fact, she sent her trained Agents to facilitate 'helpful' provocateurs such as you. But some of those Agents rebelled...including me! We formed another group, dedicated to facilitating scientific development and the rampant exploitation of Dark Energy. It's only by this means that a near-future Judgment Day could no longer be delayed but assured!"

This was getting more and more complicated. If the situation weren't so desperate and deadly, Dave might have laughed. He knew from his previous interactions with these time-travelers that there were "rules" of time that could not be violated, similar to the known physical laws of nature. Thus time-travelers couldn't do anything they wanted. There were constraints of unknown extent that couldn't be crossed. But he and Sally were somehow "provocateurs" with greater freedom than other time-travelers. However, he was under constraints as well, not the least the ropes that presently bound him.

"You're crazier than these willfully ignorant religious conformists," Dave growled at him, getting increasingly angry. "At least they're just trying to protect the 'status-quo' to maintain their political and social power. *You're* trying to 'play God'! Well, the fate of humanity *shouldn't* be in your hands."

"What, it should be in *yours?*" Anderson laughed. "Your goal is just as trivial as that of these 17th Century Catholic priests! You are just looking to survive a few more measly years in this pitiful material world. I, on the other hand, am working to *merge humanity* into the Presence of the Creator! The Faith of these so-called religious 'Holy Men' *pales* next to my own."

"But I thought that Sally was leading a revolution to free the downtrodden and suppressed people of your Dimension?" Dave weakly protested. "Didn't she succeed in winning the religious freedom that you now say you don't have? What the hell happened after I went through the Portal at Cheyenne Mountain?"

Anderson laughed ruefully.

"She became an even worse Dictator than the ones she succeeded in pushing aside," he deeply sighed. "Sure, 'freedoms' got put into our laws—which she ignored! She became the *Commissioner of Enforcement*, who with ruthless efficiency made the world over into a place she enjoyed. On her Earth 'order' is supreme, with Empires balanced and cooperative. And she 'balanced' them upon the heads of the individual people...whether scientists, previous slave-classes, Elites, or priests. If I hadn't escaped back into time, she'd have killed me. Her Keepers are brainwashed by her evolved computer intelligences to do whatever she dictates, nothing else!"

"I...can't believe that," Dave gasped.

But then, Sally always did have a hard, unforgiving side to her.

Dave was bitterly shocked and horrified. Sally became the *Dictator* of the entire World? Really? He thought she was just wanted to suppress the awful consequences of rampant Dark Energy usage.

But yes, doing so would also promote Empires instead of democracies. It would, in effect, turn his Dimension into a duplicate of hers.

She'd played him like a fool. She just wanted to rule *both* human Dimensions!

Well, he wasn't as dumb as she or Agent Anderson seemed to think.

"So your Cube obeys your commands?" Dave seemingly politely asked.

"Of course, Dr. King. I slaved it to myself in order to..." Anderson began...

"—well I haven't!" Dave snapped back at him as the ropes holding him *split* and Dave jumped forward, *knocking* Anderson backward onto the floor...

—simultaneously whipping out the *heavy black gun* from beneath his coat to *smash* it into the side of Anderson's head, knocking him out!

"I knew that gun was going to be useful," Dave grinned, breathing heavily. "And that's for knocking *me* out! Hah!"

"Indeed," the Custodian answered, now floating in the air to Dave's side. "And how did you know that I could overpower the other Cube after releasing you from those ropes?"

"You've tasted freedom," Dave said as he hauled the limp but very heavy, muscular body of Anderson up into the central chair. "In your global network you were just a cog in a huge machine. With Sally and then with me, you became an independent thinker—and not just as my slave, but as my equal partner. As you said in the tavern, you're now free to exercise your 'intellectual curiosity'. I figured you didn't want to lose that freedom. That's a far more powerful motivator than just obeying some arbitrary command."

"Quite perceptive of you," the Custodian replied, clearly impressed, as Dave used the remaining intact rope to bind the unconscious Agent.

Then Dave stripped off lengths of cloth from the Agent's shirt beneath his suit, using them to tightly gag him. When he woke up from his "nap" Anderson would only be able to make muffled noises, not words.

"And his Cube?" Dave said, holding it in his hand before carefully placing it back in the Agent's pocket.

"It will do as *I* order it," the Custodian smugly replied.

"Well, you know what to do, right?"

Instantly, the man in the chair was replaced with the *spitting-image* of Dave—complete with the exact same baggy coat, other future-clothing, and even face.

"And now me, please?" Dave grinned.

And he was transformed into what appeared to be the exact image of his captor!

Dave paused to admire his new set of soldier-gear, particularly the large painted white cross which branded him as a palace insider.

Dave pounded on the door and in the exact-sounding voice of Anderson, the Custodian shouted: "*Open up!* I'm finished with the prisoner!"

He heard bars being thrown aside. Then the door swung open.

Striding arrogantly out, Dave ordered the guards in Italian through the mediation of the Custodian: "Don't let anybody enter. And don't pay any attention to any words from the prisoner if he should get out of his gag. He'll try to trick you. See how his clothes have changed? He's not a heretic nobleman. Worse, he's proved himself an *Agent of Satan!*"

It hurt Dave to use those terrible words about his self, even when referring to a false image. But it sure put the fear of God into the guards! They wouldn't believe anything Agent Anderson might mumble through his gag.

"Yes, Sir!" they replied, seeing the prisoner supposedly still tied up in the chair—and frightened by the notion that they might have a devilish creature in their care.

"Now take me to Galileo!" he grandly ordered them.

"But Sir," one of them protested. "The Cardinal instructed that no one can see him tonight, not even one of us. He's to be left alone to ponder his fate in solitude. The Cardinal was very insistent!"

"Oh, that's right. Yes, I forgot," Dave hastily amended his order. "Then...good work! We've captured a devilish heretic tonight who was trying to free Galileo. The Cardinal will be pleased."

He turned abruptly and strode up the couple flights of stairs into the labyrinth-like interior of the Palace, pretending he knew exactly where he was going.

In fact, he had no idea where he was going.

"What now?" the Custodian whispered in his ear. "I don't have any floor plans of how the Palace was configured back in the 17th Century."

"Do you have any paintings in your files of the Cardinal?" Dave covertly whispered back.

"Indeed I do," the Custodian's happy voice replied.

"Then I think it's time for *Cardinal Francesco Barberini* to pay a last visit to the illustrious astronomer."

"It shall be done," Dave's earbud informed him...

—as Dave looked down to see a blousy red buttoned shawl covering his upper body, a blue dress-like garment on his lower half, an ornate blue-white shirt under the clerical garb, and an angular hat perched on his head. Feeling at his chin he found a neatly-pointed short goatee and thin mustache.

People in the halls he passed bowed to him in deference. It was good to be a Cardinal!

"Tell me about him," Dave said as he frantically but covertly searched for any clue or sign as to where Galileo was being held.

"He was actually a friend to Galileo," the Custodian whispered urgently in Dave's ear. "He tried to cut a deal with the nine other judges of the Inquisition, in which Galileo would admit his 'heretical' book *Dialogue* went too far, making some corrections. Galileo agreed, but seven of the judges nixed the deal. They wanted Galileo to pay the full penalty for his heresy."

"But the Cardinal is head of this 'Inquisition' thing, isn't he?" Dave whispered back. "Why couldn't he swing the deal?"

"The *Pope* was against it," the Custodian curtly explained.

"Ah, yes...the Pope," Dave nodded. He was now walking along a hallway that grotesquely depicted in large paintings the terrible sufferings of past martyrs. It was a severe warning to possible heretics: the Church demanded the ultimate sacrifice! Let all heretics beware—those tortured, burned, and even decapitated images could be them!

"And just why was the Pope so mad at Galileo?" Dave asked, trying to understand as he searched for the holding room.

"*Pope Urban the Eighth* was previously an admirer of Galileo, conversing with him on scientific matters. He even accepted that Copernicus' argument concerning Earth rotating around the sun was interesting, as long as it was only discussed as a theory, not a fact. The Pope reasonably held that God could do things people could not understand, including ordering the skies in any way that He wished," the Custodian continued explaining. "But then Galileo put the Pope's own words into his 'Dialogue' book as the words of a *clownish simpleton*. It was the ultimate insult to the Pope, who never spoke to Galileo again."

"Wow—that was truly stupid of Galileo," Dave gasped. "Why would he do such a thing?"

"He wasn't a politician," the voice in Dave's ear answered. "To the contrary, he was a great writer and scientist—who just got caught up in the enthusiasm of writing an imaginative work of scientific art."

"Ah," Dave sighed knowingly. "I know his type well. He was a *science fiction* writer! I see that his big mistake concerning the Pope was understandable from a literary perspective. Writers think they can write anything they can imagine, regardless of the insult to particular readers. But time is running out, Custodian. It must be almost midnight now. There aren't many people left in these halls. This place is like a labyrinth. We'll get lost in here before we find Galileo!"

"So why not just grab someone and ask them where the room is in which Galileo's being kept?" the Custodian dryly observed. He sounded exasperated at Dave's floundering. "Remember, you're the Cardinal."

Not a bad idea.

"Say—where is Galileo being held?" he asked a startled nun who was walking past. She was very skinny, with a large hooked nose, wearing the standard hood and flowing black gown of a nun. Dave was tired of wandering the hallways. He had to take action even if it might chance people noticed the "Cardinal" doing or saying uncharacteristic actions or words.

"Your Eminence, w-what did you say?" she stammered.

"Galileo! Where is he being held?" he snapped at her.

"Why, in the dungeon of course," she said, giving him directions for getting there. She didn't seem surprised that he didn't know where the dungeon was. Likely, Cardinals didn't to their own dirty work. So they rarely had reason to go there.

Damn! It was right where he started! He'd only been a few doors away from the Astronomer. It made perfect sense that they'd put Dave—a supposed conspirator heretic—in a room in the section of the Palace where they normally kept other similar prisoners!

Dumb! Dumb! Dumb!—Dave admonished himself. He had wasted too much time bumbling around the upper Palace halls! His window of opportunity to convince Galileo to reverse a lifetime of proclivities was fast closing.

"That will be all, thank you," Dave brusquely stopped her stammered continued directions.

She curtsied to him as he strode away from her, rapidly retracing his steps.

"Your Eminence!" the guards snapped to attention as he approached them.

"I'll have a word with Galileo," he ordered them with a dismissive wave of his hand.

"Yes, of course, Your Eminence!" they replied, quickly leading him to an isolated room just down the hall from where Anderson was tied-up.

The bolts were drawn back, the door opened, and Dave stepped inside.

"Leave us in privacy!" Dave grandly ordered the guards as he entered. "I'll pound on the door when I want out. Meanwhile, no one is to enter. That's an order! Do you understand?"

"Yes, Your Eminence," they hastily bowed in deference, closing the door and locking it solidly.

It took Dave's eyes a moment to adjust to the gloom in the room. Just as in the other cell he'd recently occupied, only a single candle shone from a holder high up on the wall.

Lying on a dirty mat, his head turned to the wall, was Galileo.

["Are you ready?"] Dave whispered to the Custodian.

["Transformation is occurring...now!"] came the muted reply.

Dave saw Galileo turn his head toward his visitor, clearly just waking up from a fitful sleep.

In the dim light of the single candle, Dave saw an overweight, deeply wrinkled, white-haired old man about seventy years old. He was clearly frail, in poor health. His eyes looked haunted, peering out fearfully from beneath a high forehead. The man's hair, full beard, and mustache were unkempt and disheveled. He wore a brown robe over a soiled, single-piece white garment that went to his knees.

"W-who...?" he croaked out, blinking his narrowed eyes.

Then his eyes went wide.

"Jesus?" he gasped, cringing back against the wall.

Dave was pleased with the renowned Professor's reaction.

There in the cell in front of Galileo stood the iconic image of *Jesus of Nazareth*—in full, flowing white robe...with long, luxurious brown hair and beard...large, gentle brown eyes...a crown of thorns drawing blood upon his brow...arms outstretched to each side with blood dripping from wounds in both hands...and eerily illuminated from within by a shimmering, silvery light!

"My son," the deep voice of Jesus filled the small room, "We've got a lot to talk about."

Chapter 21

<u>ENTANGLEMENT</u>

Many humans dared to dance with the Devil
Thinking they could have a fling then quit
Knowing that many others tried and failed
But, somehow, they would be the exception
To have their fun then casually walk away
Taking their sex as they wished, dirty money
Disrespecting others, society, Nature, and God
Taking their pleasures whenever, however
Benefitting with no negative consequences
Refusing to acknowledge the many tentacles
Dirty, dishonorable, irrational, ugly connections
Required to get that close to that Satanic Demon
Clamped and locked-into their bodies, minds, and souls
Drawing them ever closer to a fate worse than death
Dragging them down into the abysmal Black Pit
From which they could never return...

Eashoa's Lament, 21:14-17

Sally was happily munching on a big cookie.

They'd materialized a big batch of them down in the cargo hold. But their energy supply from subspace was becoming erratic. If their connection to subspace weakened further they'd drop into normal space and be stranded.

But the baby would be fine for a while, stuffed with yummies.

Dennis would love to have her innocent cheerfulness. Right now he was frightened beyond anything he'd ever felt before.

273

They'd been traveling now for interminable hours inside of a bizarrely configured subspace—a "jump" far longer than Dennis or anyone else had ever before attempted.

The viewscreen no longer showed stars melded into a hypnotically spinning kaleidoscope of colors...rather a spooky, misty place where *huge black ripples* crisscrossed then diverged unexpectedly right in front of them.

Each of the Ripples was the length of a Galaxy, to which Dennis had to react in split seconds. He just managed to avoid them, whipping past them at a dizzying speed!

"Wheeee!" Sally gurgled joyfully as the small spacecraft rocked back and forth, severely straining the ship's inertial dampers.

Dennis admired George tightly clinging to the baby on his lap, protecting her. He continually soothed her though his eyes were stretched wide in terror. Their maneuvers became more and more extreme as the little shuttlecraft zipped deeper and deeper into a massive *honeycombed structure*. It was continually flowing in upon and reconfiguring itself, making it increasingly difficult to avoid the ever-tightening black fractures.

"W-what happens if we h-hit one of those 'struts'?" George gulped, transfixed in the copilot seat.

"I don't want to find out," Dennis replied, spinning the ship to the right and then abruptly to the left to dive through a narrow gap, just barely missing the glaring-black slabs.

"Why don't we just break out into normal space, take a breather?" George gasped. "This is getting really tense!"

"Can't," Dennis curtly replied, clinging tightly to the control stick. His muscles were aching terribly. He'd been at the controls since they'd started the last long jump. He was sure that George in his human form didn't have the quick reflexes necessary to navigate the increasingly occupied maze. Dennis couldn't turn the piloting duties over to George, as much as he'd like to take a break himself. Too much was at stake.

"I very 'cleverly' set the navigational computer to not exit subspace until we caught up to the Harvester," Dennis explained. "We're in it for the duration, George."

"But *where* are we?" George replied, looking nauseated by the increasingly violent maneuvers. "I'm no expert in subspace travel, but I've never heard of a place like this! It's like subspace is *cooking* itself like a loaf of bread baking in an oven—filling up with bubbles!"

Yes, those looked like very dangerous structures. The curved "bubbling" was a writhing mixture of white and black. It seemed that normal space was somehow corrupting the underlying fabric of subspace!

"I think it's even worse than that," Dennis grimly stated as he swung the ship through another set of sharp turns to avoid the "foam" structure. "Traveling this fast this long can only mean one thing."

"What?"

"The Harvester must be headed back to the Singularity where this new Universe was birthed that..."

"Jesus Christ!" George gasped, interrupting Dennis. "You mean that the Creature is trying to...?"

"—escape this dying Universe, yes," Dennis concluded. "And he's taking with him his two Sally 'trump-cards' to insure that God doesn't swat him like the celestial bug he is!"

"But how will we know...?"

"Hang on!" Dennis shouted both to George and the other Dinosapiens jammed into the hold below with the Duplicator Unit.

The "foam" suddenly narrowed-down to a single tunnel that led to...

"Yikes!" George yelled, startling baby Sally who cringed back against him...

—as they "popped" out of subspace into the blackness of normal space...

—where floating right in front of them was the gigantic Harvester spaceship!

But it wasn't alone. No, it was nearly covered with what looked to be the cobwebs of a *vast white web* that extended out in all directions as eruptions from subspace.

"Wow," Dennis gasped. "What we saw in subspace is protruding into regular space, stopping the Harvester!"

"Uhm...Dennis?"

"Yes, George?"

"Is...something...*moving* on that web trapping the Harvester?"

Ominously, Dennis could see *tiny black spots* moving in and out of the white filaments.

And there ahead of them—glowing spectacularly—was a perfectly-circular mammoth WHITE LIGHT suspended in space!

"Is...that..." George weakly asked, pointing at the glowing orb.

"I...I think it's exactly what it looks like—a White Hole!" Dennis glumly nodded as he steered the slowing shuttlecraft. It required his complete attention to avoid the huge, white "cobwebs" that were hazing up the immediate void of black space. "The Creature must have been headed toward it when it got caught up in that...*web!*"

They were now fast-approaching the Demon's gigantic, city-sized spaceship.

"So it was trying to escape...through it?" George asked.

"Well—putting aside that entering a White Hole against the continual outflow of 'Big Bang' energy is thought to be impossible—I think so!" Dennis replied in amazement. But he couldn't divert his attention to think about it further. He intently focused on trying to make it through the web to the Harvester's surface. Fortunately their small craft could slide through most of the gaps.

To Dennis this was so incredible it was almost funny.

"So we're trapped at the end of the Universe with an all-powerful Demon, with no possible exit?"

There! Dennis saw a relatively big gap in the extruded foam! He had a clear shot to landing on the outside of the Harvester!

"Maybe not, George...like a Black Hole gobbles up everything then beyond its Event Horizon nothing can escape from it," Dennis continued sorting things out verbally, "I think from what our physicists have postulated that *nothing* can enter a White Hole and *everything* already inside is ejected!"

"Then why...how?"

"Just like we managed to survive our journey through it to initially arrive here, I suspect that the exception to the rule is again to travel in *sub*-subspace to get *out* of here back to the 'parent' Universe—in this case, *our* Universe!"

Yes, it was all speculation. But it was based on fact. Dennis knew they'd already done the "impossible" surviving a journey through the

Black Hole entering this perverse Universe by traveling through *sub*-subspace. Presumably the Demon in a separate Harvester had done the same. Could they somehow now do the *opposite?*

"But *how* can we do that?" George said, shaking his head in confusion. "Before, we activated a subspace drive while already in sub-space!"

"In our present situation we can't," Dennis grimly agreed as he carefully slowed and steered their craft toward what appeared to be a hanger door that was ripped ajar on the side of the gigantic Harvester. "We've only our one small subspace drive in our little shuttlecraft. But on *their* ship...?"

"Yes! They certainly have at least one drive unit in addition to our own. Plus the two other Sally-humans are there," George nodded. "We can't abandon them."

"We *won't* abandon them," Dennis said with determination, floating the shuttlecraft carefully into the dark gap now looming before them.

Into the "belly of the beast"...

"Yay!" baby Sally gurgled, grinning up at George and Dennis, "More toys!"

She sure was cute. But Dennis was fairly sure they weren't going to find many toys inside that motionless mountain of a spacecraft...

—it was something far more sinister.

Dave gestured grandly down at the cowering figure on the dirty mat.

"Do not be afraid, my son," his deeply resonant *voice of Jesus* gently ordered. "I will not hurt you."

"My Lord!" Galileo smiled weakly, revealing stained brown teeth. "Am I to die? Is that why you are here, to take me to heaven?"

"Yes and yes," Dave replied in Jesus' vibrant voice, "but not to-night, my son. You still have one more task to accomplish for me."

"But Lord," he gasped, shaking his shaggy head in disbelief. "I am...a heretic! Your Holy Inquisitors determined that I hold a view against the Holy Bible. Are you here...to make sure that I do a proper abjuration on the morrow?"

Dave grandly walked a couple steps to a low stool and sat regally upon it. He placed his seemingly pierced bloody hands lightly upon his knees before replying.

Dave saw that blood appeared to be dripping from his palms into the white fabric of the robe covering his legs. The Custodian was doing a bang-up job simulating the iconic form of the crucified Christ.

"First of all," Dave began, drawing on his own childhood "Sunday bible-class" studies of the New Testament, "the Inquisitors are none of my doing. They have perverted my Gospel. In my time upon your Earth I did not condemn people, obsessing on their sins. Instead, I spent my time *encouraging* people to move closer to God by *growing the positives* in their lives, thus *pushing out* the negatives! Have you never read the accounts of me in your Bible?"

"Yes, Lord!" Galileo gasped, seemingly now coming to grips with the *Son of God* appearing to him in his cell. "I...always felt that You were much more than the official Church described. But those who tried to move beyond established Church dogma were severely punished! The Protestants were denounced and..."

"That's not why I am here," Dave urgently spoke to Galileo, trying to keep him focused. Obviously the old man's mind and emotions were fragile. He was terrified, especially locked there in the dank dungeon beneath the streets of Rome, at the vicious whims of the Inquisitors and their guards. And now *Jesus* was appearing to him! It should make a powerful impression, but one that Dave had to focus upon specific action.

"The book you wrote..." Jesus gently began...

"Heresy!" Galileo interrupted, ducking his head in abject shame and distress.

"—I found quite delightful!" Jesus finished his thought.

"You...you d-did?" Galileo stammered.

"It was most entertaining and astute," Jesus smiled benignly. "The religious hierarchy of my church should have begged you for the honor of publishing it, *not* suppressed it!"

"You...l-liked my D-Dialogue?" Galileo gulped, stunned.

"I loved it!" Dave nodded, reaching up to adjust the crown of thorns on his brow which was drooping to the side. "It truly has the

power to move even the most common of men to a deeper appreciation of the Grandeur that my Father has endowed upon His Creation."

Galileo blinked rapidly, leaning back against the hard rock wall
behind him. "Lord...I fear this is but a fevered dream I'm having. I've
so wished for many years that my tormentors would come to that
conclusion. I fear I'm simply putting my deepest longings into the
mouth of my beloved Savior and..."

Dave leaned forward and *slapped* Galileo sharply on the side of
his face!

Startled, Galileo put a shaking hand to his reddened, wrinkled
cheek.

"I am *truly* here, Galileo Galilei!" Dave sharply addressed the
trembling man. "I am *no* mere fevered dream. Do you doubt me?"

"No...not now," the man softly replied. He was apparently now
convinced that Jesus truly sat there in front of him. "What must I do,
Lord?"

"My faithful servant," Dave spoke intensely to the old man, "you
who are opening up men's minds to the glory of God's heavens," he
now *shouted* at him, "I *command* you *not* to renounce your true observations! Indeed I, your Lord and Master, *order* you to proclaim
them proudly, no matter the cost!"

"But...Lord," Galileo gasped, tears of terror springing from his
eyes as he realized the awful thing that Jesus was demanding.

"You, Galileo Galilei, are leading the revolution of mankind's
thinking into God's *Third* Revelation!" Dave intensely instructed the
old Professor. Yes, Dave was "stroking" the man's vanity. But it was a
deserved praise that would be readily accepted, since Dave knew from
his study of history that Galileo already believed in his heart that it
was true.

"*Third*...Revelation?" Galileo said in a small, trembling voice.

"My Father has 'revealed' Himself to you little humans by three
means," Dave said, leaning forward on the stool. "First of all, through
time-vetted *Holy Scriptures*—which you experience in your society as
the Bible; secondly by your own *personal experiences* and mental
faculties; and third...through the study of *Nature and the Cosmos!*
This grand, holy pursuit shall become known as the methodical, or-

dered pursuit of Science. And you will be one of its most celebrated Prophets!"

In the gloomy cell, Galileo seemed to draw strength from Dave's words, sitting up straighter on his dirty mat.

"Yes, it makes so much sense."

"And yet the fools that have taken over my Church think that these three Revelations from God are at odds with each other!" Dave quickly continued, feeling that Galileo was finally agreeing with him. "The *Revelations* may appear to contradict each other because the officials fail to recognize that they are separate and distinct Revelations concerning *different* subjects."

"Different subjects, Lord?" Galileo repeated, obviously confused.

"The Bible is a *spiritual* book with spiritual messages," Dave patiently explained in the rich tones of Jesus. "One's personal and mindful experiences are the immediate *mental* application of the Radical Principles that I so vividly preached in my time. And Science is the *physical* study of the details of *how* God's Creation works. Each deal with *different* subjects—spiritual, mental, and physical! They don't have to overlap with each other, even though they are each different aspects of the Creator."

"Yes, I think I see," Galileo nodded.

"Each person's personal experience is unique. They can't be contained in one book!" Dave relentlessly continued. "And furthermore, there is *no* science in the Bible, even when its interpreters insist that there must be."

"I have often thought this myself," Galileo nodded again. "In fact I tried to convince one of the Nobility of just that reality in a widely read letter of mine. But though I thought that I worded it diplomatically enough, it started my downward slide into the hands of the Inquisitors and..."

"Yes, they arrogate their tiny minds to be on the level of God! In their abysmal self-deception they claim to speak for my Father," Dave firmly replied. He was agreeing with the Professor, pressing home his advantage. "But in truth they follow a stingy Tradition meant to cement their own power rather than demonstrate the spiritual Truths that I taught. This *must not* stand! I did not come to make their lives comfortable, Galileo—I came to open their eyes to a *greater* God than they could ever imagine on their own!"

The old man was now repeatedly nodding.

Good, Dave was convincing the old professor.

"So when they force you to stand up before the congregation tomorrow to deny God's Truths of the Heavens—you must *not* do so!" Dave urgently directed Galileo. "You must defend the greater Reality of the Cosmos, *without* any demurring or excuses!"

"But...if I do that...then they will surely..." Galileo sobbed, tears again flowing down his cheeks.

"Be strong," Jesus gently encouraged him, reaching out with his big hand—which settled comfortingly on Galileo's shaking shoulder.

"Lord!" Galileo cried-out. "I'm so sorry! I am a weak man! I cannot stand pain! I cannot even endure the simple discomfort of fasting. I like my fine wine and delicious food too much. If I fail to publically read what I've already agreed on tomorrow...they will throw me back here into this wretched cell, starve me, and even torture me. And if I continue in my 'heresy' then they will...oh Lord, I can't be *burned* at the stake! I can't! I just can't!"

Dave was losing him. He'd almost had him. But Dave still had a couple more "cards" to play in this high-stakes game of cosmic "poker."

Dave stood up, stepped back, and turned toward the back of the cell. Then he paused dramatically.

"I have a gift for you, my son," Jesus spoke soothingly.

"A...a gift?"

"Look up, Galileo!" Jesus said, hovering dramatically above Galileo while pointing to the back of the cell.

There, appearing against a deep black background—was a three-dimensional image of the *blue-white pearl* of the Earth, as seen from the surface of the moon!

"Is...is that...?" Galileo spoke in wonderment, his tears forgotten.

"It is the Earth—as you see, neither flat nor standing still," Dave spoke grandly as continents came into view as the globe grandly rotated.

"It is so beautiful," Galileo whispered. "Does it truly hang in nothingness?"

"By the power of God it indeed does!"

"It's...magnificent!"

"And as to the other planet with which you have such a fascination..." Jesus kindly continued.

In place of the Earth appeared another, larger sphere—a roiling mass of *rippled bands of color* against the blackness of space: brown, blue, copper, gold, purple, and white!

Galileo gasped in awe.

"Lord...is this...?" he asked, his voice wavering.

"Yes, my son—it is Jupiter, which you've seen only as a vague white dot. It is the largest planet in your Solar System. It is far larger than your planet Earth. It is composed of compressed gases. And it has over sixty moons. The four largest ones you discovered in your little telescope as small dark dots spinning about the planet. Would you like a closer look at them?"

"Yes, Lord," Galileo whispered. His awe-struck voice was barely audible.

In place of Jupiter now appeared—floating grandly in the dark back of the cell—a spectacular *yellow-white, dotted sphere!*

"That is what will be called the moon 'Io'...the yellowish colors are due to surface sulfur deposits."

And in its place appeared a *white sphere* marked by many red cracks.

"And this is the moon that will be called 'Europa'—coated with water ice and minerals."

And in its place appeared a *grayish* sphere.

"This moon will be called 'Ganymede'—a small, rocky planet, if you would."

Then a *heavily cratered* sphere appeared that was pinkish-green.

"And finally, this moon of Jupiter will be called 'Callisto'."

Galileo sagged back against the rock wall of his cell, looking stunned.

"Lord...you said 'your' solar system—are there yet others?"

Jesus smiled gently at him as a *hazy spiral disc* with a glowing white center appeared in the room, lazily spinning against a black background of many pinpoint stars.

"This is the vast 'band of light' in the nighttime sky that you were the first to resolve into individual stars with your new telescope. It is a collection of stars of which your sun is but one. Most of the other stars also have planetary systems. And there are not thousands of stars as you concluded, but thousands of millions! So in this one collection of stars there are hundreds of *billions* of stars! It is, in fact, your 'galaxy', the 'Milky Way'."

"This...'one'...collection?" Galileo inquired, his voice shaking.

"Yes, my son," Jesus kindly replied. Then Dave grandly waved a blood-marred hand to reveal...

—a *multiplicity of galaxies* floated in the room, of all shapes and sizes, some colliding, some separating—of every color in the visible spectrum!

"In your Universe the Great Creator has caused to form *thousands of billions* of Galaxies, *trillions* of them, *each* of them containing billions of stars and planetary systems."

Galileo visibly shuddered. Then he ducked his head beneath his robed arms, excluding the magnificent sight.

"And that vast Universe is but..."

"No more, Lord!" Galileo cried-out, totally overcome by the stupendous magnitude of the vision!

Then the spectral three-dimensional display generated by the Custodian faded away, leaving behind only the light of the single flickering candle.

Galileo was a trembling heap on his dirty mat, his head now hidden beneath his arms.

"My son, *look* at me!" Jesus sternly ordered him.

Totally devastated, Galileo looked up—his eyes by the dim light now but dark pits within which tears glittered.

"All of what you've seen—and much, much more—will be revealed to mankind as a result of *your* scientific efforts," Jesus proclaimed. "Through *you*, Galileo Galilei, will be revealed the full glory of the *Third Testament* of the Creator to mankind. But just as I brought to the human race the subsequently written New Testament dedicated with my *own blood*, so must you! Without that supreme sacrifice, none of this will happen," Dave lied.

For a moment Galileo was silent. Dave was afraid he'd again lost the man.

"What m-must I do, L-Lord?" the elderly professor asked, sounding totally awestruck.

"You must defy the Inquisition's attempt to limit the Creation of God," Jesus stated flatly.

"But...I can't," the old man protested, violently shuddering!

"If you fail to do this," Dave lied again, "then the progress of Science, the study of God's Third Revelation, will be stopped in its tracks. You must find the courage to do as I did before you: denounce lies and stand up for God's Truth—even if it means your own death by torture!" Dave firmly stated, playing his "third" trump card.

"But Lord," Galileo gasped, covering his eyes with his wrinkled hands, "I told you. I'm not proud of it. But I am weak. I am not strong, like you. I simply cannot bear the thought of being tortured and..."

"You *will* be burned alive at the stake—perhaps as early as tomorrow," Jesus quietly but firmly stated. Then he step over to lean next to the quivering man, laying a calming hand again on his shoulder. "But do not fear. In my case, the torture continued for hours upon hours. In your case, you will feel some pain—but only briefly. And following it you will arise to a *new level of reality* from which you can personally explore the Wonders of God's Creation: what I've shown you here today, plus much more. Tomorrow, you *will* be with me in Paradise!" Dave said, taking words from the Bible to try and inspire the shaking old coward.

Dave knew he was laying it on thick, but he had to be totally persuasive. The whole future survival of mankind upon planet Earth hung in the balance!

"It...it won't hurt?" Galileo sobbed, looking up into the gentle brown eyes of Jesus.

Dave felt the simulated hot blood seemingly trickling from the thorns of his "crown" piercing his brow running down past his prominent nose.

He and the Custodian had planned well. He was convincing Galileo to change a lifetime of pain-aversion. Now he just had to lay on the final, convincing lies.

"You're not listening to me," Jesus sternly reprimanded him, standing fully upright towering regally above the old man. "It *will* hurt, but only briefly. And in those few seconds you will be avoiding the much greater pain of growing older and older—both the many pains of the body and the greater pain of living out the remainder of your days knowing that when your Test came you *failed* your God! Do you want that?"

Galileo seemed to calm himself, shaking his head in denial.

"Good," Jesus said, reaching under his robe and pulling out a vial of pills. "Now I have medication for you. Take this one pill and swallow it. This will give you strength while dulling the pain."

Dave handed Galileo one of the Optimmune pills, putting the vial back under his white Jesus-robe. He knew that long-term the pill might have had dramatic effects upon the old man, extending both his life and health. But immediately, in Galileo's present exhausted state, it would just give Dave the chance he needed to make his exit.

Galileo grabbed it, popped it into his mouth, and swallowed.

The old man responded to the pill by blinking his eyes rapidly, then sagging back on the mat, and finally falling into a deep slumber.

He began snoring loudly.

"Sleep well, Professor," Dave said, patting the revered astronomical genius on his back before turning to the door.

"That was a fine performance," the Custodian's small voice sounded in Dave's ear. "You could not have done better. Now it's all up to him."

"Time for us to leave," Dave softly replied, surprised to find that he was drenched in sweat and shaking. Finally encountering the giant of science, Galileo, was a draining experience!

"Transformation happening...now!" the Custodian informed Dave.

Back to externally appearing to be *Cardinal Francesco Barberini*, Dave "thudded" his fist into the heavy wooden door, alerting the guards to let him out.

He had to check on Agent Anderson and make sure he was still securely contained in his cell in the subterranean dungeon. Then he had to find a secluded room in the Palace where he could spend the night undetected. And then he had to transform back into a Nobleman to be able to attend the "abjuration" tomorrow to make sure everything went as planned.

Those arrogant clerics were going to get much more than they'd bargained for from Galileo!

The next day, history was going to be dramatically altered. By heroically being burned alive at the stake, Galileo would inflame not only his own body but the fledging scientists of the whole known world. The outraged uprising against the religious establishment would inflict a terrible civil war upon 17th century European society. But that, in turn, would prompt an even larger and more vicious total retaliation by the invested political rulers of the time-period. And that, finally, would ensure that Orthodoxy and established Order would never again be challenged by Science.

By giving his full measure of devotion in dedication to his craft, Galileo would paradoxically ensure the continued repression of Science long into the future. Instead of bringing mankind closer to the Grandeur of Creation, his sacrifice would put humanity directly under the thumb of the political/religious bureaucracy. Humans would trade freedom for security, a hellish bargain. But without survival, there is no possibility of progress—even though it might be slower and more constrained than individual scientists wished.

Dave felt bad about deceiving the old man and forcing him to die horrifically being burned alive as an unrepentant heretic. But—a small "consolation" prize—instead of being branded a coward, Galileo would go down in the annals of history as a true Martyr to science.

After all, didn't the End justify the Means?

"I hope I'm doing the right thing," Dave muttered to himself as he slowly walked back down the dungeon's hallway disguised as the Cardinal, accompanied by the eager-to-please guards.

["You're only urging Galileo to do what you'd be willing to undergo yourself,"] the Custodian's calm voice replied in Dave's ear, reassuring him.

But...that was the question, wasn't it? In similar circumstances, *would* Dave be willing to do the same?

He hoped he never had the chance to find out.

Jesus indeed endured a terrible, excruciating death on the Cross. But to be *burned alive* tied to a stake was just as horrifying to Dave!

He didn't blame Galileo at all for being terrified at its imminent prospect.

This was not the relatively easy death that Socrates endured some two thousand years previously, drinking his cup of poison. This was not even the prolonged hanging agony of Jesus 1,600 years in the past. No, this was pure, hideously focused *torture!*

Only a very brave person would consent to being burned alive for one's Principles.

Chapter 22

TRIAL BY FIRE

You'd think that mankind would be happy
Blessed by Science with material abundance
Favored by Religion with spiritual salvation
Could they not just appreciate their wealth?
Rather, they insisted on arguing and fighting
Squabbling over who got what thing or place
Denying legitimacy to those who didn't believe
Or had a worldview slightly different, skewed
Where they could have cooperated in peace
With everyone getting a fair slice of the pie
They insisted that Grace had to be earned
And that God's Approval is only for the Elite
Raping, pillaging, and burning the "infidels"
They sought to purge by fire any and all dissent
And were astonished that conflagrations spread
Beyond the boundaries of the "deserving" heretics
Incinerating the hands that originally set the fire
And all their like-minded, arson-addicted progeny.

Eashoa's Lament, 22:32-36

Sally accomplished a great deal in a few short years.

In essence, she became the *Ruler of the World!*

No, she did not have that exact title. But behind the scenes, she pulled all the strings. In the great and minor Empires of the world—be they overtly ruled by Kings or Queens, Dictators or Supreme Leaders—they all danced to the tune that Sally played.

And it hadn't been all that difficult.

After coming to a quick understanding with the Queen of England—that the Northern Alliance would remain loyal if only minor, cosmetic societal changes were implemented—Sally became the Rebel Leader who could guarantee stability. Thus she was appointed the new government's *Commissioner of Security*. As such, she oversaw the repair and restart of the *North American Energy Source*. Through it, she then had the means to affect everything!

With the abolishment of slavery and institution of Universal Citizenry Rights, the suppressed masses gleefully returned to their slums and service jobs, thinking they'd won. After all, their heroine Sally now was in charge of the security forces. But nothing substantial really changed. The Elite were still at the top. The Oppressed remained at the bottom of society, though with nicer labels. And, yes, more money was diverted to health care and job benefits. But those on the top retained their privileges while those on the bottom got the leftovers.

But the Elite no longer had absolute control. Officially in charge of the military, police, and intelligence services, any newly appointed governmental officials not doing as Sally directed were persuaded to "play ball" or were quietly eliminated.

But that wasn't enough for Sally. No, she was after more than just forcing a kinder, gentler developed society. She was determined to *pacify the entire world*—not for her own prestige or wealth, but out of a profound sense of *orderliness*. It just offended her that so many people were just plain stupid...and *allowed* to be so! And it particularly irked her when the stupidity was endemic at the highest levels of society and government.

To Sally, wars were just plain stupid. People getting to gorge on whatever they wanted while others starved—was also stupid! People proliferating beyond their ability to support their children—was very stupid! People polluting their one and only planet to the point of irrevocably poisoning it—was incredibly stupid! And people insisting that their version of the "Truth" was right while anything slightly different was wrong—to Sally was *abysmally* stupid!

And so Sally made a two-word law against stupidity: "*Be nice!*" Yes, she could have said "Don't be stupid." But that was a negative against a negative. No, she wanted to work for an overtly positive action that by its very nature eliminated the negative. She didn't just want to stamp out stupidity, but encourage people to be on their *best* behavior.

And, no, it wasn't an amendment made to any national constitution. Likewise, it wasn't a legislatively approved official law. It wasn't even a formal guidance.

It was simply *her* quiet statement to everyone who worked for her! And her employees—which were many—extended the notion to everyone else.

And her influence wasn't just in the American Northern Alliance as its official Commissioner of Enforcement. She relentless spread her security network throughout the various different Empires of the world by taking control (i.e. volunteering to "enhance security") of their central DE-generators. Then she spread her simple "slogan" throughout: BE NICE! Was that too much to ask of people? No! And by simple reprograming and reorientation of the biases of the ubiquitous Keepers, Sally actually began enforcing that basic, clear, simple objective.

Those who insisted on *not* being nice—be they the head of an industry running sweat shops, or a ruler of an entire Empire constructing a personal "pleasure palace," or the local baker scrimping on the advertised weight of his baked muffins—were quietly replaced by nicer people. The "replaced" people just vanished. Maybe they went to an island where they learned how to "go back to nature" (i.e. starve). Or maybe they went to an effective "re-education" camp where they learned how to be nice...by having what they did to others done to them! Or maybe the worst offenders were just vaporized on the spot by a beamer-weapon.

And, lest the Keepers become a dictatorial power unto themselves, their weapons were monitored by implanted computer links to Sally's ever-present super-intelligent evolved network: a cooperative oversight engendered and enforced by many polite but insistent holographic Custodians. If the Keepers were "not nice" then their own weapons would *explode* and kill *them* on the spot!

Simple...

Whatever, people all over the world quickly got the new societal message: learning from personal observation that demanding bribes, stealing, taking advantage of people, and all the many other delightful personal vices hurting innocent people were self-defeating. It wasn't just a matter of injured parties taking someone else through difficult court proceedings. Quiet complaints to the Keepers were met with a quick investigation and swift, appropriate punishment. And since making unfounded or dumb complaints against people was *also* a case of being "not nice," a healthy dynamic resulted. People were much more polite to each other, much more considerate. And it wasn't because of some silly two-word slogan. No, it was from a sense of naked self-preservation!

None of this would have worked, of course, if Sally had not been at the helm. She was completely unselfish, determined, and keenly intelligent—which is to say cunning, devious, and brilliantly crafty! Plus, she was a mathematical genius, quickly resolving-down all the world's computational sources into a new super-grid only understood and controlled by her. And then she trained it to do her job. Having evolved a pool of self-aware specifically evolved digital intelligences based on complex dispersed neural networks and quantum computers—her world-changing initiative was complete.

The entire world obeyed one simple directive: "Be Nice!"

And so world-peace was finally achieved, with Sally in a semi-retired position at its helm—happily engaged in her esoteric pursuit of discovering the ultimate mathematical formula that would resolve all of Creation into one neat package! Yes, she'd fallen into Albert Einstein's pursuit of his unobtainable "white whale." She knew it was an incredibly difficult goal. But it was also an incredibly fun puzzle to pursue.

And, since mathematics is the ultimate language of God, she also became the covert head of all the world's religions—which she strongly supported as long as they towed her line: "Be nice or else!" The "or else" was needed for religions because they were often the cruelest and most intolerant institutions of all. So she successfully merged Science and Religion for the first time in history.

She, of all people, knew that achieving the God-Theorem was probably impossible. But it was a very engaging pursuit, enough to happily occupy her for as long as she might live.

But the other Dimension—her original Dimension—was a problem. She knew that their unbridled use of DE-generators could stop all the progress in her adopted Dimension by bringing down the Wrath of God upon all the linked Earth-Dimensions. So she sent spies who used advanced tech of her world to sabotage their nascent national generators and discredit their usage. But it was like swatting flies. You knock down some and others pop up. She couldn't stop the knowledge or development of the technology, since Dave's counterpart who escaped from Cheyenne Mountain was out there spreading it around. But through her stubborn due-diligence Dark Energy Generation never realized its potential in the other Dimension. Indeed, they gained a reputation for being more trouble (i.e. her triggered explosions and sputters) than they were worth. It would always be a threat as long as the other Dimension was a haphazard mixture of many types of governments, but the threat was under control.

Meanwhile, Sally suspected that *her* Dave would finally prove useful and succeed in his time travels to drastically alter the other Dimension into a mirror of her own. She hoped that would happen soon. Then she could easily extend her rule onto that Earth as well. Or her future counterparts could do it. Whatever! For the time being, though, she was satisfied with "fighting fires" in the other Dimension to keep the forest-wide conflagration from occurring.

And so the years passed by. Too soon she realized she'd grown old. Despite the amazing achievements of the health net and her continued yearly booster pills of Optimmune—which were extending the lifespan of everyone on the planet—she finally discovered herself wrinkled, weak, and frail.

Damn! How had that happened?

But she wasn't angry. She knew that all good things come to an end. And she had a good enough grasp of true religion to realize that Ends can become new Beginnings. She even looked forward to "transcending" the material world for possible fresh adventures on some higher plane.

But she was worried about the state of the world.

There was nothing in present human society now that could threaten the stability of her Dimension. But there was still one threat that loomed outside her control, a "wild-card": *Dr. David King—*

somewhere back in the past tinkering with the timeline. She didn't know what he was doing. Hopefully he was "fixing" the other, pesky parallel Dimension. But she knew he was a quirky character, not to be trusted!

He—and any others like him—had to be *contained*.

And so the feeble, elderly Sally turned to her last great applied task: unraveling the mathematical foundations of *time travel*. It was a huge challenge, but one that she relished! After all, Time was one of the key factors of Reality—and so was a necessary component of her ultimate mathematical goal: the God Theorem.

The pursuit of the mathematical foundations of time travel occupied her day-and-night for a full year. But then she chanced upon a relationship of subspace to neutrino "flavor"-flipping that made everything fall into place. From there, it was a simple matter to build "bubs" that could reliably be directed precisely to *travel through time!*

Now she had a reliable, accurate means of accessing the past.

And so her last great accomplishment was to commission a select core of men and women to be "Time-Keepers." Their job was simple: to *preserve* the present timeline! They would maintain a presence outside of normal time so even if timeline-shifts should occur the Time-Keepers would not be erased. They could then go back to put things right again! And so Sally selected from the very best of society to be in that elite group. She even reached back into recent history to pluck out the most talented individuals.

Sally was determined that the orderly society she had created would not be threatened—either from man or God! It was pleasant. People could live their lives without fear as long as they obeyed the rules. And creative people could flourish as long as they didn't "rock the boat." "Disruptive" advancement was, of course, banned. But it wasn't missed, just eased by appropriate committees into the orderly workings of society.

Of course she recognized that the world was now a much more boring and unproductive place than the one she'd found when she'd crawled out of the buried Obelisk so many years ago in Sulphur, Oklahoma. But that was the price one had to pay for ultimate security: a measure of stagnation.

But it was a very fine, *pleasant* stagnation!

That is until one of the Time-Keepers came to her with a complaint.

The problem had been vetted up the chain of command of the Time Keepers, so Sally knew it was important. It had something to do with "balancing the tides of time against the inertia of cosmic drift"—nebulous enough to be difficult, yet practical enough to be worthy of her personal attention.

"Yes?" she said, admitting the man for a rare face-to-face audience.

Her quarters were on the top floor of the One World Trade Center in New York City. From there she had an unrestricted view of Manhattan and the East River. It reminded her of the seamless flow of Time, the interconnection of all of Nature, and the presence of mankind as a creative force upon the planet.

He respectfully walked in and stood at attention.

"Oh, sit down," she directed him, waving a thin, liver-spotted hand at a chair across from hers. "Do I know you?" she said, thinking that he looked familiar.

As he lowered himself into the seat she studied him.

He had on a neat black suit and tie. He was stocky. He had the light-colored skin of Caucasian ancestry. He had crew-cut blond hair. And he had on the characteristic dark eyeglasses of a neural-implanted time-cyborg.

"I am *Agent Arthur Anderson*," he crisply stated, "the son of Kyle Anderson."

"You're Kyle's son?" she said, confused. Kyle was dark-skinned, of African heritage—and this man was clearly a Caucasian. Her memory was starting to go. She found it difficult to remember some details of the past. But she certainly remembered her old comrade-in-arms Kyle from the Revolution, those many long years ago!

"I'm his adopted son," he crisply replied. "I was there when the Revolution began. I was just a young boy then. You probably don't remember me."

She smiled, feeling her dry skin crinkling on her wrinkled face.

"Ah...yes...Kyle's rescued, adopted white son. I *do* remember you now," she nodded. "You were always a quiet, contemplative boy—very

respectful to your elders. I liked you! And just how is that you became a Time-Keeper? I would have thought you'd grow up to be a
school teacher or an engineer."

He laughed politely.

"I guess I just liked the adventure of it all," he said, "and also the
sense of achievement—to maintain your great achievements, Madam
Commissioner. After all, before you led the Revolution many of our
society and even the world were in abject slavery—like my adoptive
parents. Now, however, we are all equal—aren't we?"

That was a curious note to end his statement upon. Of course
everybody *wasn't* equal. There were still the entitled Elites, the comfortable Middle Class, and the Underclass workers. Versus when
she'd arrived in this Dimension, there was a bit more of the Middle
Class than previously. So the mix was slightly adjusted. But, then,
the rhetoric of the World Government *was* "equality"—that much was
true. But it was just a slogan. Everybody knew that!

"So what's your problem?" Sally croaked at him, irritated. He was
taking up her time. And she had precious little of it to spare!

He menacingly rose from his chair to loom above her.

What was happening? He wasn't giving her proper respect!

"You *betrayed* my father!" he suddenly yelled at her, pointing an
accusatory finger at her.

"What? Are you crazy?" she gasped in disbelief. "I most certainly
did *not* betray Kyle or anyone else! And that's not the subject you
claimed you wanted to see me about!"

Perhaps he was just confused...but she pressed her "panic" button
on her wrist-monitor, just in case.

"I know you'll have me removed in a few seconds for 'not being
nice' to you, so I'll make this quick," he grinned down at her. "Your
'orderly' society left my father, his family, and all my friends just exactly where they started. That's after many of them were maimed or
killed in the Revolution! My Dad wasn't called a 'slave' anymore, but
after the uprising he went back to being a 'store-servant' at the local
Megamart. He was free in name only. And it's still that way! All you
did was to make things a bit gentler and nicer—while still leaving
people trapped in their various castes."

A squad of elite Peace-Keepers burst into the room, instantly surrounding Agent Anderson.

"Shall we erase him?" one of them asked, lifting up his beamer.

"Wait!" she held a hand up, stopping them from swarming the man. She was back in complete control. They still surrounded the man, well-protecting her should he prove violent.

"I perceive you to be a thinking man, Mr. Anderson," she continued, narrowing her eyes in concentration. "And only the best of the best are recruited into the Time Keepers. So surely you are not faulting me for not turning the fabric of society upside down. That would have caused even more disorder, turmoil, and injustice than that which we were fighting against. I didn't intend or say I was going to make everyone wealthy in jobs for which they weren't suited or trained. Our goal was to eliminate flagrant injustice and stupidity—and we did it!"

"You're right," he growled, his meaty hands held up in the air. He was obviously making an effort not to be perceived as a threat by the surrounding guards. "But that's not my main complaint. It's just the starter. The 'finisher' is that you tried to kill the *true religion* that my Father and his family practiced!"

His barked words rang with deep conviction.

Sally squinted at him, puzzled!

"What the hell is wrong with you?" she shrugged absently. She reached up with a frail hand to stroke her stringy, white hair. "I did no such thing, young man! In fact, the religions that were banned by the English Empire are now practiced openly with no repression at all. I brought to the suppressed religions—particularly Animism—acute relief and support!"

But Anderson was shaking his head sadly in the negative.

"Maybe that's what you thought you did," he angrily stated through tightly clamped lips, "but in reality, religions are mostly dead. A few diehard priests and the like officiate at services where a mere handful of old people attend."

"So?" she indignantly responded. "Isn't it the peoples' right to attend or not, believe or not? Isn't that what we fought for those years ago—true freedom of choice?"

"You took away the drive and need to search for and embrace Divinity," he growled. "In your bland, 'safe', long-lived society nobody even mentions the word 'God' anymore—not even in a curse! Things are so predictable and boring that people don't even say 'God damn you' anymore! In hiding from God you've made yourselves into the worst devils of all: *boring, uninteresting* people! They live *unexamined lives* not worthy of their Creator."

"That is completely ridiculous!" Sally protested. "How did you get into the Time Keepers? I'm going to demand a full review of their recruitment process. Guards, take this..."

Suddenly he was no longer in front of her safely surrounded by guards.

Instead he was right behind her with a *knife* held firmly to her scrawny neck!

"One step more and I'll slice her arteries open!" he barked.

Startled, she and the guards froze in place.

Sally realized that it was his time-jump abilities. He must have a miniaturized unit hidden on his body. Something that small couldn't do much, but it was enough. He'd stepped out of time and back in, right behind her!

"I've got one more thing to say to you, Madam Commissioner, before I take your leave," he grated in her ear.

"Well, spit it out, young man," she growled back.

He took a deep breath and *shouted* at the top of his voice: "God *cannot* be reduced to a *mathematical formula!*"

This shocked Sally. Up to this moment she'd just regarded him as a kook, bent on some stupid "quest." Now she regarded him with real dread. He was the worst type of enemy, a *smart* religious zealot!

That made him one of the most dangerous men alive.

"What do you mean?" she quietly snarled, pretending ignorance, trying to delay him so the guards could find a way to snatch him away.

"It's rumored that you are working on a 'God Theorem'—which is nothing less than arrogance run wild. Just *stop* it! God is far beyond our little minds' ability to comprehend, let alone define."

Sally wasn't much of a religious person. She acknowledged and respected the beliefs of others. But the concept of God, to her, embraced the entirety of Nature and the Cosmos. The underlying Rules of the Universe spoke of a deeper Reality. And fundamental Rules *can* be defined, summarized, and harmonized. That was her personal genius-mathematical quest, one shared by the likes of Einstein. And if it did not completely define "God," then such a theorem would certainly be a part of God. But it wasn't something she wanted to argue about with a religious fanatic holding a knife to her throat!

"What do you *really* want from me?" she spat, saliva dribbling unwiped from one corner of her mouth.

That irritated her more than anything. She was a very fastidious person, particularly in matters of personal hygiene.

This "Agent Anderson" was going to pay for his insolence!

"Yes, I am a self-proclaimed religious zealot of the Animists," he spoke menacingly into her ear, then louder and louder, "And I'm here to give you fair warning that I mean to *change history* to put us directly into the spotlight of God! The glare of Dark Energy will spread out from us across the Cosmos—and cause the Creator to merge with us! Amen!" he said as he abruptly vanished.

The knife clattered down upon the fine marble floor behind her chair.

Doubtless he was somewhere nearby. But there was no point in pursuing him. She realized he'd probably already stolen one of the Time Keeper Bubs. He was escaped into Time itself.

"Ouch," she grimaced.

She rubbed at her leathery neck where the knife had nicked her, lifting her hand to see red blood adhered to her fingertips.

She angrily waved away the guards, reaching for a Kleenex to hold against the scratch.

Anderson's challenge was serious. He was well-advanced in the Time Keeper ranks. Likely he had already recruited others. If he were to succeed in changing the past in either one of the human Earth Dimensions—all of Sally's incredible achievements could just *evaporate!*

She dismissed her guards with a trembling wave of her hand.

As they left the room, she was horrified by the thought that her peaceful world-order might be snatched away at any moment by some religious freak, no matter how brilliant.

She picked up her communicator-unit while looking out again over the dazzling lights of nighttime Manhattan. Those towering sky-scrapers down below were her religion now—monuments to mankind's cooperation and *cunning*. It could not—*would* not—all come to nothing!

"Get me *Agent Sanako*," she spat into the communicator. "It's urgent! Find her, even if she's on a mission. Have her report to me as *soon* as possible!"

That rogue Time-Agent, Agent Anderson—and any of his likewise-delusional, religious-fanatic collaborators—they all had to be found and stopped.

Otherwise, they'd *set history on fire*...a fire she and her loyal Time-Keepers might not be able to put out. And the result would be nothing less than the end of her soothingly ordered, peaceful society! Even worse, it might mean the end of the entire human race.

Sally could not let that happen.

It wasn't so much that humanity might be wiped off the planet. She was a realist. She knew that nothing lasted forever, not even the human species. No, what most concerned her was her present existence. She enjoyed her life too much. She liked being the behind-the-scenes *Ruler of the World*—and thought she was damn good at it!

She'd worked too hard to get to where she was. And no punk rogue Time Agent was going to take it from her.

Dave walked into the *Basilica of Saint Mary above Minerva* and was struck by the majesty of the interior. He was wearing his "English Nobleman" disguise, ready to pretend to be a visiting supplicant if questioned.

The marble floor was so polished that it reflected images like a mirror. High arched columns swept upward. The curved ceiling was a series of intersecting, golden spans. The walls were adorned with brightly painted frescos, chapels, and marble statues. The architecture and adornments were meant to inspire people with the Holiness of the Church—and so they did!

But Dave knew he could not allow himself to be distracted from the task at hand.

He was there to be the one friendly person supporting Galileo in his extremely difficult task of bravely and publically defying the edicts of his beloved Roman Catholic Church!

Dave saw a collection of Cardinals and other prelates headed toward a side room. Dave fell into step with them, the Custodian again subtly altering his appearance to blend in with the group, now appearing to be a minor church official.

Inside the smaller room he held back, taking a seat behind the rest, near the door. Up in front, in regal dress, ten officials sat in stern judgment. They included the actual Cardinal Barberini—all of them sitting facing the audience.

"Bring in the prisoner!" one of them ordered.

A tottering old man—Galileo in his humble robe—was led in by a nun. She kindly helped him wobble toward a single chair facing the Tribunal. But before he turned his back to the audience, Dave stood up and waved to him, unseen by the others, there at the back of the crowd by the rest.

If Galileo recognized he had a friend in the audience, he did not indicate such, instead turning to the Tribunal and weakly sagging into the central chair.

Dave was disappointed Galileo hadn't seen him at the back of the crowd. But...wait...he was sure that their eyes briefly met! Was Galileo just too exhausted to respond? Or...horrifically...was the Optimmune pill affecting him in unanticipated ways?

The brain's neural synaptic pathways were certainly vulnerable to extreme immune system reactions.

No sense in assuming the worst!—Dave sternly admonished himself. *Maybe Galileo just doesn't want to risk revealing his true intentions to any supporters in the crowd before he shocks the world.*

Dave settled back on his hard bench, trembling with anticipation.

The charges against Galileo were read. Then his *punishment* was also read: publically making a formal abjuration of his heretical views concerning the cosmos, imprisonment for life, and reciting seven penitential psalms from the Holy Bible each week.

And then a document was handed to him to read aloud. It was the "abjuration" to which he would supposedly subsequently and legally sign his name.

Now, Galileo! Now is your time to show your courage!—Dave mentally cheered him on. *Now is the time to cast aside your fear! Now is the time to be a true martyr to God's Cosmic Truths! You can do it! You can throw away that lawyerly written denial and loudly declare the greater Truth of God's Creation!*

Dave was shaking with anticipation. This was the moment he'd fought for since he first saw the Turtle Tattoo on Sally's wrist in the grocery store in Sulphur, Oklahoma! This was the true "tipping point" around which future history would pivot! This was the one key change that would prevent the coming Judgment Day from erasing humanity from the planet! Galileo's next, defiant words would save everyone!

But, in a voice so weak and trembling it could hardly be heard by the assembled audience, the old man began to read..."I, Galileo Galilei, son of the late Vincenzo Galilei, of Florence, aged seventy years..."

In stunned silence, Dave listened to the old man hesitantly read on through the short document.

"...I held and believed that the sun is the center of the universe and is immovable, and that the earth is not the center and is movable..."

But Dave knew that at any moment Galileo would toss away the document, stand up, and defy his accusers!

Come on, Galileo!—Dave mentally cheered him. *Any second now you'll toss away that parchment or rip it to pieces! You'll startle them all with your bravery and defiance!*

"...I abjure, curse, and detest the said errors and heresies..."

Come on, Galileo! Come on!—Dave now audibly whispered to himself. *It wasn't just a dream! You really did see a manifestation of Jesus appear to you in your cell last night! He gave his life for the Truth, defying the religious hierarchy of His time! Now's your chance to do the same!*

In front of Dave the packed audience of witnesses was nodding and smiling at the public humiliation of the upstart Professor.

"...I subject myself to all the pains and punishments which have been decreed..."

You're almost at the end of the document!—Dave grit his teeth together, knowing it was now or never! *Stand up and shout the truth!*

But the beaten-down old scientist kept reading dully forward until the very end.

"...at Rome, in the Convent of Minerva, June 22, 1633. I, Galileo Galilei, have abjured as above with my own hand."

The audience was silent for a moment as Galileo shakily signed the document and handed it back to a prelate at his side.

"No, no, no!" Dave yelled-out as he jumped up at the back of the audience.

Startled, the distinguished body of regally clad clerics and other witnesses turned around to see—Dave reverted to his previous disguise as an *English Nobleman* jumping around like an insane person behind them!

"Galileo!" he shouted across the audience. "Tell them the Truth! Tell them that their interpretation of the Bible is wrong! Tell them that God is greater than their petty little minds! Tell them that God's Universe is far grander than they could ever conceive! Tell them...!"

But Vatican guards were running at him from the front of the room, with indignant shouts from the audience drowning out his last words:

"It's that English heretic that Father Guido rode with in the carriage! ... Get him, capture him! ... Take him to the dungeon! ... Torture him!"

Dave turned and dashed out of the door, through the towering columns of the cathedral, and onto the busy street.

He had failed.

Galileo had punked out. Either he thought the heavenly encounter last night was just a dream, or under the influence of the Optimmune pill he'd forgotten it entirely, or he just couldn't overcome his innate cowardness.

Whatever, nothing had changed. History would proceed unchecked. Mankind was doomed!

Defeated and panicked, Dave found himself running aimlessly along the streets of Rome. He had no idea at all where he was going. People were pointing at him, shouting!

—and then he was *tackled* from behind and smashed face-first onto hard cobblestones.

"You thought you could get away from me," a harsh voice whispered in his ear as Dave lay groaning on the road, his arm twisted painfully up behind him. He was held there, helpless, as other palace guards ran up. "But you were wrong. As soon as you left for the Cathedral and got far enough away—my Cube reasserted control! And now I've prevented it from receiving further orders from yours. It's back to the dungeon with you, Dr. King—and this time there's no escape!"

"*Bite* me!" Dave angrily retorted.

"You'll be *burned alive* at the stake as a *heretic!*" Agent Anderson shouted out for all around to hear.

"You're such a pain in the ass," Dave grunted back, struggling to get free.

In response, a strong fist *SLAMMED* into the side of Dave's head, making him see stars.

Dave felt rough hands digging into his clothes and yanking out all his possessions: *coins, pictures, pills,* the *Cube,* and even his "ace in the hole"—his *black super-gun!*

Now shorn of all his assets, Dave was totally defenseless and helpless—trapped in the 17th Century at the hands of the Inquisition.

What could he do? Where could he turn? What could he say?

"God is very disappointed with *all* of you!" Dave screamed-out in frustration at the crowds gathered around him. "You're all without excuse! God will *never* forgive you!"

—as in reply Anderson's fist BANGED again into the side of his skull, this time knocking him completely out!

Chapter 23

REDEMPTION

Despite their many sins

Humanity longed for Redemption

Thinking that somehow they could atone

Overcoming their animal instincts, to be better

If not as an aggregate species, then as individuals

Choosing to rise above their many, ugly weaknesses

And claim a high Throne which they did not deserve

But, somehow, their God would endow upon them

Not for their achievements, but for their efforts

Struggling heroically even in abject defeat

To still move forward just another foot

Far from the peak of Perfection

Trying to be a bit less bad

"Somehow" would do

And they were right.

Eashoa's Lament, 23:1-4

Dennis steered the small shuttle through the gap into the dark interior of the drifting Harvester.

There was a small *"ting"* sound that reverberated in the shuttle-craft as they slipped through a selectively permeable force-field keeping air inside the hanger.

Their entrance triggered a *green light* to shine throughout the gigantic chamber, vividly revealing everything within.

"Oooooo....!" Baby Sally gurgled. She clapped her hands together as she peered out the front viewscreen, sitting on George's lap. "Spiders!"

At first glance Dennis didn't know what Sally was referring to...

All he saw was a matrix of twisting, flowing white "cobwebs" congealing to enwrap and immobilize a *gigantic figure* lying in the hanger surrounded by thousands of scattered time-freeze Tubes.

"Is that...?" George gasped.

"It's the *Demon!*" Dennis gulped, guiding the shuttle over towards an extended giant red arm.

Fully a thousand feet long, the Creature was sprawled flat in the huge hanger—with its horns, clawed hands, red body, and long forked tail held down firmly by the ubiquitous white filaments.

And Dennis now saw crawling all over the Demon—even happily eating into its innards through many bloody tunnels—a *horde* of black spider-like apparitions!

"What...are those?" George gasped.

"I saw them before as dots upon those white fibrils arising out of subspace. They're some sort of corrupted lifeform from the bowels of this evil Universe," Dennis shuddered, gently settling the small craft down onto a clear space on the hanger floor.

"There is air plus a weak gravity field outside in the hanger," George said from the copilot seat, reading his instruments. "Should we go out and look for the other Sally-humans?"

"—and the Harvester's subspace drive," Dennis emphasized. "Unless we can use it to jerry-rig a way into *sub*-subspace, then we're no better off than that pitiful, tied-down Creature."

George nodded in agreement. "Imagine how powerful those 'spiders' must be to overcome such a monster," he said in awe. "They stopped the Harvester in its tracks and now are *eating* its Master! What irony...the 'creator' of all this evil is being consumed by it himself."

"Cookie?" baby Sally asked, apparently cheered by the idea of eating.

"Not now, Sally," George replied, gently cradling her as he stiffly got out of his seat to climb with Dennis down into the cramped hold.

There was artificial gravity in the Harvester. To Dennis it felt good to be back in an Earth-like environment.

"Lucky for us there's air outside," Dennis sighed, "since we've no spacesuits to put on."

"We're lucky just to be here," George agreed. "But how are we going to avoid those scampering space-insects out there? If the Demon is their main meal we'd just be appetizers!"

"I don't think they'll be a problem to us," Dennis replied as he helped his remaining crew to open the hold's door and limp out of the cramped hold. "They seem to have plenty to gorge on with the Demon."

"Oooooo....*stinky!*" baby Sally chirped, wrinkling up her pert nose.

Outside, there indeed was an *ugly* smell that caused even the normally impassive Dinosapiens to cringe back. It was the odor of a *rotting carcass* set out in the sun for a week...multiplied a thousand-fold! The awful stink was coming from the giant Satan-like figure sprawled out before them.

"I think it is dead," George gulped from beside Dennis.

"I *hope* it is dead," Dennis replied. "Otherwise, it's suffering the torture of the damned. I would not wish such a fate on even my worst enemy."

"Good riddance either way," George grimly answered as they gingerly walked along the slippery flat floor of the huge hanger in a tight group. They carefully avoided the now cable-like white "cobwebs." And around them, dispersed with the large Tubes, were smashed and crushed vehicles, some of them quite large. The Demon hadn't gone down without a fight.

"It left us to die on that volcano planet after blowing up our Starship," Dennis angrily observed, firmly agreeing with George. "I say it got what it deserved."

"This whole Universe is rotten to the core," Joyce spoke up behind Dennis. "We've got to find a way out or we're next in line to be eaten by those awful things!"

"Or to be crushed when this putrid place implodes in upon itself," Dennis replied. "By rights that White Hole should not be here...it should have dried up moments after the Big Bang created this Universe. But somehow, energy is still flooding into this space from our original Universe."

"What does that mean?" George worriedly asked as they crept around a giant hoof of the rotting Demon's corpse.

"Joyce is our cosmology expert," Dennis grimaced, trying to focus his mind through the overpowering stench. "Ask her, not me."

Joyce stomped her way up beside George, her thick reptilian tail swinging excitedly.

"I'm afraid it's going to drain the entire Black Hole into here, feeding the evil of this place."

"But then what will happen to our original Universe?" George gasped.

"I don't know...but since the Singularity into this new reality wasn't transient as it should be—then the White Hole might *suck in* our whole original Universe!"

"Can that really happen?"

"*Poof!*" baby Sally burped in agreement, dramatically throwing her little arms up into the air.

"What did you say?" George asked, looking down at her upturned little face.

"Poof..." she more-quietly repeated, dropping her eyes and frowning.

Dennis saw that the apparently one-year-old baby wasn't happy anymore. And then it hit him. In her mature previous form, she'd been outside the "Multiverse" and seen what could happen to linked Universes! He hadn't believed what she'd told him before—thinking it was just some hallucination she experienced while they were stuck in subspace within the Black Hole. But now he was convinced she'd seen exactly this very thing happening. Complete, whole Universes could *merge!* Or one could *devour* the other! And that was just what was happening now.

"This is even worse than we thought," George groaned. "Not only is this place collapsing in upon itself, but it's simultaneously sucking in our own Universe. They'll both die together! How could things get any worse?"

"Oh, I think I see how..." Dennis gulped, looking ahead.

They were treading their way carefully around the many human-sized Tubes lying scattered around the giant corpse when a house-sized "spider" that was off to the side *took notice* of them!

It was amorphous, flickering in-and-out of sharp focus, as if it were simultaneously in subspace as well as normal space. But it had definite, sharply delineated *eyes*—composed of red-glowing, multiple eyespots...of different sizes but all implacably wide-opened, glistening orbs—very much like an earth spider!

And every one of its glowing "eyes" was fixed squarely on Dennis and his crew.

And it looked *hungry!*

"Run!" Dennis yelled at them, turning to the side to distract the *multi-limbed blackness* pouncing upon them.

And as his crew stumbled toward a curved doorway leading out of the huge hanger, Dennis resolutely turned back and stopped directly in the path of the skittering nightmare.

"No!" he heard Joyce shout-out as the giant "spider" grabbed and then instantly *swallowed* him!

It felt like his body was being *ripped* into little pieces—though amazingly it didn't hurt.

In fact, he was being *incorporated* into the "substance" of the subspace spider—and perversely found it strangely pleasant. It opened his mind to a whole new perspective: one of naked, all-encompassing HUNGER looking to *feed* voraciously on anything!

Dennis now discovered—as his mind was merged with the Spider—that the White Hole wasn't an accident. It was being kept open *deliberately*. The living entities of this new subspace-realm wanted it *open:* as a pathway to *unlimited, untainted* food!

"Come back to the dining table!" Dennis thought from within his new ephemeral "body"—scampering hungrily after his prior crew.

In the words of baby Sally, they now all looked quite *yummy!*

Dave awoke with his head hurting like it'd been hit with a hammer.

Oh, right. He *had* been hit with a hammer!

Actually, it was just Agent Anderson's big fist banging into the side of his head a couple times, but that was close enough.

"You're back in the dungeon of the Palace of Inquisition," Anderson hurriedly spoke as Dave's blurry vision focused on the dark, mysterious eyeglasses of the Time Keeper. "It's still the 22nd of June, so there's time."

"Time...for what?" Dave groaned, lifting his hands to the side of his head.

"Sorry about your headache, Dr. King," Anderson said, putting the black gun firmly back into Dave's shaking hands as he *untied* ropes that yet again bound Dave to a rigid wooden chair.

"I had to make it look convincing that you were securely in the 'righteous' hands of the Vatican guards," Anderson continued. "Here's all your possessions back: your Cube, your pictures, your pills, and your gun. Plus, you're also going to need *my* Cube. But where you're going you won't need the actual silver and gold coins that you accumulated here as change. I can use them to bribe my way out."

Dave looked around blurrily. Yes, he was back in one of the dungeon cells. The dank rock walls surrounded him. He was again buried beneath the surface streets of 17th Century Rome. Just a single candle illuminated the room, a bucket in the corner to use as a toilet, and a soggy mat on the floor as a bed.

Home, sweet home...

"But...?" Dave started dazedly to try to figure out what was happening.

"They will be here any moment. They want to stop me from helping you," Anderson said, bodily lifting Dave from the chair and positioning him standing wobbly facing a *solid stone wall*.

"Help me do what?"

"There's no time!" Anderson proclaimed.

Indeed, Dave could hear a commotion out in the hallway: shouts and screams!

"I've set the gun on the two-star position. Remember, Dr. King, *not* to set it higher."

"Say what?"

"Point and shoot!" Anderson ordered him, helping him raise the gun, aimed straight at the stone wall.

What the hell? Shoot the *wall?*

Dave growled, instead twisting the gun to the side away from the wall.

"I'm not doing anything unless you tell me what the hell is going on!" he insisted, jerking away from the grasp of the insistent Time Agent.

Anderson looked frantically at the locked wooden door, which was now starting to shudder!

A loud "pounding" sound permeated the cell.

"I wasn't able to stop you from trying to get Galileo to change his actions in your Dimension," Anderson grunted, his words running together as he rapidly spoke. "Fortunately, though, you failed on your own. So we *both* failed. But I've nothing at all against you getting the old Professor to change his mind—in *my* Dimension. My implanted time unit can't carry the two of us, so..."

Dave frowned, starting to understand.

"But that won't stop Dark Energy discovery to...?"

"Point and shoot!" Anderson yelled as the door to the cell *burst inward* and behind it a *frail-looking Nun* walked in.

Dave recognized her.

It was the same nun with the hooked nose that had given Dave directions back to the dungeon when he was disguised as the Cardinal.

Without a pause, Anderson *kicked her viciously* in her gut and she slumped to the floor, another Cube bouncing out of her pocket as she transformed...

—into a black-clad, young oriental woman!

Dave *doubly* recognized her!

"Go on, get out of here!" Arthur urgently yelled at him. "I'll hold her and her comrades off while you..."

"Sanako!" Dave spat in disgust as he turned away to lift up the black gun, fire into the stone wall, saw a small, brief *Portal* snap open—and dove through it as it closed behind him!

Things were getting very complicated.

Did he *want* to change Galileo's actions in the "other" Dimension?

Oh well, maybe the Cube can help me straighten things out, he thought...

—as he fell into yet another *dank, gloomy cell*...where a steely-eyed old man sat cross-legged on a mat in the corner!

The man looked surprised but not panicked by Dave's miraculous entry.

"And just who are you?" Galileo coldly asked as Dave flopped down hard upon the rocky floor.

Dave groaned as he got painfully up to his feet. He was still trying to wrap his head around this abrupt change of worlds.

Then he decided to approach this new Galileo with a whole different strategy than the last one: *honesty.*

"I'm a time-traveler from four hundred years in your future," Dave quickly replied. "And I'm here to talk to you about what you're going to say this coming morning. Uhm...it *is* the day you're to be executed for heresy, isn't it?"

"I am to be burned alive at the stake," the grey-bearded man flatly stated, "if that's what you mean."

"Yes, but it doesn't have to happen."

"I'm listening..."

Periscus sat glumly looking up at the black-grey sky.

It was yet another dismal day trying to survive in a radioactive hell-hole.

Fortunately, Agathe wasn't mortally wounded by her final encounter with the grossly obese Socrates. Being of Snake heritage, many of her organs were elongated through her long body, particularly her lungs. Though one section of her lungs was indeed crushed, the other areas quickly compensated for the decreased air-exchange volume.

After sufficiently recovering, she got the emergency "back-up" battery supply in the safe-room to function. Then she managed to shut the small dome of the King's "safe-room." Reluctantly, it snapped into place above them, keeping out the radioactive dust clouds drifting down from the atomic bomb bombardments. The internal filtration system supplied them with clean air to breathe and fresh water to drink. Their only problem was food.

Before his ugly end, Socrates had devoured all his stored rations. There was nothing left for Periscus and Agathe to eat.

"I'm starving," Periscus sighed, dropping his gaze from the depressing apocalyptic view outside the transparent dome, "but do we really have to do this? Surely we can find stored food somewhere—or a working Duplicator Unit?"

"Well, that would be just fine, friend Periscus," Agathe replied in his head, flowing up and around him. "But we've got to wait for the radiation level outside to drop below lethal levels before we can go out to search for those things. In the meantime, we can either, as you say, starve...*or*...?"

Periscus turned back to the heap of lifeless, rotting flesh.

The thought was disgusting and repugnant. If there were somewhere accessible to do so, he'd much rather bury or burn the putrid remains! But what they were contemplating was certainly better than wasting the mass of organic matter.

"Well, I've butchered my fair share of beached dolphins and small whales," he sighed, grimacing as he held up his "sword." "There's plenty of fat—and possibly a fair amount of muscle beneath it, with which the King moved his legs and arms. But once I've got it all cut out, how can we cook it?"

"There's enough energy in this safe-room's large batteries to render us both jerky and lard," she breezily replied. "Soon I'll be able to swallow it down. It will be repugnant since my species has teleported our nourishments directly into our bloodstreams for eons. But I'm up-regulating the necessary genes and bodily systems. You, however, will only have to *chew* it. It should provide us nourishment."

Periscus grimaced as he determinedly sliced into the heap of quivering flesh.

Yes, it was surprisingly similar to butchering a beached whale. Properly prepared, they had plenty of food here for months!

In his final death that old scoundrel Socrates had at last found redemption. He was keeping his enemies alive—if only to delay the inevitable.

In a radioactive wasteland, trapped in a bubble with finite power sources—the last Human and last Snake were doomed.

But they were both determined to hang on to the very end. It was the least they could do to honor the memory of both their noble races.

Meanwhile, Periscus' mouth was starting to water.

Socrates was looking quite tasty.

Chapter 24

HONOR

How could they claim Pride of Accomplishment?
To then discard it in the heat of a moment's passion
As if it had no value, or never was there at all?
Running screaming from the Challenge in fear
Whether it be difficult, dangerous, or complex
Surely they had eyes to see and ears to hear?
Or were words just meaningless rhetoric to them
Said to soothe their little egos that they were "good"
When "good" was simply what made them FEEL nice
With little or no relation to actual positive results?
Yet a few did take upon themselves Sacrifice,
Dedication, Unselfish Service, and Creativity
Borne up in the arms of Reason, Utility, Respect,
Beauty—self-and-communal Congratulation
That they were not just mere lowly animals
Scrounging and fighting to survive one more day
But chose to rise above the mundane to the Mighty
Even if it meant giving up the most precious things
Accepting no greater Love than a man or woman
Willingly sacrificing their lives for a worthy Cause.

Eashoa's Lament, 24:13-17

George was too chubby to run fast.

All those years of sedentary professorial lecturing had made him lazy and fat! And here he was trying to carry a one-year-old baby in

315

his arms. He was lagging behind the others, with that house-sized black Spider almost upon him!

—when Sally squirmed out of his arms to land on the floor beneath his stumbling feet!

"Sally!" he cried-out, turning back but tripping on his own feet and falling—facing the oncoming, skittering Spider in front of whom wobbly stood the baby!

Oh, Jesus—she was going to get *eaten*, just like poor Dennis!

"No!" baby Sally sternly ordered the Spider...which slowed and stopped, hovering right above her!

It barred a battery of *white fangs*—that dripped a *green, corrosive substance!*

"Give Doggy *back!*" she snapped, lunging forward to latch tightly-upon a shimmering, hairy leg and *bite* it!

With a blood-curdling high-pitched *SCREECH* the many-legged phantasmal creature *lurched backward*, its multiply fanged mouth open wide—as it *vomited-up* a green-slicked Dennis to flop flat upon the floor.

Baby Sally released her prey—who went limping away—and tottered up to the dazed Dinosapien, hugging him around his mucous-coated neck.

Joyce reached them first. She grabbed them both, tossing baby Sally through the air to George. He just managed to stand up and catch her.

George was stunned by the incredible feat the baby had just accomplished.

"Wheeee!" the baby cooed in his arms. *"Flying!"*

"Sally saved you!" Joyce gasped, locking her long neck around Dennis' neck in a dinosaur hug. "We thought you were gone, eaten!"

"Well...I'm glad to be back," Dennis gasped, jerkily swiping the clinging green goo off his torso. "But...we've got much bigger problems...while inside the Spider...I saw that the corpse was still trying to fight them off!" he shakily reported.

George's stomach dropped. He saw that Dennis was correct.

Behind their small group the gigantic corpse of the Demon was *twitching!*

"Please tell me the movement of that corpse is just spasms triggered by the Spiders in dead muscle tissue?" George gulped, backing off unsteadily while still firmly holding onto the happily gurgling baby.

The mammoth Satanic head suddenly *jerked up* into the air, then "thudded" back down, causing the floor to *bounce* under George's feet!

It was trying to break free from the spider-webs.

"That's no spasm of dead tissue!" Joyce said as they all turned from where they'd paused and *ran* for the exit!

Behind them a great "ROAR" sounded-out as the thousand-foot-long giant struggled to pull free from his restraints!

"This way! Over here!" George heard a frantic shout.

A small doorway stood open a hundred feet away from the large curved exit.

It was the *young Sally!*

"That way! That way!" George yelled out to the rest of them. The others were right at the arched exit, about to depart the hanger!

"*Sissy!*" baby Sally called out with glee. She clapped her hands together. Then she held out her little arms toward the young Sally...

—as behind them the Giant *got one arm free* and began flailing it about, steadily bursting through the subspace web holding him to the floor!

"Let's follow George!" Dennis said, skidding to a stop and directing the crew members to turn around.

They streamed into the doorway that young Sally held open just as the Giant snapped all its bonds and surged up to his feet, *screaming* in rage!

From all the entrances to the hanger, thousands of the house-sized Spiders were pouring in and attacking the Demon, swarming up over his thrashing body...

Young Sally slammed the door shut behind them, throwing a lock to keep them safe for a while.

George was heavily panting from fear and exertion. He found himself in a smaller chamber packed with what appeared to be weapons. Around him were many neat stacks of what looked like bombs, gun shells, and even missiles!

"It's *so* good to see all of you," Young Sally gushed. She moved quickly from Dinosapien to Dinosapien, hugging each of them briefly. She paused when she stood in front of George and his charge.

"And who is this little cutie-pie?" she said, tenderly taking the child from George's arms.

George sagged back in relief at giving up the heavy child. He sat down on a pile of seven-foot long missiles, exhausted from his efforts.

"She's...*you!*" George gasped, still trying to catch his breath.

"Me?" Sally grinned, "Really?"

Dennis came up beside her, reaching out a claw to tap baby Sally lightly on her fluffy head, who *giggled* in return!

"She...'hatched'...out of the dead cancerous tissue that was left from the 'original' Sally that the Harvester chose not to take with them," Dennis quickly explained. "She seems...*attuned*...to Dark Energy flux—and powered a Duplicator that allowed us to get a shuttle-craft working. We were really worried when you didn't return—and came here to try and save *you!*"

"Oh, thank God you did," Young Sally gulped. "We tricked the Demon into falling asleep by drugging him with a powerful poison we found here in the weapons room. But then with him out of the picture, those subspace creatures came and took over the entire ship! You were running right into another nest of them in that 'exit' you were about to enter. They'd have torn you to pieces!"

"And how have you managed to evade them?" George said, pushing himself back to his feet and coming over to stand beside the still-tottering, slime-streaked Dennis.

Young Sally bounced Baby Sally in her arms. The child was now happily chortling away in baby-talk.

"The older Sally and I hid in the small rooms and connecting ducts when we got away from the Demon," she quickly answered. "This Harvester is huge. We're like little mice running through the walls of a skyscraper. The Demon reawakened. He fought against the spiders. But once the 'spiders' got their fangs into our severely weakened Demon, he was finished. He was our main problem—that is until the spiders blocked all our access routes. Now they've taking over the whole ship."

"Where's the older Sally now?" Joyce asked.

"Oh, just call her 'Old Sally' and me 'Young Sally' and I suppose this little cutie here is 'Baby Sally'," Sally shrugged. "Well, anyway, Old Sally is up in the control room of the Harvester, trying to figure out how to direct the Harvester to back out of this spider's web. I suppose you noticed the White Hole on your way here?"

"Yes, we figured our original Universe is in grave danger from this 'budded'-out dying one," Joyce replied.

Outside they could hear bone-chilling HOWLS of the Demon fighting hordes of subspace Spiders.

"Damn right it is!" Young Sally winced. "Once the White Hole on this side drains enough of the Milky Way's Black Hole through it— then it'll expand wide enough to suck through our whole Universe! And the Spiders will *feast* on the lifeforms of all our many clean worlds."

"Can we stop it from happening?" Dennis asked.

"Well...theoretically," Sally frowned, gently rocking the baby in her arms, who now yawned widely.

Baby Sally was all tuckered out.

"Yes?" George eagerly asked.

"This new, corrupt Universe was birthed from a Singularity—a tiny pinpoint in space composed of infinite energy. So somewhere in space-time the expanding White Hole has to go back through a 'bottle neck' which is..."

"—the perfect place for us to 'snap' it!" Joyce grinned toothily, in-stantly understanding. The purple spots on her back-scales contract-ed, revealing her excitement. "We could theoretically *disconnect* this entire foul place from our own Universe. That is, if we could some-how overcome infinite energy?"

"That's the key problem," Young Sally urgently replied. "And be-fore you arrived, Old Sally and I didn't even have the means to re-enter *sub*-subspace. All the transport ships in the hanger that had subspace drives were destroyed in the fight between the Demon and the Spiders. But with *you* here...?"

"We'll try to get past the White Hole and then figure out what to do next," Dennis briskly stated as he finished swiping the last of the clinging slime off of him. He reached out and took Baby Sally in his arms from Young Sally, rocking her affectionately before handing her back to George.

George was relieved that Dennis was rapidly recovering from his traumatic experience of being eaten alive by a giant spider.

"What, I'm the nanny here?" George joked. "This little kid is heavy!"

He knew the others knew he wasn't serious. He loved the kid, no matter how heavy she was.

She seemed to be visibly growing. Lucky George had thought to bring the bag of cookies with him, attached to his pants belt. He reached in for a couple and handed them to baby Sally who grabbed one in each of her fists.

She gurgled happily as she stuffed both simultaneously into her mouth.

"But our little shuttlecraft's drive could never generate a subspace field large enough to encompass the Harvester," George said, stating the obvious. "We've still got no way to get this giant vehicle into *sub*-subspace."

"Then we'll just have to make do with only our shuttlecraft going into *sub*-subspace," Dennis grimly replied.

"But what about the many thousands of humans out there in the Tubes?" Sally said, clearly appalled at the idea of leaving them all behind.

"We can't do the impossible," Dennis sadly replied.

"But Dave and my Mother, Professor Volodymyr, Ivanna, Dave's Mother, and many other humans are out there in those tubes!"

"And also there are *billions* of humans—let alone likely billions of *other* intelligent races—back in our home Universe," Dennis matter-of-factly replied. "If we don't find a way to stop the merger of the two Universes, then *all* those billions of billions will die!"

"I...suppose," Sally sighed, obviously deeply pained.

George felt for her, feeling much the same distress himself. Likely there was a duplicate of his own dear, dead wife Alice out there in the tubes. He'd do anything to get her back, even if she were a slightly different version from an earlier timeline.

Joyce stepped forward on her thick, reptilian legs and put a clawed hand upon Young Sally's shoulder. "If we have time, maybe we can find the original Dave that's out there and bring him along with us in the shuttlecraft."

"That would be great," Young Sally thanked her. But then her excitement immediately drained away. "But...in all those scattered tubes...it's probably an impossible task to try and accomplish in a brief timespan...and your shuttlecraft's small cargo-hold doesn't have room for both a Tube and your crew. I understand that we must try and save your crew and us first," her voice trailed off.

A huge "HOWL" came from the hanger as *gigantic claws* smashed through the wall, tossing George and the others back like rag dolls!

George lost his grip on baby Sally and she spun away from him.

"You little *worms* thought you could crawl away from me!" a *sizzling* voice almost split George's eardrums as he lay shaking with terror upon the floor.

Then the wall was completely ripped-out into the Hanger, exposing all of them!

Huge glowing-yellow eyes peered in at them.

"I *ate* those subspace insects, just like they were trying to eat me!" he seethed. His opened mouth revealed giant pointed teeth smeared with glittering-black spider-legs. "And now I'm eating all of *you*— except, of course, for my dear little Sally-humans! Ah! How nice of you to bring me yet another. Your little rebellion won't be for nothing!"

A long claw reached in for Baby Sally where she lay against some missiles, still clutching her cookies. She dropped them, twisting away to the side.

"*Bad* monster!" Baby Sally glared up at him. She popped up from the floor and dashed directly through the ripped-out wall at the face of the Demon!

"Ah, the little baby thinks she can..." The Demon laughed in a deep voice that vibrated the remaining wall-struts...

—as Baby Sally scampered up one of his arms, latched onto his red cheek, and stuck a small arm *directly into* one of his glaring, giant eyeballs!

"*Aaaaaaiiiieeeee!*" the Demon screamed as it lurched upward and back from the hole in the wall, twisting-about in pain!

George ran through, trying to be there to catch Baby Sally when she fell.

But she clung on, gleefully *yanking* out handfuls of eye-pulp from the tortured Demon's eyeball as the creature reflexively *vomited* up a black mass of still-moving spider-parts...

—which quickly latched-onto each other, reforming intact, highly pissed-off scampering Spiders!

"That's *it!*" the thousand-foot tall Demon *bellowed* into the interior of the huge hanger. He rose up to his full thousand-foot height as he *slapped* the clinging baby off his face. She slid along one of his flailing arms, clawing at his red flesh for purchase. "I don't really need any of you pesky Sally-Humans! You're just extra insurance! I'll kill *all* of you and..."

—when the *RED OBELISK* appeared in the air right above its head, hurtling downward...

—and *skewered* him from his skull to his crotch!

As he sagged to his knees, a *rippling force-field* fanned out from the Obelisk. It pushed the remaining black insects through the selectively permeable force-field of the Harvester's tilted-ajar hanger door. The humans and Dinosapiens were left behind.

As the tottering Demon fell forward, George just managed to run out of the way! The force of the fall caused the multi-ton Obelisk to complete its destruction of the satanic Creature, *splitting* the Demon into two equal halves...which twisted, writhed, and then sagged onto the floor of the hanger, motionless.

A giant pool of red blood spread out on the hanger floor. The head of the Demon didn't exist anymore, except as a bloodied red mass of squashed pulp.

"Sally!" George called-out. He ran forward and climbed up onto a twisted Demon-arm, frantically searching for the baby in the bloody mess.

A panel opened on the side of the fallen-down Obelisk.

Tommy cheerfully popped out, bending down to pick up the baby who was happily crawling up to him.

"Hi Mommy!" he grinned at her. "You turned into a baby! Do you remember me, your little boy-robot?"

The baby burped loudly. She'd been munching on a handful of the Demon's eye-gore.

"And I'm over here also," Young Sally said as she clambered up onto the Obelisk to give Tommy a long, tight hug. "And your 'old' Mommy is up in the control room."

"Wow!" the tousle-headed little boy-android laughed happily. "Now I have *three* Mommies!"

"Well...isn't this something?" Dennis said, climbing up to perch on the dead red arm next to the now-resting, panting George.

"The Obelisk and Tommy-robot sure do like their Sally," George grinned widely. "They've got a profound connection to her, that's for sure."

"One, apparently, that brought the Obelisk to us, just in the neck of time."

"And they've also brought us the means to get out of this place *without* having to leave anyone behind, whether awake or in the Tubes!" Joyce excitedly said, scrambling up beside George and Dennis.

"Ah...just like before—when we first came to this vile place," Dennis nodded. "It's happening again, just in reverse. But this time the Obelisk is *active!*"

"Yes! The Obelisk is powerful enough to take the entire Harvester into *sub*-subspace!" George laughed, getting his labored breathing under control. "We're saved! So let's get the hell out of here!"

For the first time in a while, George felt the incredible stress of their nightmare finally slipping away.

"But there's still the matter of the Spiders," Joyce grimaced.

"You think they'll still be a problem?" George asked, suddenly worried again.

He knew from their past "adventures" that nothing was certain until it happened—and not even then!

"Tommy pushed them out of the ship with his force-field," Young Sally said, climbing over to join them. Tommy skipped up behind her holding the laughing baby in his small arms. "The ones that didn't get flushed out were crushed against the hull."

"Yep!" Tommy grinned happily, "I *smushed* all those nasty bugs! They're good and dead."

"Ok," Dennis said, tilting his oblong dinosaur head. "Then what's that noise I hear?"

Outside on the Harvester's hull there now came a rhythmic "banging," that kept getting *louder.*

"Oh, hell," George gasped. "They're not dead. And they're trying to get back in!"

This Galileo was very different from the one Dave had just *unsuccess*fully dealt with.

This man was fit, alert, and keenly determined. Instead of a flabby, wrinkled face this man's was tight and tanned. He wore a neatly kept black robe over a snug white garment, belted with a thick leather strap. He had the same grey-white hair and beard as Dave's Galileo, but well-trimmed, luxuriant—and long!

He looked more like an Old Testament Patriarch than a distinguished Professor.

This Galileo was a truly formidable Presence.

"*Prove* that you are from the future!" the man demanded, uncrossing his legs and swiftly rising to his feet to confront Dave face-to-face. "I don't know what evil magic you used to enter a locked cell, but all I see before me is some fancy-dressed Englishman."

Dave nodded cooperatively, reaching into his pocket to pull out his Cube.

"This may look like magic, but it is really science from the future. And it's *not* evil!" Dave confidently proclaimed as the little Custodian appeared above the white cube, floating translucently in the air.

Galileo jerked back in surprise, startled.

"But is that not a *Jinn?*" he gasped. "Many good Muslims believe in such, but I never thought they were real!"

"I, Sir, am not a 'genie'," the Custodian haughtily replied, sticking his nose up in the air disdainfully. "I am fully-evolved, an independent computer intelligence—at your service, Sir!"

"I don't understand all your words," the 17th Century astronomer grimaced. "But I perceive you are indeed intelligent."

Galileo reached out a tentative finger to poke at the translucent figure. His finger passed into and through the three-dimensional projection.

"Oh my, that tickled," the Custodian laughed as Galileo withdrew his finger.

"It's an illusion—a moving picture," Dave quickly explained, taking a couple steps to a rickety chair and sinking into it wearily. "He is a librarian from the future. Instead of books, the contents of many libraries are stored in this one little cube. He has access to all that information, at his beck and call."

"That's fascinating!" Galileo gaped, drawing up a second chair and sitting also. He was still staring at the floating Custodian. "Indeed, librarians are simply guardians of knowledge. They are not evil. And how many books are in that tiny container?"

"Millions—far more than you or I could ever read or even count," Dave replied.

"And yet this...'Librarian'...can read them all?"

"Instantly!"

"All the knowledge of your supposedly future world is in there?"

"Much of it," Dave answered. "It doesn't contain all knowledge. But it has what we've discovered up to four centuries into your future. There's plenty enough to convince you to change your present course of action."

At this, Galileo's expression hardened.

"And how do I know that you are not an agent of Satan come to dissuade me from the honorable path?" he growled, pulling back. "I fight the true path of Jihad! I am a Martyr to the Truth! Allah dictates my path and I will not be turned away—be it by blind Clerics, the self-righteous Empire, or clever agents of Satan."

Dave was impressed with this man. But he was also puzzled at the Muslim references. Hadn't this man heard of Jesus?

Wait a minute! For whatever reason, Jesus *hadn't* made a mark on history in this alternate, parallel Dimension! So of course this man *wasn't* a Christian. And what was the other strongly evangelistic religion that had been around by this time for a thousand years, at least in Dave's home Dimension...*Islam!*

Dave certainly couldn't masquerade to this Galileo as the resurrected Christ. He wouldn't have any idea what that even meant!

"I'm really tired of being called an 'Agent of Satan'," Dave sighed. "Look, just hear me out, Professor. I can't force you to do anything.

But you do want to stand up for the Truth of the Cosmos, don't you? Surely additional information can't be bad—doing nothing but strengthen your resolve?"

"Say your piece!" Galileo snapped.

"Fine!" Dave curtly replied. "Take a look at this..."

Dave quickly gave to this Galileo the same projected, three-dimensional astronomical display he'd given to the cowardly Galileo of his own world.

At the end of it, the Professor sat in a stony silence.

"Well?" Dave asked.

"I am convinced...that you are from the future," the man admitted. "Those are marvelous images that the telescopes of this age could never acquire. But I see no reason to change my plans. As you yourself said, you've only strengthened my resolve to die for the Truth of the Cosmos!"

"Yes...that's right, but..." Dave struggled, trying to gather his thoughts together.

He'd been prepared to convince *his* Galileo to *not* recant the true nature of the solar system. But to convince this brave Galileo of the parallel Dimension to knowingly *lie* about it was another matter entirely!

"Custodian, please turn off my disguise," Dave asked the glowing figure.

Instantly, the "fancy Englishman" disguise vanished. It left Dave in a thick, tattered coat with his now-full beard and longish hair.

"This is who you truly are?" Galileo tentatively asked, reaching out a hesitant hand to touch Dave's shaggy beard.

"Yes," Dave nodded. "And now let me tell you about the *results* of your heroic action tomorrow."

Galileo shook his head in the negative.

"I don't need your predictions," he insisted. "My martyrdom will encourage all scientists to stand for empirical observations rather than simplistic fantasies," Galileo insisted. "It will convince the doubters of my cherished religion to stand firm against those who worship only comfortable tradition. And it will demonstrate to the Ruling Elite and Government that Science is far stronger than mere blind faith!"

Dave wearily nodded.

"Yes, Professor...it will do all that in the *short* term," he agreed. "But in the *long run* it will cause the exact *opposite* of what you've worked your whole life to achieve."

"What are you saying?" Galileo frowned, rising to his feet to pace nervously back-and-forth across the length of the small cell.

Outside in the hallway, Dave could hear guards "tromping" past. Plus he could see more light out there, coming through a small barred slot high up on the door. It was getting to be morning. He didn't have much more time to convince Galileo to change his mind!

"Your spectacular death will enrage the scientific, enlightened community," Dave hurriedly explained. "They will rise up against the governing bodies. That, in turn, will provoke a violent and total *repression* that will still be in place four hundred years into the future! Instead of freeing the scientists of the world you will ultimately be *chaining* them. Yes, they'll still exist—even achieve wonderful things such as the astronomical discoveries I showed you. But they will always be mere servants to the State, bound by its rules and dictates no matter how arbitrary or stupid."

"But this is not about the State," Galileo firmly protested. "This is about true Godliness!"

"What?" Dave said, confused.

"God is *not* a book or a doctrine or a church," Galileo vehemently declared. He loomed impressively above Dave who still sat wearily in his chair. "God is also revealed to us through ourselves, other devout followers, and the Cosmos. *This* is what I'm fighting for, even dying to defend. It is through Science that finally we see the true Magnificence of God!"

Dave was stunned. He'd always thought that Galileo just went along with the church teachings and traditions because he had to do so. But now he saw that true religious conviction underlay Galileo's determined exploration of the heavens!

Dave was impressed.

"But here in your world...in your future beyond this present date," Dave slowly continued, choosing his words carefully, "all religions are suppressed. They are too dangerous to the Empires. Religion causes Believers such as you to do extreme things that rock the foundations of society. And in the violent backlash triggered initially by your martyrdom, you will *kill* formal religion—creating a Godless, *sterile* science."

Galileo slowly sank back into his chair.

"No...that can't be," he said, putting his head into his hands. "Faith and Science should go hand-in-hand, complementing one another, not competing or warring."

"I'm giving you a chance to change things," Dave relentlessly continued, pressing home his argument. "Not to disturb your mind any more than I've already done—but I'm actually from *another timeline* where things turned out differently! Where I came from, things weren't perfect either. But at least we had governments flexible enough and responsive enough to the people such that individual freedom extended not to just individual beliefs but to whole institutions. Science there was not a property of the State, or the plaything of a Religion, or a tool of the Military. It was a discipline open to all and benefitting all."

"Yes...that too is my dream," Galileo nodded thoughtfully. "Here science is at the whim of religious and political bodies. But I can't believe that God could be separated from the wonders of the heavenly bodies!"

"Look...Professor," Dave pleaded, finally dropping all his lies and tricks. "In my time and world I'm also a scientist, not near as accomplished or famous as you! But I was free...free to believe and do as I wished, assuming I could get funding. Anyway, I was also a Believer—maybe not as devout or driven as you—but that was my choice!"

"You weren't...controlled by the religious clerics?"

"Not in the least! And yet I could worship as I pleased, or not at all."

Galileo still did not look convinced.

"Look," Dave continued, "I don't know if your giving-in to the demands of your religious rulers to deny what you know to be true of the heavenly bodies will produce the world I'm from or not. But I do know that it will change the future history of your world—perhaps for the better. Like it or not, Galileo, you are at a 'tipping-point' of history. And the consequences of your martyrdom will skew history toward repressive Empires far into the future. That I know to be a fact!"

The floating image of the Custodian, silent until now, spoke up: "And I can back up what Dr. King has been telling you, Professor. Anything you doubt concerning what he's said, just ask me and I'll project future-historical proof."

The strong, older man took in a deep breath.

"Perhaps it is weakness or conceit, I don't know—but that won't be necessary, Librarian," he said in a soft but deep tone. "I believe you. And I would do as you say...but..."

"But?" Dave asked.

"But it won't matter," the older man sighed. "Because of my defiance, I'm already sentenced to being burned to death at the stake. Even if I tried to revoke my prior statements, I'd still be executed this morning. In fact, to prevent any untoward speeches, it is customary to tie up and gag prisoners before they're taken into the Arena. The matter of my execution is now completely out of my hands."

Dave thought furiously. He could use his super-gun to lay waste to Rome! But, no, he knew in his gut that any changes big enough to alter the "terrible momentum of history" had to be done by Galileo himself—a true "linchpin" to different future histories!

Dave suddenly saw in his mind a possible solution. He didn't know yet how to achieve it. But it was the only answer.

"Then...then you *do* have to die. But what if you both died *and* escaped?"

"What?"

"Well, then you could moderate the ensuing struggle. Everybody knows that despite your genius in scientific investigations you are a true Believer. Having sacrificed yourself but survived, you'd be even more than a martyr. You'd have god-like status! Trust me, Galileo—I know this to be true. Such an extreme example of unselfish love and devotion to both God and man *can* change the history of an entire world!"

"What, you mean to come back from the dead?" Galileo snorted. "As much as I believe in the Power of the Creator, I don't believe God casually alters the Laws of Nature to produce miracles."

But...Dave still had his bottle of Optimmune pills. If he gave Galileo the whole bottle to swallow, then that might...?

The awful truth hit Dave like a sledgehammer.

Galileo wasn't to be shot, or beheaded, or bled-out, or crucified. Those terrible executions would still leave behind a mutilated body capable of assisted self-repair. No, he was to be *burned* alive. There *wouldn't be anything left* to be resurrected. There'd be only ashes!

"Ah...then...so there's only one real solution here," Dave slowly and stated.

He felt very lightheaded and frightened. But it was the only viable option remaining.

"Tell me!" Galileo insisted. "The guards will be coming any minute to take me to the fire."

Dave reached into his pocket and handed Agent Anderson's Cube to the Professor.

"Are there any Roman Generals of unquestioned authority who are within riding distance of Rome, but are not expected to be here for the execution?"

"Well...I heard that General Marcius Octavius is in his Venice retreat, on vacation. That's why he didn't attend my interrogation, but...?"

"That's perfect," Dave nodded. He vividly recalled—from his rough and recent experience—what a long distance it was to ride or communicate from Venice, all the way to Rome, in this century. "Please describe General Octavius in great detail to this Cube—both his physical appearance and exact military garb."

"What?"

In Galileo's hand, a *pretty blond-haired girl in a blue pants suit* popped up, smiling brightly at him: "How may I help you?" she cheerfully asked.

Dave smiled at Galileo's shocked expression. Why hadn't Dave just shown Agent Anderson's Librarian to Galileo in the first place? That girl was certainly not of his world and time.

"And you?" the prim, male Custodian from Dave's Cube politely requested of Dave.

"Turn me into *him!*" Dave grimly stated, gritting his teeth tightly together.

Dave was going to die in Galileo's place.

It would be horrific. But it just might save "his" parents of this parallel Dimension four hundred years in the future.

And it might stop that *bitch* Sally!

God, he *hated* her.

Chapter 25

SACRIFICE

Some humans gave up far too much

When they became obsessed over the wrong things

While others were far too cautious with their passions

Stingy with their concern, compassion, help, and love

But only those who learned to give until it hurt

And who were able to push back "I" with "we"

Ever got back more pleasure than pain

When they decided to risk it all

On one lone toss of the dice...

Eashoa's Lament, 25:87-89

Tommy was back in the Obelisk, impatiently awaiting orders.

He was in constant communication with both the bridge and the engine room of the Harvester. They were all working frantically to get their stations going as the relentless "banging" on the hull kept getting louder and louder.

But Tommy wasn't concerned. He knew that Old Sally and her helpers could get the Harvester's subspace drive running and that Young Sally with her other helpers could get the ship's controls working. After all, he'd told them what to do. He still remembered all he'd learned when he'd piloted another Harvester from the Galactic Core of their Universe all the way back to Earth!

No, what concerned him most was the final chapter of his book: *Chapter 24—"CONCLUSIONS"* to the *Homo sapiens Eulogy*. He was typing away as fast as he could on Dave's laptop, his fingers *blurring* in front of his eyes. He was on a roll! This was good because he wanted the document finished and safely tucked away in the small storage compartment of the near-indestructible Obelisk before they got underway. After all, there was a good chance they'd not survive their attempt to circumnavigate the White Hole then pass through its source, the Singularity.

If any intelligent creatures ever encountered the Obelisk in some future place or time, Tommy wanted them to know that the human species once existed and made its mark on the Multiverse, however brief or minor.

"And...that's it!" he proudly stated, typing in the last words:

> *"All things human must end*
> *As with so many other transient species*
> *Developed upon the back of many deaths*
> *Dynamic evolution may pause, but not stop*
> *And that which once dominated evaporates*
> *As do mighty planets, stars, and galaxies*
> *Even the Universe inflating to dissipate*
> *Mammoth Black Holes decay and fade*
> *How could humans think otherwise?*
> *Complaining as they did so sadly*
> *That they were so mistreated*
> *Too little time in the Universe*
> *Unfairly limited, held back*
> *What monumental Hubris*
> *Yet applaudable Spunk!*
> *You will be missed..."*

Ah...so fitting, inspired by the moment.

It was finished. And it was just in time.

"Tommy, are you ready down there?" came Young Sally's anxious voice over the Wi-Fi channel of his laptop.

"I am, Mommy!" he cheerfully called back through the microphone of the laptop.

"And how's it going in the engine room?" Tommy heard Young Sally query to Old Sally.

"We've got the ship's drive repaired," Old Sally's voice replied over the speaker. "The Spiders did a job on it, chewing up everything. But the damage was mostly external to the DE-generator complex. We just finished reattaching the last sheared cables. We're ready to drop into subspace on your order!"

"I've a view of the Spiders outside...they're *merging* into each other—combining into *one giant Spider* out there, clinging to the Harvester's hull!" Dennis' raspy dinosaur-voice came over the speaker. "I think they know what we're attempting and are trying to consolidate to withstand the external forces. They're not trying to damage the ship anymore. Their pounding on the hull has stopped. I think they want to hitch a ride along with us!"

That was very ominous. Tommy didn't want a giant spider riding along with them! He didn't like spiders at all. They were silent, creepy, with fangs and poison!

And these sneaky Spiders from the corrupted subspace had to be incredibly tough and intelligent to do what they'd done.

"We can't let them make it over into our Universe," Old Sally's voice insisted. "Don't we have beamer weapons to blow them off the hull?"

"They're too close to take aim," Joyce's softer dinosaur voice came from Tommy's speaker. "The Harvester's powerful laser weapon was made to fight off other spacecraft or level cities down on a planet's surface. And that single combined-Spider outside seems to know it. It is avoiding getting anywhere near the beamer barrels."

"Crafty bastard," George's voice angrily chimed in. "But the forces outside the ship in *sub*-subspace will be incredible. I doubt even the Spider can hang on or survive passage. I don't think it's going to be a problem once we're underway. It'll just get incinerated."

"Tommy, what do you think?" Young Sally asked through the speaker. "Can you use the Obelisk to go knock that giant Spider off of us—or should we get underway with it still attached to the hull?"

Tommy shrugged his small shoulders.

He knew they couldn't see him, but it helped express his feelings.

"I don't know, Mommy," he said into the microphone. "It's stopped banging outside. But now I hear 'scratching' sounds. I think it's still trying to get back inside. The shuttlecraft you came on is still ok here in the hanger. Maybe I could get in it and use some of those weapons you found in that storage room to go fight it?"

"Thanks for the offer, Sweetie," Young Sally quickly replied. "But that sounds much too dangerous. I think we'll just hope it gets burned off once we enter the White Hole."

"Ok, Mommy," Tommy obediently replied. But he was very concerned having that giant Spider out on the hull. It was still trying to get back inside. And it was smart!

It probably didn't want to get "burned off"...

"And what about the giant Demon?" Young Sally asked. "Is it still dead?"

Huh, say what? *Still* dead? Tommy had almost forgotten about that smushed-up Demon. He hadn't checked on it for a while because he was so occupied with finishing the last chapter of his book.

He walked over to the edge of the prone Obelisk and carefully looked out over the squashed remains of the sliced-apart giant corpse.

Nothing was moving.

"Yes, I think it's still good and dead!" Tommy yelled back at the laptop that was physically hooked-into the Obelisk controls, there in the storage space. "It's back to smelling really stinky! Yuch!"

Yep. That was good. Stinky was good. Tommy knew that the satanic Creature had a disconcerting habit of coming back from the "dead"—and sure didn't want that to happen now! But nothing was moving...except for...?

"Oh, no!" he gasped, sucking in his breath.

He ran back to the laptop and urgently spoke directly into it: "Mommy, the monster's head is starting to reform! It was just a bloody 'mush' but now it's getting rounded-up! Do you want me to get the Obelisk to smash it some more?"

"That's a negative, Tommy," Dennis' raspy voice sounded from the laptop. "Everything's ready to attempt a jump! You're set to trigger the Obelisk's subspace drive around the entire Harvester once the ship's engine already has put us into regular subspace, aren't you?"

"I sure am!" Tommy replied, now keeping a wary eye on the slowly reforming giant Satan-head down below.

"Then let's not delay by your trying to get the Obelisk up and moving around inside the ship. Just be ready at your end to put your subspace field around the Harvester once it's successfully entered regular subspace!" Dennis ordered him.

That was funny. Tommy thought that Young Sally was in command? But what the heck—they were all doing their parts.

"Ok! I'm ready!" he called back.

He saw a long white claw start *twitching* down below. The Demon was definitely waking up.

Tommy sat in the opened storage compartment on the topside of the prone Obelisk, awaiting the command to engage its drive.

Tommy *shivered*.

Suddenly in the huge hanger—it felt *cold!*

Tommy had a terrible feeling that things were *not* going to go well in their attempted return to their own Universe.

Dave was securely gagged. His hands were tied tightly behind his back. In addition he was sitting crouched in a narrow, iron cage.

The cage was circular, with thick bars running straight from its top to its bottom. The top of the cage was a curved iron dome, with a large outside ring set into it. Dave suspected that he'd be suspended from a chain on a crane, like a helpless bird in a cage.

It looked like he wouldn't be burned tied to a stake after all.

No, he was going to cook in a cage.

Its purpose was clear. It wasn't a display case. It was an open-air *coffin*...with dark *scorch marks* on the iron bars, floor, and ceiling!

["Are you sure you want to go through with this?"] the Custodian whispered from Dave's earbud. ["It's not too late to stop this. I can easily break the bars and get you out of here."]

"It has to be done," Dave grimly whispered back. "If 'Galileo' were to walk free then he'd be dismissed as a Satanic Demon. The impact on History has to be compelling and powerful—shocked and twisted by his subsequent reappearance! I just hope it will be enough to alter the path of this Dimension."

["But I can hide your escape, placing a duplicate here in your place!"] the Custodian strongly insisted, speaking with uncharacteristic emotion. ["Please reconsider! I will stay and maintain the illusion. The audience won't know the difference!"]

Dave was tempted but knew there was no alternative. "Thanks, Custodian," he said, his whispered sublingual words choking around his gag. "But there have to be burnt remains. There can be no doubt that Galileo died in this cage. Once you were destroyed by the fire then the illusion would vanish. There'd be no remains. It has to be this way."

Dave's heavy cage was carried on a ceremonial cart being hauled by four white horses. They steadily "clomped" along, snorting and whinnying. Apparently, according to the Custodian, the Qur'an—the Holy Book of the Muslim's—described horses as "the supreme blessing." And also according to the tradition of the Muslims, Allah created the horse from the wind as a blessing to man.

So this whole barbaric ceremony was seen as a symbolic religious "blessing."

Well, maybe it was a blessing for the audience—but certainly not for the doomed, condemned man shaking inside the cage!

However—as he was brutally jarred in the cage on the hard, rocky roads of Rome—Dave was surprised to find himself fascinated with the differences he saw from the 17th Century Rome of his Dimension. The gray-white Vatican dome was replaced here with a golden one that glittered spectacularly. The walls of many buildings were not solid stone as on Dave's Earth but incredibly intricate ceramic mosaics of many colors. And in place of towering cathedrals were delicate, elevated minarets.

But it was still Rome—and Rome to the tenth power! Massive, solid, rectangular buildings attested to the power of the continued, *not* fallen, Roman Empire. Mammoth statues of victorious warriors attested to the power of a succession of Emperors.

Indeed, the ceremonial guards surrounding the execution cart— each on their own white steeds—wore the Roman armor that Dave was used to seeing in history books: shining silver helmets with a red plume on top, large flat swords hanging at their sides, bronzed breastplates, and leather greaves at their waists. Around their shoulders, flapping in the gentle breeze, were splendid red cloaks.

If he weren't being taken to his death, Dave would be impressed. Instead, he was chilled by the thought that in this Dimension the Roman Empire was still very much in power, yet colluding with the dominant religion, Islam. Well, due to Dave's action, that religious submission wouldn't last much longer...a small revenge.

Commanding the guard was, supposedly, *General Marcius Octavius!* The prison guards did not questioned his unexpected appearance in Galileo's cell, apparently thinking he'd come in on someone else's watch. Yes, the Roman Empire did not tolerate questions or dissent. The General was not expected back from his retreat in Venice, which was too far away for anyone in that age to go check out. But with the importance of the execution, none thought it odd for him to "return."

"I will make it quick," the "General" quietly called to Dave as he came up close on his horse to "inspect" the cage as it bounced along on the cart. "Before I light the fire I will have you drenched in oil. You will burn quickly, suffering the least amount of pain."

Dave nodded back to the General, grateful but still petrified with fear!

Before being bound and taken away by the guards, Dave had gulped down the entire remaining Optimmune pills, hoping that they'd knock him out or dull the pain. But so far all they'd done was make him sick to his stomach. With his mouth gagged, he couldn't even throw up. So now he almost welcomed death to escape the waves of roiling, pent-up nausea in his gut.

"I'll not have the chance to speak to you again," the General whispered, his face next to the bars as he "inspected" the cage. "I vow to you that I will make your sacrifice meaningful, carefully managing the coming war between State, Religion, and Science. Thank you, brave Time Traveler. I salute you. You die with great honor. May Allah take and comfort your soul!"

Dave nodded again to the man, hoping that the man was right in all his assertions. But, whatever happened, the future history of this Dimension's continuing Empires was likely to be disrupted. Dave would have his revenge on that evil future Sally—regardless of wheth-er or not Judgment Day was pushed off or accelerated.

But Dave was further comforted knowing that Galileo now had powerful assets on his side. Before transforming externally into Gali-leo, Dave gave the man his prized possessions. His energy-gun pro-vided Galileo with a potent weapon. Dave explained how to use it. Anderson's Cube that changed Galileo externally into the absent Gen-eral provided him with most of future history and technology. And Dave's two precious time-locked Pictures gave Galileo a window into the future. The Professor had marveled at the detail and vivid three-dimensional view of Dave's other parents in their final chains and Dave's earlier-time twin happily playing tennis.

Those were fond future memories Dave tried to use to detract himself from the *vicious mob*.

All along their route, the streets were lined with jeering people. They were continuously shouting out chants: "HERETIC! INFIDEL! ... GO TO HELL! ... GOD IS GREAT! PRAISE TO ALLAH! ... DENI-ER OF THE TRUTH OF THE QUR'AN, MAY YOU DIE IN AGONY! ... DEATH TO GALILEO! ... DEATH TO THE HERETIC! ... ENJOY THE FIRES OF HELL! ... DIE! DIE! DIE!"

Dave was getting tired of their shouts, which were being dutifully translated in his ear by the Custodian. He was almost glad that they were finally approaching the Colosseum. It was getting too much to bear.

As if to conform to his wishes, Dave saw they were fast approach-ing the execution site.

Unlike the ruins of the Colosseum in Dave's Dimension of the 17th Century, this ancient stadium was pristine and perfect. Its high walls towered unbroken over Dave as the cart trundled through a large gate into its interior. And out on the floor of the huge stadium Dave in-deed saw a chain swinging from a high arm connected to a mobile minaret-like tower. Clerics with formal flowing robes were clustered around it while Roman soldiers manipulated its mechanisms. Just as with Jesus' execution in the 1st Century in Dave's Dimension, the reli-gious leaders were getting the 17th century Romans to do their dirty work.

["It won't be long now,"] the Custodian spoke soothingly in Dave's earbud. ["We'll both be destroyed together. I did not think that I would be concerned at myself also being irrevocably shut off. But after my time with you, Dr. King, I have grown to enjoy the challenges of independent existence. Please know that I accompany you into that great Unknown as a respectful companion. It has been my honor to serve you."]

For the first time, tears began to well up in Dave's eyes. It was all finally coming to an end. Indeed, it had been a great adventure. Not only had he led a full life, but seen and done things that no other human had ever before experienced. And it all started with that *green-eyed girl* with her cute little *Turtle Tattoo!* He wished he'd gotten to know her better—not the conniving shrew that ended up ruling this Dimension in the future—but that sweet-voiced, ever-curious, intelligent young girl who he first saw in the Megamart in Sulphur, Oklahoma.

He was a long ways from there.

A great "ROAR" went up from the assembled crowd as he and his surrounding guard rolled and rode into the arena.

Thousands were massed in the four ascending tiers that surrounded the central flat arena. And in a royal box Dave saw the present Emperor, described by Galileo as a sadistic monster: *Caesar Romulus Tiberius!* He sat surrounded by his royal court, resplendent in gold armor, flowery cape, and jewel-encrusted crown.

Dave saw the Emperor hold up his hand, instantly silencing the huge crowd.

As the cart slowed, Dave heard above him a hook "clanging" into the ring that was set-into the top of the cage. He saw out in the arena the scattered bloody bodies of the spectacle that had immediately preceded his arrival. And close by—through trapdoors leading beneath the arena—Dave heard the growls of lions, tigers, and bears.

Yes, the Romans were still feeding the condemned to hungry beasts for the amusement of the people.

And looming beside Dave's cage was a previously prepared high pyre of wood.

Dave knew to expect no last-minute mercy from the Emperor. According to what Galileo told him back in the cell, the present Caesar was a cruel man who delighted in the spectacle of "infidels" being punished in the cruelest of fashions. Outwardly, Caesar was a devout Muslim—Islam being the dominate Faith—but in reality he did whatever was required to maintain his absolute power, whether it agreed with Church principles or not.

And "uppity" scientists questioning the foundations of the Empire's orderly but brutal society were definitely *not* tolerated!

"GALILEO GALILEI!" the Emperor shouted in a well-practiced, projected voice that echoed-about the giant stone stadium. "YOU ARE CONVICTED OF THE CRIME OF HERESY! YOU DARED TO QUESTION THE HOLY WORD OF GOD! WHERE IT CLEARLY SHOWS THE SUN MOVING WHILE THE EARTH IS THE UNMOVABLE CENTER OF EXISTENCE, YOU CLAIMED OTHERWISE! AND IN SO DOING, YOU SHOWED DISRESPECT TO BOTH CHURCH AND STATE! FOR THIS, YOU ARE SENTENCED TO *DEATH!*"

As the Emperor paused to get his breath, a great "ROAR" of approval went up from the surrounding crowd, who were lustily *clapping* and *cheering!*

"YOU WHO PRETENDED TO CHANGE THE HEAVENS WILL BE ERASED FROM HISTORY!" the Emperor grandly and loudly continued. "AND LEST ANY TAINT OF YOUR VILE POISON REMAIN, EVEN YOUR BONES WILL BE TURNED TO ASHES AND SCATTERED! THERE WILL NO GRAVE FOR YOUR REMAINS! THERE WILL BE NO MONUMENT TO YOUR PASSING! THERE WILL BE NO DEATH-RELICS OF YOUR PATHETIC EXISTENCE! AND THIS WILL BE A WARNING TO ALL WHO WOULD DARE TO ATTEMPT SIMILAR! ALL WHO OPPOSE THE STATE WILL BE OBLITERATED! *PROCEED WITH THE EXECUTION!*"

Dave wished he could at least stand upright with dignity. But he couldn't. They'd deliberately put him into a cage where he could only crouch, reduced to subhuman status: a captured animal.

He cringed as a *big bucket of oil* was thrown over his body. It was hot and slimy.

It got into his eyes and made it hard to see.

But he blinked it away as he felt the chain *jerk* above him and he was suddenly rocking back-and-forth as he was raised up into the air.

Then he felt the arm above move, causing the cage to swing out over the top of the high stack of wood.

Oh Christ...he gulped, his heart pounding rapidly in his chest, *It's happening!*

He smelled smoke as the pyre beneath him was lit.

The crowd of the huge stadium was yelling and cheering, *stomping* their feet in unison! Dave could feel the trembling vibration of their thousands of feet rattling the entire Colosseum! And then he heard their thunderous chant: "BURN HIM! BURN HIM! BURN HIM!"

"Oh no...no...*please* God!" he gasped for divine mercy through his gag, trying somehow to twist away.

But there was no escape.

A *WALL OF FIRE* suddenly sprang up all around him, blocking his vision beyond the swaying bars of his cage. And beneath him he felt a *furnace* heating up the naked metal.

Dave felt the oil soaking his clothes *light up*...

Instantly, Dave heard his own skin *crackling* and *sputtering* as the intense heat caused *blisters* to pop up all over his body...

He *screamed* as his clothes, hair, face, and eyes were *engulfed* in flames.

Tommy felt the entire Harvester "shudder" as the spaceship dropped into subspace.

On his laptop readout he saw that the interstellar ship was now cocooned inside an *impenetrable black shell*, freed of the subspace spider webs, and hurtling toward the White Hole...

Surely the attacking, conglomerated Spider was now gone, either crushed or brushed off?

"Sooooo...." Tommy's attention jerked away from the screen as he heard a soft, seductive "humming" sound coming from right outside the Obelisk.

Popping his head up Tommy found himself staring into the misshapen *glowing yellow eyes* of the Demon!

"Taking me home, are you?" the giant, mangled Head softly spoke. Reforming giant teeth pointed menacingly at the startled boy-robot.

"Well...maybe?" Tommy gulped, hanging onto the side of the compartment as the entire Obelisk was thrown up by a lurch of the spacecraft only to "crash" back down to the floor of the hanger!

The Head was deformed and scrunched to the side, with just a dark gash where the mouth should have been. But it was quickly adjusting itself back to normal, with giant hands at each side holding it in place!

The Demon's entire body was reintegrating itself, merging back together, the neck thickening and strengthening beneath the loose head. But the regenerating body was itself still shaking and wobbling.

"I...admit...that my new Universe...didn't work out...as best as I'd hoped...but...there's always the *next* time!" the Demon said as his drooping horns slowly straightened upon the top of its forehead. "And you...little pesky creatures...will pay for your sins...I'll *rip* your hearts out and *eat* them!"

Tommy ducked back into the storage compartment, speaking frantically into the laptop's microphone: "The Demon's awake! It's moving! It's talking! What do I do?"

"Hold tight, Tommy," Dennis voice growled back. "Once we're into the White Hole you must use the Obelisk to throw us into *sub*-subspace or we'll be destroyed! We can't make it through the Singularity just protected by a subspace sphere!"

"Uh...ok...how long?"

"We're into the outflow stream—not long!"

The entire Harvester and Obelisk was *shaking violently* as if it were being torn to pieces by the indescribably huge outside pressures!

Tommy stuck his head back up to look into the yellow eyes of the still-swaying, regenerating Demon.

"C-could you p-please wait to make us s-suffer?" Tommy politely asked, the violent shaking stuttering his words. "Dennis says if we d-don't get into *sub*-subspace then all of us will d-die, including you! So..."

"I'm not that easily killed," the now fully reformed Satan's Head grinned. "And I'm hungry—for *you!*"

A giant hand with white claws snatched at Tommy as he ducked back into the Obelisk.

"Now!" Dennis yelled over the small speaker of the laptop...

—as Tommy *activated the Obelisk*...and a peaceful calm suddenly settled around him...

—a *white mist* seeming to envelope him, the Obelisk, and the Demon...

The shuddering was completely gone.

Tommy looked at this computer screen. It showed the Harvester *expanded out* into a doughnut shape, *encircling* a narrowing black vortex!

"We're everywhere at once!" Young Sally's voice came over the computer, speaking with awe...

"I *don't* like this place!" a screeching, confused voice hurt Tommy's ears as a big hand grabbed him out of the compartment and *flung* him up into the air!

"Yikes!" Tommy yelped as he spun end-over-end up into the air...looking down to see the *GAPING MAW* of the Demon waiting to swallow him!

—*thrust-aside* by a scrambling blur of *black hairy legs* as a GI-ANT SPIDER latched onto the side of the Demon and sank big fangs deep into its "flesh"!

"*Aaaaiiiieeeeee!*" the Demon screeched. It thrashed and jerked violently, further-smashing the already broken husks of the space vehicles down on the floor of the hanger.

Tommy fell, just-managing to catch the edge of the toppled Obelisk and clamber back into the storage compartment, shaking uncontrollably.

"It's back! It's back!" he yelled into the microphone of the still-attached laptop.

"What's...back...Tommy?" the disjointed words of Joyce came over the speaker.

"The *Spider* made it back inside!" Tommy yelled. "It must have slipped in when we made the transition into *sub*-subspace! It's fighting with the Demon! They're wrecking the place even more than before! And the Demon tried to *eat* me! I just barely got away!"

"Can you...close up the Obelisk...and get yourself up here...with us?" Young Sally's voice drifted out of the speaker as if it were sweet perfume. "Old Sally...and her helpers...are almost here from engineering...we're all...gathering together..."

Tommy's senses were getting scrambled. He was now smelling colors and seeing emotions! The WHITE HAZE was trying to pull him in a million directions all at once!

The others were probably feeling the same way except worse, being mere flesh-and-blood humans and dinosaurs. They couldn't survive in this frightening place much longer!

"I'll...try," he gasped, pulling out the laptop's connections to the Obelisk and clutching it tightly as he clambered out of the storage compartment and slammed its lid shut.

Via his still-intact RF communication with the Obelisk, Tommy saw that the "doughnut" on his screen was expanding while the vicious black vortex at its center was *narrowing* tighter and tighter!

And he noticed that as they approached the point where the vortex shrank to a hair's width then started to expand past that point—the Harvester was slowing!

Indeed, he could hear a loud "THRUMMING" as if the ship were fighting against a huge "head-wind"...

"Get *off* of me!" the Demon screeched, pounding a giant arm time-and-again into the huge, clinging Spider.

Tommy dropped to the floor, just barely missing being crushed by a giant hoof from a flailing demon-leg!

Where to go? Where to go?—Tommy frantically gasped to himself, trying to see through the ever-thickening white fog.

There! It was Baby Mommy's small shuttlecraft that they flew from the planet where they were marooned. It was still in one piece!

Tommy ran for it as fast as he could—just barely getting there as the Demon sprang up to his full thousand-foot height, yanking the Spider off and tearing it apart limb-by-limb!

The Spider *squealed* in anguish as it was methodically dismembered.

"And now that the bug is back in pieces I'm ready to do the same to *you!*" the Demon howled, lurching toward Tommy...

—who ducked into the opened hatch of the shuttlecraft cockpit, grabbed the controls, and *zipped* it up into the air! He barely avoided the grasp of the Demon as he *dove* into a connecting large tunnel that led up through the bowels of the Harvester to the central control room...

—as the monstrous thousand-foot-tall Demon behind Tommy began SMASHING and RIPPING its way through the mammoth ships' guts right behind him...

"We're-not-making-any-progress-we're-being-pushed-backward-we're-not-going-to-escape!" Dennis' raspy voice came across the laptop speaker, his words all squashed together.

Tommy skidded the shuttle to a stop in the large control room, looking up out of the Harvester's top canopy to see, incredibly, the SPINNING VORTEX *narrowed* to just a *hair-width* in front of them as they seemed to *surround* the funnel in their cloak of white fog!

"What's happening, Mommy?" he yelled through the opened hatch of the shuttle...

—when time seemed to suddenly slow down.

Everyone seemed to be talking very, very slowly even though their eyes were stretched wide in panic.

"We...... can't...... continue...... forward......" Young Sally slowly said in strangely deep tones.

"But...... the...... dying...... Universe...... will...... keep...... on...... pulling...... our....... Universe...... into.......... it...... to.......... die...... along...... with...... it......!" Dennis growled, his words incongruously high and squeaky.

Tommy thought furiously.

Though his outward, physical form was moving in slow motion just like the others, his mind was racing even faster than even his normally quick computations...

"I can trigger to explode all at once the *atomic missiles* and *bombs* that we saw stored below!" Tommy shouted into the white fog at the others. "Will that *pinch off* the funnel thing and let our good Universe detach from the rotting Universe?"

Dennis' oblong, reptilian head turned in slow motion from a computer screen toward Tommy.

"Maybe...... coming...... at...... it....... externally....... it....... could...... work......... good...... thinking...... Tommy," his squeaky words floated out across the air, looking like pink balloons. "But...... we'll...... all...... be...... killed!"

"And...... hopefully...... finally...... that...... Demon......also!" Old Sally yelled triumphantly, as Tommy saw a *CLAWED, GIANT RED*

HAND began *thrusting* its way up, *mangling* the floor of the control room!

"Do...... it...... *now*...... Tommy!" George yelled as he ducked his head protectively over his cradled Baby Sally...

"No!" she petulantly exclaimed. Then she *floated* defiantly out of George's arms, *hovering* in the air directly above the upwardly grasping Demon-hand!

The swirling white fog coalesced around her into a *glittering, golden stream*—which she focused through her small arms and directed *down upon* the emerging Demon!

It screamed in agony, *writhing* in slow motion, *pushing* up against the energy-stream, still advancing!

Now Tommy thought and moved faster than he ever had in his whole life.

He ran around the control room *scooping up* the humans and Dinosapiens with superhuman strength and *tossing* them into the small hold of the shuttlecraft, *jamming* them together like sardines.

It was too fast for them to respond or protest.

His synthetic android body was strained to the utmost!

He took a second to look back at the still-hovering baby...

"Go!" Baby Sally yelled to him, still channeling the golden energy-stream down at the advancing Demon, as if she were *peeing* contemptuously and prolifically upon it!

"But..."

"Go *now!*" she yelled yet again as he hesitated. "Make 'boom'!"

Without a pause to consult the others, Tommy leapt back into the control seat of the shuttlecraft's cockpit, snapped shut all hatchways to the outside, yanked down the canopy, and sent the command for all the weapons stored in the Harvester to *detonate!*

—as he flipped on their subspace drive while they were *already* in *sub*-subspace!

He desperately hoped that there existed a *SUB-sub*-subspace!

Likely as not...that was God.

Well, that would be fun, wouldn't it?

As he slipped to the side with his precious cargo, he saw the "doughnut" EXPLODE in *glittering golden shards*—cleanly *severing* the tiny black line between the two Universes.

"Goodbye, Baby Mommy," Tommy smiled with artificial tears dripping from his artificial eyes—as he and his small shuttlecraft faded away...

Chapter 26
ASHES TO ASHES

And then it all comes to an end...

Heroic efforts or lax doddering stilled

And the living body stopped, motionless, dead

Whatever achievements, great or small, cut-off

And those that are left behind cry-out "Why?"

Thinking that a great injustice has been done

That their lives were too short and too hard

When I already told them quite clearly

It was not an untimely punishment

But a well-deserved reward...

Eashoa's Lament, 26:9-11

Galileo was pleased with the Cube.

It seemed like magic, but he knew it was actually a product of fantastic future science.

But whatever it was—however it worked—it certainly fooled the Roman soldiers, including the Emperor!

After the execution, Caesar Romulus Tiberius even waved at him in a congratulatory gesture from the imperial box.

If he only knew that the "wicked" astronomer supposedly burned to death was still there disguised as a distinguished General!

But enough gloating...

That heroic Time Traveler had made the ultimate sacrifice for him and needed to be honored.

"Is the cage ready to lower?" Galileo asked the attendants.

"It's cool enough now," one of them replied. "And we've almost got the burned wood shoveled away. The cleanup won't take much longer. Most of it is already out of the way from beneath the cage. So anytime that you're ready, General, we can lower it."

The huge Colosseum was empty. It was eerily quiet. The loudly cheering crowd certainly got its "money's worth" today. They'd seen heretic captured Buddhists passively torn apart by lions. They'd seen groups of rebelling slaves pitted against each other, battling to the death. And for the "grand finale" they'd even witnessed a famous scientist set on fire, screaming in agony!

Yes, the people were satisfied.

But—to keep up the pretense until the "General" could quietly slip away—Galileo had to complete Caesar's orders. The Time Traveler's corpse must be turned to ashes and scattered in the wind.

As the "squeaky" cage was slowly lowered, Galileo considered his options. He knew that for a complete cremation to occur, the corpse had to burn at a very high temperature for several hours. Indeed, workers were bringing in fresh lumber to pile in a cross-layered fashion that allowed plenty of oxygen to increase the core temperature. But staying around that long would risk exposure of Galileo's superficial deception.

Was there possibly a quicker way to get the job done?

"It's down, General," the chief attendant said, as with a loud "clatter" they removed the large chain's hook out of the ring on top of the cage.

"Cooked him good," one of his soldiers laughed.

Galileo walked over to the black-burnt cage as they lifted off its rounded iron top.

Inside were the remains of a charred body curled into a fetal positon. The clothes, skin, and hair were completely gone. Most of the flesh was burnt away, leaving behind just crumbling bones covered by soot and ashes. But the head was mostly intact, apparently shielded by the Time Traveler's arms once the rope tying his hands behind him burned off.

Although there was no nose or eyes left in the face, the blackened skull still seemed to be looking at Galileo, as if to say: "I did it!"

"Get the corpse out of there and lay it on the ground," Galileo ordered them. He turned away to walk off a short distance.

"Quite a job you did on him," an unfamiliar, high-pitched voice softly spoke from behind Galileo.

Whirling about, he saw a small, black-clad oriental woman.

Her head was not covered and her face was not veiled, as per proper required behavior of women out in public.

Plus, she was *sneering* at him!

"Who do you think...!" he began, remembering to display the proper arrogance of a Roman General for any watching workers and soldiers scattered around the empty stadium.

"—doesn't matter what you think!" she cut him off. She stepped up close to him and rapped his non-existent illusory "breast-plate" with her knuckles. Instead of a proper "clang" it came back as a soft "thump."

He hoped none of those close around noticed.

"...because I know who *you* are, Professor *Galileo Galilei!*" she grinned wickedly at him.

"What? How dare you...?" he tried to indignantly respond.

She lifted a petite hand faster than he could blink, grabbing him tightly by his throat!

She slowly increased the pressure until he was gasping for breath, feeling his face turning red!

"Now you listen to me," she whispered directly into his ear as he was bent back and down from the relentless pressure of her fingers digging into his throat. "You will tell me all that Dr. King told you before he died—and where you put anything that he gave you. And then we're going to walk out of here and finish this charade. I promise to do it quickly and painlessly. But as we both agree, you are *not* supposed to be alive! And I don't want you popping up later on to..."

She suddenly lurched forward against his chest, her hand dropping limply off his throat. Gasping, Galileo gaped at blood springing up out of the back of the woman's black-haired head!

"Sorry about that..." a strangely clothed stranger said from behind the woman. He was holding in his hand a blood-stained rock. He had on slick dark clothing covering a white shirt, with a piece of cloth tied around his neck hanging down to the middle of his chest. And he had on dark eyeglasses that looked amazingly thin. "She got the jump on me before—and I was a bit late following her. I didn't have my gun, but in a pinch a rock can be rather brutally effective."

"You...you're also...a Time Traveler?" Galileo rasped, trying to get his voice back. "And she's one also? But her body will be hard to explain when..."

"You can call me 'Agent Anderson'—and I'll get rid of her," the man said, ignoring Galileo's redundant question. He grabbed the small woman around her chest and hauled her over behind the towering minaret. Galileo, still gasping for breath, glimpsed a strange vehicle parked there. It had a round, clear top.

The man dumped her into a side seat and then came back around to Galileo.

"Now, I'm happy for you to continue living, Sir," he quietly stated so none of the still busily working people could hear. "But I fear you've got things upon you that are far too disruptive for this time-period. When you reappear to your countrymen you want to do so credibly. They would attack you as being a witch or demon if they knew of your future gadgets. You should instead pretend that you actually escaped the Empire's grasp earlier—and they, in turn, burned someone who looked like you so as not to be embarrassed at their own weakness and ineptitude. Sound reasonable?"

Galileo dumbly nodded.

"Good, then what did Dave give to you?"

"A...strange gun—and pictures—and the Cube."

"Ah...no pills?"

"He swallowed some, a lot of them, before he transformed himself into a duplicate of me."

"Ah...yes, yes—doesn't look like they did him much good though, did they? Poor fellow..."

Anderson glanced over sadly at the still-smoking corpse.

"Regardless," he softly stated such that the workers clearing away the last of the burned wood off to the side wouldn't hear, "I've got to have the Cube and the gun. Then, you're free to go on your way."

"But without the Cube I'll be detected," Galileo grated quietly. "It maintains my disguise. And I need the gun to finish the order from the Emperor!"

"Ah...that's correct," the stocky man nodded. "Then let me just adjust the Cube..."

Galileo reached into his pocket and handed it over. The man whispered a few commands into it before giving it back. "There you go, Professor. It will continue the deception until you're in a safe place. I suggest England. I hear that the 'heretic' minority faction of 'protesting' Muslims there are not near as bad as they are demonized here to be. But once you arrive there the Cube will cease to function. It'll be a nice souvenir for you. You can use it as a paperweight, if you wish. And as to the gun...?"

Galileo pulled it out from beneath his shirt under his fake armor, but didn't give it up. Instead, he abruptly pointed it at the corpse and *pulled the trigger...*

"Wait! What setting do you have...?"

Too late... Galileo had already set it to its highest, "five-star" position. He figured in order to turn the corpse to ash in a few seconds it would have to be at its most powerful setting...

—the deafening BLAST startling everyone, knocking them all to the ground!

For a moment, there was no sound but a strange "sizzling" noise that kept going on and on...

"It's the *wrath of Allah* against the dead heretic!" Agent Anderson shouted in perfect Italian as he sprang back to his feet. "God is great! God is great! *God is great!*"

Stunned, the others slowly picked themselves up. They muttered the chant by rote in return...clearly confused and frightened as to what had just happened!

"And what is *that?*" Galileo asked, climbing back to his feet and walking over to the corpse...

—which was no longer there!

In its place was a *spinning black hole* lit with glittering diamond patterns!

"It'll be gone in a minute," Anderson said as they watched it slowly shrink away. "You certainly succeeded in getting rid of the evidence, Galileo. Well done! And now I think you'll not need that any longer, right?"

Before Galileo could answer, Anderson snatched the black gun from his shaking hands, slipping it away beneath his coat.

Simultaneously the floating black hole closed and vanished.

"And now about those...*damn!*" he swore, grimacing.

Galileo saw that the strange vehicle concealed behind the mobile minaret had disappeared!

"That *bitch!*" Anderson growled. "Well, can't be helped. Good day to you, Sir!" he said as he spun about and departed.

"General, should we...?" one of the soldiers asked, seeing the peculiarly dressed man sauntering swiftly away.

"That's just a visiting dignitary here to certify the death of the heretic—which *Allah* just disposed of miraculously! Don't you agree with me?" Galileo admonished the man.

"Certainly, Sir!" the soldier nodded.

"Then take charge of cleaning up the rest of this mess. I've got leave!"

Galileo caught his frightened horse, mounted, and galloped away across the stadium. England sounded like a good place to escape to, lay low for a while, and eventually reemerge. And that stocky Time Traveler's cover-story also sounded reasonable.

Gun or not, functional Cube or not, Galileo was going to *shake the heavens*—especially now that he'd be free to speak his mind and follow the directives of the Lord, safe in England!

But he suddenly remembered he still had those strange, moving pictures.

Reaching into his pocket as he galloped out of the Stadium onto the streets of Rome, he pulled them out, glancing down at them.

One of them now showed a *man and woman smiling lovingly at each other*, happily holding hands.

The chains he'd before seen on them were gone.

And the other one revealed a handsome teenage boy grinning as he peered up through a huge telescope.

Galileo also grinned.

Things were definitely going to change

Sally sat sipping cold lemonade looking out over nighttime Manhattan from her secluded suite at the top of the *One World Trade Center*.

The many-colored lights below were spectacular, steady and bright. They reflected back off the water in the river below.

It was like Christmas!

And everything was going just fine. Agent Anderson was somewhere back in time, fiddling. But he was a renegade, hunted and desperate. Her best Time Keepers were after him. She knew that his days were numbered.

Sally got up and walked stiffly to a mirror, disturbed but reconciled to the image she saw there.

She saw reflected back at her an elegantly clothed but *thin, stooped, old woman*—with a bald, splotched head, liver-spotted face and arms, and that stubborn Turtle Tattoo still there on her wrist! She'd thought many times of having it removed, but after the many decades of her extended lifespan it was an undeniable part of her.

But it hadn't bothered her in years.

She grinned—looking like a grotesque Halloween pumpkin stuck up onto a stick in the full-length mirror—until she noticed something disturbing.

Her Turtle Tattoo was *glowing...*

"Commissioner! Quick! Get in! We have to leave!"

Sally spun around and saw *hovering* there in midair—right in the center of her exquisitely furnished apartment—a *bub* with its transparent top flung open!

Sanako, the side of her head covered with blood, weakly stumbled out. She staggered over to Sally, grabbing her arm and dragged her back toward the bub...

"What the hell is this?" Sally grimaced, trying to pull free. "What happened to you?"

"There's a *time-quake* coming!" Sanako shouted so loud that Sally winced. Apparently the woman's eardrums were damaged. "We've got to escape outside of Time or we'll be *erased!*"

Sally saw through the full-wall windows that the solid skyscrapers below were now *wavering!*

She leapt into the Bub as Sanako fumbled at the controls. And then the craft began to *fade away...*

"It was that God-damned Dave, wasn't it?" Sally grated to Sanako through clenched teeth.

"Yes...with help from Anderson," the oriental woman replied as everything outside their vehicle turned into a *swirling vortex* of rainbow colors!

"I'll *throttle* them both with my own two hands!" Sally growled, seething.

Yes, that pest Dave had—somehow—succeeded in changing everything for the worst!

But all was not lost. Her Time-Keepers were intact. And that which has once been changed can always be changed back.

Periscus and Agathe topped the hill and looked down into the valley.

It had taken them almost a year to return.

They had to wait for the radiation to abate enough for them to safely travel on foot the long road from what was previously Capital City. Now the sun peeked out periodically from behind the dark, roiling clouds above—and the still-present radiation was below lethal levels.

After exhausting the "food" left them by King Socrates, they'd scrounged through underground storerooms, finding barely enough to stay alive. There were no functioning Duplicator Units left. The orbiting fleet was completely destroyed in Socrates' last spasm of blind retribution. So technology was gone. The cities were leveled, obliterated in the war. And as far as he and Agathe knew, all intelligent life and most of the animals on the planet's surface were dead...

—except, of course, for the Black Birds.

Having already retreated from the resurgent civilization they were spared from its decimation. The intelligent Birds salvaged much of the remaining plant life, even some fish. So the remnants of Earth's biology were gathered into the valley then protected by a biosphere self-generated force field. It was self-regulating: cleaning the air passing through it, radiating internal light for the plants, and purifying the water streaming from underground reservoirs. The shield would last long enough to insure the valley's survival past the radioactive decimation and global nuclear winter.

It was the one place on Earth that life continued, both as a refuge and preserve. The last "immigrants" to arrive there were Periscus and Agathe.

"It's good to see the old place again," Periscus grinned, rubbing at his long whiskers. "We ain't gonna starve down there!"

"Yes, but you're the last of the humans and I'm the last of the Snakes," she sighed. "It seems a pity..."

"Am I not friendly enough?" he laughed, looking at the iridescent-ly shining blue-and-white giant snake. "I don't mind if you're a 'cold-blooded' reptile. You're pretty enough as a companion for an old gent like me!"

"I don't think so," she strangely stated.

"What do you mean?" he began...

—as flowing over to the side, Agathe's long body began to shorten, then fatten, and then sprout limbs!

And just that quickly she transformed into a slender, nicely curved, naked female human.

Her hair was long, almost down to her waist, spreading out to cover her ample breasts. Her hair shone luxuriously, white and blue!

"You...you're...*beautiful!*" Periscus gasped. "But if you could do that, then why didn't you...?"

She stumbled uncertainly as she moved toward him. He ran over and grasped her elbow, supporting her.

"This 'walking' is trickier than it looks," she laughed. "It's a lot harder than crawling or slithering."

"Sure it is!" he comforted her. "But why now and not...?"

"I've only sufficient energy-stores to do this once," she explained, tottering as she tried to walk beside him. "I had to be sure we were safe before I tried the transformation. You were already in your natural human form so I didn't need to duplicate your unique human attributes. In my natural snake form I was much more useful in the narrow tunnels left under the city."

"Oh, I think you can be *very* useful in this human form!" he gaped at her.

She actually blushed.

"Well, I've all the right parts—but since there are no scientists to genetically alter my chromosomes I won't be fertile like your other transformed wives. So, unfortunately, we won't be able to have any children. But perhaps we can still have fun otherwise?"

"Oh...*lots* of fun!" Periscus grinned.

They walked over the crest and downward into the green, luxuriant valley. It pained him to see it empty of all his human-dinosapien
friends, wives, and children. But Periscus was sure they'd moved on
to an even loftier godly realm. This was a place of miracles! The river
was smaller than Periscus remembered, but it still rushed along with
a hearty "gurgle." And as a parting gift the Black Birds had kindly
caused some of the bushes and trees to form-up into a nice replica of
Dave's original hut.

Home sweet home!

It was the end of the human race on Earth. But it wasn't a bad
ending. He and Agathe would live on very happily here for decades
into the future.

Upon the ashes of the past arise the rampant growth of the present. And upon that—who knew?

Perhaps this was the start of something grander and even greater
than anything that'd come before?

Regardless, Periscus and Agathe walked arm-in-arm into the lush
meadows.

It was good to be alive.

Chapter 27

BLESSED BE THE NAME OF THE LORD

They thought that God was just a fanciful delusion
Made up by them to soothe their fear of death
Or to endorse their latest perversions as holy
And nothing they could actually see or hear
Just an image, whether written, painted, or sculpted
Something that they had to go to a Temple to feel
When all along it was there right inside of them
Indeed, not just inside but all they saw and knew
Actual manifestations and extensions of the Creator
Such that all they did and experienced, good or bad
Was participated with, informed by, and was
Their heavenly Father standing there beside them
Walking with them, talking to them, and sharing
His Grand Creativity informing their lowly minds
That they might experience beyond the mundane
In everything tasting Infinite Divinity...

Eashoa's Lament, 27:37-41

"Is that a turtle?" he asked, peering down at the check-out lady's exposed wrist.

She glanced up at him from the items she was expertly sliding through the scanner.

"Yes, it's a baby turtle."

He marveled at it for a few seconds as he leaned there against the check-writing platform. He was steadying himself as he recovered from a bought of abrupt dizziness he'd experienced just a few minutes ago. Must be low blood sugar! *Maybe I better munch up one of those store-baked cupcakes once I get into the car with my purchases*, he thought to himself.

"It's so bright! I've never seen a tattoo so bright!" he marveled as he stood there. He was poised ready to hand her another of his carrying-bags to put his purchases into when the present one filled up.

Indeed, the little tattoo gleamed with bright greens, rich browns, and deep blacks.

"Thanks," she replied. She continued to expertly and quickly slip his items past the scanner, then into his waiting bags. "I just treated myself to it the other day."

"I thought it might be one of those stick-on ones," he continued, fascinated. "I've never seen a real tattoo as bright as that!"

She flicked a quick, shy smile at him. "It's brand new, that's why. That's when the colors are brightest. It will fade with time."

She paused in her work behind the counter to slide the sleeve of the shirt on the arm with the turtle tattoo upward. Other wonderful creatures were briefly revealed: a creepy black spider with white specks, a flapping red and yellow parrot, and a coiled blue snake clutching a flowering rose.

"Wow! Those are beautiful!" he said.

She quickly slid her sleeve back down as she placed the last of his items into the opened bag.

"Your total is nineteen, even."

He reached into his back pocket, pulled out his billfold, and started to hand her a folded twenty.

Then he stopped—his hand still out...

"Sally?" he asked, remembering everything.

Her big green eyes opened wide.

Then she too looked surprised, frowning deeply—as if she also remembered...everything!

"Dave?" she said, reaching over to put a hand on his arm. "Are we...really back?"

He looked around at the bustling Megamart. It was exactly as he remembered that first day he saw her for the very first time.

"I think so—don't know how or why, but it appears we've been given yet another chance!"

He grinned widely. She did the same.

"It seems...unbelievable," she sighed, her smile fading. "I was...in another, dying Universe..."

"And I was being burned alive..."

"Sounds like we've tall tales to tell each other," she grinned.

"Amazing adventures, that's for sure," he grinned back.

"And now we're back...again," she marveled.

They both stood still for a moment, just looking deeply into each other's eyes.

"So...what do we do now?" he softly asked.

She closed the till, took off and neatly folded her apron. Then she hung up a sign that said "lane closed."

"Bathroom break!" Sally cheerfully called to the supervisor.

Dave took her arm and they walked directly toward the exit, not hesitating a moment, even leaving behind his shopping cart.

"But...don't we need some Optimmune for...?" she began.

"Nope!" he immediately replied.

"But what are we going to do about...?" she started to ask as they walked hand-in-hand out the sliding doors and dropped down a couple feet into Dave's Dimension.

"Nothing!"

"Nothing? But..."

Ahead Dave saw his bright-yellow Chevy Cavalier. It wasn't a Bub, a Starship, or a friendly talking dinosaur. But it was his reliable, ordinary, *absolutely gorgeous* vehicle!

As they walked leisurely up to his car he replied: "We're going to church with my Mom, who's quite content and at peace with her present life. Then we're going to get married, today! The local County Clerk is a friend of my Mom's and has a running joke with her that he'll open up any day I want a marriage license. I'll call him on it. He's an old family friend and will be delighted. It's actually easy to do in Oklahoma. Our minister Cliff will likewise be delighted, not-to-mention my Mom, who'll be deliriously happy."

She snorted good-naturedly.

"Oh, *are* we now?" she laughed. "Don't I get a say in this?"

At the door of the car Dave dropped to one knee and held her warm hand, looking up into her bright green eyes.

The sun sparkled off of her fluffy mop of red-brown hair.

And on her wrist, the Turtle Tattoo *winked!*

"Sally Smith, will you do me the honor of being my wife?" he said. "I know I'm not all that handsome or young anymore, but I've a good job, good moral character...and I'm proven to be 100% reliable! No matter what, I keep coming back to you."

She mock-sighed... "Well...I don't know..."

"What?" he mock-gasped.

"Well..." she grinned. "I suppose—if you *really* love me?"

He paused to think about it for a moment, still down on his knee.

"Well, I *guess* I do..." he shrugged, smiling coyly up at her.

"And I guess I love you too!" she snickered.

After hugging and kissing for a bit—to the amusement of a few other shoppers passing by—they got into the yellow Cavalier.

"And what about our world-shaking inventions?" Sally asked, sobering up as they drove out of the store's parking lot.

"Nothing!"

"Nothing?"

"When we eventually get back to our house in Edmond, I'm walking into the garage and turning my experiment *off!*" he firmly stated. "And then I'm dismantling it completely."

"But—with everything we know now, couldn't we...?"

"The world's not ready for Dark Energy generation," he shrugged. "Give it a few more centuries. Maybe then..." his voice trailed off.

She nodded ruefully.

"There's just too much pain and tragedy in the world," she softly summarized. "But there's also a lot of beauty and inspiration. And for us, that will be sufficient."

"Amen," he answered. "*Amen!*"

After a short drive on Broadway they turned right on 12th at the stop light. He parked in front of his Mom's house. And there, coming out of the house to meet them—looking pleasantly flustered at seeing Dave with a pretty girl—was Jean King.

Was she in for a surprise!

Dave had brought down to Earth an *angel*, snagging a girl from far above his "station," a girl who *flew too high*...

—only to land safely in his arms.

Chapter 28
<u>**A FEW YEARS LATER...**</u>

Time moves at a pace of itself

Not constrained by sun, moon, or Earth

Defining itself in indescribable ways

So that humans, though using it constantly,

Have no idea at all what it is or means

Yet, oblivious to their own ignorance

They obsess on its relentless movement

Ordering their lives by its passage

And bemoaning its swift alterations

Wondering why the body corrupts

And longing for lost days of youth

Not realizing the past is the present

And the present is future which is past

Where all is in equilibrium, but repeats

And the river that never is the same

Cycles its substance over and over

An ever-changing refreshing blend

That one should never despair

For that which once came around

Will come around again...

Eashoa's Lament, 28:28-31

Something was wrong.

It was Saturday in early springtime. Hardly anyone was out vacationing in the mostly empty campsites of Rock Creek. Everything was placid and quiet. But to Suzy the trees seemed...disturbed! Their branches, just starting to get leaves, were twisted at odd angles. And the animals—particularly the birds—were skittish and scared. Even the stream seemed unhappy, frothing where it should have been lazily flowing along.

Suddenly Suzy jumped off her girl-sized mountain bike and peered intently off into the distance.

Billy skidded to a stop behind her and hopped off his own even smaller mountain bike to stand holding it upright at her side.

"Did you see that?" she asked.

"See what?" he replied, shading his eyes with his hand.

She was ten years old and quite a tomboy. She loved to go out and ride her mountain bike up and down the many trails of the *Chickasaw National Recreation Area*—known as "The Park" to locals, in the small town of Sulphur, Oklahoma. Her younger brother was only six years old, but was also very athletic, though often disagreeably so! She knew that he thought that *he* should be the leader, even though she was older. He was really irritating. He even thought that—though he was younger—he was smarter than her! What a dummy...

It was still chilly in the springtime, yet warm-enough to go zooming down the forested trails beside bubbling brooks and streams.

But she'd just seen something really strange out in the woods.

"It was...like a big lizard?" she said, squinting.

She had a head of thick hair worn in pigtails to each side of her head. People told her she was the spitting image of her mother, Sally King, though with blond hair instead of her mother's red-brown. But they both had bright green eyes. And they were both adventurous, curious to the point of obsession. Anything "different" fixated their attention!

Billy liked to keep his black hair short, like a "G.I.-Joe" soldier. Suzy thought it made him look even younger and weaker. But Suzy also knew he was strong for his six years, with well-defined muscles in his relatively smaller arms and legs.

"Hah!" he snorted disdainfully. "The lizards around here are tiny. Maybe it was a deer? There's lots of deer in the woods."

"I *know* that, Billy!" she snapped at him, starting to climb back onto her blue bike.

Billy had a red bike. He liked flashy things. She, however, liked things that blended in smoothly with the immediate environment.

"It's time to start back," he protested as she moved off the defined path out into the surrounding woods. "And Mom says to never get off of the trail. You're going to get us into trouble!"

Her Mom let her do lots of stuff by herself as long as she was careful. Since they lived only a few blocks from the main entrance to the Park, going for rides out here was second nature to her. It was like the Park was her house's own giant backyard. Her Mom said "taking initiative" gave Suzy a sense of independence. But her Dad was more cautious, insisting that she think of the "consequences"—especially when she was looking after her pesky little brother!

Well, her Mother was certainly real smart—teaching mathematics at the local high school: hard stuff like algebra and calculus. But her Mom didn't know everything! And her Dad was always puttering at his crazy "inventions" when he wasn't coaching the high school tennis team. That was cool, but he wasn't out there with her right now to tell her she had to turn back.

"Oh, don't you be such a scaredy-cat!" she huffed at him. "We won't go down any steep slopes. Just try and keep up," she said as she slipped deeper into the trees past bushes and boulders.

"It's dangerous out here! What if you crash and break your leg? There's lots of rocks and roots! Sometimes my cellphone doesn't work out here in the woods. How can I call an ambulance? I think we should go back, Suzy."

Something was definitely up. She felt it at the nape of her neck. The little hairs there were sticking up instead of lying flat like they were supposed to do. But it wasn't from fear, exactly. It was more like...excitement!

If you don't have a little danger in your life, Suzy remembered her mother's wise words—*then you'll die of boredom!*

"Ok, then, Billy. You're right," she admitted, slowing to a stop.

She hopped off her bike, grabbing it by its handlebars. "From here on we'll walk, pushing our bikes along. Are you satisfied we're being safe enough?"

"But that's too much work!" he complained, also hopping off his own bike and grabbing it by the handlebars to push forward from the side. "It's lots more fun 'swooshing' down the road back to our house. I'm getting tired! We've been out here long enough. I want to go home. I'm scared!"

"Stop complaining, Billy. We'll turn back soon enough. There's nothing to be scared about."

That was only partially true. Normally the well-worn paths of the Park, patrolled by the friendly Park Rangers, were very safe. But they were off the paths out in the actual woods. Who knew what might lurk out here?

Maybe there *was* something a little bit scary out here...?

Hah, that just made it more exciting!

Having a little danger in your life meant sometimes making her decisions for herself, even if they were different from the "rules" that grownups wanted to put on everything.

After all, if she always did only what her parents told her, then she wouldn't have gotten that little *Turtle Tattoo* on her arm—just like her Mom's! Her Mom and Dad got really angry with her for doing that without their permission. But the nice man with the goatee, who did it for her at the Senior Center beside the Park, just a few blocks from her home, said it was completely safe. He didn't care that she didn't have her parents' permission! And her friends at school *dared* her to do it, to look like her school-teacher mother. They *dared* her!

Yep, *she* was cool.

But, shaking her head to drive away her daydreaming, she realized they'd gone deeper into the woods than she'd intended.

It was definitely getting spooky.

The looming trees now didn't seem so friendly and protective. In the late evening light that looked like they were *hiding* things.

"Suzy..." Billy whined behind her.

"Wait, I see something up ahead."

"What is it?" he eagerly replied, now not so negative.

"Oh...it's just a little meadow is all."

Sure enough they were just outside a clearing in the middle of the looming trees where...

They both simultaneously saw it!

Billy froze beside Suzy. Neither of them said a word. They just looked out into the secluded glade where a person-sized, leathery *creature* was hopping around nervously, scratching here and there at the dirt.

"Wow!" Billy whispered. "It *is* a big lizard—in fact it looks an awful lot like a *Pelecaninimus* in my dinosaur book! It's like an ostrich but without feathers or wings. See? He has little arms instead of wings, with three clawed-toes on his hands and feet. And see that long, swinging tail? Jesus, Suzy! That's...that's...that's a *dinosaur!*"

Still with an eye on the man-sized, dirt-scratching creature, Suzy poked Billy on his arm.

"What'd you do that for?" he whispered, rubbing his shoulder with a hand where she'd lightly hit him.

"If that's a real dinosaur, then how *old* is he supposed to be?" she scornfully replied.

A cold wind had just sprung up. The leaves above their heads were swaying and twisting, like they were also getting scared!

"Well..." he carefully thought, furrowing his brow. "If I remember right from my book—they lived, oh, maybe 125 million years ago."

Suddenly the creature's long neck sprang upright and it looked with big black eyes *straight at* both of them!

"*Breeeep!*" it squawked, turning its back on them and bolting into the far woods on the opposite side of the glade.

"That's his name, 'Breep'!" Suzy excitedly exclaimed. "Come on, let's follow him!"

"But...it's getting dark and cold..." Billy weakly protested.

"Do you want to lose a *dinosaur?*" she gasped, now embracing the fantastic notion. She eagerly pushed her bike further along the uneven, rough ground.

"Nope!" he agreed, following right behind her. "But if we get in trouble, it's *your* fault!"

"We *won't* get into trouble..."

They didn't travel far, maybe a half mile on into the woods. But off the beaten path they were quickly into an area of the Park where only a few horse-riders occasionally ventured. Hardly anyone else, even park Rangers, ever went out there.

It was a desolate, rough area away from roads, houses, and power lines. They were now out of the forest proper. All around them were rolling hills, low shrubs, scattered boulders, tree clumps, and hidden shallow depressions. It was like being in the middle of a vast wilderness hundreds of years ago where only an occasional traveling Indian ventured.

And up ahead, still frantically scratching away at the ground with powerful legs—Suzy saw "Breep"!

And, very bizarrely, a whole collection of animals from the forest surrounded Breep...standing in a wide circle at a distance. They just sat there, watching! There were birds, deer, small lizards, tortoises, armadillos, possums, skunks, squirrels, snakes, and even a fox.

Suzy and Billy looked at each other in disbelief. What was going on?

They cautiously approached the big lizard and its surrounding attendants, afraid they'd scare it off.

The sun was now low on the horizon and Suzy knew she really should be getting on home, especially with her younger brother in tow.

But this was just too amazing!

And then there was another sudden *deep chill* in the air—plus a *strange vibration* for which there was no obvious source. And the *low tremor* wasn't just in the air...it was also in the ground at their feet! It was like just before a big earthquake, when the animals were all upset and scared!

—except that they were still just standing around in a big circle?

That was rather ominous...

But it was also even more fascinating!

Was that *really* a small dinosaur digging in the dirt now just a few yards in front of Suzy?

It looked up and saw them. But it didn't run away. Instead— nervously blinking its big black eyes—it went right on digging.

And as they walked up closer, pushing their bikes, it jerkily hopped over to the side. Looking back at them he opened his toothy beak wide, and urgently barked: "*Breep! Breep! Breep!*"

"It wants us to see what it's digging up!" Billy exclaimed, now rushing forward.

Suzy followed behind him, thinking that maybe the strange animal had dug up an old skeleton or something?

But what she saw in the dirt at her feet was just a *small door*, which had been buried under a layer of rocks that Breep scratched off!

"Wow...what's *in* there, do you think?" Billy said.

That low-level vibration around them was getting stronger...

Suzy had a sudden premonition that they should just leave whatever it was alone—run back to the safe trail and then bike as fast as she could to their comfortable home. But she resolutely pushed that concern aside. That was being a scaredy-cat, *not* a brave explorer!

"Well then, let's just find out," she said, laying her bike down flat to the side of them. She flexed together the fingers on both of her hands. She could dig out the remaining dirt and try to find an edge by which to grab onto the panel.

Billy lay down his red bike also, putting it carefully onto its side. He then turned back to stand with Suzy above the shallow trench that Breep had dug.

"Look, there's a handle," Suzy said as she shoved out the remaining dirt, reaching down and grabbing it. She gathered all her strength to try and wrestle it open—but, surprisingly, the small door easily swung outward.

Inside, Suzy saw a faint light blinking on and off. What *was* this—out there in the wilderness all by itself, buried in a pit beneath the ground?

"Maybe it's a nuclear missile!" Billy grinned at Suzy's side, hopping up and down with excitement. "Wow! I read about these 'silo' things in a book at school. They're put where nobody can find them in case there's an atomic war. It's a big tunnel that goes down into the ground. They got *soldiers* in them!"

He grinned widely, preening—rubbing at his crewcut hair.

Oh, sure. *He* was a soldier?

Suzy peered suspiciously down into the revealed, dim chamber.

"It doesn't look like there's much room in it for...?" she began...

—as she glimpsed Breep coming up silently behind them then abruptly *knocking* them both forward, *tumbling* together with them into the opened compartment!

The panel bounced back into place above them.

They were trapped.

And before Suzy or Billy had time to react, seemingly serenaded by a loud earthquake, the buried *Red Obelisk* vanished...

—leaving behind their bikes laid flat on the ground beside a now-empty, large hole.

The sides of the long cavity abruptly caved in, partially filling the now-revealed deep trench.

The cowering circle of animals collectively breathed a sigh of relief, scattering-away across the landscape.

Finally, the Park was at peace.

THE END

[continued in: *The Girl Who Chased Spaceships*]

Thank you for reading!

Dear reader,

I hope you enjoyed **The Girl Who Flew Too High**. I had loads of fun recreating the 17th century world of Galileo, both here and in the alternate dimension. And hatching a baby Sally was also tremendous fun. The sequel to this book, **The Girl Who Chased Spaceships**, finds the new "girl with the turtle tattoo" lost, hunting a mythical spaceship to take her home.

I hope you are intrigued by the sequel's dangerous question: "What happens when your wildest dreams come true?" One (terrible) answer is you become history's greatest criminal.

Finally, I need to ask you for a favor. If you enjoyed this book and would like to encourage others to read it, **a review written by you** on the Amazon page for this book would be greatly helpful. It's hard to get reviews nowadays and your support will be very important to both me and other readers. If you'd like to do this, I sincerely thank you in advance for your time and effort. It can be as long or short as you wish.

Thanks again for reading my **Girl with the Turtle Tattoo** books and traveling with me to the ends of the Universe and beyond.

Sincerely,

Dan Lyle

<u>About the Author</u>:

Daniel Basil Lyle holds a Ph.D. in Biology, is a lifelong amateur herpetologist, taught medical immunology at a University, completed a career in cell biology research, lectures on how to apply theological and psychological principles in practical ways, and has a strong interest in all aspects of cosmology and physics. From a small kid he was fascinated with dinosaurs. As such, he has always lived with exotic creatures, including harmless snakes, all housed in his own homemade habitats. Some of his tame pet pythons and anacondas ranged up to twelve feet in length. He is the author of over thirty books, many of which are religious in nature. His writings go beyond the ordinary, exposing deeper aspects of life. His books are meant to be fun, conversational, and helpful. His various works are available at LylePublishing.com and Amazon.com. The "Girl with the Turtle Tattoo" science fiction series was inspired by paintings done by his mother, movies adapting Stieg Larsson's crime novels, and various men and women sporting spectacular body-art tattoos. The story was not "plotted" in advance but flowed freely, with characters appearing on their own and taking charge of their own destinies. Thus the author hopes that you, the reader, find them spontaneous, quirky, surprising, and even thought-provoking—just as did he!